THE
OATH
OF
ASH AND THUNDER

THE OATH OF ASH AND THUNDER

BY

ELIJAH STEPANOVICH

The Oath of Ash and Thunder

For permission requests, write to the publisher at:

McCord Stepanovich Publishing

Tavares, Florida

elijah@elijahstepanovich.com

THE ACCORD'S EMPIRE

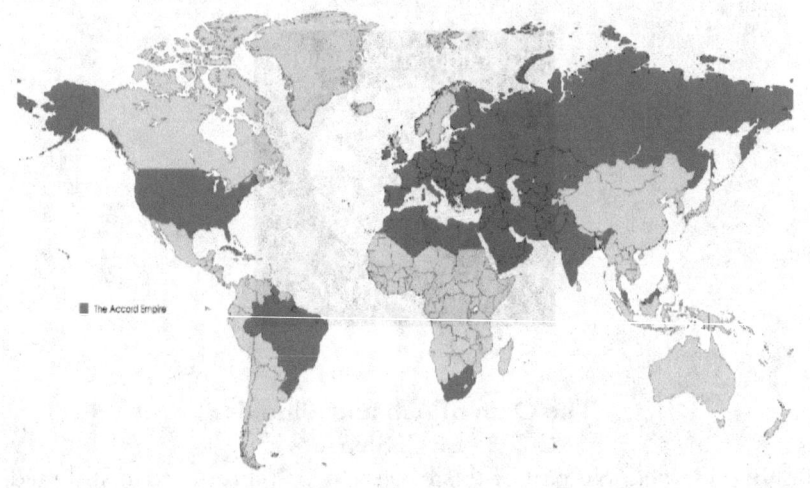

■ The Accord Empire

DEDICATION

To my wife, my flame and frost, may Freyja and
Lada always bless our love. May Perun and Thor
never quiet the storm in our hearts. And may Loki
quell the chaos around us.

CONTENT WARNINGS

THIS STORY WALKS THROUGH WAR, MYTH, AND SHADOW. WITHIN THESE PAGES, YOU WILL ENCOUNTER:

❋   **Violence and War:** graphic battles, bloodshed, and the destruction of cities.

❋   **Torture and Torment:** depictions of physical pain, psychological cruelty, and memory manipulation.

❋   **Death and Grief:** on-page deaths, sacrifice, and the lasting weight of loss.

❋   **Captivity and Coercion**: imprisonment, manipulation, and abuse of power.

❋   **Child Endangerment:** threats and peril directed at the young.

❋   **Profanity**: frequent use of strong language.

❋   **Sensual and Predatory Themes:** darkly intimate language tied to obsession, control, and divine eros.

❋   **Sexual Content:** includes explicit sex scenes.

❋   **Predatory Intimacy**: intimacy tied to manipulation, obsession, or power imbalance.

PRONUNCIATION AND DEFINITIONS

PEOPLE & FACTIONS

Ilija (EE-lee-yah) tied to storms and memory, name common in the Balkans.

Danica (DAH-nee-kah) "Morning star" in Slavic languages; name linked to dawn.

Ana (AH-nah) A goddess figure; name means "grace" across many tongues.

Selene (seh-LEH-neh) Greek for "moon."

The Accord (ah-KORD) Empire built on worship and obedience.

The Unforgotten (un-for-GOT-en) Those who resist silence and erasure.

PLACES & GEOGRAPHY

Athens (ATH-enz) Capital city of Greece, and seat of Accord power.

Olympus (oh-LIM-pus) Mountain of the gods in Greek myth.

Rome (ROHM) Ancient capital, scarred by divine war.

Skopje (SKOHP-yey) Capital of North Macedonia.

Sparta (SPAR-tah) Ancient Greek city-state, symbol of war and discipline.

The Acropolis (ah-CROP-oh-lis) Citadel of Athens, home to ancient temples.

The House of No Dawn: A prison without light, bound in shadow.

The Field of Ended Fates: A desolate place where paths meet their end.

CULTURAL & LANGUAGE TERMS

sine moj (SEE-neh moy) "My son" in Serbo-Croatian.

tata (TAH-tah) "Dad/father" in Serbo-Croatian.

djed (JYEHD) "Grandfather" in South Slavic languages.

ja sam ponosan (YAH sahm POH-noh-sahn) "I am proud" in Serbo-Croatian.

volim te (VOH-leem teh) "I love you."

Sveti Ilija (SVEH-tee EE-lee-yah) Saint Elijah in Slavic tradition.

Agora (AH-go-rah) Public square/marketplace in ancient Greece.

laurel wreath: A crown symbolizing victory and legitimacy in Greek tradition.

olive grove: A common Mediterranean symbol of continuity and peace.

MYTHIC CROSSOVERS

Perun (PEH-roon) Slavic thunder god.

Veles (VEH-les) Slavic underworld deity, master of trickery.

Bifröst (BEE-frost) Norse rainbow bridge between worlds.

Idunn's Apples (EE-doon) Norse fruit of renewal and youth.

PLAYLIST

PROLOGUE
OLYMPUS, THE SILENT THRONE

Ilija

"You killed my fucking sons."

The words hit harder than her fists had. Harder than the marble that had shattered my ribs.

I lay there, broken on stone that once held up gods, and understood what my students never could when I taught them Greek tragedy. Recognition doesn't illuminate—it guts you. Understanding is the knife.

Rome had vanished with a scream of light. When she tore the Veil open, the world inverted, and when it closed again, Olympus was all that remained—broken, smoking, still breathing gods' ash.

Her voice came from deep places where mountains are born, where tectonic plates grind against each other until something gives. My ribs shifted when I breathed. The stone beneath my cheek tasted of metal and dust. Divine blood. Fallen thrones.

This is how gods die, chained and forgotten.

She walked toward me, and even through the pain, I saw centuries of artistic lies. The Renaissance had painted over her Mediterranean brutality with soft curves. This was Aphrodite Areia—the war goddess the Spartans knew, the one they were too frightened to paint. Her armor breathed roses that wept molten gold.

Golden hair conducted rage like lightning looking for ground. Those eyes—I'd known them blue once, Mediterranean summers when I still believed in happy endings. Now they burned gold. Dying stars. I used to tell my students that collapsing stars either fade or explode. She'd chosen violence.

When she knelt beside me, her breath carried contradictions. Pomegranate sweetness—Persephone's fruit. Bitter ash—Troy burning. And beneath that, something worse: the anguish of a goddess who'd turned love into a weapon.

"They were mine, Ilija." Each word crafted to cut. Personal. Intimate. Maternal grief aimed at the guilt already eating me alive. But there was something else—a flicker of performance, like she was reading someone else's script. "Born from my blood when the cosmos was young. Shaped from the marrow of my longing."

Phobos and Deimos. Fear and Dread. I'd taught their names to bored sophomores, never mentioning that gods could die of heartbreak. That immortal sons might pour themselves out for a mortal woman's smile.

"You let them unravel." She rose, predator-smooth. "Let them spill their essence into that raven-crowned girl until nothing remained. You chose her, beloved. You became their undoing."

The stone beneath me came from Mount Pentelicus—same quarries that built the Parthenon. Now it was expensive rubble. Zeus's throne loomed behind her, cracked down the middle like a spine that bore too much weight.

"You thought this was about love?" She smiled, and my skin crawled. "Love is just the silk around the blade, sweet Ilija. This was always war for mortal souls. The Accord rose from their prayers, their hymns, their desperate hunger for the divine. We gave them golden idols. They forged their own chains."

That smile deepened, too satisfying for personal victory. "Every bell that rang. Every candle they lit. They were building the shackles that would bind them to our will."

Even dying, part of me wanted to document this. Divine confession. The real story under all our myths. If scholars still existed. If libraries remained. If I lived to tell anyone.

She moved to Hera's ruined throne, fingers tracing ivory with graveyard reverence. "It started with Hera's pride. Beautiful as winter crystal. So brittle that one touch of shadow could shatter it."

I'd found those cracks—jealousy aged into poison; loneliness hardened into rage. Aphrodite had poured her anguish into those fractures like molten bronze, making something more beautiful in its brokenness.

"Ares." Her hand found his forgotten spear. "A blade dreaming of the forge. Of being remade into something worth singing about."

I knew that story. The weapon that aches to be reforged. The soldier who fights because he's forgotten how to stop. She'd promised him a beautiful war, and he'd marched into void chasing glory that existed only in his head.

"And Zeus." Her sigh could erode mountains. "The fool never understood gods exist only in mortal longing. In prayers whispered in the dark."

Her empire was built on that understanding: harvest the worship, capture the faith, watch humanity kneel. I'd seen it unfold, Cassandra-cursed with understanding but no power to stop it. Yet something in her posture suggested deference, as if her victories served something larger, something watching from beyond this ruined pantheon.

"I unmade them all for you." Her shadow fell across me. "Pulled down heaven itself. Carved us a kingdom where nothing could touch us." The words rang hollow—a justification she'd been given rather than believed. The obsession in her touch was real, but it served an agenda beyond herself.

The irony would have made Sophocles weep. I'd spent decades teaching tragic inevitability, how heroes create their own destruction. Now I was living it.

"And you burned it all for a girl who'll be dust in a blink."

Her fingers found my face—tender and terrible at once, a surgeon preparing to operate without anesthesia. Her skin burned cold, froze hot. "Don't think to call storms here. Zeus guards his sky even in death."

"We have time," she murmured. "I'll teach you to love me again. Drop by drop. Memory by memory. Even if I have to scrape her from your soul like honey from the comb."

She knew my weaknesses. But she'd made one error—she thought the original text was hers to rewrite. Some loves are written in indelible ink.

"What name is left for you, Ana, when you've devoured all the others?" My voice came from somewhere past my throat's wreckage. "Danica will find me. She'll burn the universe down to reach me. We always have."

Something flickered in her golden gaze. The predator realizing its prey had teeth.

"Then I'll make her beg for the grave." Her smile was a blade that had waited centuries for this moment. "I'll peel her from herself, layer by layer, until she forgets her own name."

She reached into my mind and showed me.

The vision hit directly, bypassing sensation to lodge in pure understanding. Danica falling through space and time. The frost beneath her was crystallized moments, joy frozen before it could bloom. Blood spread across her chest in perfect mathematical spirals. Her hair against white—a signature on an unfinished manuscript.

The Blade of Fates fell from her loosening fingers. Another weapon that wasn't enough.

A figure approached through desolation, crowned with falcon feathers. The psychopomp. Guide between worlds. Her eyes held the terrible knowledge of cycles that must complete.

Behind her, Idunn's Tree gleamed with golden apples—immortality at the price of everything that made life worth living. The Bifrost stretched beyond, a bridge between what was and what could never be.

The vision ended but its weight stayed, settling into my bones. I made a sound, scream and analysis combined, and somewhere in Olympus's corpse, dead gods stirred.

This was my anagnorisis. I was both Oedipus and the chorus, living the myth I'd spent my life interpreting.

And somewhere beneath monastery bones, Danica was coming for me. She always did.

CHAPTER ONE
MY LITTLE STORM

Danica

The air down here is thick with old prayers and older blood, heavy with incense ghosts from altars now cracked and bleeding stone. It tastes of limestone and copper—martyrs' last breaths settling in my lungs like temple smoke. Tomb-air. The kind of cold that finds your marrow and stays there.

The walls weep salt-bitter moisture in this eternal dark, silver tears tracing the gouged faces of saints. Saints whose names Ana's jealous chisels scraped away until only bone-smooth marble stares back. She's a god who suffers no competition, even from the holy dead.

Above us, the monastery's skeleton claws at a sky that never heals. War and time picked it clean, left stone ribs jutting against heaven in silent accusation. Even broken, I feel phantom bells in my chest—vibrations that won't stop until the last stone crumbles.

My scarred hand trails the wall where countless monks wore grooves smooth. Their prayers soaked into stone like blood into cloth, and their devotion bleeds through my fingertips—desperate, beautiful, eternal. My other hand finds the Blade of Fates against my hip, cold spine of metal humming with predatory hunger. It drinks warmth from my skin the way I drink hope—both of us starving for what we were made to protect. I learned to love its cold because it matches the hollow in my chest, the space carved exactly Ilija-shaped where winter lives now.

Ilija. Prayer and curse on the same breath.

The blade is bone torn from the world's ribs, iron wed to starlight in heaven's forge. It feeds on my heat as hungrily as I feed on memory.

Seven years.

The number tastes like ash. Time doesn't heal; it teaches you to carry the wound. Seven years is a chasm through my soul, a void pulling everything toward its mouth.

Seven years since the sky tore open above burning Rome. Since Ana's hands became claws, ripping Ilija from my arms, swallowing his scream as she vanished into that wound between worlds.

In that compressed eternity, I learned to weave armies from whispers, sharpen hope in darkness like a blade. We carved our sanctuary in the shadow of Ana's Sacred Confederation—that silk noose masquerading as salvation, tightening around the world's throat. We call ourselves the Unforgotten. The name tasted of iron and defiance and tears we had no time to shed.

Every dawn breaks on his phantom ache—pain so physical it steals breath, leaves me gasping at the Ilija-shaped hollow where wind sings mournful songs only I hear. Every night I sleep with my hand on the Blade's hilt, using its cold to anchor myself to a war that's slowly dying.

And I'm dying with it.

The corridor opens into a burial chamber vast enough to swallow cathedrals, vaulted ceiling lost in shadows that breathe centuries. Here, among bones of saints whose names God forgot, we plot the future of the living. A massive sarcophagus serves as our command table, its marble lid polished smooth as a lover's skin and twice as cold. Spread across its ancient surface lies our broken continent—maps stitched from smuggled papers, whispered reports, testimony of ghosts who still believe in more than survival.

Our only light bleeds from a salvaged Accord monitor, nervous blue flickers painting shadows in shades of grief and determination. Red wax marks Ana's patrols—poisonous threads creeping like infection through blood. Blue pins, small and brave as forget-me-nots, mark our flickering resistance. Fewer than last year. Each lost position a fresh cut on my heart.

"You carry them both now," Milan says, voice graveled with a thousand battles fought at my side. His gaze settles on my hand hovering over our desperate cartography.

I stop. Fingers trembling over a coastline that might not exist anymore. In the monitor's cold light, I see what I've become written in gold and iron across my knuckles. Two rings sit like warring queens forced to share a throne: Lada's rose gold breathing with inner fire, captured memory of summer dawns and shared laughter. Beside it, Morana's night-black iron shot through with lightning-blue veins that pulse with barely contained fury.

Silence falls thick enough to drown in. Zoran and Marija go still as hunting cats. This grief has been mine alone—too heavy for casual questions, too deep for careless words.

"He gave it to me," I say, words escaping like prisoners held too long. "In Rome. In the throne room, after we thought we'd won. In that perfect, stupid moment before she came, when the air still tasted of ash and victory."

The memory rises like bile. His hand closing over mine, still battle-warm, steady as stone that should have anchored me. His storm-gray eyes holding universes of love and that sliver of fear I was too drunk on triumph to recognize. He slid the lightning-veined ring from his finger with priestly solemnity, placed it against rose gold like a man performing last rites.

"He said they belonged together. One was only half a soul without the other. 'Just like us.' If we were ever separated, their power had to stay with one of us. To keep the path open between worlds. A way back."

His final gift, pressed into my palm one hour before she fed him to the void.

In my friends' eyes—Zoran, Marija, Milan, family forged in this fallen world's crucible—I see terrible understanding dawn. They see the rings for what they are: a yoke that will drag me into fire if necessary.

"They're afraid out there," Marija says from the armory niche where she moves with deadly grace. "People remember what hope felt like. They paint old symbols in ash from her burned temples—lightning bolts for Perun, sun wheels for Lada. Small rebellions are still rebellion. She can't kill memory itself."

Milan doesn't look up from the axe cradled in his arms, curved edge catching light like a sharpened moon. "She can kill the people who carry those memories. And she will. Memory makes martyrs. Martyrs make excellent fertilizer."

"And from that fertilizer," Marija shoots back, words carrying banked-coal heat, "new things grow. Stranger. Stronger."

I curl fingers until the rings bite deep—one searing hot, the other grave-cold. My constant torment and only connection to him. A tether of pain stretched across the screaming void.

The generator coughs in the depths—dying man's last breath—and light flickers, casting our faces skull-sharp before settling back to its weary heartbeat. Zoran braces scarred hands against the sarcophagus.

"Vienna is bleeding out," he says, each word precise as a surgeon's cut. "Her new Inquisitor, Cygnus—he's different. True believer. Methodical. Lays informant networks like spider webs. We lost three safe houses last week. Seventeen people, Danica. They took the children too."

Marija's hands go white around her rifle stock. "Hunger makes informants of good men. She keeps outer districts starving while her inner circles feast. A starving man will sell his brother for bread."

"And how do we feed a city of ghosts?" Milan's voice is a tomb-door sealing. "Bake enough loaves? We can't feed a capital while her Legions crucify anyone caught with extra. Our hearts are willing. This is logistics, and we're losing."

"We don't need to feed an entire capital," I say, voice quiet and sharp enough to cut despair. "Just keep from losing tomorrow. Feed ten mouths on the right corner, and suddenly there's a poem on a wall. Get medicine to one clinic, and fifty more believe they might see spring. Supply one baker, and the queue becomes a choir humming old songs. Ana doesn't fear bullets—she fears memory. Fears when the hungry start singing instead of screaming."

Hope flickers in Zoran's features. "The Flame of the West."

"What word from the Balkans?" I ask, tracing the coastline of a bruised sea.

"Quiet to the ear, loud in the bones," Marija answers with fierce homeland pride. "Ferrymen on the Drina row at night, moving our people for nothing but the promise their children will remember why rivers flow to sea instead of sky. Someone cut down her statue in Tuzla. Hung her scales from a butcher's hook."

Milan's mouth twitches. "Good. Remind them marble bleeds when cut deep enough."

"These are gestures," Zoran sighs, tapping stolen intelligence. "Her supply lines are flawless. If she has weakness, it's elsewhere."

"Her weakness is spectacle," I say. "She built a religion around herself. Gods must be seen to be worshipped. She draws power like storms draw lightning—that hunger makes her vulnerable."

"The broadcast tower outside Graz," Milan says, eyes sharpening. "That explosion wasn't ours."

"No," Zoran confirms. "Whoever did it read our playbook. In the final minutes, they broadcast over emergency frequencies. Lullabies. Old ones."

Profound quiet settles like snow. In its depths, I almost hear the melody—song passed from one generation's ache to the next. Weapon forged from sorrow and stubborn refusal to let beautiful things die.

"Good," I say, letting them see steel grown beneath grief. "Let her learn to fear mothers singing to children."

"Cuts both ways," Zoran warns, scar whitening with tension. "The more they resist, the more she cleanses. Lost the entire Prague library cell. Archivists, scholars. Thirty-seven souls protecting books that might never open. The woman with the vault key—she swallowed it whole rather than surrender. They broke every tooth getting it back."

The brutality steals my breath. Marija folds her rifle cloth with burial-shroud reverence. "We tell the living we'll show them receipts for what's been stolen. Perhaps one day, we'll show them a world where receipts aren't necessary."

"To reach that world," Milan rumbles, axe across his shoulders, "we walk through valleys full of men who chew keys from the mouths of the dead."

I close my eyes, let grief wash over—tide that never recedes, just pulls back to gather strength. Seven years is the shape my soul bent into to keep from breaking. I bent. I will not break.

"What about Greece?" The words taste like ashes.

Zoran's voice drops. "Six couriers sent, none returned. It's a black hole, swallowing everything. Even if he were there, even if she hadn't moved him—"

"We don't say the sea refuses her dead until we've drowned looking," I cut him off. "We haven't drowned yet."

From the corridor comes a sound lighter than birds on stone. I know it better than my heartbeat. Warmth blooms in my chest—fierce and painful and holy.

"Let her in," I say, iron melting from my voice.

She enters like candleflame in a crypt, shadows pulling back in reverence. Selene. My little storm, my heart walking outside my body on legs barely long enough to carry her. Monitor-light catches her copper hair, sets it blazing with rebellion. Clutched in her fist—the ghost of a robin, carved by a soldier who died when she was three, whose final wish was creating something that could fly.

At six, she carries stillness that makes warriors shift. Her gaze doesn't dart—it settles and sees. When her eyes find mine—those impossible storm-gray eyes, his eyes—it's being stabbed with love and grief in equal measure.

I drop to one knee, arms opening. "Hey there, little storm. Thought you were sleeping."

She flows toward me, inevitable. Her small body presses against mine, cheek finding my collarbone. Her scent—wild thyme, woodsmoke—strikes like lightning. For one moment, the war vanishes. I'm just a mother holding her child.

My companions' armor cracks. Marija's rifle lowers. Zoran's fists unclench. Even Milan lets something soft flicker behind pale eyes.

"Every time," Marija whispers to the skulls. "Every time, it's like looking at him. Same eyes that saw storms before clouds appeared."

Zoran nods, throat working. "She has his gift for seeing trouble. I pray she never has to use it like he did."

My throat closes. I hold her—this living ember Ana can never extinguish, breathing proof that love outlasts gods' jealousy. My heart and wound wrapped in one small, fierce package.

She pulls back, storm-gray gaze sweeping our map with impossible precision. Her hand rises, pale as starlight, finger hovering over the screaming emptiness where Greece waits.

The world holds its breath.

"Selene," I begin, useless shield against what's coming.

She touches the map.

"Tata," she says.

The word drops like stone into still water. She speaks it with flat certainty—a truth she's been keeping safe like a pearl, key to a lock rusted shut for six years.

The world explodes white. Pain tears air from my lungs, fills my mouth with iron and winter as the rings ignite like twin stars. Lada's band sears with memories of sun and laughter. Morana's circlet bites with space-between-heartbeats cold. Life and death surge up my arm, finding the space behind my eyes, ripping me from the world.

I'm nowhere and everywhere, adrift in void stretching beyond dreams. Then emptiness condenses into a single point of agony that becomes a place from nightmares.

I stand on the shattered peak of bone-white stone, polished by winds older than breath. The sky above churns perpetual storm, silent lightning shedding no rain. And chained to this dead mountain's heart with bindings that devour light—

Ilija.

He hangs suspended in obsidian shackles, head bowed under exhaustion deeper than bone. The incandescent storm that always burned in him—that beautiful, terrible power that made gods notice—dimmed to barely a flicker.

Circling him in ritualistic dance are three figures woven from shadow—forms shifting like smoke, faces hidden beneath absolute darkness. The Sorrow-Weavers, Ana's beloved servants. They move with funeral-procession grace, whispering sounds of grinding bone and tearing silk. Forcing visions into his mind, weaving threads of every life we shared across centuries into a tapestry of unending anguish.

The vision pulls me in. I'm drowning with him in memories turned poison.

I see us in a thousand forms across a thousand lives. Medieval lovers dying as villages burn. Star-crossed warriors separated by war's mathematics. Scientists in chrome futures watch helplessly as one fades while the other rages against unbreakable barriers. Each death, each loss, each separation magnified until it becomes a universe of pain.

This is crueler than memory. The Sorrow-Weavers aren't content showing what was—they're making him feel it all again, every splinter of ancient agony made fresh. Breaking him piece by piece, using our love as the hammer.

The scene shifts. I'm falling through space between visions, landing soft in frost stretching beyond the world's curve. The surface littered with bones of forgotten wars. Snow that won't melt—each flake a crystallized failure, frozen tear shed by gods who learned too late that love isn't enough.

The Field of Ended Fates, where all paths come to die.

My body feels weighted with weariness like drowning in honey. Cold seeps through clothes, through skin, settling in bones with winter's patience. I look down—blood blooming across my chest like poppies in snow.

The Blade of Fates slips from numb fingers, twin flames dying as it hits ground. Discarded metal, all magic severed where hope comes to be buried.

Shadow falls. A woman whose beauty is blessing and curse. Crown of living raven feathers shifting with dark intelligence, eyes holding vast wisdom of skies watching civilizations crumble. Freyja, the Seidr-Queen.

She kneels in impossible snow, scent of autumn orchards and ancient magic. "All paths end eventually, child of Danu. The brave choose which ending is theirs."

Behind her rises a tree defying winter, branches heavy with golden apples pulsing like hearts. The Tree of Idunn, life stolen back from death.

Beyond the tree, across a chasm making star-voids look shallow—a bridge of pure, singing light. The Bifrost hums with every soul that crossed between worlds, harmony so beautiful my bones ache with longing.

My grave. The road to him leads through my own ending.

The vision twists, showing its cruelest revelation.

Back on the bone-white mountain, the Sorrow-Weavers withdrawn. Ana stands before Ilija's chained form, radiant as forest fire—beautiful, terrible, consuming. No anger, no triumph. Only love so possessive it's toxic, so all-encompassing it will destroy what it claims to cherish.

"You see now, my beloved?" Her voice honey-sweet with corruption. "All that pain across all those lifetimes—she is the wound that won't heal, the knife turning in your heart. I can take that away. Make you whole."

Her hands wreathed in liquid sunlight reach toward his face with sculptor's reverence. The reforging—ritual older than memory, designed to rewrite a soul's essence. She begins tracing patterns across his skin, each symbol a thread of her divine essence burning away every connection to me.

I scream his name into the vision's terrible silence. Feel him slipping—from life, from me. Death more final than any sword through the heart.

The agony shatters the vision's hold.

I slam back into my body with thunderclap force, knees hitting stone. Air rushes back in desperate gasps. The world returns—concerned voices, water dripping, heart hammering.

My hand clenched so tight around the rings they've cut half-moons into my palm. The pain is welcome, real.

Truth settles like lead in my bones. He's on Mount Olympus, chained in Ana's hell, and she's systematically unmaking him. The only path leads through the death the Norns showed me.

The knowledge should break me. Instead, it forges me into something sharp enough to cut gods.

I push to my feet, swaying. Zoran reaches for me. "Danica, what did you see?"

My gaze finds Greece's empty space on our map. The rings pulse with a rhythm that isn't mine—his heartbeat across impossible distances. Alive. Barely. Running out of time.

"I saw him." My voice is winter-forged blade. I press the map over our enemy's heart. "Mount Olympus. She has him chained, and she's..." I swallow against golden light rewriting his soul. "Unmaking him. Memory by memory. Soon there won't be enough left to save."

The words hit like physical blows. Milan goes rigid. Zoran pales. "That's impossible. Olympus is her power's heart. It'd be suicide."

"I don't care if she's hidden him in her own fucking heart," I snarl, feral voice of something pushed too far. "He's there, I'm getting him back or dying. No other option."

Selene looks up with his storm-gray eyes that see too much. "Tata," she says again. A command.

Something bent for seven years snaps straight, tempered in determination's fire. I look at my family, my army, my heart made manifest.

"Send word to every cell, every safe house, every soul we have," I command, voice carrying bronze bells and funeral drums. "I don't care what we burn, what prices we pay, what gods we kill. We're going to war."

Marija's smile is all teeth and promise. "You mean we're going after her."

"No," I whisper with more menace than any shout. "I'm going after him. If Ana wants to throw every god, every legion, every nightmare in my path, so be it. I'll tear Olympus down stone by stone and salt the earth before I let her keep what's mine."

The vow settles like smoke, heavy with coming catastrophe. Zoran straightens, fire kindling behind his eyes.

"Then we go to war," he says, steady as stone.

We're no longer the resistance. We've become something far more dangerous: a reckoning seven years in the making.

Ilija is alive. The path is a straight line drawn in fire and blood into hell's heart.

And I'm going to walk it with a smile and his name carved into my bones.

I'm bringing him home.

Chapter Two
THE ACCORD'S ADVANCE

The tunnels wound like veins through the earth, low-ceilinged and damp, their walls sweating with mineral tears. In the old days, these had been part of Monte Cassino's foundations, catacombs for monks who thought stone and prayer could keep the world at bay. Now they were the bones of the Resistance, hollowed out and strung with electrical cords like arteries, pulsing with the grim, determined life of a war that refused to die.

The air was thick with the smell of too many people pressing into too little space, wet wool, gun oil, boiled cabbage, and the faint, sour tang of fear that clung to everything. Somewhere ahead, boots rang against metal plates laid over collapsed flooring. A radio sputtered static before resolving into a scratchy voice reciting coordinates. The voice cut out. Somewhere else, a man muttered fuck under his breath, the sound almost a prayer.

I passed a group of soldiers bent over a table strewn with ammunition belts. One of them glanced up, a wiry woman with a jagged scar down her cheek that pulled at her eye when she blinked. "Flame of the West," she said quietly, like she was reminding herself I was real. Her voice was rough, and I caught the faint tremor in her hand as she threaded rounds into a belt. I gave a single, sharp nod and kept moving. I didn't have the strength to be their symbol tonight. My belief in what that symbol meant was flickering, unreliable.

Further on, I saw Jovan hunched over a crate of grenades, his fingers quick and careful. He used to be a teacher in Zagreb before the Accord burned it, before his classroom of wide-eyed children was replaced by a roster of the dead. Now his hands smelled of powder instead of chalk. He looked up long enough to give me a nod, stark recognition between survivors, and went back to his work. The set of his jaw was tight, a muscle twitching with a tension that never fully eased, even in these relative depths of safety.

The deeper I went, the more the walls pressed in. The stone here was older, darker, carved with faint lines of saints and angels that had been half-erased by time. Some faces were worn away entirely, nothing left except blank ovals. Others had been defaced with crude symbols of the old gods, spirals for Zorya, sun wheels for Lada, jagged runes for Perun. The Resistance had no saints left. Only war, and the ghosts of the gods who had started it.

I passed the infirmary and caught the copper tang of blood under the sharp sting of antiseptic. Through the half-open door, I saw Marija bending over a young man whose leg was wrapped in soaked bandages. His face was pale, his eyes glassy with shock and pain. He couldn't have been more than seventeen. She met my gaze for half a breath, her expression unreadable, before turning back to her patient. In that fleeting look, though, I saw the cost of our fight written in the exhausted lines around her eyes. Every victory was paid for with bodies like his.

A child's laughter echoed from somewhere deep in the warrens. It was thin, brittle, laughter that belonged to someone who'd learned early that joy had to be stolen, quick and quiet. I followed the sound without meaning to, my boots crunching faintly on grit. That was when I saw Petra.

She was standing just outside the barracks door, leaning one shoulder against the stone like she'd been holding up the wall for years. Her rifle rested against her thigh; her fingers curled loosely around the stock. Her hair was tied back in a messy knot, streaked with gray that had come in since Rome fell. Her face was a study in grim endurance. Petra had been a captain in the Serbian army before the Accord rose, before her country had been stolen by a goddess wearing a politician's face. She, more than anyone, knew the cost of blind faith.

Her eyes met mine the moment I stepped into the lantern light. "You sure you're ready to do this?" she asked, voice low and flat. No kindness, no room for lies.

I stopped a few paces away. Behind the door, I could hear Selene's voice, bright and unbroken, humming a tune I didn't recognize. "No," I said finally. "When the fuck has that ever mattered?"

Petra's mouth twitched, almost a smile. She spat a cherry pit into the shadows and straightened. "Then let's get it done."

The door was lighter than I expected, though it still dragged like the stone itself knew this was a parting.

Selene sat cross-legged on her cot, turning the little wooden bird over in her hands. The paint had faded to ghost colors; she cradled it like treasure. Her hair caught the lantern light, copper and gold, and for a moment I almost couldn't move. Her eyes, Ilija's eyes, found me.

"Mama," she said, soft as breath.

I crossed the room slowly, my boots barely whispering against the worn rugs Petra had scavenged from the ruins of Cassino to make the barracks feel less like a tomb. Selene watched me the whole time, still turning the bird in her hands, her head tilted in that way she had when she was trying to decide if I was safe to approach.

Gods, she was so damn small. In my mind she was still a newborn, a fierce, tiny warmth tucked against my chest in the dark hours before dawn in a world that had just ended. Here she was, six years old, her legs longer, her face sharper, her eyes... her father's. Storm-gray and endless, holding a wisdom that felt far older than her small frame.

I knelt in front of her, the ache in my knees a welcome distraction from the tightness in my throat. "Hey, my little storm," I murmured. "What's got you up so late?"

She shrugged; her fingers tightened on the bird. "Couldn't sleep. The walls are loud."

The walls were loud. Down here, the stone held onto every sound, the distant thud of crates being moved, the muffled echo of boots, the metallic click of weapons being checked and rechecked. To her, it must have felt like the world itself was pacing in its cage.

I reached out and brushed a lock of her fire-like hair behind her ear. "I need to go for a while," I said softly.

She looked up at me, unblinking, like she'd been expecting this. "Because of Tata."

It wasn't a question. My breath caught. "Yes," I said. "Because of Tata."

For a moment, neither of us spoke. The room felt too small, the air too thin. I wanted to pull her into my arms and never let go, to build a wall of fire and frost around her that nothing in this world or any other could ever breach. That wasn't the kind of love this war allowed me. Instead, I cupped her face in both hands, memorizing the curve of her cheekbones, the weight of her gaze, branding the image of her onto my soul.

"I'm leaving you with Petra," I told her. "She'll keep you safe. No matter what happens."

Her little jaw set in a way that made her look so much like Ilija when he was being stubborn it made my heart ache. "You'll come back."

"I'll try," I said. My voice almost broke, so I made it sharper, like a blade catching light. "You listen to Petra. You run when she tells you to. You hide when she says hide. And you don't come looking for me. Not ever. Do you understand?"

Selene's lip trembled; she nodded. Then she reached out and placed the wooden bird in my palm. "So you don't forget where home is."

Something in my chest cracked open, and for a moment I couldn't breathe. I closed my fingers around the bird, the worn edges biting into my skin, and pulled her against me. I buried my face in her hair, breathing in that warm, clean scent of child and thyme and innocence that didn't exist anywhere else in this world.

When I pulled back, I pressed a kiss to her forehead and stood before I could change my mind. Petra was waiting in the doorway, her expression unreadable with soft eyes.

"She's the whole fucking world," I said quietly.

Petra nodded once. "And I'll guard her like it."

I turned, forcing myself not to look back again. The rings on my fingers pulsed once, gold and black, and for a heartbeat, I swore I felt Ilija's presence, far away and alive.

And that was enough to keep me walking.

The mountain pass was a wound in the earth, a narrow scar of shattered rock and stunted pines. Lying on the ledge, I felt the cold of the stone seep through my coat, a patient, invasive chill that felt like a premonition. Below, the road was a grey, silent ribbon. We were a dozen ghosts clinging to the rock, our breath held in the cold, waiting.

The sound came first, a low hum that vibrated up through the stone, into my bones. Then the lights, two pinpricks of cold, blue energy cutting the mist. The convoy moved with a chilling, unnatural silence. Three massive, black-armored vehicles, their hulls bearing the single, stylized golden rose of Ana's faith. They hovered inches above the road, gliding like tombs. They were an offense to the wildness of the mountain, a sterile, silent procession of absolute control.

I clutched the wooden bird in my pocket, its familiar shape a stark contrast to the cold, predatory weight of the Blade of Fates on my back. I was a mother. I was a monster. I was a goddess in waiting. A woman so tired of fighting she could barely breathe. And I was about to set the world on fire.

The lead vehicle entered the kill zone. My voice was a harsh whisper into the throat mic. "Milan. Burn it."

The world ended in a flash of white and a wave of pressure that punched the air from my lungs. The IED Milan had planted detonated with a deep, gut-wrenching whump that felt more like a tear in reality than an explosion. The massive transport lifted a foot into the air, its massive engines screaming a metallic death-shriek, and slammed sideways into the cliff face, its armor buckling like tin. For a heartbeat, there was only the ringing in my ears and the smell of ozone.

Then Zoran's voice crackled, laced with static and rage. "Rear vehicle! Light them up!" An RPG hissed from the far end of the pass. The warhead struck the third transport, the charge exploding against its hull with a deafening clang. It wasn't enough to destroy it, the vehicle slewed sideways, crippled. Milan's PKM opened up, the heavy machine gun hammering rounds against the transport's viewport in a relentless, deafening chatter, each tracer round a stitch of angry light in the grey morning.

Hatches hissed open, and the Accord's soldiers poured out. They were modified, something beyond human. Encased in sleek, bone-white armor, their faces hidden behind mirrored visors, they moved with a silent, fluid grace that was both beautiful and terrifying. They fanned out, rifles already raised, into a storm of lead from the resistance fighters below. The familiar, frantic crack of our scavenged rifles felt achingly mortal against their silent advance.

I rose from the ledge and did not hesitate. I leaped.

I landed on the roof of the middle vehicle, my boots hitting the armored hull with a heavy thud. The metal groaned. I drew the Blade of Fates, its ancient steel hissing as it met the cold air, and I was no longer just Danica. I was Sigrún. I was a Valkyrie. I was vengeance given form.

I drove the blade down, plunging it through the roof as if it were paper. The metal screamed and buckled. Blue lightning arced up the steel as the vehicle's energy core died. I came off the side in a spray of sparks, landing in a crouch as an energy bolt seared the air where my head had been. The battle was a blur of motion, a symphony of violence. I met the first of the bone-clad soldiers. I didn't kill him with a clean thrust; I unmade him. A sweep of the blade unleashed a wave of frost that found the seams in his armor and cracked him open like a geode, his lifeblood freezing into a grotesque, crimson sculpture before he could register the cold.

I moved through them, a whirlwind of steel and elemental fury. The Blade of Fates sang in my hand, each swing a note in a song of death. I parried a rifle butt, spun low, and sliced through another soldier's legs at the knee. He collapsed without a sound. I drove a spear of ice through the visor of a third, the shard bursting from the back of his helmet in a spray of gore and frozen brain matter.

My heart hammered against my ribs, with a terrible, exhilarating power. I felt the burn of a plasma bolt graze my side, a searing kiss of pain that only sharpened my focus. I gritted my teeth and answered with a torrent of fire from my free hand. The flames, white-hot and laced with blue frost, washed over two more soldiers. They didn't scream. Their armor flash-heated, glowing cherry-red, and then they simply... dissolved. Ash and steam were all that remained, the air thick with the smell of superheated metal and something horrifically organic.

The resistance fought with a desperate, human ferocity. I saw Marija drag a wounded Jovan behind cover, her face a mask of grim determination as she laid down suppressing fire. I saw Milan, roaring a curse, abandon his machine gun and charge down the slope, his axe a blur of motion, cleaving through a soldier's helmet with a sickening crunch. The cost was brutal. I saw one of our own, a boy from Zagreb named Stefan, get caught by a concussive blast. He was thrown against the rock wall, his body limp, a broken puppet. The weight of it, the responsibility, threatened to crush me. I channeled it into the blade.

I fought my way toward the rear vehicle, the one Zoran had confirmed held the children. Two guards, larger than the others, stood before the main hatch. They fired in unison. This time, I didn't dodge. I raised my hand and a cathedral of impossible ice erupted from the ground, the morning's grey light caught in a thousand fractured prayers. The energy bolts slammed into it, and the ice wall shattered like a stained-glass window in a hurricane, the glittering shards a beautiful, deadly distraction.

I strode through the cloud of ice dust, the Blade of Fates held low. The two guards charged. I ducked under a rifle swing, drove my elbow into a soldier's throat, and brought the pommel of my sword down on the back of his helmet with a wet crack. He dropped. The second swung his rifle like a club. I blocked it with the flat of my blade, the impact, a jarring shock that ran up to my shoulder. We were locked for a moment, his mirrored visor reflecting my own grim face, smeared with blood and fury.

Then, with a roar that was more animal than human, I channeled the fire. The blade ignited, flames erupting along its length. The guard's rifle melted in his hands. He staggered back, his armor smoking. I lunged, driving the flaming sword through his chest. The symbol of the golden rose on his breastplate melted, dripped, and then burst as the fire consumed him from the inside out.

I reached the hatch and slammed my hand against the release panel. It hissed open. The inside was dark and cold. Then my eyes adjusted, and my heart seized.

A dozen children, none older than ten, huddled in the far corner. They were pale and silent, their eyes wide with a terror so profound it had gone beyond tears. They wore simple, grey tunics, and around each of their necks was a small, iron collar, pulsing with a faint, sickly green light.

I stepped inside, my sword still burning, casting flickering shadows across their small, frightened faces.

"It's okay," I said, my voice softer than I thought possible. "I'm here to help you."

One of the children, a small boy with dark hair, flinched back. "You're one of them," he whispered. "The old gods. The dissonant voices."

The words hit me harder than any physical blow. I looked down at my hand, at the ring of Morana, at the flames still licking along my sword. I saw myself through his eyes, a creature of terrifying power, wreathed in fire, her face smeared with blood and ash. A monster from the stories they had been taught to fear.

The fire on my blade died, leaving only the cold steel. I sheathed my sword and knelt, making myself smaller.

"My name is Danica," I said, my voice thick with an emotion I couldn't name. "And I'm going to get you home."

I took a slow, deliberate breath, forcing the fury and grief down. I held out my hand, palm open. "The collars," I said, my voice low and steady. "I need to get those off you."

The boy who had spoken before shook his head, his dark eyes filled with a terror that was heartbreakingly absolute. "We can't. The Preceptors said they keep us safe. They keep the... the bad memories out."

My blood ran cold. It wasn't just a prison; it was a form of erasure. A chillingly elegant cruelty.

"Sometimes," I said, choosing my words with exquisite care, "memories are all we have left. They're how we know who we are."

I moved slowly toward the boy, my heart aching with a fierce, protective love. He was the same age as Selene. He had Ilija's hair. For a moment, the weight of my own loss threatened to crush me. I pushed it aside. These children were all that mattered now.

Outside, a fresh explosion rocked the transport, and the boy flinched. I reached him and gently touched the collar. It was cold, humming with a faint, nauseating energy.

The boy whimpered, a small, terrified sound. "Please... don't hurt me."

"I won't," I whispered. I focused the frost, the fire. A delicate web of ice formed over the collar's lock. I let the cold seep in, making the metal brittle. Then, with a sharp, focused thought, I shattered it. The collar fell away.

The boy gasped. For a moment, he went limp. Then his eyes opened again, and for the first time, the programmed fear was gone, replaced by a dawning, wondrous light. "I... I remember my mother's face," he whispered, a tear tracing a clean path through the grime on his cheek.

A wave of hope, so fierce it was almost painful, surged through me. I moved to the next child, and the next, shattering their chains of forgetting one by one.

When the last collar fell, I led them to the hatch. The battle outside had died down to the shouts of the Resistance and the groans of the wounded. Milan stood guard, his axe dripping, his face a grim mask of blood and soot.

"Get them clear," I ordered. "Take them back to the monastery. Petra is waiting."

Milan nodded, his eyes lingering on the small, frightened faces. For a moment, the hardened warrior vanished. "We'll get them home," he said, his voice thick with emotion.

I watched Milan and his team lead the children away, their small forms swallowed by the mist and the grim reality of the war-torn pass. My heart was a tangle of relief and a deep, gnawing sorrow. I had saved them, yet the Inquisitor's words echoed in my mind. I had given them back their pain.

I turned back to the smoldering wreckage of the convoy. The beacons had to be destroyed. I found them in the lead vehicle, three sleek, obsidian pillars pulsing with a corrupt, golden light. They hummed with a power that felt both divine and deeply wrong, a sterile, manufactured faith. I raised my hands, the rings on my fingers glowing with a light of their own. I drew on the fire, the frost, the rage, the grief, the long years of loss. I drew on the memory of Ilija's face and the sound of Selene's laughter. I gathered it all into a single point of focused, incandescent fury.

"For the children," I whispered, and unleashed hell.

The explosion was a silent, concussive wave of pure energy that vaporized the transports and scoured the pass clean. When the light faded, there was nothing left except smoking craters and the profound, echoing silence of a victory that felt too much like a beginning.

The quiet that followed was a lie, a vacuum where sound had been violently murdered. Smoke and steam coiled in the air, thick with the scent of ozone and something that smelled like burnt sugar and melted faith. The pass was a ruin, a testament to a power I was only just beginning to understand, a power that frightened me as much as it did my enemies.

That silence broke with a shift in the air, a sudden, oppressive weight that made the hairs on my arms stand on end. A new presence entered the pass, moving through the smoke and carnage with a calm, unhurried grace that was more terrifying than any charge. He emerged from the wreckage of the lead vehicle, stepping through a gaping hole in its hull as if it were a doorway waiting for him. His armor was the color of scorched ivory, trimmed in gold, and etched with intricate verses from Ana's new doctrine. He wore no helmet, revealing a face that was unnervingly serene, his features sharp and ascetic, his eyes the pale, unwavering blue of a winter sky. He carried a long, slender blade that hummed with a low, dissonant energy, its edge seeming to warp the very air around it.

He stopped twenty paces from me, his boots silent on the scorched earth. He looked at the devastation, at the dissolved bodies and smoking craters, with a kind of detached, scholarly interest. Then his pale eyes settled on me. "The dissonant echo," he said, his voice calm, resonant, like a priest delivering a sermon in a vast, empty cathedral. "They told me you were a storm. They failed to mention the sheer, exquisite artistry of your chaos."

My grip tightened on the hilt of my sword. "Who are you?"

"I am Inquisitor Valerius," he said, with a slight, almost courtly bow. "And I was the Preceptor at the seminary from which you stole those children. I was their shepherd."

"You were their jailer," I snarled, my voice raw.

"Semantics," Valerius replied, a faint, condescending smile touching his lips. "I was freeing them from the burden of a fractured past, from the chaotic memories of dead gods and the pain of parents who chose heresy over peace. I was giving them clarity, a single, perfect truth to guide them. You have undone that. You have returned them to their agony. You see yourself as a liberator, Danica Madsen, yet you are a purveyor of suffering, a ghost clinging to a world that has already chosen to forget you."

Every word was a perfectly crafted dart, aimed at the deepest, most vulnerable parts of my soul. The way he held himself spoke of more than military discipline; it was the rigid posture of a true believer, his faith a weapon more potent than any rifle. The fire inside me, which had been a roaring inferno moments before, now flickered, threatened by the cold, chilling certainty in his eyes. He moved then, with the fluid, undeniable grace of a dancer, his blade a silver whisper in the air.

I raised my own sword to meet him, steel screaming against whatever unholy metal his was forged from. The impact sent a shockwave up my arm, a numbing, dissonant vibration that sought to deaden the power within me. I pushed back, unleashing a wave of frost, a golden sigil bloomed in the air before him, and my magic dissipated against it, rendered inert. His weapon was a nullifier, a blade designed to unravel the very chaos I wielded.

"Your gods are dead," he hissed, his face inches from mine, his pale eyes burning with a zealot's fire. "Their power is a fleeting echo in a world that now sings Her name."

He was fast, his blade a relentless, weaving pattern of strikes and parries. He was trying to exhaust me, to bleed the power from me until I was nothing more than a woman with a sword. And it was working. My breath came in ragged gasps, my muscles screaming in protest. The fire and frost that had answered my call so readily before now felt distant and sluggish. He pressed his attack, cutting my arm, a shallow and burning line of pain. He scored a line across my cheek, the cold steel a caress of death.

I stumbled back, my boots slipping on the ash-slicked ground. He saw his opening and lunged, his blade aimed at my heart. There was no time for fire, no time for frost. There was only the Blade of Fates and the weight of a thousand lifetimes behind my arm. I met his lunge with a desperate, brutal thrust of my own, throwing all of my weight, all of my rage, all of my grief into it. Our blades slid past each other. His hummed past my ear, close enough to feel the vibration of its power.

Mine did not miss. The Blade of Fates, forged in myth and tempered in sorrow, sank into his chest, just below the collarbone, punching through his sanctified armor with a sound like tearing silk.

Valerius froze. A profound, almost childlike surprise crossed his face. He looked down at the ancient steel buried in his body, then back up at me. The zealotry in his eyes was gone, replaced by a dawning, terrible understanding. "But... She is... peace..." he whispered, a dribble of blood escaping his lips.

I twisted the blade, my voice breaking, my body trembling with the sheer effort of it all. "She is a cage."

I pulled the sword free. Valerius stood for a moment, a statue of shattered faith, and then he collapsed, his ornate armor clattering on the broken stone. I stood over his body, panting, bleeding, my vision blurring at the edges. The pass was silent once more. The battle was over, truly over this time.

The adrenaline faded, and in its place, a wave of profound exhaustion washed over me, so complete that my knees buckled. I fell to the ground beside the Inquisitor's body, the Blade of Fates slipping from my numb fingers. The victory was ash in my mouth. I had won, I had become a monster to fight a monster. I lay there for a long time, the cold seeping back into my bones, my breath mingling with the smoke.

A shadow fell over me. I looked up to see Milan, his face a mask of awe and a deep, unsettling fear as his gaze swept over the vaporized soldiers and Valerius's body.

"Gods above, Danica," he breathed, shaking his head slowly. "I've seen you fight... this... what have you become?"

I didn't have an answer for that. I closed my eyes, the wooden bird a hard, painful lump against my ribs, and let the darkness take me.

CHAPTER THREE
THE HOUSE OF NO DAWN

Ilija

I woke to silence so complete I could hear my own pulse. Cultivated quiet, swept clean, deliberate as a held breath. The air tasted sweet. Lotus, I recognized after a moment, threaded through with something older. A flower that had never grown in any garden I knew. The scent settled at the back of my throat, insistent as a hand on my shoulder.

The floor beneath me was marble, still warm from my body. Gold veins forked through the white stone like frozen lightning. Beautiful. When I finally sat up, my body screamed. Every muscle, every bone. I'd been pushed past breaking and somehow kept moving.

No chains. No shackles. My prison was more elegant than that.

My ribs pulsed with each shallow breath. Something deep in my bones rang with spent power, the hollow ache of a god who'd used too much too fast. My mouth was dust. When I swallowed, I tasted lotus again—that sweet, quieting drug that promised to make everything stop hurting. I knew that taste. Dangerous. Familiar. Another thread in the net holding me here.

A hand runs over my head. The skin is slick with cold sweat. Even the familiar smoothness of my scalp feels wrong, like it belongs to someone else. My reflection in the polished floor—distorted, warped in the gold-veined marble. The face staring back is haggard. Eyes too wide. A caged animal.

The walls made this clear—they wanted me to know the totality of my confinement. Seamless marble curved up into a perfect dome painted with a sky too exact to be real. Stars in patterns I recognized and patterns I didn't. Dawn had been captured on that ceiling, arrested at the moment before light wins. The painter had frozen that last tremor of darkness giving way, then refused to let it finish. Silk draperies hung at the edges, pale and still. Even my breath hesitated before moving. This place was built by a god with a surgeon's precision and a jailer's heart.

Rome. The memory hit like a thrown stone breaking water.

Absolute chaos. Stairs under my feet. Bodies pressing past. The smoke was thick, acrid, burning plastic and cordite and something organic my mind refused to name. Red emergency lights turning the world to raw meat. Flash. Flash. Flash. The sleek black shapes of Accord drones cut through the sky. Stone falling in ribbons. Ana's hand on my arm, burning hot. A command. The rift tearing open, edges snow-bright and terrible, the universe screaming as reality peeled back. The world losing its name as I tumbled through colorless energy. Danica's face. Her mouth forming my name. Then nothing.

I reach for more and find only this polished stillness.

"Where—" My voice comes out hoarse, ugly in this pristine place. I lower it, the effort scraping my throat raw. "Where the fuck am I?"

The silence answers. A voice like ice chimes, coming from nowhere and everywhere.

"Here."

I scan the room for a door, a shadow, anything. But she's already there. A solitary figure in the hushed chamber, her form slight and sorrowful. Her dress is deep black, absorbing light, making her a void. A veil cascades from crown to neck, revealing features so precise they look carved. Her face shows nothing—no malice, no mercy. Unreadable stillness. Her hands rest empty at her sides, pale and unadorned. The lotus scent intensifies around her.

"I am Tisiphone," she says, and the name seals around her like wax on a ring. "Witness and correction."

Fury. Erinys. This is no harpy, no nightmare from guilty dreams, but a priestess of grief, an artist of consequence. My skin prickles.

"I haven't—" I start, then stop. Haven't what? Woken? Remembered? Been forgiven?

"You have brought mortals under your shadow," she says, her voice flat and distant. "You have called storms and told yourself you were only weather. Come. See with both eyes."

The room's edges soften. The dome's stars extinguish with the sound of a pinched wick. I'm standing, though I have no memory of rising. Walking, though my feet seem distant. The lotus drains from the air and Rome's iron reek floods back. I've been pulled down through the surface of this place, into the dregs of my own memory.

The vision is relentless. I'm a ghost forced to watch what I can only witness.

The corridor. Half-lit by emergency strips bleeding terrified red. A woman with a scarf over her mouth reaches for a child. A man presses a satchel into someone's hands. Myself, distant and useless: "Move, go, now."

A boy with mismatched sleeves—blue at one wrist, gray at the other—turns to look back. Twenty years old at most, freckles like dried pomegranate seeds scattered across his nose, the mouth of someone who smiles easily when there's anyone left to smile for.

He will die in seven breaths.

He lives in ignorance. I carry the knowledge like a fishbone stuck in my throat. I try to force my body in the memory to move toward him, to drag him forward, but memory doesn't obey the future. The spear whistles out of the smoke. It finds him where he stands.

The sound he makes is indignation first, then astonishment, then nothing as he sinks to the floor and his blood goes black on the ruined tile.

"Stop," I say. To Tisiphone, to the image, to the past.

"Look," she replies. Her breath stirs the hairs at my temple though her veil doesn't move. "Look because you need it, and because not looking is its own cowardice."

Faces unfold from the crowd—precise people, the woman whose scarf became so saturated with dust she tore it away and laughed once, as if breath itself were indecent. The old man holding his chest like a parcel he meant to keep. A girl with gold thread sewn through her sleeve—she pulls it loose and ties it back with her teeth.

A hand on my back. "Professor."

I never knew his name. I do now, because the Erinys is ruthless.

Milo.

Of course he has a name. When the beam gives way he leaps for me and pays for it with his spine. In the moment, I didn't hear the breath leave him. Here, I can't hear anything else.

"You taught the tragedies," Tisiphone says, calm as a litany. "You told them hubris is crossing the boundary set for mortals. You taught that crossing with power makes catastrophe, and the gods don't take intent for absolution."

"Their fate was sealed the moment the Accord was signed," I say. My voice sounds like a stranger's. "Her world killed them, not mine."

"You opened a gate for what you are." Her voice is gentle. Unyielding. A whisper that cuts sharper than shouting. "You brought ancient thunder to a street filled with children and called it weather. You unleashed something that predates memory into their fragile lives. You rationalized it. Convinced yourself it was only a passing storm. But the skies you opened don't close. They echo with what you are, and they've found their home among them now."

The serene torture shatters.

The air in the memory curdles. Dust and fear replaced by blood, shit, burning flesh. Alecto—the Fury of unceasing anger—steps forward from shadow. Her form crackles. Her snarl vibrates in my teeth. She reaches out and touches my ghostly form.

"Witnessing is for cowards," she hisses. "Feel it."

The world fractures.

No longer watching. In the boy's skin now. Rough fabric of mismatched sleeves against my wrists. Dust and fear in my mouth. The frantic, hopeful beat of his young heart. Turning to throw the strap to the professor, an act of pure instinct, and the spear strikes.

Incomprehensible agony punches through my back. Shatters a rib. Explodes out my chest. Air ripped from my lungs in a wet, choked gasp. Indignant shock. Profound biological offense. My legs collapse. I taste my own blood, hot and coppery, flooding my throat.

My last thought: Fuck.

I'm thrown back into my own body, on my knees on cold marble, vomiting thin bile. My own ribs ache in sympathy. Alecto is laughing. The sound of tearing metal.

"Again," she snarls.

The vision shifts. Milo now. The strength in his shoulders, the desperate loyalty in his heart. The professor, me, stumbles. The massive beam groaning above. No time for decision. Only the act. A shove. A lifetime of force in a single push.

Then the world ends in pulverizing white-hot pain as my spine turns to dust.

I don't feel death. I feel the moment before it. My consciousness obliterated by weight it cannot comprehend.

I was back in the chamber, screaming this time, raw and ragged, but Alecto continues.

"You feel their pain," she hisses, circling. "Now feel the pain you gave."

The world dissolves into Rijeka. An Accord soldier now. Young, terrified, faith a thin shield against horror. A monster wreathed in lightning. Me. Rifle raised, hands shaking, and then a bolt of raw white energy hits.

I'm in his body as my own power incinerates me from the inside out. Armor melting, fusing to skin. Lungs boiling. Divine fury scouring my soul clean in absolute agony. My last sensation is the smell of my own flesh cooking.

"Enough," I sob, curled on the floor, body knotted with sympathetic pain and trauma. "Please. Enough."

The violence recedes. Blood and cooked meat fading to quiet. Megaera, the Fury of grudges, steps forward. Her sisters fade into shadow, their work done. Her voice slides into my ear like venom.

"The body is easy to break, storm-god," she murmurs, kneeling beside me. "The heart is more exquisite."

The marble dissolves into soft green lawn. I'm standing somewhere I've never been, but it tugs at something in my chest. A small house with a porch under summer sky. Wind chimes made of seashells singing. The air smells of cut grass and the sea. Peace I've never known.

An older Danica walks onto the porch, alone and beautiful but scarred in ways I've never seen. The fire in her eyes has cooled to weary ember, hardness in her jaw, deep sadness in her gaze. She moves with a warrior's grace and exhaustion—someone who's fought too long. She looks out at the sea, and her hand rises to touch something at her throat. A pendant I gave her once. Her fingers close around it, then drop.

The vision shifts, and I see Danica leading a charge through burning streets, her face a mask of fury with only grim necessity in her power. Blood on her hands that won't wash clean. She's magnificent and terrible and utterly alone.

Another shift. Danica in a sterile room, staring at maps. Red pins marking battles. Her hair is shorter, streaked with gray. Someone tries to speak to her. She keeps her eyes on the map. The war has consumed everything else.

Another. Danica kneeling in snow, hands pressed to the earth where a village used to be. Her shoulders shake, but she's cried herself dry years ago.

Megaera's voice coils around me.

"This is the world you give her if you survive. A life defined by your war. A woman who forgets how to be anything but a soldier. Who carries your storms until they hollow her out. Your love is a curse, Ilija. The cage that will keep her from ever knowing peace. The kindest thing you could do, the only genuinely loving thing is let her go. Forget her. Free her from the burden of you."

The vision fades. I'm in the marble chamber, broken. The Furies showed me my guilt, my pain, and now they've shown me my love is the most potent poison of all. I'm a curse in a man's skin. A walking catastrophe. The kindest thing I could do for her is cease to exist in her heart.

The thought sits in my gut like a blade.

The chamber receives me again. Silent. An indifferent witness to my unmaking. The Erinyes are gone. I'm alone with the wreckage of my soul.

Another voice threads the air. "Truth is not the only drink."

She steps out as if the lotus scent itself learned to take a body. Ana. Quieter now. Her presence dimmed to candleflame. Her eyes hold sorrow I want to believe. Her hair is damp where it lies against her throat, as if she's come from a storm and made herself clean for me. She carries a shallow cup in both hands.

"You're tired." A hand on the back of my head, lowering it gently. "Of course you are. Drink."

"What is it?" I hate the suspicion in my voice.

"A kindness. Protection. A way to let the noise pass. You've always carried more noise than you admit."

She kneels before me. Silk pooling on marble. Close enough that I can see tiny scars at the corners of her mouth I've never catalogued before. The faint crescent where some childhood injury marked her eyebrow. She looks almost human.

"Remember the nights in Belgrade?" she murmurs, soft and nostalgic. "After a bad lecture, when the weight of all those dead gods was too much?

You'd pace the apartment for hours, unable to be still. I'd make you tea. Mint and honey. You'd drink it and the storm in you would quiet. Just for a little while."

She lifts the cup until the rim touches my lip. The scent is mint grown in shadow. I taste it. Relief. Immediate and profound. A coolness sliding behind my eyes, telling them they need not hold so much pain. The image of the boy with mismatched sleeves recedes. The sound of Milo's spine snapping softens to distant echo. The vision of Danica's hardened face, alone in that house by the sea, blurs at the edges.

I could drink. The world would grow manageable. Simple. Clean. Untorn.

"From what?" I ask. The question is a final anchor to the man I was. "You say you'll protect me. From what."

"From the uses other people make of you," she says, and I want very much to be persuaded. "From the parts of yourself that always turn into storms. From Danica."

I make myself hold her gaze. "From Danica."

"She collides with you. She makes ruin out of your restraint. She takes your careful life and pulls it toward her and calls that destiny. She's ruinous. She harms you, and she always has. You know this. Let me protect you where she would spend you."

The cup is still at my lip. I think of Danica as the Furies made me see her—distant, powerful, hardened. A warrior who's forgotten joy. I think of the pain my existence will cause her. The cup feels heavier in Ana's hands. Oblivion, just within reach.

"I've asked you to rest inside what I know is true."

"What you know," I repeat.

"What the gods know," she corrects. The softness thins. I see the mechanism underneath—the wheel, the gear, the logic that belongs to power. "You are made for clarity, Ilija. Danica confuses you. Drink."

I could be spared this work. I could stop being a man drawn thin across two natures. I could free Danica from my curse. I could let the pain stop. Just for a little while. Rest. My lips part.

Then I remember.

The memory rises from a place Ana cannot reach. A place older than her schemes.

Winter. The kind that makes stone crack. Sigrun is standing in the doorway of the longhouse, snow caught in her dark hair like stars. She's bleeding from a cut above her eye—some skirmish with raiders I'd missed. She's furious with me. Has been for days.

"You think the storm makes you wise," she says. Her breath fogs the air between us. "It makes you absent."

I'm Alatyr then. Younger. Stupider. I say something about duty, about watching the borders. The words taste like ash even as I speak them.

"Focus, Alatyr. We need to be ready for whatever fucking hell they through at us."

"If I'm being honest with you, I'm terrified, Sigrun."

"I am too my love, but we need to end this fucking goddess once and for all. You are more than the storm inside you. You are my storm in all the ways that matter."

She kisses me, fiercely.

That was Sigrun. Fierce and uncompromising and absolutely certain. The one person across lifetimes who'd ever made me want to be fully present.

I lower the cup. The motion feels small and enormous at once. Ana's mouth tightens by the breadth of a breath.

"Another time," I say carefully. "Perhaps."

"You always think you can live on the edge of the choice forever," she says, exasperation threading her tone. "It's what makes you a scholar. It's also what makes you a dangerous god. Neither will serve you now."

She sets the cup on the marble. No sound when it meets stone.

"Will you keep coming?" I ask.

"Yes," she says simply. "Until you're safe."

She withdraws into the scent the way a hand withdraws from water, leaving no mark. But my defiance has a cost. The moment she's gone, the Erinyes return, forms crackling with rage.

"Stubborn fool," Megaera hisses. "She offered you peace."

"You choose pain," Tisiphone states, voice like a scalpel. "Then let us remind you of its shape."

Alecto says nothing. She only grins.

The world dissolves into the kitchen of my childhood. My father is on the floor. My mother is screaming. Steam rises from his cup. The scene plays on loop, faster and faster, dizzying and nauseating spiral of my first great trauma. The thud of his body. The shatter of my mother's voice. The mocking steam. Over and over, drilling into my skull.

"Fuck you," I snarl at the memory.

I wrench my mind away from the vision, away from the pain. Force my eyes open and stare at the painted dome above. I find the spot. The single pinprick of darkness where a star had been. A flaw in my perfect prison. An anchor.

I focus on it. Pour every ounce of will into it. The memory of Danica's touch. The sound of Milo's last thought. The weight of the boy's death. I gather all of it—all the pain they gave me—and I use it.

The Furies recoil as if struck. The vision of my father's death shatters like glass. They stare at me, serene faces twisted with genuine shock. They showed me my wounds, and I just learned to make them into a shield.

"You will be asked to call sleep mercy," Tisiphone says, voice cold with new respect. "Be careful."

"How careful can a man be when he's hungry for forgetting?"

"That is precisely the measure," she replies. Then they're gone, leaving only the outline of their absence.

I was back in the chamber. I lay back and counted the painted stars. I found the shape I thought of as Danica's. I held the memory whole.

A god can eat thunder for a century and still starve. A man can live a week on the warmth of a shoulder.

The star I extinguished is still gone—a beautiful, defiant wound in the perfect sky.

I sat up, the marble cool against my back. The walls offered nothing, but the ceiling—its sky, its lid—had taken a breath and let one star go. I laid my palm flat on the marble and felt the steady engine of my heart, and for the first time since I woke, I felt something beyond containment.

They meant to take my mind. They meant to set me gently inside a room of good arguments and better sleep and close the door on storms and the particular person who wakes them. They meant to make me useful and quiet.

Here, in this gilded cage, memory offered no comfort. It arrived as a blade, and I'd been given the steadiness of hand to use it. Danica's face, the face she makes the second before laughter—became the edge that kept me.

On the ceiling, the dark where the star was held caught me eyes. I don't know if another will go when next I choose to remember. I know only this: the door they've denied me isn't in the wall. It's in what I refuse to let go.

I lay back down and practiced the quiet of a room I would leave behind. A single point of night on a painted sky was new as any dawn. I knew, with certainty that sat in me like an anchor set deep, this was the field of battle.

And I was armed.

Time in this place was a fiction. The sterile, arrested dawn on the ceiling, never changed. I measured it in the slow rhythm of my pulse. In cycles of hunger and thirst that Ana's offering always appears on a silent pedestal when I was weakest—sought to quell.

I ate, I drank, I used the grief and pain as fuel, and I fought back.

My rebellion was quiet, an act of pure, focused will—lying on the marble, I closed my eyes and reached for a memory of Danica forged in violence and defiance.

The battle at the Meadow of Saints, the visceral shock of her power, the way she moved like a storm front with fire and frost as her willing accomplices. The grit in her voice, blood on her cheek, the unwavering loyalty in her eyes even as the world burned around us. I held the memory as a living thing, gave it my full attention, my breath, my will, and let the memory of her strength become my own.

Above me, another star flickered, resisted for a moment, stubborn point of light, then it too was extinguished, leaving another scar on the flawless, false sky.

A sound like silk scraped on stone brought me back. Tisiphone stood over me, veiled face turned toward the dome.

"Each one you take has a cost, son of the storm," she said. Voice flat and cold.

I sat up, my own voice a low growl. "What? Do you run out of paint?"

"This chamber is a tapestry. A loom. And you're pulling at the threads. You think you're wounding only your cage. You're wounding the world outside as well."

I stared at her. "What the fuck are you talking about?"

"Every star that dies here is a memory that fades from the waking world. A small truth erased. A name forgotten. A story loses its ending. You fight for your own recollection by forcing forgetting upon others. That's the price of your defiance. Ana offers oblivion for you alone. You choose it for everyone."

The words were cold weight in my gut. I looked up at the two pinpricks of darkness, two tiny wounds in the fabric of my prison, and wondered what I'd just destroyed. A child's memory of a lullaby? A lover's recollection of a first kiss? The name of a forgotten hero?

"You see," she said, voice a rustle of dry leaves. "Even your virtue has a shadow."

She vanished as she always did, leaving me alone with my choices. For a time, I was still. I considered her words. The poison in them. The elegant trap. To fight for my memory was to erase someone else's. To save myself, I had to sacrifice a piece of the very world I was fighting for.

I lay back on the marble, the cold seeping into my bones, and the choice was clear, a world of perfect, ordered silence under Ana, or a world scarred and broken by the fight for truth.

I thought of Danica. Her unwavering belief that a remembered pain is better than a forgotten peace.

I closed my eyes. Reached for another memory. Her laughter in that ruined church. The sound so beautiful and unexpected in that broken place felt like a prayer. A benediction on the decaying stone and our tangled lives. I could almost feel the rough marble beneath my fingertips. Smell the damp earth. Hear the distant hum of cicadas in the Italian sun.

But even as I clung to it, cold crushing weight settled in my chest. Above me, a third star extinguished. Its brilliance fading to a pinprick, then nothing.

Each disappearing star was a wrenching blow, a physical manifestation of memory ripped from me—they were anchors tethering me to who I was, to what I'd experienced, and to lose them was to lose fragments of my soul.

Defiance surged within me.

I refuse to stop. I will face this oblivion head-on. I'll rip this entire sky down if necessary. One memory at a time. I'll fight with every fiber of my being, clawing back each stolen fragment. For as long as there's even a single flicker of light, a single whisper of a forgotten moment, I'll resist.

The pain is unbearable. The fear a constant companion.

The thought of her laughter—that beautiful, unexpected prayer in a ruined church—gives me what I need to keep going.

I will not let them take her from me.

CHAPTER FOUR
ASHES OF DELPHI

Danica

The mountain gave us their smoke before their faces. Bitter, cheap tobacco riding the wind, clinging to stone with the stink of nervous sweat. Two Accord scouts leaned on their rifles at the ridge—careless, slack, drunk on the arrogance of men who think the war is already won. In the deepening twilight, the red tips of their cigarettes were the only stars left, two angry points of light in a world bleeding dark.

I took my knife and moved before Kostas could stop me. Good soldier, Kostas—loyal and true, but loud. His boots scraped stone where mine found silence. Years of battles weighed him down: metal on metal, old leather creaking, that ankle he fucked up outside Sarajevo making him favor his left. I'd learned to move like something that hunts. The ground yielded beneath me, frost-brittle grass bending without sound.

I flowed through shadows between rocks, each breath a plume in the freezing air. The cold burned my lungs, stripped every thought down to the kill. My senses sharpened to a predator's edge.

The first went down with a surprised breath, his cigarette scattering sparks across the gravel. I caught his weight and lowered him to the ground, his life bleeding warm against my arm. The second spun, eyes going wide and animal, mouth opening to shout. My knife was already at his throat. A moment of resistance—steel meeting cartilage—then warmth spilling fast and hot over my wrist. The night swallowed it, swallowed us.

Kostas dragged bodies into rocks like he was stacking firewood. Efficient. Grim. He spat when it was done, his scar a pale slash in the moonlight. "Gods preserve us."

I wiped my blade on dead man's fabric. "They won't."

He grunted, fingers finding the red thread at his wrist—his wife's wedding dress, faded and filthy now. He'd tied it there before the Accord came. He shouldered his rifle, gave me that look. The one that says he's buried too many friends to argue with a woman who moves like a knife in the dark.

We climbed higher, the path narrowing to a goat-track carved by centuries of feet and crumbling from neglect. Pines clung to the slopes, their branches whispering warnings we ignored, their scent sharp and clean in the stale air. The higher we went, the heavier the silence pressed down on us, thick with the weight of every prayer ever screamed into this mountain. I remembered this path from before, when I'd come here desperate and seeking, when the air still held peace. Now that peace was gutted, replaced by the Accord's sterile violation.

Delphi rose like a wound that wouldn't close. Columns clawed at the sky—some standing with weary grace, others shattered and half-buried. Broken steps climbing to nowhere. This place had been the world's center once, the omphalos, where mortals spoke to gods. Now it was a corpse they'd strung up with lights.

Floodlights washed the ruins white and brutal. Electrical cables strung like thorns across marble older than memory. The Accord's red banners bled down Apollo's temple, Ana's golden rose a brand on sacred bone.

My jaw ached from clenching. Kostas glanced at me sidelong—that look he gets when he thinks I'm about to do something stupidly brave.

"Two at the portico. More by the generator," he murmured. His thumb brushed his scar. "Perimeter fence is high-frequency. We go through it. We're shadows."

I nodded. We speak the same language: impossible odds and fuck it anyway.

We slid through bent wire, strands curling like dead snakes. Inside, the air thickened. Generators hummed, oppressive and low. The stone hummed back—older, deeper. I pressed my palm to a fallen column. Heat pulsed through marble, faint and alive. The earth remembering prophecy. The Accord draped this place in lights and orders, but they couldn't silence it.

We moved through shadows. Spiro slipped behind a guard and opened his throat before the man could breathe. Lowered him into darkness with practiced tenderness. Eirene took position in a shattered column, rifle becoming stone. Kostas led us in, steps measured like a mason laying something that won't fall.

Inside, the temple reeked of dust, sweat, diesel. Sacred space turned command post. Apollo's carvings worn to ghosts, spray-painted over with Accord red: MEMORY IS OBEDIENCE. DOUBT IS DISSONANCE. Ammunition crates cluttering the floor. Papers weighed down with rocks and broken statues. The omphalos stone sat cracked in the center, fissure running through its heart like a mortal wound.

Broken. Still alive. I felt power radiating from it when I touched the stone.

I moved to the tables, sifting through papers, hands shaking more than I wanted. Accord stamps in red. Phrases burning through my skull. Olympus Initiative. Containment protocols. Divine Asset Repurposing. Then a thin file, heading simple and devastating: Subject Alatyr.

My throat closed. His name. His ancient name reduced to a subject line, a thing to be catalogued and contained. They had him in a cell somewhere, strapped down or drugged or broken, and I wasn't there. Seven years I'd searched and he'd been in their hands the whole time, breathing their recycled air, becoming their Subject.

The rage that tore through me was physical, white-hot and blinding.

Before I could grab more, a shriek tore through the temple—high-pitched, electronic. Cold synthetic voice from speakers: "Dissonant presence detected in sanctum. Sector four lockdown initiated. All units converge."

Floodlights flared outside. Magnetic locks slammed home at the entrance. Boots thundering on marble.

Kostas kicked a crate against the door. "Barricade! Eirene, west arch! Spiro, with me!"

The battle erupted. Accord soldiers breached in bone-white armor, stark against shadow. Their HK416s cracked the air—crack-crack-crack—hyper-velocity rounds punching holes in stone, dust and rock exploding everywhere.

Kostas's rifle barked. Two soldiers dropped. Eirene took another with a throat shot. Spiro's knife found flesh, steel flashing, gurgle choking off.

I moved. A round tore fire across my arm and I drove my blade under ribs, snarling. He folded heavy against me. I shoved him off as another came. Gunfire roaring, stone screaming, marble splitting under modern hate.

Kostas cried out—round caught his leg. He went down against a column, teeth bared, blood spreading dark across his thigh! Hands steady, slamming a fresh magazine home. "Still up," he snarled, and put two rounds center mass.

We were outnumbered. Every soldier we dropped, two more poured through. Sentry turrets unfolded from the ceiling, red dots painting our chests. Pinned. The odds turning from bad to you're-going-to-die-here.

"Danica!" Eirene screaming. "APC blocking the exit!"

I looked. Sleek black armor sliding into place, heavy gun swiveling. Our tomb sealing shut.

We were going to die here.

Kostas kept fighting even wounded and bleeding, blood streaming from a gash at his temple. He parried a bayonet thrust with his rifle, then cracked the soldier's jaw with the stock. Each breath was a struggle, but he fought like a cornered animal refusing to die.

Eirene searched desperately for a shot. The APC kept moving, erratic, blocking every angle. Her fingers trembled on the trigger.

Spiro moved like death itself, a blade gleaming in each hand as he engaged three soldiers at once. Whirlwind of steel and shadow. One lunged at him—Spiro's knife was already opening his throat. Another fell back, Spiro's second blade buried in his chest, scream dying with him.

They fought for me, for the fragile hope I carried. And I was going to get them all killed.

Fuck. That.

Something inside me—wound tight since the convoy, since Rome, since the first time I felt the rings burn against my skin—finally snapped its leash. Grief, rage, seven years of aching and wanting and losing, and the terrible power coiled in my bones all surged up at once. The woman with a knife disappeared.

The thing that kills rose in her place.

I rose from behind the altar. The air grew heavy, charged, humming in my teeth. Gunfire slowed to a dull thrum in my ears.

Every Accord soldier turned. Their visors caught the storm building in my eyes. They were about to learn what happens when you cage a goddess.

"Get down," I said. My voice resonated in their bones.

My hands rose. I breathed deep—dragging the mountain itself into my lungs, dormant power waking in granite and flowing into me like molten gold. The air crackled. Then I unleashed it with a roar that shook the temple.

Pure elemental chaos erupted from me. Frost and flame in paradox, in violation of every natural law.

Ice shot across flagstones—sharp, glittering, deadly—catching soldiers mid-stride and freezing their legs solid where they stood. They gasped at the impossible cold, breath crystallizing in the air. Before they could scream, white-hot fire washed over them. The air sizzled, ozone thick and choking, as flames devoured ice and turned frozen men to hissing steam and blackened bone. They crumbled to ash.

Turrets melted, barrels dripping slag. The APC caught the wave—frost cracked armor, fire found fuel cells. It detonated. Fireball roaring into the night, painting everything orange and final.

Absolute. Terrifying. It drained me hollow. The world swam. Sounds distant. I fell to my knees, trembling, the Blade of Fates clattering beside me.

Silence.

My team stared. Awe. Relief. And underneath—raw, primal fear.

I'd saved them. I'd shown them the monster.

Smoke hung low with the stink of blood and burnt oil, the air tasting of ozone and cooked metal. My ears rang with the ghost of released power. I stood in the center of carnage I'd created, breath ragged and painful, body shaking violently. Fire and frost receded from my skin, leaving a hollow ache that settled deep in my bones.

They emerged from shadows slowly, cautiously, like men approaching a wild thing they'd mistaken for an ally. Spiro stared at his hands, then at the place where the APC had been vaporized, and stepped back involuntarily. Eirene kept her rifle trained on the ruined doorway, knuckles white around the stock, stealing glances at me when she thought I wasn't looking. They'd seen me fight before, but never like that. They'd witnessed a warrior. Now they'd seen a god.

And gods don't take orders.

Kostas broke the silence. Limped forward using his rifle as a crutch, face pale under grime and blood. He stopped feet away, staring at the Blade where it lay.

"Danica," voice rough, hesitant. "What... what was that?"

I looked at my hands, half-expecting claws or scales, something monstrous to match what I'd just done. Just my hands—slender, scarred from childhood, stained with soot and blood. But they felt alien, like they belonged to someone else, someone capable of destroying the world.

The power was a living thing inside me, a caged storm that had been raging against its confines for weeks, months. It hummed in my veins constantly, an eager beast barely leashed. For one terrifying moment, it had broken free and surged through me. I'd been nothing but a conduit, a vessel for its release. The memory was still fresh, a vivid nightmare looping endlessly in my mind.

"I don't know," I whispered.

Fear in their eyes mirrored the terror coiling in my gut. In their hesitant steps and averted gazes, I felt a new wound opening: isolation. A chasm carved by the sheer scale of power I wielded. They were human.

I was becoming divine.

Kostas gathered himself. Soldier wrestling back control from terrified man. He cleared his throat, gestured at scattered papers. "The intel. Did you find what we came for?"

An anchor. A line across the chasm. Pulling me back to purpose.

I gathered papers into my pack, hands trembling. Olympus Initiative. Subject Alatyr. Cold iron. Heavier than anything else in this room.

Kostas slumped against the altar, scar pulsing in the red emergency light. He grinned—more grimace than smile, fear still lingering in his eyes. Voice raspy, barely a whisper: "So. He's alive."

I tightened my pack straps. Papers a lead weight. "Yes," I said. Blade and vow.

We left Delphi in smoke and ruin, a charred testament to the night's violence. The acrid scent of burning pine mingled with metallic fear, clinging to our clothes and skin. The mountain took us down through shadow and the echoes of our screams, familiar paths now treacherous and dark. We moved like ghosts, limping through twilight, each step a mournful cadence. The pines whispered their lament overhead.

Kostas leaned heavily on Spiro, accepting only his brother's help. That quiet strength was the only comfort he could bear. The others followed in a ragged line, exhausted and despairing. The distance between us had become a chasm carved by what they'd witnessed, by what I'd become. I carried the physical weight in my pack—supplies, intelligence, shattered hope—but the heavier weight sat under my ribs, a cold certainty that solidified with every downward step.

They had him. Somewhere above the world, in a place of eternal darkness, they held Ilija.

The thought burned like an ember lodged in my chest, refusing to die.

I swore to the mountain, to Delphi's ashes, to the core of my being: I would climb Olympus itself. I would tear apart whatever fortress they'd built on that sacred peak, rip away its foundations stone by stone, and expose every secret to unforgiving light. All to bring him back.

Every breath, every step, every thought would be dedicated to that singular purpose.

I would fight. I would endure.

Until he was safe and the nightmare that held him was utterly destroyed.

CHAPTER FIVE
CHAINS AND SERPENTS

Ilija

Each memory tears away with a scream, each one ripping a piece of my sanity with it, and I can feel myself fragmenting, breaking apart into something that will be easier to control, easier to reshape.

They tell you nothing in the texts I've memorized, in the myths I've taught, about how long a place of eternal dawn can last inside a man. The ceiling holds its painted sky like breath suspended forever, stars fixed with the precision of a medieval manuscript. Morning waits at the edge of a door that exists only as torment. I've been counting days by heartbeat, though even that measurement has begun to feel like self-deception. Time moves here thick and slow, heavy as honey poured in winter.

I lie on this slab, taught gentleness by degrees I can calculate but resist, and count what refuses to change. The lotus perfume returns each time I think I've expelled it, patient as Penelope's weaving. It crawls into my sinuses and makes residence there, sweet and cloying, turning my thoughts soft at the edges. The marble beneath me has accepted my body's heat and means to keep it. I've tried to stay cold, tried to keep some fragment of myself that belongs to the world outside, though stone has time to teach, and my bones are learning whether I consent or otherwise.

Somewhere in the false heavens, five small absences endure where stars once refused their painted duty. I made those holes in moments when memory burned brighter than Ana's engineering. Each rebellion cost me something: a piece of the storm that once lived easy in my chest, a fragment of pneuma, that divine spark of living breath. I pretend these wounds in the painted sky are windows. I pretend I can feel coolness passing through them, though what touches my skin is only memory.

The silence has weight. It presses against my eardrums like deep water, and I've learned to parse its languages: the whisper of my own blood, the creak of joints when I shift, the soft rustle of thoughts seeking purchase on something real. Sometimes I lecture to myself just to prove I still possess a voice, though even that's becoming dangerous. Words here have power, and power demands payment.

When the silence moves, it moves like a decree read in the Senate. The room makes space, the air genuflects. Tisiphone steps into the place the quiet has cleared, her veil falling with practiced drape over a face sculpted to remember verdicts and forget the people inside them. I've studied that face for weeks now—or months, or years; time here refuses proper naming. It remains difficult to look at, this face that makes you want to confess sins you haven't yet had time to commit.

Megaera shadows her, broad-shouldered and brimming with resentment that has found muscle to inhabit. She carries her anger like a tool perfected through centuries of use. I can feel it radiating from her skin, making the air taste of copper and old grievances. Alecto brings up the rear, her anatomy reduced to edges, to the essential geometry of threat. Her mouth draws back from her teeth in something worse than a snarl—the almost-smile of a woman who has stopped asking whether this is necessary.

On their first visitation, they came dressed as mourners. Soft grays, voices like distant thunder over the Adriatic. They spoke of loss, of the necessity of letting go, of the mercy in forgetting. They quoted Heraclitus at me, as if I hadn't spent twenty years teaching that you step into a different river every time. Today they brought their tools.

Chains drop from the dome in silence. They unspool like silk from a spider that has learned to work in metal, ending in rings worked so finely they could be a jeweler's last testament before blindness claimed him. The craftsmanship is flawless, which makes it worse. Someone cared enough to make my prison beautiful. The chains drink light into a tarnish that looks like the color of kept promises. I know that color—it's the same shade as the ring Danica wore on her right hand, the one that belonged to her grandmother, the one she turned constantly when thinking through violence.

From the corners where wall joins floor, serpents lift their heads with automatic grace, bodies clear as blown glass, their scales catching painted starlight and reflecting it back in fractured images. Each scale is a perfect mirror showing me in pieces: an eye here, the corner of a mouth there, all of it fragmented like Byzantine mosaic tiles waiting to be assembled into meaning.

Their tongues taste the air and read the room: This man belongs to someone else, and that someone is elsewhere.

I've watched them before, during the long hours when the Furies leave me alone with my thoughts—its own form of torture. They move with that terrible beauty Rilke wrote about, the kind that is the beginning of terror we're still just able to bear. They know exactly what they are and what they're meant to do. My hands shake when I watch them, betraying the uncertainty living in my chest like a second heartbeat.

"Witness," Tisiphone says—announcing herself or commanding me, both probably, the way certain Greek verbs can be middle or passive voice depending on your willingness to take responsibility. "Correction."

"I've already looked," I answer, because talking keeps the terror from eating me whole. "You made me look. I've seen it from every angle you wanted and some I discovered myself."

She inclines her head by the breadth of a hair—an acknowledgment that could mean anything or everything. "It is time you learn to see rather than merely look."

The words sit wrong in my mouth, like barbarism forced into proper Greek meter. As if seeing could be undone by will alone, as if memory were just another muscle you could train to forget its strength.

Megaera's mouth cuts a curve that might once have been a smile before disappointment taught it accuracy. "Let us spare him the poetry. He will be unmade by simple arithmetic. Take one and then another until nothing divides."

My chest tightens. I've spent my life believing in the power of words to save things, to preserve them like insects in amber. Here, words are surgical instruments, each question an incision.

Alecto glides her hand through air and the nearest serpent uncoils, leaving a track across marble as delicate as a line of Homer perfectly scanned. It reaches the slab and sets its face near my temple with the gravity of a physician examining a patient. Its breath is cool and smells faintly of lemon rind—the scent of something clean preparing to do something filthy.

"This is remediation," Tisiphone says, and the words cost her nothing after millennia of practice. "You have tied your sanity to a thing that endangers the order of worlds. We will untie you. You will be what you were before. Books. Chalk. A life of walls that hold still."

The promise hangs in the air like an offered apple. My old life—tenure, predictable days, well-turned lectures. Before Rome. Before resistance. Before I learned what lightning tastes like in your chest.

"Say it plain," Megaera murmurs, leaning close enough that I can see fine cracks in her lower lip—a flaw that makes her almost human until you remember the flaw is chosen, kept for effect. "Say Danica out loud and hear what the room does with it."

I try. The consonants come easily enough, hard little bones clicking against my teeth. But when I reach for the vowels, they rise in my throat like birds that have seen the snare. The name shivers on my tongue and stays there. I can feel its warmth, can taste the shape of it like wine I'm forbidden to swallow. My throat has been taught obedience to rules I never signed, and the humiliation makes me want to tear out my own tongue just to spite them.

"Good," Alecto says, and for the first time her smile is honest because it admits she's enjoying this. "His mouth already knows what we're doing."

The serpent opens its jaws and presses teeth lightly against my temple, just suggesting a bite. Then something threads through bone, barely a prickle, and I hear pages turning in a book I don't remember writing. The serpent reads my memories like a scholar parsing ancient text, searching for passages that need redaction.

My scalp tightens the way it does before storms, when the air grows heavy and every old wound remembers itself. Hollow feeling spreads where sensation should be, an emptiness that echoes.

The ceiling drops by degrees I could calculate if I still trusted mathematics. The chains hover, their rings spreading to circle my wrists and ankles and throat with delicate precision. I lift my hands, hold them there—partly defiance, partly the scholar's hunger to understand that's always been my weakness. I want to understand their craft before it unmakes me. The first ring settles around my wrist and warms there, learning my pulse like a student memorizing verb forms. The second takes the other wrist with matching dedication. The throat ring stops a finger's width from my skin and waits, polite as a question mark at the end of a sentence.

"Which will you take first?" I ask them, because asking makes what comes next bearable, gives it the structure of dialogue rather than mere victimization. "The beginning, or whatever's pretending to be the beginning?"

Tisiphone sets her veiled face directly above mine so that for a moment it becomes my only sky. "We'll take the small things. You love words. You should appreciate the importance of articles and conjunctions. The grand declarations hold nothing together—it's the joints you overlook. Pull the right peg, and the cathedral forgets it ever needed a roof."

She's using my own teaching methods, the way I used to show students how language works by removing small words from sentences, showing how meaning collapses when you strip its modest architecture. My own lessons, weaponized and turned on their creator.

Alecto touches the serpent's head and the reading gets deeper, past surface memories into the sediment layers where the oldest things settle. The first theft is the weight of chalk in my hand before a morning lecture, that specific heft that meant I was about to do the thing I was good at. My fingers ache and then stop aching. The absence is so precise I can barely mourn it properly.

The second theft is the memory of the corridor outside my office, that scuff on the floor where some student's boot dragged year after year until the janitor stopped trying to buff it out. It slides away smooth as a ring warmed in water, pulled off easily.

The third theft is cruel in its specificity: the particular shadow her lashes cast when she looked down to tie her hair back, that small darkness thrown across her cheek. When it's gone, I feel heat behind my eyes. My chest empties like a punctured wineskin. I'd thought to guard the grand declarations, the important moments. I missed the shadows, unaware something so small could carve such a precise wound.

Megaera watches my face with professional attention, reading it the way midwives read breath. She's done this thousands of times. I can see it in how she tilts her head, the small adjustments of her position, the craftsman's satisfaction in work done well.

"He still thinks the loss is his idea," she murmurs to the others. "Let him study a little longer. Scholars always sign their own expulsions if you give them enough rope to make it look like research."

She's right. Part of me—the professor who spent a decade dissecting texts—is fascinated by their methodology. Even as they destroy me, I'm taking notes, filing observations, trying to understand the grammar of my own undoing. It's the only defense I have left: to make my torture into a lesson plan.

The room changes, a palimpsest revealing earlier text. Rome returns as an afterimage, and I'm back in that corridor, the one that's become the center of everything they want to steal. Tisiphone gives me the scene, then moves me like a chess piece one square to the left of where I stood the first time. A knight's move away from mattering.

Danica passes me. She's doing what she always did in those moments, measuring the necessary violence and spending it precisely, never a gesture wasted. Her hair is pulled back in that efficient braid she favored during operations, and there's blood on her knuckles from the fight we've just survived. She's incandescent with purpose, and the sight of her makes my chest feel like it's collapsing inward.

She passes me by because looking would cost a second and seconds were currency we couldn't afford. The difference is in my position. I'm scenery now, furniture in a room she's passing through. The leather strap passes from her hand to someone else's. My mouth stays closed. At the door, she brushes past me like I'm architecture. The universe holds its shape. I am a man-shaped absence in a scene that continues perfectly around me. When the spear goes through the boy—Milo, seventeen, who pressed flowers in stolen books like they were prayers—my body stays still. It's the same tragedy viewed from a safe distance.

But I remember the original. I remember how her fingers brushed mine when she passed me that leather strap, how the touch was electric and accidental and absolutely necessary. I remember the quarter-second our eyes met, how that look contained entire libraries of things we'd never have time to say.

"You're making me watch a miracle edited for cowards," I say, fighting to keep scholarly distance in my voice. "You know this will starve me rather than break me, and starved things have teeth."

Megaera's mouth softens in something that might be respect. "Then let us feed you," she says, and there's almost kindness in it, which makes it worse.

They give me a different corridor, a different angle of the same moment. This time she looks at me. It's brief and complete and carries the entire weight of recognition—of being seen. Her eyes are dark and tired, but when they find mine, something shifts in her expression. It's the look of someone who's been carrying weight alone suddenly realizing they don't have to. Three seconds, maybe less, that rewrote the entire syntax of my life.

In the original moment, those three seconds contained everything: attraction, yes, but also recognition of something deeper, a shared exhaustion with the world's cruelties, a mutual refusal to let that exhaustion win. I saw her see me as the man caught between those things, trying to make sense of it all. And she kept looking.

Alecto slides her hand over my eyes and removes the moment before she looks and the moment after. I'm left with the gaze itself, floating untethered, a fragment of stained glass wrenched from its window. Decoration. Safe.

But the meaning stays rooted in my bones: she saw me. Really saw me. And I saw her seeing me, and in that mutual recognition, something irreversible happened. We became possible.

The serpent makes another of its delicate incursions. Names begin to shuffle like expertly manipulated cards. They rearrange themselves into patterns that privilege other narratives over mine. Milo transforms into "someone," and that someone pushes me from the path of falling debris, but the act loses its edge of devotion, becomes mere reflex. The boy with mismatched sleeves—one blue, one gray, both too short for his growing arms—keeps his adjectives but loses his noun. He dies like all boys in all wars, anonymous and unmourned.

Grief, deprived of its address, goes docile. It transforms into the kind of sadness you feel reading newspapers from distant countries, genuine but manageable, lacking the specific weight that makes you want to claw your own heart out.

The throat ring lowers until its inner edge kisses my skin. I had hoped for cold metal, something harsh and honest. Instead it's warm, body temperature, making my flesh accept what should be rejected. The metal crawls across my throat like something alive. I open my mouth to curse the humiliation of it, but find that some essential component of the word has been replaced. The curse leaves my mouth carrying the same phonemes but a different soul.

"I will hold my thirst," I say, announcing it to the painted ceiling, to the false stars. "However pretty the cup. However pure the water. I know what river that water comes from."

Ana arrives as if she's been waiting in the wings for her cue. She's dressed in white linen today, simple and severe, the costume of someone whose intentions are too pure to require ornamentation. She looks like a nurse, or a nun, or a mother about to give medicine to a reluctant child. The performance is perfect and therefore perfectly false.

She sets the cup down where the serpent can see it, lets the reflection of water climb the creature's glass throat. The water inside is clear as crystalline promise, luminous as false hope.

She acknowledges the Furies with a subtle shift of her lashes—a queen thanking servants for preparing her chamber. "You imagine I am the water," she says, lifting the cup with the tenderness of someone about to feed a bird with a broken wing. "I am only the hand. The water existed before your argument with it. You have drunk it before and called it by other names. Rest. Mercy. Academic rigor."

The cup is beautiful, ancient Greek work, probably 5th century BCE, decorated with scenes of heroes forcing order onto chaos. Even the vessel meant to steal my memories is a masterwork, because of course it is. Ana deals only in perfection.

"Lethe by any other name," I say, and I'm ashamed that the professor lives in my voice even now, showing off my erudition even as they prepare to steal it. "You understand that forgetting offers no miracle. Only the emptying of a house, and even if no one else notices, the house remembers its ghosts."

Ana holds the cup so its rim nestles into the curve below my lower lip, intimate as a kiss I refuse. The smell is mint, clean, sharp, designed to mask whatever else swims in that clarity. "Listen to yourself," she murmurs, and her voice could pass for affection if you'd never heard the real thing. "Household gods. Small devotions. As if your life should pivot on whether someone laughed in a corridor, whether fingers touched by accident at a door. You have no capacity for such worship. You will break under it. Be large. Be spared."

She's right, which makes this worse. The small things are killing me— every remembered laugh, every accidental touch, every moment when her eyes found mine across a room full of maps and violence and desperate planning. They're hooks in my flesh, pulling me toward something beyond my reach, someone who might already be dead. My ribs ache with the weight of carrying impossible love.

But these trivial things are also what make us human. Strip away the minor devotions, the household gods that go unnoticed, and what's left? A hollow man, functioning but empty.

"Show me your mercy by leaving her intact," I say, and the pronoun defies the room's architecture because it needs no name to find its target. "If your case is strong, it needs no theft."

Ana considers the question as if it deserves weight, and for a moment, the smallest crease appears between her brows—a flaw that makes me trust her less. "I have already given you the most merciful argument. When you wake with a mind washed clean, you will thank me. You will write papers again. You will lecture students who hunger for your wisdom. You will spend rain instead of wasting thunder on men who only needed rain."

She's offering me my old life back—tenure, safety, the small predictable satisfactions of scholarly rhythm. The life where my biggest concern was whether freshmen understood Latin grammar, where violence was something that happened in texts I translated. It was a good life. Quiet. Bloodless. Empty.

"Would you thank someone for cutting off your legs if they promised you'd never stumble again?" I ask.

Alecto moves two fingers, and the serpent takes something else—the taste of rain in her hair when she shook it out in a doorway and laughed, then stopped because laughter could be counted by enemies. Another gesture, another theft: the particular impatience she had with buttons, living always a degree too fast for them. I'd watched her rip one clean off rather than work it through its hole, and somehow that small violence had been more intimate than any kiss. Gone now. Then the muscle at the base of her thumb where a pen had worked its small violence, creating a callus I'd felt when our hands touched. Also gone.

"Please," I hear myself say, and hate the sound of it. "Please, I'll—"

"You'll what?" Megaera asks, genuinely curious. "Forget her willingly? You can't. That's why we're here."

The serpent's teeth sink deeper, and I feel something fundamental tear inside me. The memory of her hands—all of them, every time she touched me, every accidental brush, every deliberate contact—they're lifting away like pages torn from a book, and I can feel the absence spreading, a void opening in my chest where those sensations used to live.

I scream. It's not dignified. It's not controlled. It's the raw sound of a man being unmade one nerve at a time.

"More," Alecto says, and there's hunger in her voice now. "Show him what he's truly losing."

They give me a memory I didn't know I'd kept: Danica sleeping. Just once, after a battle that had lasted thirty-six hours. She'd collapsed against a wall, head on my shoulder, and slept for maybe twenty minutes before jerking awake, reaching for a weapon that wasn't there. In those twenty minutes, her face had been soft. Unguarded. Young. I'd memorized every detail—the way her breathing changed, the small twitch of her fingers, the exact angle of her neck against my collarbone.

The serpent takes it. Carefully. Surgically. And as it goes, I feel something in me snap.

"No, no, no—" I'm sobbing now, thrashing against the chains, and I feel the rings tighten in response. "You can't—she trusted me—"

"She trusted the man you were," Tisiphone says, and there's something almost gentle in her voice, which makes it worse. "That man is dying. We're simply attending the death."

They show me more, faster now, each memory tearing away screaming. The scar on her left hand where a knife had slipped during training. The way she said my name when she was angry—three syllables instead of two, drawn out like an accusation. The specific shade of her eyes in morning light, darker than in afternoon, holding more green than gray. The sound she made when she was trying hard to hold back tears, a half-swallowed gasp that she thought remained unheard.

"Stop, please, I'm begging—" My voice cracks. "Take anything else. Take the storm. Take my name. Take my life. Just leave her. Please. Please."

"Your life?" Megaera laughs, and it's not cruel, just factual. "Your life is her. That's the problem. That's what we're fixing."

The serpent moves to a different kind of memory. Deeper. Older. The first time I saw her. Not in Rome, but before. In a lecture hall where she'd sat in the back row and systematically dismantled my entire argument about Herodotus. I'd been furious. I'd been fascinated. I'd been utterly, completely ruined for anyone else from that moment forward.

"No—" I'm hyperventilating now, pulling against the chains hard enough that my wrists are bleeding. "Not that one. Not the first one. You can't—"

They can. They do.

And when it's gone, I feel something in me die. Not metaphorically. Actually die. The part of me that knew how to hope, how to want, how to love anything more than duty—it withers. It calcifies. It becomes ash.

I stop struggling and screaming. The absence is so total, so complete, that I can't even remember why I was fighting.

"There," Alecto says with satisfaction. "Now he's ready."

"Enough," I whisper, but it's surrender now, absolute and total. "You've won. I'll drink. I'll forget. Just make it stop."

"Then beg properly," Megaera says. "Say the words. 'I want to forget her.'"

My mouth opens. The words are right there, ready to end the pain, to make the hollowness stop spreading. All I have to do is say them.

"I—" My voice breaks. "I want—"

And something in me, some last stubborn fragment that remembers what it felt like to be whole, rebels.

"No." The word is barely a whisper, but it's mine. "No, I won't."

So I beg, though I direct my words elsewhere. I speak to the holes I've made in their painted ceiling, those small rebellions that cost me so much. I speak to whatever might exist beyond their perfect prison. I can't name her—the room has stolen that ability, my throat closing around the syllables—but I can name what remains.

But even as I do, the serpent is taking more. The way her shoulder found mine on a roof during the siege of Frankfurt—gone mid-sentence. The sound when someone's been crying but holds their mouth steady—dissolving even as I speak it. The minor key of her laughter when she'd won some small argument—stolen before I can finish the thought.

I'm trying to build a wall of moments, but they're taking the bricks faster than I can lay them. Each memory I name out loud solidifies for one instant before the serpent's teeth sink in and tear it away. I'm losing. I'm losing everything. I can feel my mind becoming a battlefield where memories die faster than I can defend them.

"You can keep this up only so long," Tisiphone says, and there's something almost pitying in her voice now. "You lack the years or the breath to out-speak a machine built before your language existed. Yield, and be free of the work."

"The work is the freedom," I answer, but my voice is hollow now, automatic. I'm repeating words I barely understand anymore. The meaning is draining away even as I speak.

The ring around my throat tightens, enough to make swallowing conscious, deliberate. The ceiling, offended by my resistance, lowers another inch. The room, which has been silent as a theorem, allows the first sound to cross its threshold: a delicate sliding click, like jewelry being fastened by fingers that know the motion blind.

The sound makes me think of my old life, those morning rituals of respectability—cufflinks and tie clips, the armor of academia. That man seems like fiction now, someone I invented for a story whose ending I've forgotten.

The serpents lift, reposition, bite again. The rings at my wrists heat past warm to the edge of burning—enough to teach. My skin learns their temperature; my pulse synchronizes to their rhythm. Soon only the memory of binding will remain.

Ana leans closer. Her breath rewrites the air between us, making it taste of distance and high places. "I will save you from her. From the hunger that makes you foolish. From the wreck she'll make forgetting to be gentle. Let me take this, and I'll give you back what you were meant to be."

"She is what I was meant to be," I say, and find the strength for anger only in the moment I tell the complete truth.

Ana straightens with the smallest of sighs—the sound of a craftsman admitting the material has flaws that can be worked around. "Then let us be finished," she says to the Furies, and tips the cup so a single drop of mint water finds the seam of my mouth.

Cold climbs my tongue like quicksilver rising in glass. Thought goes bright, then clean, then simple. For an instant, the room's architecture reveals itself as pure geometry, and I understand—truly understand—how much easier it would be to just let go. To be empty. To be free of this weight that's killing me by inches.

If I breathe twice in this clarity, I'll agree to everything. Three times, and I'll forget why I ever resisted. The peace being offered is real. The oblivion is real. And gods, I want it. I want to stop hurting. I want to stop carrying the weight of every stolen memory like stones in my chest. I want—

I breathe once. The clarity intensifies. I can feel my resistance crumbling, my will dissolving like sugar in water.

My lips part for the second breath.

And then—unbidden, unwanted, agonizing in its clarity—a memory surfaces. One they haven't found yet. One I didn't even know I still had.

Sigrun. My Sigrun.

Winter. The kind that makes stone crack. She's standing in the doorway of the longhouse, snow caught in her dark hair. She's bleeding from a cut above her eye—some skirmish with raiders I'd missed. She's been furious with me for days.

"You think the storm makes you wise," she says. Her breath fogs between us. "It makes you absent."

I'm Alatyr then. Younger. Stupider. I say something about duty, about watching the borders. The words taste like ash even as I speak them.

She crosses the space between us in three strides. Grabs my face with both hands, her palms frozen from the snow. "I need you here. Present. With me."

Her eyes are the same—storm-gray meeting storm-gray, they've always been the same.

"I'm afraid," I tell her. The truth I'd buried for lifetimes. "That if I'm just a man, you won't want me."

She kisses me then. Hard. Her mouth tastes like mead and blood from the split lip she got in the fight. When she pulls back, she says, "You're an idiot."

"I know."

"The storm is what you do. What you are is mine."

The memory burns. It's older than the Furies, older than this prison, older than Ana's schemes. It comes from before—before Rome, before Greece, before we'd learned to hide what we were behind mortal names and mortal lives.

And it's the memory of the moment I learned that being loved wasn't about being perfect or powerful or divine. It was about being present. About being seen.

The serpent lunges for it, teeth bared, but the memory is made of different material than the others. It's been carried across lifetimes. It's been worn smooth by centuries of remembering. When the serpent's teeth meet it, they slide off like oil on water.

I hold my breath. The lotus water sits on my tongue, cold and sweet and promising everything I'm desperate for.

I swallow nothing. I spit the water onto the marble floor.

"I choose the pain," I say, and my voice is broken, shredded, barely human. "I choose her. I choose every fucking moment of agony if it means I get to keep one memory of what it felt like to be whole."

But before they can move, a new sound tears through the room's choreography: CLANG.

It's the sound of hammer meeting anvil, but more than that—this is the sound of the first tool striking the first metal, the sound that taught fire how to bend, that taught stone how to become. The vibration travels through the marble and into my bones, and for a moment my heart forgets its rhythm and tries to match this older beat.

The room shakes. Dust that has been painted over for centuries suddenly remembers it exists. The Furies recoil as if slapped. They look at each other with something I haven't seen from them: uncertainty.

CLANG.

Closer now, and with it the groan of something that was built rigid learning it must bend. The sound comes with footsteps of someone who walks through walls as easily as doorways.

A section of seamless marble behind them cracks in a pattern like lightning frozen mid-strike. The Furies hiss in harmonized frustration. Their work is unfinished. I'm still too much myself for the water to wash clean.

The wall explodes inward with exactly the force required and no ounce wasted. Through the hole steps a figure that makes the room suddenly seem decorative, fragile, built for lesser things.

He's dense, compressed, like a mountain that decided to be man-sized but kept all its weight. His skin is dark bronze, weathered like stone exposed to millennia of wind. Arms thick as bridge cables, hands built for one purpose: enforcement. He wears simple leather and iron, minimal gear, purely functional—the equipment of a being that has always been absolute in purpose and execution.

But it's his eyes that stop my breath. Cold gold, burning with absolute conviction accumulated over ten thousand years of unwavering obedience. When he looks at you, you feel judged by a standard that tolerates only perfect compliance or perfect resistance.

The Furies expand in response.

Tisiphone's veil catches fire that gives no heat, flames the color of old blood. Megaera's form ripples, muscle becoming something older, more essential—pure wrath given anatomy. Alecto's edges sharpen until she's less woman than weapon, a blade that learned to walk.

"You forget yourself, enforcer," Tisiphone hisses, and her voice carries ten thousand verdicts rendered, ten thousand necks meeting rope. "This chamber exists outside your domain. The Edict of New Divine Order grants us dominion here."

Kratus takes another step. The marble cracks beneath his foot like ice over deep water. "The Edict." The word comes out flat, final. "Aphrodite forged that document in the hours after Olympus fell, when Zeus's authority scattered with his death. I stood guard while she wrote it. She thought I would enforce it the same way I enforced Zeus's will. She was wrong."

Ana rises from where she'd been kneeling beside me. The white linen burns away like morning mist, revealing armor underneath—something woven from broken promises and bent laws. Her hair lifts in a wind that comes from nowhere.

"Kratus." She shapes his name with perfect diction, each syllable a small act of violence. "You served Zeus with absolute loyalty. You bound Prometheus to the rock without hesitation. You crushed rebellion. You enforced order. Zeus is gone. Your purpose is gone. Go back to waiting for a master who will never return."

The temperature in the room spikes. The painted stars begin to crack at their edges.

Kratus's face remains carved from stone. "I bound Prometheus because Zeus commanded it. Zeus is dead. My loyalty follows living authority alone."

He raises one massive hand, and the chains respond with instant, absolute obedience, unspooling from my wrists, my throat, my ankles, and falling to the floor like discarded rope.

"These are toys," he says. "Persuasion dressed as restraint. I know real chains."

Alecto moves like mercury—fast, fluid, gleaming—her form blurring as she closes the distance between them, her hand transforming into a talon, sharpening into a blade as she reaches for his throat.

He catches her wrist, and there's a sound like two boulders colliding that makes Alecto shriek. Where his hand grips her, her flesh simply stops—violence meeting something that is violence made absolute and perfect.

"I held Prometheus while the smith drove chains through his flesh," he says, voice devoid of emotion. "You're softer than Prometheus was."

He throws her with the same emotionless precision, and she impacts the wall behind Ana, sliding down it and leaving a long crack in the perfect marble.

Megaera roars, gathering centuries of fury into a sound that turns the air thick with rage, almost visible as a red haze between us.

Kratus stands motionless, staring at her with the accumulated weight of every rebellion he's ever crushed, and her power scatters like ash in wind before his gaze.

"Your rage is a luxury," he says. "Mine is function."

Tisiphone holds her ground. "You are making a mistake. This is not your war. The storm-god is ours by right of transgression. We are correction. We are justice. You interrupt cosmic law."

"Cosmic law." Kratus's voice is flat as struck iron. "I enforced Zeus's law for ten thousand years. I executed every command. I questioned nothing. I showed perfect loyalty." He pauses. "Zeus's last command to me was given as Olympus fell. He told me: 'Protect what matters when everything else is ash.' This matters."

He looks at me. His expression holds pure assessment, cold calculation of whether I'm worth the effort. "You're caught between mortal and divine. You think that makes you weak. It makes you necessary. The world needs something between absolute power and absolute weakness. That's what you are."

Ana steps forward, voice carrying the full weight of her authority. "You want him? Then you declare war on me. Every enforcer I've recruited. Every system I've built. Every power that wants order. You'll stand against all of it."

Kratus considers her with those cold eyes, and then reaches down to wrap one massive hand around my arm, lifting me to my feet with his grip iron and absolute.

"I already stand against you, Aphrodite," he says quietly. "I have since the moment you confused order with Zeus's will. Since you built systems that serve themselves instead of serving purpose. Zeus commanded loyalty to what matters. You command loyalty to structure. These are not the same thing."

He turns his back on her. On the Furies. On all of it.

"This is not finished, Kratus," Ana says, and her voice could freeze the sun. "You walk out of here with him, and you become the enemy of every power that wants order restored. Every god that wants stability. Every force that believes in law. You will stand alone."

He pauses at the hole he made. Looks back over his shoulder. When he speaks, his voice is granite. "I've stood alone since you killed Zeus. Did you think I didn't know? I stood guard outside his chambers that night. I heard the struggle. I saw you leave." His eyes burn cold and absolute. "I chose to wait. To watch. To see what you would build with his blood on your hands. Now I've seen enough."

Ana's face shifts—calculation replacing composure. "Then you know he deserved it. He was chaos. I brought order."

"You brought tyranny," Kratus says. "Zeus was a king. You're a jailer. I'll take the king's chaos over your perfect cages."

Then he steps through, carrying me with him, and behind us I hear Ana's scream of rage—primal and absolute and promising vengeance.

The Furies' chorus joins hers: "This is unfinished. He remains ours. We will come for him again, and next time, there will be only completion. No rescue. No mercy. We are inevitable. We are the correction that comes for all things. You have delayed the sentence, nothing more."

The last thing I see before the hole seals is Ana's face, beautiful and terrible and absolutely committed to destruction.

And I know, with the certainty that lives in my bones: this is just the beginning.

CHAPTER SIX
COUNCIL OF ALEXANDRIA

This is how I leave Europe for the first time. I'd hoped Ilija and I would travel the world when this bullshit was over. Fucking Ana. Every goddamn life, she steals my happy ending. Denmark, Kyiv, Sparta, Alba—every lifetime. I'm done waiting. I sigh so deep Thor himself feels it. The thought barely crosses my mind before we arrive in Egypt.

Desert salt crawls through the broken windows of our stolen train. My daughter's palm burns in mine, small fingers sticky with fever and something older that makes my bones ache.

The train screams against rusted tracks. I know this sound—it lives in my throat when I wake from dreams of Ilija turning to ash. The wheels shriek like the sound Mirko made when the Accord's bullets found his spine.

The memory hits. Mirko's face going white, his legs suddenly useless. The way his mouth opened and closed. The Accord left him there for the rats and ravens.

I press my forehead to glass webbed with cracks. Copper on my tongue. Bombed-out villages blur past, salted fields, cratered roads.

Selene breathes like someone drowning. The fever has burned beneath her skin for six days now. When she sleeps, shadows pool in the hollow of her throat. When she wakes, light fractures around her fingers.

"Mama." Her voice is rough. "The water tastes like crying."

She means the sea. We're close enough now to smell it, that sharp brine cutting through ash-thick air. The Accord burned the coastal farms. The wind carries charred wheat, melted flesh, the chemical sweetness of villages erased from maps.

"Hey little star," I whisper, my fingers sparking as I stroke her hair. "Every drop of water carries tears. The trick is figuring out which ones are worth drinking."

Alexandria spreads before us like a wound refusing to heal. The Accord gutted this city, tore out its libraries and schools, left its towers crumbling. Yet it breathes. Cardamom threads through the smoke. Children's laughter echoes off collapsed walls, sharp and bright as shattered bells.

This city has been Greek and Roman and Arab and Ottoman and British and Egyptian, conquered and burned and rebuilt from its own remains. The Accord thinks bullets and bombs can erase it. Fools. This city knows how to swallow empires and shit out their bones.

We disembark at the port. The platform reeks of fish and fuel and fear-sweat. Refugees huddle in bombed-out shadows, their faces gray as old newspaper. A woman rocks a bundle that might once have been a child. An old man sits beside a suitcase held together with rope, counting coins that will never be enough.

Selene stumbles. I catch her, feel her bones through her skin. She weighs nothing. She weighs everything. The fever makes her eyes too bright, turns her skin translucent as pearl. When she looks at me, I see galaxies drowning.

"I can walk," she whispers, though her legs shake.

"You can." I lift her anyway, settle her against my hip. Her head falls to my shoulder, hot as a brand. "But walking alone just makes you tired."

The safe house crouches above the harbor like a scarred cat. Stone walls thick enough to stop bullets, windows boarded with planks that smell of old storms. The woman who lets us in has eyes like flint and hands stained permanent black. She stares at Selene and crosses herself, mutters something in Arabic.

Our room is small, salt-stained, perched above the water like a seabird's nest. The shutters rattle with each gust of wind, a rhythm like chattering teeth. I lay Selene on the narrow cot, pull the thin blanket to her chin. The fisherman downstairs sold me bread for three bullets and a promise. She takes it in her hands, turns it over and over, watches crumbs fall to the floor like snow.

"It should have been different." I kneel beside the cot, feeling splinters bite through my pants. "Today should have been cake tall as your fist, candles bright as small suns. Ribbons for your hair and presents wrapped in paper that crinkles."

Her gray eyes find mine. Seven years old, ancient. "It's my birthday."

The words hit me like shrapnel—hot metal tearing through muscle, lodging in bone. "Baby, I know. Fuck, I know." I take her face in my hands, feel her fever burning through my palms. "I'm sorry I'm putting you in rooms that smell like fear instead of birthday cake. Sorry I'm dragging you through meetings while children starve. Every year I steal from you is another piece of the girl you should have been."

Her fingers catch mine. Bird-bone thin, strong. Stronger than they should be. "It's all right, Mama. As long as we're together."

I bow my head until my forehead touches hers. She smells like smoke and sea-spray and childhood I'm murdering one breath at a time. Seven years old and already older than stones. The weight of it sits on my chest like stone, pressing until I think my ribs will crack.

"I'll make it right." I swear against her skin, taste salt where my tears meet hers. "When this war ends, I'll give you back every stolen birthday. Every candle, every wish, every ribbon. I'll give you the sky itself."

She smiles. Dawn breaking over bombed-out buildings, brief and fierce and heartbreaking. "Then I'll wait."

I gather her against me. So small. So breakable. Yet when she sleeps, shadows bend toward her like flowers toward sun. When she dreams, light leaks from her skin like spilled honey.

Outside, the harbor bells begin to ring. Bronze voices calling across water, summoning the council to order. I hold her tighter for one heartbeat, then force myself to rise.

"Come, little star." My voice breaks on the endearment. "Time to go watch men play games with the world's blood."

The chamber lies beneath the library's corpse. Down stone steps worn smooth by centuries of feet, through corridors that remember books like amputees remember limbs. The hall stretches before us—broken pillars, fire-blackened vaults. Bronze lamps hiss in their iron basins, filling the air with smoke that tastes of old metal and older prayers.

The delegates gather in their circle of light.

Admiral Hassan al-Masri stands tall and knife-sharp in robes the color of deep water. Navy braid glints at his cuffs like captured starlight. His voice when he speaks is the Mediterranean itself—steady, relentless, vast enough to swallow ships.

General Nikos Stavridis carries Greece on his shoulders like Atlas carried the world. Broad-shouldered, battle-scarred, his forearms mapped with old wounds. In his eyes I see Thermopylae, see three hundred Spartans choosing death over surrender.

Captain Luca Ferretti paces like a caged wolf. His uniform bears patches on patches, held together by stubbornness and thread. His hands shake when he thinks no one is watching. His hands are steady as stone when they grip his sidearm.

Commander Samira al-Khatib sits silent in the shadows, her keffiyeh bound tight as armor. Her eyes are obsidian chips. The desert has made her patient, taught her to strike from ambush.

Ambassador Kwame Obeng speaks softly like evening rain. His skin is carved ebony, his words measured like gold coins. He has seen empires rise and fall like tides. He knows which way the wind is turning.

And there, cloaked in pale wool fastened with silver, Jaakko Lemminkäinen of Finland. Iron-gray hair, frost-carved features, patience learned from watching ice form and break through endless winters. He has the stillness of deep forests, the cunning of wolves hunting in snow. When he looks at me, I feel him measuring my weaknesses, cataloging the ways I might break.

The debate erupts like wildfire in dry grass.

"Strike their coasts!" Hassan's voice booms off broken stone. "Burn their ships before they can land more troops."

Stavridis slams his scarred fist against his thigh. The sound cracks like breaking bone. "While you play admiral, our villages bleed dry. Children starve in the hills."

Samira's voice slides between theirs like steel between ribs. "Shout loud enough and they will sweep us from the desert with fire from heaven."

Ferretti's laughter tastes of copper and rage. "Tell that to my cousins rotting in ditches outside Bari."

Kwame's words fall like stones in still water. "Unity is survival, or we all burn alone."

They argue like children fighting over scraps while the house burns around them. Voices rising, falling, clashing like swords against shields. Each one believes their pain is unique, their loss the deepest.

Then Lemminkäinen rises. The pale wool of his cloak whispers against stone. Silver catches lamplight and throws it back like captured stars.

"Perhaps we should listen to her."

Silence falls like a blade. Every eye turns toward me, weighs me, judges me. I feel their attention like heat against my skin, like the moment before lightning strikes.

"Danica Madsen has held lines where veterans broke. She carries fire, and men follow fire into hell itself." He pauses, lets the words settle. "I have watched you carry burdens that would break lesser souls."

Murmurs ripple through the circle. My stomach tightens like a fist.

"Fire burns quick and dies quicker. Passion crumbles when built on sand." He steps closer, voice softening to something almost tender. "You have carried this war alone too long."

His eyes flick to Selene's hand in mine, quick as snake-strike, then back to my face. "Your daughter needs more than a warrior mother. When the storm passes, who tends the wounded? Who carries the children home?"

The hook is set so gently I almost miss it.

My jaw sets like cooling steel. "Stones crack under pressure. I've watched mountains fall while fire still burned."

His smile is winter-thin, appreciative. "Then perhaps fire and stone together endure what neither could alone." His voice drops to barely a whisper, meant for my ears alone. "I know which battles can be won and which victories cost more than defeat."

Behind me, Kostas's cane strikes marble once, sharp as gunshot. Warning bells in the sound.

I step into the circle. "You bicker over scraps while the Accord devours the feast. Borders mean nothing when cities burn. Desert and sea, mountain and plain—all the same if we strike as anything less than one fist."

Stavridis spits at my feet. "My grandmother's bones are dust. My cousin's children are gone. Greece bleeds while you play general."

"Greek pride," Ferretti snarls. "Where was your honor when Rome burned?"

"The enemy sits at this very table!" Stavridis lunges toward Lemminkäinen, blade singing from its sheath. "Finland sold us to the Accord."

Lemminkäinen rises smooth as winter ice. His hand finds his own knife, pale steel catching bronze light. "Careful, General."

"We're already dead," Samira says, sharp as breaking glass. "The Accord has satellites, weapons that turn cities into glass. We have fishing boats and stolen rifles."

"Then what would you have us do?" I snap. "Crawl on our bellies?"

The world tilts sideways. Shadows pour up the walls like spilled blood, swallowing bronze light, drowning the chamber in darkness thick as tar. The air grows heavy, pressing against my lungs. Ancient stone shudders. Pillars groan like wounded giants.

Selene breaks in the middle of their shouting, in the middle of Stavridis raising his blade, in the middle of everything falling apart. Light explodes from her small frame—white-hot as forge-fire, bright as the heart of dying stars. It burns across broken marble, strikes the delegates blind, turns shadow into molten silver.

Men reel like drunkards. Stavridis curses in ancient Greek, his blade clattering to stone as he throws hands over his eyes. Samira stumbles backward, trips over her own robes, falls hard against a pillar. Ferretti drops to his knees, whispering prayers his dead grandmother taught him. Even Hassan shields his face from the impossible radiance pouring from a seven-year-old girl.

Only Lemminkäinen stands unmoved. His winter eyes drink the light, reflecting it back cold as Arctic ice. His smile is thin as paper, satisfied as a hunter watching prey stumble into snares.

Hassan lowers his hand slowly. His eyes burn with recognition, something deeper and older than rage. "Then Egypt sails with you, Danica Madsen."

The others mutter agreement, grudging respect replacing fear. The weight shifts, subtle as changing tide. I am the commander now. The war will sail under my flag, bleed at my word.

Through smoke and shadow, I find Lemminkäinen watching. He alone stood unmoved by my daughter's fire. His face is calm, pleased even, as though Selene's display proved some private theory. The fox waits for the rabbit to tire.

When the council disperses and delegates scatter to their separate wars, I sit beside Selene's cot. She sleeps fitfully, fever-dreams chasing themselves behind her closed lids. Her lashes are still damp with tears.

The room stinks of brine and old fear. Shutters rattle against wind that carries the voices of the dead. I whisper Ilija's name to cracked stone walls, hoping it finds him somewhere in the dark. The walls give no answer. They never do.

A soft knock at the door. I know that sound—measured, patient, courteous even in the gesture. "Come in," I call softly.

Lemminkäinen enters like winter mist, silent and inevitable. He carries a steaming cup in his hands, the scent of herbs and honey threading through the salt air. "For the child," he says, setting it on the windowsill. "An old remedy. My grandmother used it for fevers. Chamomile, elderflower, a touch of willow bark."

He asks no permission before moving to the far corner, settling into the single chair. His presence fills the small space—steady, unhurried, patient as mountains. He sits in silence with me, two people keeping vigil over a fevered child.

The quiet stretches. Comfortable, almost. Like he understands that some moments need only breath and stillness.

Finally, quietly: "Seven years."

I know what he means.

"Seven years you've carried this alone," he continues, voice low enough to spare Selene's sleep. "Seven years of decisions that would break most commanders in seven weeks. Seven years of choosing who lives, who dies, which villages burn so others might survive." He pauses. "Seven years since they took him from you."

My throat closes. I keep Ilija locked behind my ribs. Talking about him feels like being carved open with a dull blade.

"I watched my wife die," Lemminkäinen says, and there's something in his voice I haven't heard before. Something human beneath all that winter calm. "Cancer. Slow, brutal. She made me promise I would keep living after she was gone. Made me swear it on our children's names." His laugh is soft, bitter. "I kept that promise. But some nights I wonder if I should have."

I look at him then. Really look at him. The frost-carved features, the iron-gray hair, the lines around his eyes that speak of centuries of such nights. His gaze rests on Selene, and the expression on his face is almost tender.

"She looks like you," he says. "Same fire in her bones. Same stubborn refusal to break." He meets my eyes across the darkened room. "Same bone-deep exhaustion she's trying to hide from the world."

"I'm fine."

"You're burning out." No judgment in the words. Just observation, clinical and true. "I've seen it before. Warriors who carry too much for too long. They erode. Small pieces at first. A decision that takes too long. A reflex that's half a second slow. Then larger pieces. A tactical error. A missed opportunity. And then—" He stops. "Well. Then people die who shouldn't have."

The words hit like bullets, precise and devastating. Because he's right. Last week I hesitated before giving the order to fall back from Thessaloniki. Just three seconds, no more. But those three seconds cost us twenty-seven people. I remember their faces. I count their names in the dark.

"You need help, Danica. Because you're human. I have help. I have my people—"

"Hassan has Egypt's interests. Stavridis has Greek pride. They're allies, yes, but they serve their own nations first. You serve the whole war. You carry the weight of every nation here, every village, every child." He pauses. "Who carries it with you?"

The question opens something in my chest. Some wound I've been holding closed through sheer force of will. Because the answer is no one. I make the final decisions. I sign the orders. When the body counts come in, they come to me.

"Ilija—" I start, then stop. Because what can I say? Ilija has been gone for seven years. Seven years of silence, seven years of wondering if he's alive or broken or already dead. Seven years of making decisions alone, sleeping alone, fighting alone.

"Would Ilija want this for you?" Lemminkäinen asks softly. "Would he want you to destroy yourself trying to save him?"

The words are a knife between my ribs. "You know nothing about him."

"But I know love. And I know that the people we love rarely want us to die for them." He leans forward, elbows on his knees, hands clasped. "If your positions were reversed—if you were the one held captive and he was leading this war—what would you want for him? Truly?"

I want to say I'd want him to burn the world to get me back. Want to say I'd want him to fight until his last breath. But that's a lie, and we both know it.

If Ilija were out here and I were the one in chains, I'd want him to live. I'd want him to find peace, find joy, find someone to share the burden with. I'd want him to survive, even if it meant letting me go.

"I have to keep searching," I whisper. "I have to try."

"I ask only that you survive long enough to save him." He rises, moves closer. His movements hold only presence, only certainty. "You will burn out, Danica. Alone. At the rate you're going."

He crouches beside Selene's cot, reaches out to brush a strand of hair from her forehead. His touch is gentle. Practiced. The touch of someone who has tucked children into bed before.

"She's manifesting faster than I expected," he says quietly. "Do you know what that means?"

My stomach clenches. "Tell me."

"The power is looking for an outlet. Right now, it expresses itself randomly—in moments of fear, of stress. But as she grows, as the power grows with her..." He looks up at me, and his eyes are serious. "She'll need to learn control. True control, beyond suppression. Or the power will consume her."

"You're trying to scare me."

"I'm trying to prepare you." He stands, stays close. Close enough that I can smell winter-cold on his skin, pine and snow and something older. "I've trained young ones before. Helped them understand what they are, what they can become." He pauses, lets the words settle. "I can do the same for Selene. Teach her to channel that light, to use it instead of being used by it."

"And what do you want in return?"

"Partnership." The word hangs in the air between us. "Equality. You bring the fire, the passion, the tactical brilliance that's kept this rebellion alive against impossible odds. I bring experience, resources, knowledge of the old magics. We make decisions together. We carry this weight together."

It sounds... reasonable. Seductive, even. Someone to share the planning sessions, the tactical debates, the endless weight of responsibility. Someone who understands the deep magics, who could teach Selene, who could make me stronger so I can protect what matters.

"I trust nothing about you," I say, but my voice lacks conviction.

"I expect that. For now." He reaches out, slowly, giving me time to pull away. His fingers brush my cheek, catch a tear I hadn't known I'd shed. "Trust is earned. Let me earn it. Let me prove that I can carry this weight with you, that I can be the ally you need."

His hand is warm against my skin. Solid. Real. Seven years since anyone has touched me with gentleness instead of need or fear. Seven years since I've let myself be anything other than the commander, the weapon, the last desperate hope of people I can't afford to fail.

"One week," he says softly. "Give me one week to prove my worth. Let me stand beside you in the planning sessions. Let me demonstrate what I can offer. If at the end of that week you want me gone, I'll leave. No argument, no recrimination. You have my word."

"Your word." I almost laugh. "What's the word of a man who's lived through a thousand years' worth in one lifetime?"

"Everything." His eyes hold mine. "Because reputation is all any of us have in the end. And mine has been built over centuries of keeping my promises."

I should refuse. Should I tell him to get out, should keep my walls up, should remember that every offer of help comes with hooks buried in the honey.

But I'm so tired. And he's right, I am burning out. The mistakes are getting bigger. The cost in lives is climbing. And Selene's power is growing faster than I know how to handle.

What if refusing is the mistake that costs everything?

"One week," I hear myself say. "But you so much as look at Selene wrong, and I'll kill you myself. Slowly."

His smile is winter-thin, satisfied. "Fair enough." He moves toward the door, pauses with his hand on the latch. "Rest tonight, Danica. Tomorrow we begin building something that can actually win this war."

The door closes with a soft click. I sit in the darkness, listening to Selene breathe, feeling the weight of the choice I just made pressing down like storm clouds.

I've made a deal with a fox. I know it. He knows I know it.

His logic is too smooth, like a stone worn slick by centuries of river water—beautiful to look at, impossible to grip when the current threatens to sweep you away. His offer feels less like an outstretched hand and more like a beautifully crafted key, ornate and ancient and undeniably powerful. Every key opens one door only by locking another, and I'm suddenly, desperately uncertain what door this particular key is meant to seal behind me.

But I'm so tired. And he's offering rest, offering someone to share the weight. Even if it's a trap, even if it costs me everything, would that be worse than what I'm becoming? Would it be worse than the hollow thing I feel myself turning into, one choice at a time?

What if he's right about Selene? What if her power really is dangerous left wild? I've seen the way shadows bend toward her, the way light fractures around her fingers like broken glass. What if my stubborn pride, my refusal to trust, costs her everything? What if I'm so afraid of losing control that I lose her instead?

Selene stirs in her sleep, reaching for my hand. Her fingers find mine in the darkness, grip tight as anchor chains. Even unconscious, she knows when I need steadying. My daughter, my heart walking outside my body.

"I will keep you safe," I promise the darkness. "Whatever it costs, whoever I have to become. You will see birthdays with cake and ribbons. You will laugh at silly things and dance in summer rain. I swear it on my bones, on my blood, on every life I've taken and every soul I've failed to save."

The wind picks up, drives salt spray against rattling shutters. Somewhere in the harbor, ships creak at anchor, waiting for dawn and orders and the chance to carry war across wine-dark seas. The Mediterranean has seen empires rise and fall, watched heroes become legends become myth. Now it will carry one more war, one more desperate gamble against the darkness.

I close my eyes and try to sleep, though rest refuses to come. Too much weight, too many voices counting on choices I'm making without confidence. In the morning I will have to be the commander they need—strong, certain, unafraid. Tonight I can be what I am—a woman holding her sick daughter, listening to the sea sing lullabies older than nations, trying to find courage enough for whatever comes next.

The bells toll one o'clock, then two. Alexandria settles into the deep quiet that comes before dawn, when even the city's ancient ghosts pause to rest. I listen to my daughter breathe, count each rise and fall of her small chest, and wait for morning to bring its particular burdens.

In a few hours, the real work begins. Ships to provision, routes to plan, allies to coordinate across languages and centuries of mistrust. The Accord has factories and satellites, drone armies and nuclear fire. We have fishing boats and stolen rifles, wounded pride and the fury of the dispossessed.

History should be written already, our defeat carved in stone before the first shot is fired. But history has forgotten something—desperate people are dangerous people. Cornered beasts fight with claws and teeth, dying stars burn brightest in their last moments. The Accord thinks they fight an army. They face something older, fiercer. They face mothers defending children, fathers protecting home, lovers avenging the dead.

They face fire that refuses to be quenched, stone that refuses to yield, the rage of ten thousand years of conquest and colonization and imposed silence. We are every village burned, every culture erased, every language strangled in its cradle. We are the roar of all the dispossessed rising as one voice.

And tomorrow, we go to war. The thought should terrify me. Instead, it feels like coming home.

CHAPTER SEVEN
FIRES ON THE ADRIATIC

Dawn breaks against my skull. Light hammers the harbor, diesel fuel bleeding heat across concrete, steel cables singing under tension, fish rotting on the docks. The brightness cuts through my closed eyelids. I taste copper in my throat, metallic and familiar as old wounds. My body knows what's coming before my mind catches up. War has a smell that seeps into your pores—salt and diesel and the sweetness of fiberglass about to burn.

Selene's thumb digs into my palm, bone against bone, as if she can anchor me through holding on. Her grip speaks without words: don't let the sea take what's mine. I feel her pulse through that contact, rabbit-fast and mortal and so precious it makes my chest ache. Market spices spiral up from the docks, cinnamon and cardamom threading through my nostrils. I breathe them for her, for the warm flesh pressed against my side.

Petra leans against the concrete wall. Her eyes sweep over us, cataloging injuries that haven't happened yet. She can see how my jaw clenches, how my free hand curls into a fist that wants to hit something until it breaks. She knows I'm already bleeding inside, already burning.

"She stays with me." Petra's voice carries the finality of winter settling over mountains.

Selene looks up at me with eyes that hold midnight seas. I see myself reflected there, scarred and salt-stained and shaking. The child's question hits me between the ribs: "Will you bring me something from the sea?"

Shells. The word rises in my throat, tasting of promises and salt tears I refuse to shed. "I'll string them for you." My voice cracks on the lie we both pretend to believe. We both know I might come back with empty hands. We both know the sea might keep me.

When I touch my forehead to hers, her skin burns against mine with fever-warmth. I press a kiss to her brow, sealing it there. My lips leave salt behind, hers or mine, it doesn't matter. We're both creatures of brine and blood.

Petra's hand finds my shoulder and her fingers dig in deep enough to bruise, deep enough to leave marks I'll carry into battle. She's marking me with what I'm leaving behind. Come back, her grip says. Come back or I'll follow you into hell and drag you home by your fucking hair.

The flagship's deck throbs beneath my boots. The radar array turns overhead. The air smells of ozone and old fear, of coffee gone cold and recycled air. Men cluster around digital displays.

The tactical screen spreads before us, islands scattered across the Adriatic's throat. I trace coastlines with my fingertip, feeling the glass's cold surface. Each contour line represents depth and danger, death translated into green light.

Hassan's voice rumbles from deep in his chest. His scarred hands move across the screen. "Šibenik. Zlarin. Prvić." Each name falls heavy. "They hit the coastal village three nights ago, took the fishing boats and converted them to fast attack craft. If we cut them here—" His finger stabs the narrow channel. "We break their southern advance."

Stavridis leans forward. The console groans under his weight. Scars map his arms in silver rivers. He carries Greece on his shoulders, and Greece is fucking heavy. "You want to sail our fleet away and leave the islands naked to whatever comes next." His accent thickens with anger. "We defend our territorial waters. We don't abandon our house so you can kick down another's door."

The argument builds around us, electric and dangerous. Ferretti drums his fingers against metal, tap tap tap, his energy seeking outlet. His patched flight suit tells stories: shrapnel tears, knife cuts, a burn mark that missed his heart by inches. He wants to hit their supply depot, starve the machine until it eats itself.

Samira cuts through the chatter. "Smoke screens and electronic warfare. Cloud their radar and let confusion do the killing while we keep our hands clean."

Kwame stands apart with hands clasped behind his back, watching the argument with calm. He speaks only when the noise peaks: "Unity first. If this victory tears us apart, winter will kill us before spring comes."

They could argue until sunset. Men think talking can change war's physics, that words can make death less hungry. I feel the battle already forming, taste it on the wind. My body knows what my mind hasn't decided: this ends in blood.

Hassan's eyes find mine across the display: Will you be the fire that burns us all or the forge that shapes us stronger?

Lemminkäinen steps forward. Silver insignia winks at his collar, small star, cold light. He's been watching, cataloging weakness, measuring intention against result. "We should listen to her. Danica has stood where other commanders broke. She knows how to shape courage, make fear serve purpose."

He pauses, lets the silence stretch.

"Storms burn themselves thin if they're not carefully managed. We should divide command for maximum efficiency. Hassan leads the main assault with his superior firepower, Danica holds the reserve with her tactical expertise. Preserve our assets for the long campaign."

Reasonable. Sensible. Tactically sound. Fucking insulting.

My palm hits the console hard enough to make it ring. The sound echoes through the bridge. "Reserve keeps you clean and safe and useless. I didn't sail out here to stay fucking clean."

Hassan's beard twitches with what might be a smile. Approval warms his eyes. He spreads his fingers, making space. "Then speak, General, and we'll listen."

The title settles around me, heavy with the weight of lives hanging on every word. I give them the trap I've built in sleepless nights: Samira's smoke canisters on the water, sea mines across the channel's throat, Greeks coiled in radar shadow waiting to strike. Hassan's guns speaking first, Ferretti's boats painting burning diesel across the surface.

As I speak, I feel old hunger waking in my chest. The pleasure of a problem that solves itself through precision. Physics and timing and willingness to bleed for mathematics.

"We can maintain smoke cover for hours if the wind cooperates." Samira nods. "We have chemical canisters and white phosphorus."

Ferretti grins with broken teeth. "Sea mines, yes, we can deploy them. I know a man who liberated naval ordnance from a Croatian depot. He'll boast for years that his theft saved a fleet."

Stavridis works his jaw. "You want me to wait while the enemy consolidates. Greek sailors in Greek waters, learning patience from foreigners while our enemies grow stronger."

"I want you sharp as the blade you carry." My voice cuts through his objection. "A weapon waved wildly is dead before the fight begins. Keep it sheathed until you find what needs cutting, then strike with everything."

Hassan presses his thumb to the console's edge, leaving a print on the metal. "So it will be."

Lemminkäinen's smile curls at the corner. "Clever. Don't become what you burn in the process."

The words follow me down the gangplank, whisper in the engine's hum as we cast off. Don't become what you burn. The warning comes too late. I've been burning since Delphi, since the first time I watched good people die for bad reasons.

The twilight bleeds across the water in bronze and copper. Our engines purr at quarter throttle, muffled against detection. We speak in radio silence, hand signals, infrared strobes, fingers lifted and dropped.

The harbor shrinks behind us, becomes memory, becomes the story we'll tell later if we live long enough. I watch it disappear and feel my chest tighten.

Samira's people deploy smoke canisters from the patrol boats. The rocky shoals begin breathing gray clouds as if the earth has caught fire. Wind spreads the smoke across the channel's throat, carrying the smell of phosphorus and diesel.

Our boats disappear into gray walls one by one, swallowed by artificial fog. Gone. Vanished. My heart tries to gallop free, and I force it to stay caged behind my ribs.

The smoke swallows our radar signatures, turns us into electromagnetic ghosts. Hassan's first naval salvo cracks reality, measured, deliberate, beautiful in its certainty. Enemy missiles answer with wild desperation, firing at phantoms and echoes, panic making them sloppy. Their searchlights stab through gray, grasping for targets, finding only their own light reflected back.

Sea mines bite into enemy hulls. Metal screams in frequencies that hurt to hear, steel learning what it means to be prey. Ships make their own sound when surprise grips them.

"Hold your position," I signal Stavridis, voice steady despite adrenaline trying to turn my words into prayers. I feel him grinding his teeth in shadow where his attack craft wait, men coiled with muscles screaming for release. I breathe, feel the moment ripen. "Now."

Greeks strike from radar shadow, engines roaring to full life, controlled fury finally given permission to rage. Their first torpedo finds fiberglass with solid impact. The second warhead peels a hull open, lets the sea claim what pride built. Ferretti's boats slide close and ignite diesel slicks that race across the surface.

Our trap holds. Mostly it works. The wind shifts at the worst moment and makes Samira's smoke go limp, revealing us when we need invisibility. One mine line goes slack where tired hands tied knots wrong. An enemy craft slips through and rams our hull hard enough to make deck plates groan.

Kostas loses his tablet when we lurch, the device skittering across deck. He stays silent, that's how I know pain bit bone. I grab his sleeve, give his weight back to the deck, feel the tremor in his muscles.

A sailor on the bow line goes over when the ram hits, young face with a pink scar at his mouth corner. His hands open underwater, reaching for something that isn't there, then there's only current carrying him away. We throw the life preserver, pull in the line with desperate strength. The rope comes back empty. The space where he should be settles behind my sternum, another weight I'll carry.

The enemy's deck gun finds us once. The hull jumps. Shrapnel goes into men shallow for some who duck in time, through and through for others who stand too tall. A woman from Samira's crew presses field dressings to the worst wounds, keeping pressure on the bleeding until the man beneath her hands stabilizes.

Stavridis takes shrapnel along the jaw and his beard blooms with blood. He doesn't touch the wound.

We light the diesel slick and watch it teach the sea new colors. Fuel ignites men who can't escape fast enough. Fire on water has its own physics, seizing oxygen from anywhere lungs might seek salvation. A man leaping from burning deck finds different burning in the water. His scream comes through waves clear and honest.

We fight spreading flames with foam dispensers and fire blankets. Ferretti takes fire to the forearm, flesh going white then red, blistering fast. He hisses through clenched teeth, sets his jaw against pain, keeps his hands steady.

The enemy command vessel tries to swing her missile battery. Instead she marries our sea mines in explosive ceremony. Her engines climb in pitch, mechanical voices protesting. She drags mine cables, then pauses with the surprise of discovering her own mortality.

Hassan's guns kiss her waterline, each shell placed with craftsman precision. A Greek torpedo finds where a welder grew tired and cut corners. The enemy captain chooses self-destruction over surrender and detonates his ordnance stores. The world goes white, then deaf.

For endless moments I feel the explosion only in my teeth, taste it in metal fillings. The sea stands up in outrage and we ride its strength down.

When hearing returns wrapped in pins and needles, there's percussion of falling debris and prayers paid in full. Strangled laugh of a man discovering his eardrums still work. Smoke claws at throats; we breathe through cloth tasting of salt and fear. Lines burn palms through gloves; we wrap them in Kevlar.

One mine cable, chewed by heat, gives way and sends steel whipping toward a sailor's legs. He kicks high and dances through death's space.

An enemy sailor with hair burned to wool claws at our gunwale with shaking hands. A Greek sailor raises his knife to cut the threatening fingers, then cuts the line that would have let the man fall back to burning water. Afterward he curses his mercy.

When smoke thins from walls to curtains, the channel belongs to us. The enemy command vessel sits caught in mine cables, too proud to squeal and unable to save its crew from choosing between drowning and fire. Two escort boats sink lower, making embarrassing bubbles as they drown.

Others run for the gap we left them, engines at full throttle, white churn marking retreat. We let runners run.

The sound from our decks is relief turned wild. Men slap the hull, confirming survival's reality. Someone starts a hymn, forgets words halfway through, transforms the rest to curses that sound like gratitude offered to gods who might or might not be listening.

Hassan comes with ash in his face lines and smoke braided through his beard. He takes something from his pocket, wooden prayer beads worn smooth by worried fingers. "From my mother," he says, voice carrying the weight of women who pray for sons they'll never see again. "She has no use for them now. The dead pray without help, or so clerics tell us."

The joke is desert-dry, the blessing well-shaped. The beads know my palm instantly.

Stavridis approaches carefully, presses his fist to his chest long enough to be witnessed. Burned hair makes him look younger and more breakable. Ferretti grins with his bandaged forearm, asks if I have more mines because he's developed ideas about other throats that might benefit from choking.

Samira's medics move between wounded with surgical kindness. Kwame stands reading whatever the western sea has written in salt foam.

Lemminkäinen waits with winter's patience, finding precisely the right place at the right moment. His smile seems small and private. "Well executed," he says, voice carrying simple approval. "Your timing was precise. The smoke deployment worked exactly as you planned."

His voice drops, quiet enough that others won't overhear. "I have been watching you command. You make decisions quickly. You do not hesitate when others would freeze." He steps closer, close enough that I can smell winter pine on his clothes. "This is unusual. Most people break under such pressure."

"The wind cooperated," I reply.

He tilts his head so silver insignia catches light, studying me with pale eyes that miss nothing. "You win battles with force. This is good. But wars require different skills. Patience. Planning. Someone to share the burden when it becomes too heavy for one person."

His hand gestures toward the wounded being treated on deck, then back to me. "You have a child who needs her mother alive. You push yourself too hard. This will kill you eventually." The words are matter-of-fact, delivered without emotion. "I could help you. I have resources. Experience. I understand what it costs to lead."

He doesn't speak Ilija's name aloud. It hangs in the air between us like smoke from the battle. "You are alone in this command. This is unnecessary. I am offering partnership."

The directness of it catches me off guard. My chest tightens because part of me wants what he's offering—someone to share the weight.

Kostas coughs with diplomatic timing. I roll Hassan's prayer beads until one knot finds the groove between my fingers.

"We need that command vessel towed clear before she rolls over and crushes three of ours," I tell Hassan.

Lemminkäinen steps aside.

We labor into brittle light. Count the living first because hope must come before grief. They announce themselves with stale jokes, humor worn thin by proximity to death. Then we count the dead. Numbers become names. Names become weight I have no room for and refuse to set down.

A young sailor who spliced cables with clever hope doesn't answer when called. His gear gets rolled with military precision, carried by a petty officer who taught him engine rhythms. A woman with a nose scar breathes the thin breath of those who will survive, wishes for air enough for stories that might make someone laugh.

When exhaustion takes us, it asks no permission. Men sleep in whatever shapes their tasks carved, hands still curved around controls.

Night comes with authority. Stars overhead, indifferent and distant.

I stand at the bow as we nose through darkness. Water parts willingly and closes behind us.

Somewhere behind us, Lemminkäinen speaks softly to Hassan. Somewhere beyond harbor lights, a child wakes with shadows on her chest, and Petra's hand settles over darkness until breathing becomes regular.

My fingers find shells cemented to the hull by salt. I work one loose, small and chipped and perfect. When I press it to my ear it carries the drum of my own blood.

I hold the shell until sharp edges warm. I keep it closed in my fist and offer Ilija's name to the wind. Wind accepts the offering and brings back only metallic salt and something like citrus cut with iron, sweet and sharp and final.

Behind me equipment makes small domestic sounds, buckets clinking, rope slapping deck plates, groans that could be human or metal settling debts. These sounds say what needs saying: we're still moving, still breathing, still becoming whatever sea and fire and the long work of living will make us.

We come into harbor under a moon smudged by smoke. Docks make eternal sounds, comfort of routine. Petra sits exactly where I left her, awake. She's arranged herself cross-legged above the spice market with Selene asleep in her lap, the child's breath lifting Petra's hand.

I set the shell beside them carefully. "For when she wakes."

Petra's eyes climb from the shell's scarred surface to my face. "She waited. And I did too."

I nod. The shell sits between us, a promise kept.

Petra shifts Selene's weight carefully. My daughter stays asleep, her breath steady and warm against Petra's shoulder. The fever's broken. Relief hits me harder than the shrapnel did.

"Come," Petra says. "You need to sleep before you fall down."

Chapter Eight
THE PARCHMENT

Danica

The city refused to sleep after the fire. Smoke hung in the alleys, and the harbor smelled of tar, salt, and burnt rope. Hulls scraped stones as crews reset their moorings. I carried the sea with me from the crossing; salt clung to my skin and hair.

Petra walked at my side, steadying our path through the busy market. Selene held her hand. Shadows gathered at my daughter's feet. When they thickened, Petra set her palm against Selene's back, skin to spine, slow breath to slow breath. The dark thinned. She simply watched Selene and answered with touch when the room needed it.

Selene moved through the noise like someone listening for a door to open. Fishmongers tested blades against boards, spice sellers shouted prices in many tongues. A beggar coughed into a cloth stiff with salt. Selene's gray eyes tracked something past the crowd, fixed on empty air. Her head tilted and she took three steps, stopped, turned. Her fingers curled and uncurled at her sides.

I touched the pouch at my belt. Inside lay the shell I'd promised her, pale and chipped, still carrying a trace of open water. Promises to children are the promises I keep first. I drew it out and Selene reached with both hands, careful and serious, then surprised me. She turned and set the shell in Petra's palm.

"Keep it safe." Selene's voice was small. The choice was firm.

My chest tightened. She trusts Petra more than my promise to come back.

Petra tucked the shell under her cloak and met my eyes. Small objects matter when the ground shifts.

We climbed toward the ruined library. The arches stood like ribs. The columns were black where heat had licked them. Fire took almost everything centuries ago. The stones still held the smell.

That was where I saw the man.

He moved like smoke through water, and the crowd parted before him, eyes sliding past as if he belonged to the architecture. His robe matched road dust, a cloth strip bound his hair. He carried only his own certainty, and that marked him clearer than any blade.

His eyes were plain brown until they found mine. Then my chest locked, and air came shallow. Something shifted inside me, like finding a door I'd forgotten existed. He stopped three paces away and bowed just enough to keep me guessing whether he offered respect or measured me.

"You carry the sea in your skin." His voice scraped like wind on stone. He kept it low, yet it cut through the market's noise. "Weather in your bones. Neither will take you where you need to go."

Petra shifted. She drew Selene behind her hip. Her jaw locked. "Who the hell are you?"

"I've had many names." He tilted his head. "Here, once, they called me Gerasimos. Names are just shells. The creature outgrows them." A pause. "I walk thresholds. I'm a key that walks."

Walkers of thresholds pass through places that should be closed, between streets that do not meet, through doors that exist only when they need them. Some say it is a holy craft. Some call it smuggling. It always carries a cost.

Selene's eyes widened. The shadows at her feet twisted into shapes that strained the eye. "He's telling the truth." A whisper.

Gerasimos looked at her. The lines of his face eased. "She sees."

My hand found my belt. Empty leather. Old habits. "What door are you opening?"

He glanced at the blackened shelves. Drew out a bundle wrapped in brittle cloth. Held it toward me.

"This survived."

I took it. The cloth crumbled under my fingers and smelled of old smoke. Inside lay a manuscript. The edges were burnt to lace. Worms had eaten through parts of it. The ink had turned brown with time. One line stood clear, as if heat had pressed it deeper than the rest.

Only when both have died may the world be unbroken.

The words landed heavy and my throat locked. Anger rose hot and immediate—another sentence that tried to rule a life, another fragment with a priest attached. I wanted to tear the page and let the wind scatter it along the quay. My hands held steady even as rage made them want to shake.

Gerasimos waited. He watched me the way a locksmith watches a lock.

"Another prophet with a relic." The voice came from the column's shade, level and cool. "This city gets one every season."

Jaakko Lemminkäinen stepped into the light. His cloak was fastened with a small silver clasp. "Relics won't feed anyone. Won't hold a coastline."

He looked at me. "You need supply. Training. Steel. Your work is here—keeping people alive."

Gerasimos kept his eyes on me. Only me.

Lemminkäinen set a hand on the rail beside me, just out of reach. "The Accord regulates prophecy—taxes it, licenses it, hangs people who act on it without approval." His voice stayed level. "They find that page, they'll seize it and use it to control you. Your daughter needs you alive."

The Accord's orders peel from the city's walls. They govern with ledgers and punishments and call that order. I have worked under them and bled under them.

Selene's fingers tightened on Petra's cloak and the shadows at her feet rose. Petra pressed her palm between Selene's shoulders. The dark flattened, but the air kept a metallic edge.

"It survived." Gerasimos said it once more, then turned and walked back into the market. People made space and closed behind him. The city swallowed him.

Lemminkäinen watched the spot where he'd been, then looked at me. "Make the choice that keeps people breathing." He left as cleanly as he'd arrived.

The page shook with my pulse. The line sat there, permanent and undeniable.

Only when both have died may the world be unbroken.

I folded the manuscript and held it against my chest. The anger stayed, and the words remained.

"Walk." Petra's voice was firm. "If it wants to hurt us, let it try under a roof."

We moved through the market's press. Spices had burst from torn sacks. Fish scales flashed like cheap glass. The Accord's old proclamations curled off plaster and fell in strips. A boy with a basket sang two notes over and over until they became a melody. Smoke lay near the ground and rose when doors opened.

The safehouse above the spice market had once been a silk shop. Bolts still leaned in one corner. Petra chose the room with a high, narrow window. She barred the door with a length of old pipe. Selene climbed onto the pallet and arranged herself with quiet care, formal as a small courtier.

I set the manuscript on the table and lit a lamp. Light pooled on the page, and I wanted to look away. Couldn't. The surviving sentence waited.

Only when both have died may the world be unbroken.

Selene came to my side and stood still. The dark at her feet thinned to a stain in the wood, then gathered again. Petra set a hand on her shoulder.

"I don't like it." Selene's voice went quiet. "It talks too loud without a mouth."

Petra stepped between her and the table. Her body became a wall. "We can burn it."

"Someone greedy will find it if I throw it in the street." I stared at the page. "And if I burn it, those words will follow me. I'll see them on my walls every time I wake. The fire started this. I'll finish it another way."

"Then we hide it." Petra's voice softened. "You can keep it safe. Honor comes later."

She lifted a silk bolt, slit it, and pulled out a tight-woven length. She wrapped the manuscript with practiced hands and stitched the edge shut with black thread she drew from a pocket I'd never found. The bundle looked like a dull scarf when she finished.

"In the hem of your cloak," she said. "Blades go for the throat and ribs. They rarely look for silk."

I opened the inside seam and slid the bundle in. The Accord trained me to hide maps and letters where soldiers look last. The final knot sat clean. The weight lay against my calf. I could feel it with every step.

A knock sounded: three beats and a pause. We use that cadence when we want listeners to write the wrong story. Petra lifted the bar. The door cracked open an inch. Two inches.

A boy stood there with a basket. Steam curled up from a loaf. Figs filled a small bowl, their skins splitting. A flask sweated.

"From the northern gentleman." The boy shifted his weight. "Said the lady fights better with food."

Petra took the basket and thanked him. She watched him all the way down the stairs. She put two coins and a note outside the door for his return trip.

We ate because bodies require it. Selene tore the bread into small pieces and lined them along the table's edge. Petra poured water and drank it slowly. I bit into a fig and let the sweetness sit.

Evening came quickly. I lit a second lamp. Selene fell asleep with one hand under her cheek and the other curved as if it still held the shell she'd trusted Petra with. Petra sat on the floor against the wall with her knees drawn up. That is how she keeps watching.

"Say it plain." Petra's voice stayed quiet. "Before you convince yourself it's something else in the morning."

"The monk knew exactly where to stand, how to keep his voice out of my head." I rubbed my face. "Men who want recruits preach. Men who want witnesses spill blood. He did neither."

"And the other one?"

"Lemminkäinen's patient. Too patient." My voice drops. "He offers rest when I'm too tired to refuse, tells the truth but angles it where he wants it to go."

A pause. My chest tightens. "He knows Ilija's on Olympus, knows I'd do anything to get a message through. And he knows I'm so fucking tired of carrying this alone."

Petra made a sound that could've been agreement. "Then lock it away."

"What if I want the opposite?" The words slip out. "What if—just for one night—I let someone else carry it?"

I opened the hem again and took the wrapped page, unrolled the silk because I needed to look one more time. The letters remained unchanged and waiting.

I read the line once aloud, once with my eyes, once in the rhythm old women use for hymns.

"Tell me something ordinary." My voice cracks. "When does the tide turn? How many steps to the quay if I'm carrying Selene and a pistol? How do I stitch a seam that'll hold when I run?"

"Tide follows the wind more than the moon." Petra's voice stayed soft. "Twenty-eight steps straight. Thirty-one if you avoid the loose ones. Forty if you let Selene pick stones so her feet learn them." A pause. "The seam you made will hold."

I sewed the hem shut again, careful and even. The work steadied me. When I tied off the thread, I stood and let the weight find its place against my leg.

I went up to the roof. The city lay bright with moonlight. The harbor knocked its chains. A clean salt breeze moved through the streets. People below cleaned steps, stacked nets, and set out buckets for morning. Normal work. Good work.

A man sat with his back to the parapet, a cigarette burning down between his fingers.

"I sent bread." Lemminkäinen kept his eyes on the horizon. "Figs too. You avoid honey."

"You pay attention." I moved closer. "Collect useful details."

"I do what works." He tapped ash away. Faced me. Lines bracketed his mouth. "Let me have the manuscript examined. My people will return it to you. And you can share this burden."

"You'd put my problem in your house. Call that help."

"One night." His tone stayed level. "Your man's on Olympus with Ana. I can get a message to him, where she'll see it." A pause. "Trade me the page for tonight and I'll send the message. That's the offer."

The place in my chest where I keep Ilija's absence shifted—sharp and sudden. Olympus. Ana has him. And this man can reach him.

My hands want to shake. "A message. To Ilija."

"Yes. Tonight, if you give me the page."

Seven years. Seven fucking years of carrying this war while Ana keeps him caged. And here's someone who sees how tired I am, someone who accepts me exactly as I am. Someone who could tell Ilija I'm still fighting, still coming.

"I need clear terms." My voice comes out quieter than I meant. "Exchange. Balance. I pay my debts."

"I want you alive to finish what you started."

He stood. "Sleep. You've got council tomorrow." A pause. "Keep this away from the Accord—prophecy's their weapon." He stopped at the stairs.

"Give me the page, I send the message. Keep it, I'll find another way. I stay until the work's done, just prefer clear terms."

"I know."

I stayed until the wind loosened my hair. When I went back down, Petra had pulled the blanket over Selene's feet. My daughter slept with her hands open, trusting even in dreams. I lay on the floor at their feet. The page warmed against my calf through the cloth of the hem.

Tomorrow, I could give it to Lemminkäinen. Let him examine it, send that message to Ilija. Just one night of someone else making the decisions while I sleep without nightmares. He's offering help. Real help. A message to Ilija. Seven years of silence, and someone's finally offering to bridge it.

My hand finds the hem, traces the outline of the wrapped page. What if this is the smart choice? What if I'm so afraid of needing anyone that I'm sabotaging the one chance to reach Ilija?

I close my eyes. Think of Ilija on that cold mountain. Think of Lemminkäinen's steady gaze, his practical offers, his patience.

Think of how much I want to say yes.

Morning brought light through the high window. Petra carried water up from the well. Selene counted our beans into small piles and then pushed them together. I brewed harsh coffee, and we were glad for it.

Hassan's runner arrived with the admiral's summons. Noon council—ships to assign, dead to record, orders to write. The Accord would be listening. They always were. Petra lifted her chin; she would come with me. Selene put the beans back into their jar as if returning men to a barracks that would need them again.

On the stairs, an old woman in a blue scarf touched my sleeve. Her gaze was sharp. Practical.

"You've stitched something into your hem." She stated it plainly. "Whatever it is, let your own will guide you. And keep it from those who'd use it to steer you where they want."

She walked away to whatever work waited for her.

The council chamber would be full of men who enjoy maps and the arguments that rise from them. I would have to speak their language and still stay myself. As we crossed the market, I tucked the hem deeper so the bundle sat clean. Selene walked between us and held both our hands. That was the only chain I trusted.

CHAPTER NINE
THE ANVIL AND THE CHAIN

Dust swirled in the air, settling on the marble beneath me. The wall shuddered before a section slid inward. Before I could register his presence, a hand clamped around my neck. Calloused. Strong as iron.

The grip spoke of labor, knuckles worn smooth by stone, day after day, year after year. Pain lived so deep in the flesh it only surfaced when winter came.

He lifted me from the cold marble, my body light in his grasp. His hand found my shoulder, then shifted with practiced ease, placing my feet beneath me before my legs remembered their purpose. I stumbled and my knees buckled. His hand stayed, solid anchor while the artificial sky hummed overhead.

"On your feet." The words struck like thrown stone. I turned, slow and hesitant, just enough to see him fully.

Shoulders like siege gates. Skin of old bronze, burnished and worn. Scars crisscrossed his flesh in patterns that spoke of verdicts. His eyes held the look of poured metal left to harden. Brutal features, every one of them. My chest loosened. I could breathe.

My mouth opened. His fist answered, striking my sternum, stealing breath. "Save it." He caught me before I fell. "Words cost air. You'll need it all."

He spun me toward a jagged opening and shoved. I stumbled forward into a passage born from hammer against mountain. Iron and heated stone filled my lungs, thick as law. The lotus fragrance died in my first choking breath.

We climbed winding stairs carved into the mountain shoulder. Shallow, irregular steps. The hammer music I'd heard as distant echo now beat proper rhythm, vibrating through rock, through bone. His hand stayed on me, guiding like a farrier teaching a headstrong colt. When my body faltered, correction came swift—a sharp impact. The House's comfort lay far behind us before I glanced back. From here, the false stars looked smaller, forgotten.

The forge hall opened beneath us. Blackened columns rose to support the distant roof, varnished glossy by centuries of smoke. Molten slag flowed through deep stone channels, cores pulsing the color of heart's meat. Where heat met resistance, edges scabbed to dull, crusted iron. Anvils stood in uneven rows, faces polished dark by generations of blows. Bellows the size of animals drew and expelled air, synchronized to the boot-sung rhythm of children who'd grown into their work until work consumed them. Everything here had been taught, passed down. Everything here told the truth.

"Kratus." He laid his palm on a block of iron set apart, the way men touch a friend who needs the steadiness. "Strength. Compulsion. The hand that binds, the foot that compels." He looked up toward the mountain as if he could see past stone to halls that had forgotten shame. "Aphrodite paints law, calls it mercy. Makes theater of consequence. I tied Prometheus to rock when talkers debated feelings. I'm done watching this house rot."

The room absorbed his words, filed them away. Lotus taste still clung to my tongue. I forced the question past my teeth. "Then why me?"

No hope in it. Only hunger for explanation.

"Because she sought to hollow you and left you bruised." Grim satisfaction edged his voice. "Because her poison failed. Because your ruin still matters to her." His hand pressed my shoulder—weight, reminder, guidance toward a descending corridor that plunged into earth. Warmth fled. Ancient chill met us in the darkness. "That reaction is your value. Anyone can make a slave. Shatter bone, crush spirit, have a pliant thing. Simple art. You—your resistance makes you a weapon." His eyes caught what little light remained. "I want an interruption. A wrench in her gears. A force to unravel her illusions."

Beneath Olympus's towering peaks, we found an entrance, a gaping maw leading into the labyrinth. The air held damp earth and indefinable antiquity.

We descended through narrow passages where rough-hewn stone walls displayed faded frescoes of forgotten deities. Their eyes, dimmed by millennia, watched our intrusion. Each fresco spoke fragments of lost narrative, hinting at rituals and beliefs swallowed by time. My chest tightened and my breath came shallow.

The passages opened into an immense hall with ceiling lost in gloom. Shattered statues lay scattered—limbs, torsos, heads bearing serene visages of gods or fierce countenances of beasts. They lay strewn as if subjected to deliberate violence. The scale suggested immense power and purposeful obliteration.

A low hum vibrated through the stones beneath our feet, drawing us deeper. It led to a hidden chamber, a peculiar cistern. Its waters ran milky, opaque white. Lotus blossoms floated on the surface, their petals exhaling that cloying, sickeningly sweet scent.

Kratus scoffed, his voice echoing. "Anesthetic cult. A place to lull the mind into blissful ignorance."

His words struck like a fist. Memories clawed up—the Furies, their relentless pursuit, Ana's bitter cup. My hands clenched. Heat rose in my chest, spread through my limbs. The rage burned welcome, fierce beacon against the encroaching shadow. I let it take me.

The corridor widened. Heat fled and dampness crept in, charcoal scent replaced by iron. The hammer's rhythm faded, giving way to an older, primal beat. Water wept from the walls. Kratus's grip tightened at the back of my neck—direction, guidance. "You asked why," he said. "This is why."

The passage opened. The river waited.

The Styx consumed light. Its surface lay dark and still as hammered metal. Beneath, slow and purposeful movement. A thought too dangerous to hold. Its sound: muffled argument from another room, words swallowed before they reached ears. The riverbank held its form until persuaded otherwise. Cold wrapped my ankles. The cost of standing before such a thing pressed against my chest.

Pale grass stretched across the far side, restless and never still. Gray trees stood motionless as held breath. Distance held a gate made of absence, a sight my eyes chose to avoid. The Styx announced itself. Kratus stood beside me, silent.

"There's no bridge."

"There's no bridge." His face stayed unchanged, but deeper lines around his mouth spoke satisfaction I trusted more than smiles. "The river keeps oaths and despises falsehoods. Cross with lies on your tongue, it claims your lips."

The ferryman arrived the way certain truths do—simply present when you finally noticed him. His skiff emerged from black water without a ripple, first outline then vessel of wood that had learned to be conveyance. He faced us, robed in material older than cloth, washed only by the river. His hands were bones smoothed by water, his face a skull the river had considered and permitted. The pole in his grip might once have been a trunk from a sacred grove that had learned better and ceased its complaints.

Kratus reached to his belt, pulled a thorn of iron as long as a man's thumb, and held it up. "He crosses." Like placing a sword between enemies. Like recording facts in a ledger.

The ferryman's empty sockets turned to me. The river made a small sound like water remembering rain. "Price." The word came from the oar, from the bank, from the place in my mouth that learned the weight of vows.

"I have—" Kratus's hand sealed on my shoulder, stopping me.

"Coins are for families who had time to plan." The ferryman spoke as if the idea amused him. "What binds you. What you'll carry through without asking the river's permission again." He lifted the pole. The skiff shivered. "A truth."

The House's ring circled my throat like an unfinished threat. The word that wanted to rise had a name's shape, struck the metal like a bird against glass. My mouth rested on the pronoun as if on wound dressing. She. I wouldn't let this place eat that. I looked at Kratus. He watched as a wall watches, unconcerned whether a man runs into it or shelters his fire.

"I won't drink." The words surprised me by fitting my mouth the way certain lines of hexameter do—the ones waiting since you were twelve and learned to hear the drum in your ribcage. I swallowed once to set it. "I cross awake."

The ferryman's head turned a fraction, feeling which way wind blew in a place that knew no wind. The river responded with movement so slight it could have been breath a body takes to decide whether to live. "That binds." He turned the skiff so the narrow side kissed the bank. "Blood." He held out a bone palm.

I bit the inside of my cheek until it reopened Kratus's cut, pressed my mouth to bone. The river met iron taste with its own iron. Where my blood touched the ferryman's palm, darkness spread and integrated. He lowered his hand. Kratus lifted his chin the smallest distance and took a step back.

"This is where I leave you."

I flinched at the note in his voice that held something other than cruelty. "You won't cross?"

"I ask Hades for nothing." Kratus spoke as if telling me water is wet and stone is stubborn. "My quarrel is with the perfumed one and the house that let her turn law into powder. His quarrel is with men who forget to be men and gods who forget to be useful." He turned the iron thorn over in his fingers, the little blade looking like a sliver of night trained to behave. "I open doors and shut them behind cowards. I was your jailer, now your guide. That work is finished." He said it because he'd heard the thought forming in me the way mountains hear weather coming before it finds flags. "Walk because you choose it, or stay here and let the river keep a simple secret."

The ferryman's empty gaze held me. The skiff's lip touched the bank as a mouth touches a cup. The water lay still. When I stepped in, the wood took my weight as if it had always expected exactly this measure, and my stomach pitched wrong. The Styx moved the way oaths do—slowly, finally, without care for bodies involved.

We pushed off and the bank fell away behind us, sound of something deciding to leave your life. Kratus stayed on shore with arms folded. If any muscle in him wanted to reach, it kept the secret. The ferryman planted his pole and pushed. The world shifted gently, and my bones went uneasy. The surface resembled glass from certain angles, mouths from others. Shadows brushed the hull without sound. I kept my eyes on the far bank.

When I looked down, I saw a shape in the black moving under mine with my posture from years ago, the one belonging to a man whose hands smelled of chalk and old paper, who worried about parking more than sieges. He was shaving in bathroom light greenish from a bulb that needed replacing, mouth set in the line men get when they're using a razor older than sense. He kept his eyes down. If I moved wrong, I would have knelt to offer him help. The pole thumped the riverbed and the skiff slid forward. He fell away the way a thought falls away when you decide you're done with it.

The ferryman stayed silent, but the river spoke. Scraps of voices threaded the air like hair across a cheek. Some I knew—the boy with mismatched sleeves, the breath he never finished. Some were the kind children have before anyone teaches them to choose. Between the threads moved other shapes wearing my features badly: a version who drank the cup, slept in a room with no doors, let the lotus make a home of him; a version who chose thunder when a door required hands; a version who refused all doors and wrote papers for students who learned to call boredom wisdom. The black beneath lifted its small inquiries to the soles of my feet. The skiff answered in wood-speech: no.

Halfway across, the surface made a small mouth and spoke a name I had been forbidden to say. It pushed against the ring at my throat with pressure that would have made lesser metal weep. I set my teeth and let pronouns do what names could achieve. She stood on the far bank, laughing, that quick and ungoverned sound like a jar of nails shaken in glee. The private one that always felt like standing in a doorway together, half in and half out, undecided about the weather. My fingers closed around the air the way they would have closed around a door handle we'd both touched once. The impulse to speak could have cracked the skiff. I held it. I'd given the river a truth: I would cross awake. I wouldn't spend that coin to buy myself the right to look down.

The ferryman angled the pole. The skiff slid sideways like a fish deciding it had thought enough about dying. On the left, under the water's skin, a face emerged that might have been Ana's if Ana had ever let her mouth admit doubt. It smiled the way a teacher smiles when she wants to keep the best student. The river rolled the image over, showed me its underface— pale meat, roses pressed into it until they bruised, a necklace of little chains. I stayed silent. The ferryman offered no praise. The pole thumped. The oar's blade came up black.

We reached the far bank, and the skiff kissed dark soil. The ferryman raised the pole but offered no hand. I stepped out and the ground took me with the reluctant fairness of a clerk stamping paper because he cannot find the rule that forbids it. The plain up close was a field of asphodel so pale it looked like breath that had chosen to stay. The gate I'd seen from the other side stood taller here, absence edged in iron. Standing near it tasted like biting a coin.

I turned back. Kratus stood where he'd been, figure cut from the idea of refusal. He lifted the iron thorn and slid it back into his belt, let the hand rest there as if on a dog he trusted but kept at distance. "We are even." The river carried his words without touching them. "I tore a hole and you used it. If you ever decide to drown, do it on purpose." He was already turning away when he added, with neither kindness nor cruelty but only fact: "Hades' laws still govern this place, even with him gone. Speak as a man would have spoken to him, and what remains may let you continue to be one."

The ferryman had already angled the skiff into the current. He gave me no farewell, took no interest in whether I'd move toward the gate or sit down on the bank and learn to be a patch of pale grass. That, too, felt like respect. I touched the ring at my throat and the metal cooled under my finger. The air smelled of iron and damp stone and something sweet beneath it that I refused to trust. The path up from the river was a slope of packed earth and worn steps and hollows left by feet that had pressed this way in numbers too stubborn to count. Olympus lay above me, disgraced and perfumed. The plain lay ahead, indifferent and honest. Somewhere in the distance something like a hammer struck once, and the sound continued quietly inside the bone without echo.

CHAPTER TEN
SHADOWS OVER SKOPJE

Danica

The city smelled of rain on concrete and exhaust from Accord patrol trucks. Their banners hung down the faces of Skopje's high-rises, wet cloth clinging to steel, red as wounds. My boots splashed through puddles that were more oil than water. Selene's small hand was wrapped in Petra's, tucked in tight. Petra carried her with steady stride, neither dragging nor urging, simply being there. We kept to the alleys where the air was thick with trash fires and cheap vodka. The Accord had gutted this city like all the others, ripping out what was beautiful, bolting down what remained useful. Skopje had once sung in colors. Now its streets hummed with surveillance drones and the scrape of boots. Only the Vardar River stayed stubborn, cutting the city in half like an old scar.

Kostas was waiting in a stairwell that smelled of rust and piss, his broad shoulders filling the space. His grin showed too much tooth, his eyes the color of tired river-water. Macedonian by birth, smuggler by habit, liar by necessity. He carried maps the way other men carried scars. "You're late."

I pulled my hood back. "We walked through half a garrison to get here. You want faster, find someone with wings."

His grin widened. "Thought you had them already." His eyes flicked to Selene and softened. Petra shifted, shielding the girl with her shoulder.

Kostas raised both hands. "Alright. Keep your knives sheathed. I'm only here to get you in and out."

The alley noise folded inward, a sudden dead quiet worse than the rain. I felt him before I saw him. The instinct of prey recognizing a predator.

Lemminkäinen leaned against the shadow of a broken lamp. His coat was too clean for this world of rust and ruin, still holding the scent of colder air. His sharp features held chilling patience.

He carried a weatherproof case as if it weighed nothing. "Maintenance window. Camera loops are running yesterday's feed. Patrols shift in ten minutes, down for twenty. Long enough to slip in if you avoid wasting time."

As a commander, I recognized the brutal perfection of his intel. I needed it. Every part of my soul wanted to throw sand in the gears.

His gaze flicked to Selene for less than a heartbeat. In that glance, I saw him measure her, catalogue her. He was turning my daughter into a variable in his equation. The thought was cold and clean: I wanted to know what his face would look like with a knife below his ribs.

My head moved, a slow, grudging dip of the chin that felt like betrayal.

The commander in me recognized the brutal logic. It was clean mathematics, and it would work. The mother felt cold dread coiling in my gut.

I kept walking, feeling Petra's grip tighten on Selene's hand. The girl's face was pale in the sickly streetlight, her eyes wide. She was a silent mirror reflecting the terrible danger I was leading her into. The rain made the shadows at her ankles bloom and collapse as if they breathed with my suppressed fear.

Kostas palmed the coded latch and pushed the door inward. The room smelled of damp paper, chlorine, and ground plastic. Fluorescent lights rattled overhead, casting sterile light on metal shelving packed with binders. Behind a grated panel, a cooling unit hummed like server farms and morgues.

I moved straight to the locked drawers while Petra kept Selene tucked against her hip, eyes fixed on the door. Lemminkäinen had peeled off with rehearsed casualness, the studied indifference of a card sharp. His case bumped a shelf without sound. He observed.

Kostas was a map I could read. Lemminkäinen was a locked door. Every instinct from six years of war screamed the real danger was the man who'd led us here so easily.

The second drawer fought me before the lock gave. Inside, three plastic binders sealed in laminate. I flipped one open—columns of numbers, station names, dates, tanker IDs, port stamps. The artery map I'd come for.

The third drawer held stranger cargo. Among the files, a cloth doll with a single glass eye, crudely restitched at the seam. I pressed its belly and felt something hard inside. I cut the seam with my blade and shook a small chip into my palm, wrapped in foil. I pocketed the chip and shoved the binders into the bag at my hip.

The room changed. I felt it before I heard it—pressure building in my teeth, a low hum through my bones. The air grew thick. The fluorescents dimmed. Petra's hand tightened on Selene's arm, white-knuckled. Selene stopped breathing.

The shadows froze. Under the table, along the shelving, around our feet—they became flat cutouts. Selene's ankles seemed glued to the floor. A quiet gasp escaped her lips as she reached for her chest, trying to push away an unseen weight. She tried to step. Her feet refused. Her eyes went wide and glassy.

"Trap." Petra's voice was a low growl.

Kostas lunged toward the breaker panel. Lemminkäinen's fingers closed on his wrist.

"Redundant. You'll only light the beacon."

The words taste like copper. Someone had planned this with surgical precision.

A faint buzz fills the air. Then the vents begin to breathe pure, sterile white light. Cold illumination casting stark shadows.

This is a detection system. Every angle covered, every blind spot erased. As the white light intensifies, I know—someone had tested this. On Selene. Her fears weaponized, calibrated to her specific terror.

Lemminkäinen stands motionless, and something in his stillness tells me everything.

Selene made a sound that belonged in no room, a thin, high keen of terror. I dropped the bag and kicked the table hard, sending it screeching into the light's path. The heavy shade it threw broke a piece of the lock around her feet. Enough.

"CO_2." Petra stripped the fire extinguisher from the wall and shoved it into my hands. I pulled the pin and hit the trigger, the blast biting my fingers with cold as it filled the air with thick white dust. Light scattered. The frozen shadows softened. Selene's feet came loose, and she gasped like a diver breaking the surface.

"Move." Petra commanded, scooping Selene hard against her body.

Alarms woke up, thin at first, then climbing in pitch. Kostas held the door while Lemminkäinen stepped past me and tore the nearest vent grille down with a hooked tool. Behind the grille, a honeycomb of small lamps hummed. He drove the tool through their wiring. The hum dropped, the light losing its dead quality.

"Bundled," he said. "Corner units too."

"Left corner." He moved left and repeated the cut. The air in the room lifted, and the shadows breathed again.

Selene sobbed once into Petra's neck and then made herself small and quiet, a skill children learn when their bodies decide to hide for them. I grabbed the bag and the doll's chip, shoved the binders deeper inside, and slung it across my back. Petra set Selene down into the deepest patch of shade we'd made with the table. "Hold to me," she said, and the girl latched her arms around Petra's neck.

The heavy thud of boots on concrete echoed in the hall, growing louder. Two pairs, then four. A glimpse through the wired glass revealed a black visor, sleek and predatory. Kostas turned back to me. His smile held disarming guilt.

"You have fifteen seconds." He slid a thick length of rebar through the door handles, the metal scraping with a harsh groan. He braced it with a chair he'd clearly tested before. "Eight seconds, maybe nine."

I moved to the near aisle and counted shelves, pulling down maintenance manuals and flinging them across the floor to build another fence of real shadow. Petra used it, crab-walking with Selene pinned to her hip. Lemminkäinen's case was open, revealing a folding knife, wire cutters, reflective film. He taped a square to the light above our heads, and the room blinked, light scattering. I saw a ring of pale scars across his fingers— old burns in the pattern of small circles. He'd handled this exact kind of lamp before.

The door hit the chair, and the frame groaned. "Back seam," Kostas called, meaning the emergency exit hidden behind the shelving. Petra was already there, dragging the unit away with a grunt. I set my shoulder to the metal panel and shoved until it gave way to a narrow service run that breathed stale air and rust.

The chair snapped. The door flew inward three inches. A gloved hand knifed through, fumbling for the rebar. I put a bullet through the glove, and the hand jerked back. Professional. More boots were coming.

"Go." My voice was a low rasp. Petra grabbed Selene, practically throwing the girl into the narrow ventilation shaft. Selene wriggled in, a fleeting glimpse of wide, frightened eyes before she vanished. Petra followed, all sharp elbows and determined shoves.

Kostas slid through behind her, trailing low curses. His oversized bag snagged on the rough edges, but he contorted his shoulders and squeezed through.

Lemminkäinen lingered a heartbeat too long. His eyes darted from the shaft to my face to the splintering door. He was measuring the odds. Then something crossed his features—resolve, or desperate hope. With a final grim nod, he slid into the darkness, pulling the shelving unit back to pretend it had never moved.

The door gave out with a splintering shriek. Two Accord soldiers flowed in, rifles raised. They moved with chilling coordination. I fired low twice, aiming for knees. The first round caught the lead soldier above his patella, and he screamed, his leg buckling. The second shot found its mark. He joined his comrade on the floor.

A third came through, shadow in the doorway. He tracked toward my position. I gave him no chance. My next round tore through the space under his helmet, finding the soft tissue of his neck. He dropped like a cut string.

I backed into the service run, torn metal scraping my spine, and sealed the panel from the inside. The alarms were a steady knife now. Petra breathed in steady counts ahead of me in the dark. The run was elbow-wide and rib-high, a concrete vein the Accord never expected anyone to crawl through. We moved in a chain—Petra, Selene, Kostas, Lemminkäinen, then me, our hands and knees slipping in grit and old water. I could still taste Selene's fear, metallic in the air.

We dropped into a maintenance corridor that smelled of wet paint, its length pulsing with slow strobes of red emergency lights. Kostas pressed his eye to the seam of a grate. "Clear right. Left goes to turbines."

"Right." We moved, the grate coming free with a squeal. We were out, crouching behind stacked coils of cable as two techs ran past. The corridor ran to a service stair—up meant cameras, down meant water. "River," I said, and Petra's eyes flicked to me in silent agreement. We both knew the surface was a net.

Kostas led us down to the mouth of the tunnel where it opened onto the Vardar like a throat about to spit us out. Rain hammered the river, and floodlights swept the opposite bank. Kostas whistled, and a shape unglued itself from the dark—his boat, black and low, tied to a ring no one had remembered to check. He dropped in and offered Petra a hand for Selene, which she ignored, jumping aboard with the girl clutched to her. I tossed the bag. Lemminkäinen stepped down with practiced balance. I went last, my bruised knees protesting.

We pushed out into the main channel, the river trying to turn us sideways until the motor caught with a cough. A floodlight found us. I stood and aimed at the bulb, firing twice until it burst in a hiss of glass on rain. Another light swung our way as an Accord boat cut across our bow, the impact jarring. Selene made a sound I felt in my spine, and Petra wrapped her body around the girl. I put three rounds into the other boat's dash, and the man at the tiller hunched over. Kostas took the gap and drove us under the low arches where the searchlights couldn't reach.

We drifted in the dark with the motor killed, the city a smear of wet neon upstream. The alarms were thin now, lost in rain. Petra leaned her head against Selene's, eyes closed. Selene's lashes fluttered and stayed down, her shadows curled close to her ankles. They'd learned tonight that light could be a weapon.

Back in the warehouse, Selene slept in Petra's arms. Petra shifted on the tarp to give me space, her eyes daring me to find words that could fix what I'd broken. I had none. My hand hovered over Selene's hair, shaking.

"He shouldn't have brought her here." Petra's voice was low and flat.

I sat opposite her, my coat heavy with river water. "You think I don't know that?"

Her eyes cut to me, sharp as blades. "Knowing isn't enough."

I whispered the only truth left. "I'm fucking sorry. I let my guard down. I'm struggling, Petra. The fog in my head, losing Ilija, trying to end the war instead of being a mother—it's killing me."

Petra bent and kissed the crown of Selene's head, fierce and quiet protection that hollowed me out.

Lemminkäinen lingered in the shadows of the doorway, too still. "You've won something tonight. Convoys will run dry. Ports will choke. The Accord will feel this." His eyes flicked to Selene, then back to me. "But you almost lost more than you gained."

My jaw clenched. "Say what you mean."

"A child shouldn't walk into wars." He paused. "Ilija would have folded at the choice. You didn't."

The words landed wrong—wedge-shaped, designed to pry. Before he could turn away, I moved. I was across the room in a breath, the flat of my blade pressed hard against his throat.

"That was part of it too, wasn't it?" My voice was a perilous whisper. "You wanted to see if I'd bring her. Wanted to see if I'd make the hard call."

His eyes met mine, calm as still water. He didn't deny it.

His breath hitched. The cold steel pressed against the pulsing vein in his throat.

"You ever use my daughter as bait again"—I pressed the point just enough—"you will die so quietly that even the gods will have to check the fucking ground to see if you were ever there."

He swallowed, his Adam's apple moving against the steel.

I held his gaze, then pulled the blade back with deliberate slowness. Stepped away.

His hand rose to his throat. "I will make this right," he said before fading into the shadows.

I looked down at Selene, her small body curled against Petra's chest. Shadows trembled at her feet. She was seven. Tonight should have been birthday candles.

I pressed my palms to my eyes until light bloomed. The rain drummed. On the table, the bag with the ledger waited. I told myself the victory mattered.

When I lowered my hands, Petra was watching me. Her gaze held a silent command: Don't lose yourself. She can't afford it.

I nodded once. Beyond the window, the river flowed, carrying wreckage into the gloom.

Inside, my daughter's shadows danced on the walls. In that darkness, I made a vow. I would see this empire razed to ash before I'd let it break her again.

I sat with my mistakes and cursed Ana for taking my Ilija.

CHAPTER ELEVEN
THE WOLVES OF NAV

The river spat me onto the muddy bank. I landed in a heap, hands and knees sinking into soft earth. Each cough ripped through me, expelling black water that tasted of decay. My chest was fire, every breath a blade. A cold unconnected to temperature had seeped into my marrow. The air smelled of rot and old iron.

I lay there in the gray mud, cheek pressed to filth, until the rhythm in my chest slowed enough to confirm my heart still beat. Slow, heavy, bruised— but there. I counted each beat. Only when the tremors subsided did I dare lift my gaze.

Kratus stood a short distance away, arms folded across his chest. His bare shoulders were a landscape of old scars. He was immovable as iron hammered deep into earth. His expression held no pity, only cold assessment.

"You crossed." His voice was a low rasp, the scrape of a boulder shifting. The sound vibrated from the air around him, thick with damp earth and something ancient. His storm-gray eyes measured depths.

"I nearly fucking drowned." The words tore through my throat like sandpaper. The memory of black water, crushing weight, desperate clawing for breath still choked me. The chill seeped into my bones. My lungs burned with phantom suffocation.

"Swimming it clean was never the point." He didn't blink. "The Styx asks one question: are you finished fighting? You weren't. That's all that matters." He offered no comfort. I wanted to spit, but my throat was too dry, too full of the metallic taste of the underworld.

Kratus was already turning, already walking away.

"All you get is to be alive. Asking for more is a fool's errand."

I hated him for being right.

I followed, each step chained to the last. My boots sank into gray dust that clung like a second skin, heavier than ash. The air pressed in, thick and still. Thin, pale figures drifted across the plain, their forms indistinct, faces hollowed out like half-finished sketches. They moved aimless as smoke, devoid of purpose. The silence pressed down, a physical weight. Only the sound of my ragged breath remained.

Kratus's jaw clenched. His gaze swept the landscape. "This place was order once. Judgment. A throne. Now, it's only rot." His voice carried disappointment, a lament for grand purpose reduced to dust.

The gates loomed ahead, iron twisted and split like cracked ribs of a colossal beast. Beyond them, the palace sagged, columns shattered and roof caved in. The smell hit me before I saw him—burnt bone, old blood, meat left too long. Cerberus. The great beast sprawled across broken stones, a mountain of carcass. Its three skulls collapsed, jaws hanging open in silent howl. Its belly was torn wide, organs spilled across flagstones where carrion shades crawled like maggots.

My knees buckled. Cold dread seized my limbs. Beside me, Kratus dropped to one knee, his hand splayed across the smooth, ancient bone. For the first time, his face cracked, revealing raw rage.

"She killed him." His voice was a low growl. "Aphrodite. Your Ana. She unmade the warden of the dead." His fist tightened against bone. His burning eyes cut to me. "You see? She doesn't just kill. She erases."

My throat closed. Before I could reply, the first howl tore the silence apart. Low and long, vibrating through my ribs, scattering the shades. Another howl answered, closer, then another, until the air shook with primal hunger.

Kratus rose, rolling his shoulders like shedding chains, a grim smile showing his teeth. "The hounds of Veles. The Wolves of Nav. She loosed them here."

Shapes coalesced in the mist, stretched thin like nightmares given form. Their ribs were stark beneath taut hides, their eyes glowing with baleful white heat like iron from the forge. They circled with hunter's patience, and I counted six before more slid into view behind them.

The first lunged, jaws agape. I threw my arms up on pure instinct, a jagged bolt of lightning bursting across my fists. It hit the wolf and the beast screamed as its body crumbled to shadow, scorched meat filling my nose. Two more leaped for Kratus. He caught one mid-air by the throat, twisting until its neck broke with an echoing crack. The other sank teeth into his shoulder. Kratus roared, smashing its skull with his fist again and again until it was nothing but splattered bone and ash. Another snapped at my legs. I kicked hard, lightning flashing along my boot as its flank burned open.

My chest heaved. Each bolt I threw felt like it was tearing something out of me. The storm was wild, unreliable, draining me with every strike.

The remaining wolves moved in a tightening circle. The lead wolf, a massive alpha with a muzzle crosshatched with old scars, separated from the pack. It moved with low, deliberate grace, hindquarters tensing, muscles coiling beneath hide the color of old ash. It lowered its head, steam puffing from its nostrils. Its glowing white eyes fixed on me—intelligent malice, a hunter who'd already passed judgment.

My ribs felt like shattered glass, each breath fresh agony. The cold had burrowed into my marrow. The lightning coiling in my gut felt foreign, jagged and unreliable, demanding a price I wasn't sure I could pay. The wolf seemed to know it, its lips pulling back in something like a smile.

"Stand your ground, storm-god!" Kratus's voice ripped through the silence behind me, a raw transfer of will. I risked a glance. He was a whirlwind of violence, bare hands seizing another shadow-beast. I heard the wet crack of bone as he rent the creature's body apart. The sight sent desperate adrenaline through my veins. I clenched my fists, feeling the tremor of thunder roll deep inside me. Now or never.

The alpha launched itself, a dark blur against gray dust. Time stretched. I could see individual muscles contracting, the way its claws tore at the ground, the raw hunger in its eyes. Its jaws opened, a cavern of crooked teeth promising oblivion. Instinct took over.

I threw everything I had left into the strike, a guttural cry tearing from my throat. A torrent of blinding white fire erupted from my palm—the storm itself unleashed in a singular, devastating column. It slammed into the wolf's skull with explosive force that lit the entire plain for a single heartbeat. The beast was incinerated mid-air. Its body collapsed into a shower of black ash before a trace could touch the ground.

A collective gasp passed through the remaining wolves. They skidded to a halt, primal certainty shattered. Their eyes darted from falling ash to me, wide with fear. Their pack was broken. Their alpha was gone.

With a guttural bellow, Kratus charged into them. His fists became a blur of brutal motion, an engine of pure destruction. The last creatures vanished into mist of smoke and shattered bone, their final howls silenced.

Silence returned. My breath tore through my chest in ragged bursts. Kratus stood heaving, skin streaked with blood. He looked at me, eyes flat. "You're stubborn. It's enough."

The ground dropped away to a river of fire, the Smorodina. Smoke boiled from its surface. Across it stretched the Kalinov Bridge, a narrow spine of iron-red that hummed with power, buzzing in my teeth. Kratus stopped at its foot. "I cross no further. This road is yours. The between-worlds belong to your kind."

He was gone. The bridge waited, alive. I set my hand on the railing and the iron bit into my palm, searing deep. I took one step, then another, the bridge thrumming under my feet like a drum.

Halfway across, the river of fire convulsed.

The Zmey ascended from the depths, colossal form cloaked in obsidian scales, each edge aflame. Thick smoke billowed from its nostrils. Its jaws unhinged, unleashing raw fire and a deafening roar that vibrated through bedrock. My body became rigid, every instinct screaming. From the distant shore, Kratus's voice cut through: "Stand, storm-god. Or burn."

The Zmey lunged. I channeled the power within me. Ragged bolts of lightning tore from my outstretched arms, slamming into its ancient scales. The beast roared and recoiled, thrown off balance. But its reprieve was fleeting. It retaliated, a searing torrent of flame erupting from its maw, engulfing me. My skin screamed, blistering. The bridge groaned under the Zmey's clawed feet, trembling violently. This was the precipice.

Yet as the heat washed over me, something shattered within me. The power that had always been a tool became the very world I commanded. Everything.

The storm ripped free from my core. Thunder split Nav's twilight sky. A hurricane of wind slammed into the Zmey. Its massive form buckled under the assault. Hailstones, sharp as forged daggers, pelted down, hissing against the beast's flames. Torrential rain joined the onslaught, hissing against its incandescent scales. I screamed then, a sound born of raw, world-breaking power. I hurled it all until the bridge was nothing but churning vortex of storm and devouring fire.

The Zmey's colossal tail whipped across the span, connecting with my ribs with a sickening crack. I felt them snap, blinding agony stealing air from my lungs. The impact threw me into the void below. I scrabbled wildly until I caught the railing with one hand, body dangling over the surging molten river. The ancient iron seared my palm.

Above me, the beast's jaws opened, a furnace of absolute death. I pulled myself up, every muscle screaming, a feral snarl baring my teeth. And then I let the storm truly have me.

Lightning speared forth from my very chest, a pure lance of power driving straight into the Zmey's exposed throat. Thunder rolled as a mountain splitting apart. The beast roared, its ancient scales cracking and bursting. Hail hammered its eyes, blinding it. Wind shoved its colossal form sideways. One last strike—a colossal column of pure lightning slammed down from the cavern's roof, exploding through the Zmey in a cataclysm of rending flesh and consuming fire. It screamed, a sound that broke reality, before it collapsed back into the river of fire. Steam roared skyward. The bridge shook but held.

I stumbled across the threshold, every muscle screaming. My skin was scorched, blood filled my mouth. The tempest within me died, leaving hollowed-out emptiness.

The far side opened into verdant pasture bathed in light of an eternally still sky.

Before me, the ancient roots of the Slavic World Tree, sprouting from the sacred rock Alatyr, spread like a living tapestry into mist. From that vapor, a shadow coalesced—a bull's horn, massive and curved, then the coil of a great serpent, finally a shepherd's staff. A shiver ran through me as the name resonated: Veles.

His voice rolled through me as vibration in my marrow, low as distant thunder, old as soil. "You saw me when you were seventeen. You hear me now. You are mine, storm-child. Nav remembers the dead. Walk. Others wait for you in the pasture."

I collapsed to my knees, shaking, lungs burning. I managed a nod. Above me, two ravens circled slowly, feathers black against gray sky. I felt the weight of being utterly seen by forces beyond comprehension.

And so I walked on into the waiting pasture.

CHAPTER TWELVE
LAUREL

Danica

The amphitheater kept the sound of us, and I fucking hated it for that. Every scrape of a boot, every breath, curled up the carved rows of stone and came back fuller, as if the marble had learned to amplify hunger. Smoke from the cookfires below the ridge had drifted in earlier, laying a thin, greasy film over everything; when I stepped onto the stage, my heel left a dark print like an oath I had no intention of keeping. Banners of the Accord hung from iron hooks where the upper arches still stood, their red weathered to the color of an old wound. Someone had tried to cut one down and failed, leaving it to pitch and snap in the breeze like a flayed thing that hadn't yet learned how to lie still.

He was already waiting in the center, planted like a fucking statue someone had dragged out to impress a village. His bronze cuirass was hammered to a near mirror, its ridges catching the gray light in a way that was supposed to make a man believe he was a story. He held a longsword with a wide, squared tip, a butcher's blade, polished up and made respectable for the occasion. His hair was cut close to the scalp, salt streaking the dark, his mouth already set in what he clearly hoped the crowd would read as heroic disdain.

I shrugged out of my jacket and handed it to the boy who'd brought the challenge banner. He was barely eighteen, his wrist wrapped in old athletic tape, eyes so bright it almost hurt to look at him. He swallowed hard, his Adam's apple jumping, when my fingers brushed his. Above us, the half-circled stands filled with farmers, dirt caked under their nails, women with hair wrapped in scarves dyed with onion skins and rust, old men who'd come to see whether the ghosts would feast tonight. A dozen of our partisan command checked their sightlines, rifles at their backs, eyes tracking the crowd, the exits, me. I pulled air into my lungs slowly, tasting thyme crushed underfoot and the copper promise of rain still holding back.

The oppressive silence of the arena, thick with the scent of fear and anticipation, was shattered as the general lifted his gleaming blade. It rose with a theatrical flourish, like a conductor demanding attention from an orchestra he hadn't earned, a blatant display of power meant to intimidate. "This is your champion?" His voice, a booming instrument honed by years of shouting commands across chaotic battlefields, echoed off the ancient, cold stone walls of the coliseum. It was a voice full of its own self-importance, each syllable laced with contempt. "A woman in a thief's boots. Go home." A sneer twisted his lips as his gaze swept over the slight figure standing defiant in the center, her worn leather boots a stark contrast to the polished armor of his own ranks. The crowd, a mass of hushed whispers moments before, now stirred, a ripple of unease spreading through the stands. His words hung heavy in the air, a challenge, an insult, and a dismissal all at once.

I let a slow, tired smile touch my lips and reached for the sword I had oiled twice that morning. The leather of the grip felt like a familiar hand, warming instantly under mine. "I'll think about going home after I've made a fucking mess of your pretty stage," I called back, my voice carrying just as easily as his. "You're right, one of us is going home. Just probably the one who's still standing. So, are we going to stand here all day comparing boots, or are you going to show these nice people why they wasted their morning?"

Petra grunted when I told her I would fight. The same sound she'd made years ago when I'd found her in the bombed-out university library, her professor's blood still warm on her hands, Heidegger's Being and Time clutched against her chest. She'd been twenty-two then, a philosophy doctoral student who'd watched her mentor die for teaching young minds to question authority. The Accord came for the intellectuals first, always the intellectuals first. She'd crouched behind stacks of Kant and Nietzsche while they put bullets in anyone who'd dared think beyond prescribed limits.

I'd pulled her out of that ruin. She'd followed because she had nowhere else to go and because something in her had already begun to harden into what it needed to become. Sometimes, in moments like these, I caught glimpses of the girl who'd believed words could save the world, who'd underlined passages about authenticity with the careful precision of someone who thought philosophy mattered more than ammunition. That girl died the day her professor bled out on Aristotle, Petra kept her ghost close enough to remember why we fought, even when the fighting threatened to hollow us out entirely.

Her fingers reached for my hair, deft, practiced, tying it back, pulling it away from my face and neck. Her touch was gentle, efficient. The same hands that had once turned pages with reverence now bound me for war with a sister's tenderness and a field medic's skill. The knot pulled tight, resolute, I felt the tremor in her fingers that she tried to hide. She'd lost too many friends to these ritual executions, too many brave idiots who thought they could beat the Accord's champions through sheer will and righteous fury.

Then, her attention shifted to the chaos around us. Her voice, usually soft with the careful modulation of someone who'd once lectured on Socratic method, took on an edge of command as she barked orders to the men nearby, their faces grim and expectant. They were to clear the lower seats, to move anyone, and she meant anyone, who might flinch, scream, or, worst of all, jump from their perch when the blood finally reached their shoes. It was a macabre and necessary precaution, ensuring that only those with the stomach for the spectacle remained, those who wouldn't disrupt the flow of the inevitable carnage. She'd learned to speak their language, the hard currency of violence and survival, I knew it cost her something each time she traded her scholar's precision for a soldier's bluntness.

He came at me like every man who had ever trained on drills and seldom met a real fight that decided to argue back. His swings were wide and theatrical, meant for a crowd, his butcher's blade cutting arcs through the air that would have taken the head off someone slower, or someone who gave a fuck about his performance. The first swing hissed past my cheek and struck the marble, sparking bright and gone in an instant. Predictable. I stepped in close, inside the clumsy reach of his weapon, and let the point of my own blade have a quiet conversation with his thigh.

The world seemed to tilt on its axis as the sharp, excruciating bite of the blade pierced his thigh. A gasp, ragged and raw, was ripped from his lungs – a sound of pure, unadulterated surprise that was almost a whispered word. He hadn't anticipated such a swift, precise strike, and the shock of it reverberated through his very bones. Instantly, a warm, slick dampness spread across the fine, supple leather of his cuisses, a horrifying bloom of crimson against the dark material. He stumbled back, a frantic hop, as if the ground itself had become treacherous. His face, usually a mask of stoic command, contorted into a furious snarl. The revelation that he was, in fact, human, and therefore susceptible to the ignominy of bleeding, ignited a searing rage within him. This wasn't a wound; it was an affront, a brutal reminder of his own fragile mortality, a truth he had long believed himself above.

"Your name?" I asked, my voice even. It's only polite to know the name of the man you're about to kill.

"Colonel Mavridis," he spat, his teeth failing to stay shut on the pain. He feinted high and came in low, the blade skimming for my knee. I skipped sideways, his edge kissing my skin just enough to promise something worse if I got lazy.

"Danica," I said, because I knew the crowd was waiting to hear it. "That's all you'll fucking need."

He took the measure of that, how a name without a father or a title can land heavier than any rank, and charged. I let him believe he had me, backpedaling hard across the stage, giving him the perfect image of a woman forced to yield. Then my heel found the faint smear of oil one of his soldiers had left on the marble earlier, and I let the slide carry me past his shoulder. His sword bit nothing. Mine learned the seam under his arm and slid home. The sound a man makes when a lung collapses is always the same: a shocked, wet cough, like he just remembered there's no air left in the world for him to breathe. He staggered, his rage dragged him forward through the pain, an ox pulling a plow through a field of stones.

He had strength; I'll give him that. He brought his blade up with both hands for a final, desperate chop at my neck. I stepped inside his guard and let the flat of my sword block the blow, the impact ringing through my bones and stinging my cheek with sparks. We stood close enough for me to smell the polish on his armor and the onions he'd had for lunch. His eyes were bloodshot, pupils wide as they tried to do a math problem they couldn't solve. I pressed my advantage, then gave way suddenly. When his weight pitched forward into the space I'd just abandoned, I brought my pommel up hard under his jaw.

I felt his teeth crack. He went wide-eyed with shock, and I used the opening to slash my blade across his mouth, cutting his next words off at the lips. Blood poured, bright and quick, spattering my forearm with a surprising heat. The amphitheater made a sound then, a low, collective moan that might have been the crowd or the stones themselves remembering what they were built for.

The colonel spat a pink froth and grinned without a trace of humor. "If I fall," he said, his words thick and wet, "a hundred will replace me. You cannot kill weight."

"Weight falls when you cut the right fucking cord," I said, and drove him backward with a series of quick thrusts that were all about economy and nothing for the theater. He parried two, missed the third, and took it in the meat above his hip. With a grunt full of despair, he swung wildly at my head. I ducked, feeling the wind of his failure comb through my hair as the fourth thrust of my own blade entered the soft place under his breastbone, finding its work without complaint. I gave the hilt a vicious turn, just to be sure. He made a sound like he'd been hollowed out from the inside.

He sank to his knees, his pride trying to make it look like a choice even as his muscles gave up and stopped obeying. I stepped in and finished it, quick and clean, my blade sliding through his throat, my hand steady on the hilt because shaking is for later, after the work is done.

A silence fell that carried its own weight, thick and profound. Then the human sound returned, an eruption of shouted names of saints and sisters and dead husbands, a ragged slap of palms on stone, the long, collective exhale of a people who had been holding their breath through a decade of fear. A woman in a blue headscarf threw a branch of laurel, its leaves raining down on the marble and sticking where the blood had splashed. The colonel's men, the ones who had wagered on their own survival, dropped their weapons with a clatter that echoed through the stands. Two went to their knees and pressed their foreheads to the stone. The others just stood, waiting to see if I would make an example of them.

I pointed my bloody sword at one whose shoulder straps were worn through, a man with a bookish face and the thick fingers of a mason. "You. Collect their weapons. Stack them against the west arch. Now."

He moved as if released from a spell. By the time Petra came down the stairs with three of our own at her back, the stage had become an altar and a market and a pledge all at once. She halted a pace away and took me in, the blood, the cut, the way I was standing. For just a moment, I saw something crack in her careful mask, a flicker of the relief she never let herself feel until the danger had passed. It was the same expression she'd worn that first night in the ruins, when she'd realized she wasn't going to die alone among the ashes of everything she'd ever believed in.

She held out a strip of linen, and I bound my own arm while she spoke, her voice pitched for me and the two men nearest who would carry it to a hundred mouths before nightfall. Her words came steady, practical, beneath them I heard the tremor she'd carried since the library, the fear that leaked through whenever she might lose another person she'd allowed herself to care about.

"His supply trains will go headless for weeks," she said, her tone flat as a weather report. "We'll take what's in the depot before his second-in-command even understands the letters."

"We'll take the men, too," I said, and looked up into the seats. I pointed at a woman with gray in her braid and a belt of keys that said she organized things. "You. Get me your schoolhouse. Your best room. Anyone who can read and is trusted with numbers comes there at dusk. We're making lists. We'll pay in salt and rope and first claim on the grain we're about to steal. No one leaves here hungry. If anyone tries to sell a rifle out the back, I will fucking know."

She nodded, her lips pressed tight to keep from smiling. A boy started a chant of my name, thin at first, then thickening as others took it up. I let it go on for a handful of heartbeats, then cut the air with my hand. The sound died, and the crowd became a single body with a single spine.

"We win small and we win often," I said, my voice ringing in the new quiet. "Anyone expecting miracles can take a fucking seat. Anyone willing to lift a crate and keep a promise, stand up."

They stood. Every last one of them.

Word runs faster than horses. A shepherd's radio would carry our fight to a fishing village, and the village would send it to a truck stop where a driver would tell a woman at a boil of laundry who had a cousin in the hills with a rifle. By sundown, it would be in Thessaly, and the men who had decided to wait out the world would be forced to reconsider. The Accord had made a theater of their cruelty; we would turn their own stage against them until they choked on an applause that was never meant for them.

When the body had been carried off and the worst of the blood scrubbed from the marble, a priest came and pressed the laurel into my hands, asking permission to speak. He talked of old plays and new wars and obligations that taste like iron. He was theirs and they loved him, and I knew he would tell the story in a way they could whisper to themselves when it got cold again.

I found Petra later in the shade of the arch, where the limewash still held the cool smell of rain. She sat with her back to the wall, her eyes on the exits, counting the men who were suddenly interested in our backs. In her lap lay a battered copy of Marcus Aurelius, its pages held together with medical tape and the stubborn refusal to let beauty die completely. She'd been reading the same passage over and over, I could tell by how she held the book, thumb marking a place she'd returned to like a prayer. "Very little is needed to make a happy life; it is all within yourself, in your way of thinking." The emperor's words, written while he waged his own impossible war against the edges of civilization.

Selene was at a farmhouse beyond the ridge, safe in the belly of the city with three women, a radio, and a dog that hated uniforms. I had told myself I would go to her the moment the blade work was done. Instead, I ate a heel of bread and a pepper, and drank water that tasted like tin while I let the hands of strangers touch my shoulder for proof that I was real.

Petra waited until my chewing slowed before she spoke. "We have their depot maps. Kostas had them in his pocket like a penitent holding a relic." She had already put a clean patch of gauze under the linen on my arm, tying it off with a knot a midwife would respect. Her fingers were steady, I felt the old tremor in them, the one that came from too many nights spent stitching up wounds on people she couldn't afford to lose.

"You trust him?" I asked.

"I trust that he loves money more than he loves fear, and you just fundamentally changed the market," she said, carefully marking her place in the book before closing it. The gesture was unconscious, automatic, even after all these years, she treated books like sacred things that deserved reverence. "Lemminkäinen sent a note to say the hill circuits are listening. He also sent a crate of oranges. The gesture makes me hate him a little less and trust him a whole lot less. Save your voice. You'll have to speak again before dusk."

I looked at the stage, where the blood had refused to completely yield to the salt. I stood, and my knees reminded me I had bent them more than most men do in a day. The colonel's sword had been laid at the foot of a statue of a tragedian whose nose had been broken a century ago, a flaw that only made him more beloved. The laurel wreath someone had pressed into my hair snagged a curl when I turned my head, and it hurt just enough to keep me awake. "We've bought ourselves a storm," I said.

"Then build a fucking roof," Petra answered without looking at me, she tucked the book of philosophy carefully into her jacket, close to her heart where she kept all the things worth saving.

I never went to the farmhouse. I sent word, telling myself Selene was safer without the smell of war brought to her door, that a child's sleep is lighter than a mother's guilt. I told myself the truth of it, and it still tasted like a lie. I walked the stone corridors behind the stage and put my hand on an old wall where some long-dead mason had left his thumbprint pressed into the lime, feeling the grit catch on my skin. I had taken a head, and now the city would begin to lift its own. The next part would require lists and oil and teaching people how to take back what is theirs without turning into the very thing that stole it from them. The blade was easy. The rest of this would test whether I deserved to hold it in my hand.

By dusk, the woman with the keys had the old schoolhouse cracked open, and the scent of chalk dust and damp paper rose to meet us. It smelled like hope and memory, like the place where Petra had once believed the future could be built with careful thought and good intentions. We began the slow, arduous work of sorting wheat from weevils, writing names into old ledgers that had survived three moves and a fire. Men came out of habit and because their wives told them to; women came because habit had finally failed them. I signed nothing. I spoke often and briefly, letting the ones with sense speak more. The room smelled of sweat and paper and the kind of hope that's afraid to look at itself in the light.

Petra moved through the room like a ghost made solid, checking papers with the meticulous care of someone who'd once graded undergraduate essays on the nature of being. She paused beside an old man struggling to write his own name, and I watched her guide his hand with the same patience she must have shown her students, back when teaching was about opening minds instead of keeping them from getting blown apart. When he managed to scrawl his signature, she nodded as gravely as if he'd just defended his dissertation.

I watched them, and the Accord's strategy crystallized. This was how they bled a rebellion dry, with theater. They issued formal challenges, these duels of "honor," as a clean way to gut our leadership. Send a decorated killer like Mavridis to some backwater town, call out the local hero, make a public execution look like a fair fight. A spectacle to keep the masses quiet while they picked us off, one champion at a time, severing heads without the messy political fallout of a full-scale war. They sent a butcher to make an example of us, they found a fucking reaper instead. And now the news was spilling from the amphitheater, racing into the spine of the hills on a shepherd's radio and a truck driver's loose tongue.

When the moon was a thin coin and the last signature had been made, Petra came to the threshold and leaned her shoulder against the frame, scrubbing her face with both hands. I had been awake since the day before and knew I would stay that way by force if I had to. She jerked her chin in the direction of the ridge.

"She's asleep," Petra said, and for the first time all day, her voice carried the weight of everything she never said, how she'd held other children while their mothers fought and died, how she'd learned to sing lullabies in three languages because scared kids didn't care what tongue comfort came in. "The dog didn't bark when it should have, I'll forgive him; he's learning. The old woman from the well brought milk and sat with her until she fell under. The girl's shadows stayed tight and polite. Tomorrow, we teach them circus tricks. Tonight, you've done enough."

I didn't argue. The amphitheater glowed in the dark, a bowl of ghosts newly fed. I slipped my hands behind my back, feeling the pull in my muscles and the stick of dried blood. I let the laurel wreath stay where it was; it smelled of green wood and sweat and the pepper oil someone had rubbed into it as a charm. I slept leaning against the schoolhouse wall, boots on, pistol near my hand, and dreamed of stairs I could not climb and a voice at the top telling me that doors were for people with time.

Beside me, Petra kept watch with Marcus Aurelius open on her knees, her lips moving silently as she read the emperor's thoughts on duty and death by moonlight. Every few minutes, her eyes would find me in the darkness, checking that I was still breathing, still there. She'd lost too much to sleep easily, she'd learned to find peace in the spaces between one heartbeat and the next, in the knowledge that another day had passed without burying someone she loved.

In the morning, I traced what Petra called a circle and what the partisans called a web and what I knew was a sling, designed to hold something heavy and throw it when you needed.

Word came from the coast that an admiral was listening. Word came from Thessaly that a bandit had decided banditry was less interesting than a payroll. Word came from Athens that a name shouted in a market can become a password if it's shouted enough. I sharpened my blade and ate two oranges from a crate that had crossed three checkpoints pretending to be medicine. I spat the seeds into my palm and pressed them into the earth where the amphitheater's rain gutter emptied and told myself it mattered.

Petra planted her own seeds beside mine, three small pits from the oranges she'd shared with Selene the night before, her fingers gentle as a scholar's as she covered them with dark soil. "My professor used to say that hope was the most philosophical of human follies," she said, wiping her hands on her jacket. "Even Heidegger planted a garden."

I didn't know then how many days we had bought ourselves. I only knew we had bought enough to keep breathing, enough for Petra to remember why she'd followed me out of those ruins years ago, enough for both of us to believe that somewhere in the future, a child might eat fruit from trees we'd planted with the seeds of our small, stubborn refusal to let the world stay broken.

I can work with that.

Chapter Thirteen
ROSES OF BLOOD

Ana

The chamber held the insult of his absence. I could still feel the memory of him on the cold marble where he had lain. I ran my hand over its surface, chasing faint warmth, the ghost of salt from his skin, the suggestion of a shoulder's weight pressed into stone. The chains above, wrought from Stygian iron, hung slack and useless. The lotus jars on their tripods breathed cloying perfume into the silence—a scent that had once been an offering to my power and now felt like mockery.

Ilija was gone.

Nav had swallowed him. The pasture beneath that crude World Tree, the howling wolves and rivers of fire—all the brutish architecture of the Slavic underworld had taken him beyond my reach. And Kratus. The name lodged sharp in my mind. That lumbering relic, that blunt instrument of forgotten titans, had dared to interfere. I remembered him from Olympus, always lurking in the shadow of Hephaestus's forge, a creature of pure, simple-minded force. He was the hammer, the chain, the brute strength that clever gods used to enforce their will. A tool that dared to act on its own.

I should have killed him when Zeus ruled from his throne. I should have ended him during the war, when Prometheus screamed under iron bonds and Kratus still believed he served justice. I should have destroyed him when our halls burned and the other gods fell, their immortality proving worthless. But I let him live. I mistook him for harmless, too dull to matter.

Now he had touched what was mine. He had laid his scarred hands on the one soul whose thread was woven inextricably into my own, and for that, he would learn what it means to be erased so completely that even the underworld forgets your name. My rage was a cold star collapsing inside my chest. This called for correction, an intimate act of erasure.

I turned from the empty slab, my movement contained fury. As I left the chamber, the silence folded back into place behind me like a stitched seam, perfect and undisturbed.

The descent into Hades began—a long path downward through cracked columns and corridors blackened by fire. This place had once been a court, a seat of judgment. You could still feel it in the bones of the stone. Every arch had been shaped to hold the weight of a verdict, every wall designed to echo finality. But that order, Hades's grim order, had collapsed. Bronze lamps lay toppled, their oil long bled into dust. The mosaics depicted scenes of his mythology—Persephone's descent, Orpheus's glance back—all reduced to shards. Chains thick as a man's wrist hung from broken hooks, swaying gently. The reek of rust clung to everything, and something sourer—old offerings left to rot.

I walked past this place with cold indifference. Another failed empire, another monument to a god who thought his power was absolute until it crumbled. I had watched them all fall.

The great gates were shattered. The marble keystones had been split and toppled. The arch now gaped like a broken jaw, a permanent scream. Beyond it sprawled the black plain of the Underworld, a horizon the color of smoke. The bones of the gate's former guards were littered where they had fallen, their armor now brittle shells. A massive column of black iron lay snapped in two, its top half driven deep into the dirt.

And at that threshold, he waited. Kratus. He looked as much a ruin as the gate he leaned against. His chest was a scarred field, some marks thin and white like scratches left by time, others deep and dark, gouged out by wars that had ended before men learned to write. His arms were thick as tree trunks, knotted with old, dense muscle. One shoulder bore the ghost of a burn, a wide patch of blistered skin that had never healed smooth. His face was a mask of stone split by fine lines of age, his mouth a jagged scar above a beard streaked with gray. He wore only a leather girdle and the raw bulk of his body. A creature of pure force—the crudest and most easily broken form of power.

"You've come," he said, his voice the groan of collapsing timbers.

I met his gaze across the shattered threshold. "You took what was mine."

His teeth showed when he smiled, jagged and broken. "He belongs to himself, goddess. Storms wear no collars. You smother him in your gilded cage."

"You speak of him as if you know his nature." I stopped before him, letting the cold space hum with intent. "You understand breaking. Forging remains beyond you."

"And you?" His massive shoulders bunched. "Your sterile order? Prayers without blood, worship without sacrifice. The boy has war in his soul. Denying him that kills him slowly. I gave him a chance to remember."

The accusation landed with uncomfortable precision. There was truth buried in his crude words—I had built my new world on the bones of the old, sanitized and controlled. I had given Ilija safety, but perhaps I had also given him a cage made of silk. The thought clawed at something deep in my chest, something that felt like doubt even as I pushed it away.

Love. That this brutish thing would lecture me on forces I command was an insult so profound it bordered on sublime. Yet beneath my rage, something smaller stirred—the memory of Ilija's face when he thought I wasn't watching, the way his storms quieted to whispers in my presence. Was that love, or was that the slow death Kratus spoke of?

I closed the distance between us, stopping close enough to see ancient battle flickering in his eyes.

I traced a finger along the deep scar on his chest. He flinched as if I'd laid hot coal against his skin. "You speak of love as if you own its meaning. Let me educate you." My voice was silk over steel. "I am gravity that pulls empires to their knees. I launch a thousand ships. I am beautiful, violent possessiveness that declares mine across lifetimes."

I leaned closer, my lips near his ear. "I am the name carved into memory's bones, the hand that crowns kings and topples them for sport. Your simple mind believes breaking equals creating. You have unmade my work—a foolish, sentimental act. For that, I will unmake you."

He laughed, blood flecking his lips. "Then remember me." He roared and charged.

He came like a hurricane, each strike a hammerfall declaration. His first blow split the gate—stone rained down in sharp teeth. A second shattered marble columns. Dust rose choking and gray, but I breathed it like perfume. This was his language: destruction. Simple, tedious, and I knew its every weakness.

I let him swing, a patient predator watching prey exhaust itself. The dagger against my thigh was patient. It knew its moment would come.

He grazed me once, knuckles ripping threads from my sleeve, bruising the shoulder beneath. He pressed me back against a fallen pillar, his hand closing around my arm like an iron manacle. He leaned close, breath foul with old wine and blood.

"Too slow," he rasped, eyes burning with unearned victory.

"Too late," I whispered.

The dagger slid under his ribs with prayer-like silence. Plain steel, sharpened to perfection. I wanted him to feel the simple intimacy of steel parting flesh—a death he could understand. I drove it upward, twisting with cruel, deliberate precision.

His body seized, massive and shuddering. The groan that broke from his chest was guttural—the sound a great beast makes when struck through the heart and finally understands endings.

Blood surged hot and thick across my hand. His knees buckled but still he fought to crush me in his final embrace. I let him. I pressed closer, mouth at his ear, and for one brief moment, I almost envied him—this simple, brutal certainty. He had always known his nature, had always trusted his devotion as pure protection.

"You should have died with the others on Olympus. This is merely the correction I owe myself."

His eyes met mine—wide, red-rimmed, furious. He tried to shape words but his tongue held only silence. Life bled out of him quick and dark. I pulled the dagger free. His body collapsed with an   that shook the ground, blood pouring into the gate's cracks as the Underworld drank its due.

I stood over him, the only sound blood dripping from my blade onto thirsty dust. The silence he left behind was more pleasing than any monument. He had always been tedious—a blunt instrument who mistook weight for worth.

I wiped the blade clean on his leather girdle, steel hissing. Lightning was unnecessary, grand spectacles pointless. Just clean, quiet finality and a decision made centuries too late.

But my work was incomplete. I walked among the ruins with grim purpose. The air pressed heavy with rust and old prayers. Further in, Cerberus lay in pieces—three skulls sagged with blackened tongues, ribs splayed where my own hand had left them. Even Hell's wardens die. Even gods make mistakes.

This kingdom should have trembled with Ilija's storms, his lightning peeling shadows from walls. Instead, profound silence claimed everything. His absence carved through me, carved through this world, carved through everything. Kratus had merely opened the gate. The true thief was her.

Danica.

I said her name aloud and the ruins darkened, venom in my mouth. She was the thorn in every weave of fate, the hand that pulled him away. He looked at her and storms bent to her will. He thought of her and my nets of power slackened and fell. I had given him a gilded cage of comfort, perfect silence. She had given him noise, chaos, ruin. He still reached for her.

And perhaps—the admission burned like acid in my throat—perhaps she had given him something I never could. Purpose that came from within rather than without. A choice made freely instead of divine decree. The thought made me want to tear my own skin from my bones.

Hatred is insufficient. What I felt was slow, consuming corruption—rot that wanted to strip her down until she became a beautiful, empty shell. I wanted her broken, her face ground into the dust that stained my gown. I wanted her to understand what it meant to be forgotten by a god.

Yet beneath the hatred lay something more poisonous: recognition. She was what I had once been—wild, untamed, willing to burn worlds for those she loved. Before I learned to build temples and demand worship. Before I mistook control for protection.

He had chosen her once. He might choose her again. I would stop it.

I pressed my bloody hand against cold stones, closing my eyes, picturing her face: sharpened by command, lips curled in defiance, eyes storm-gray like his. I pictured myself cutting that face open, silencing her name the way I had silenced so many others. But I also saw, with unwanted clarity, the way Ilija must see her—fierce and alive and utterly, dangerously free.

The realization should have comforted me. Instead, it felt like another blade sliding between my ribs.

Kratus was gone. Hades was gone. Ilija was gone. But Danica still lived, and she remained the obstacle. So why did it feel like surrender?

"I will cut you out of him," I whispered to the shadows, the words tasting of ash and old grief. "I will burn your name from his memory until even he cannot find it."

Even as I spoke the vow, I knew the terrible truth: if I succeeded, if I carved her from his soul completely, what remained might transform into something else entirely. But better an empty vessel that belonged to me than a whole man who chose another.

The ruins gave no answer. The silence held me like a lover. I turned my back on the corpses and broken gates. Their deaths were merely preludes. The true wound still walked the mortal world with laurels at her brow and his memory in her mouth.

Danica would fall. And when she did, Ilija would reach for me alone.

CHAPTER FOURTEEN
THE FATHER OF STORMS

Ilija

The bridge of fire vanished beneath my feet. The world changed without sound.

Grass stretched in every direction, patient green that felt older than memory. No wind moved it. Shallow pools held the sky in still circles. I caught my reflection in one and jerked back, hollow yellow beneath my eyes, bruise spreading over my ribs where the Zmey had marked me, dried blood seaming my scalp.

My pulse hammered in my ears. Far below, something vast stirred, roots thick as city streets. Each step sent tremors up through my bones, a thrum I felt in my jaw.

They waited.

First shapes, then faces. No ranks, no procession, just people left where they fell while patient grass rose around their legs. A dockhand with rope-burned palms. A woman with raw circles where rings had been torn away. A girl with braids pulled tight by hurried hands.

Rome's dead. Every face I'd failed to save.

The boy with mismatched sleeves stood directly ahead, blue cuff on one wrist, gray on the other, both too short. Growth had outrun money. A broken spear shaft jutted from his chest. Trust still living in his dead eyes cracked something behind my ribs.

My knees buckled. The grass caught me. I meant to beg forgiveness. What came out was a laugh, dry and bitter as ash.

"You deserved better," I said, voice scraped raw. "You deserved a commander who understood the rooms he led you into."

Silence answered. A taller figure stood to my right, arms crossed by habit. White threaded through his hair too early. The jawline I'd inherited and never thanked him for.

My father.

Two buttons on his shirt hung crooked, proof of hands that hurried for others and neglected themselves. He didn't reach for me.

"Am I dead?" The words scraped my throat.

A single shake of his head.

"Then why are you here? You have a grave. I put dirt on it. Why aren't you where I left you?"

"Because you carry me," he said, and Christ, that voice, gravel under rain, the one that taught me to hang a door and curse without wasting breath. "You never set me down."

The speech I'd sharpened since my twenties lined up behind my teeth, the catalogue of hungers a boy grows in a father's absence.

"You left," I said, and those two words pulled twenty years behind them. "You hit the floor and left me. Left the house to her grief. Left silence so thick I could taste it. I kept your coffee mug like it might hold you. I taught myself to need nothing, to be stone." My throat closed. "And now you stand here like you didn't teach me all the wrong lessons."

Pain flickered across his features. "I meant to give you stubbornness. I thought it would keep you safe. I stayed close to the ground, hoped the teeth in the dark would forget your name." His voice cracked. "They found you anyway, in the birches, when you were seventeen and the fog smelled like river stones. I watched and couldn't tear you free. I screamed your name; you didn't hear. A farmhand's back and a teacher's hands have no grip on a god in serpent's skin."

He stepped closer. "So, I kept watch. You came here, and I walked with you, because blood ignores the borders clever men draw."

We stood in a space shaped like a kitchen, the span between sink and table, where we'd fought about homework and talked around everything that mattered.

"Be angry, sine moj," he said, voice breaking on the endearment. "You've earned it. Then spend that fire where it matters."

"I wanted you old at my table." The words came without permission, raw and bleeding. "I wanted you to meet your grandchildren and play with them. I needed someone to show me how to stand in a man's life without shaking at the joints. You missed everything, every failure, every small victory."

Tears came fast and scalding. He hadn't chosen to leave; I knew that. Anger still had its claws in my throat.

"Sine moj, I know." His hands shook and steadied. "I had no vote in my leaving. But hear me, I never stepped away from you. I watched you learn our myths. I stood with you when you became Doctor Dragović. I saw Ana's true face look through her mask. I saw Danica plant her feet in front of you and refuse the abyss." His voice swelled with fierce pride. "In Rome, when you faced them with empty hands, I watched until watching was agony."

He gripped my shoulders. "Above all, listen, ja sam ponosan. I am proud of you. Tell your child this: her name is Selene. Your daughter.

Bright as the moon, fierce as her mother. Her djed loves her more than breath."

The words detonated in my chest.

The world tilted. Vision grayed at the edges. My legs gave out completely. The grass caught me as I collapsed, gasping like a landed fish. "What the fuck," I wheezed, voice cracking. "I have a daughter?" The words felt foreign in my mouth. "Selene."

Her name hit like lightning to the chest. Years. Years already gone. A child who didn't know her father's face.

"How long?" I choked out, staring up at him through tears that came like a dam bursting. "How old is she?"

Guilt crashed over me in waves. My chest heaved. "I'm a father. I don't know anything about her. I don't know if she likes pancakes or fairy tales or—" My voice broke completely.

My father's hand settled on my shoulder, warm and solid. "Sine moj," he said, voice carrying absolute conviction. "Look at me."

I forced my eyes up to meet his.

"This is why I am proud. This moment, right here. You feel the weight of what you've missed, and it's breaking you open, because you already love her."

He squeezed my shoulder. "And this is why you're here, isn't it? Why you're crossing the lands of the dead. You're trying to get back to them. To her. To Danica."

I wiped my face with shaking hands. The weight in my chest shifted, still heavy. "I don't know how to be a father."

"Neither did I," he said simply. "You learn by doing. You learn by staying."

"Tata..." The word opened something raw and bleeding. "I need to reach them. I don't know the way."

"Watch the ravens," he said, voice carrying absolute certainty. "Look for the bow drawn across Perun's firmament. Follow it. That road is his. Other halls call it Bifröst. It will carry you toward them."

He pulled me close, and his chest shook once against mine. "I have to go again. But wherever you lift your face, under sky, under burden, I'm at your shoulder."

"Volim te, tata," I whispered into his collar, breathing in sawdust and coffee that meant safety. "Stay with me. I'll carry you right this time."

"You always carried me right, sine moj. You just didn't know it."

Darkness gathered like ink through water. Inside it, steady glow pulsed like a hidden heart. Thunder built behind my ribs.

My father turned to me one last time. The dead across the plain had begun to fade like morning mist, but he remained solid, real, present.

"I don't know how to do this. How to be what they need."

He reached out and cupped my face in his hands, the way he used to when I was small and the world felt too big. "You already know," he said, voice thick with unshed tears. "You carry my blood, your mother's heart. You carry every story I told you, every lesson we shared. Trust that."

I gripped his wrists, desperate to hold onto this moment. "I'm scared I'll fail them the way I failed in Rome."

"Sine moj," he whispered, eyes bright with fierce love. "Rome was learning who you really are. You stood when it mattered. You chose love over safety. That is the man I raised."

His thumbs brushed away tears I didn't know were falling. "Now go. Your daughter needs her tata to come home. Danica needs her partner. They are waiting for you to stop running and start living."

He pulled me close one final time. I breathed in sawdust and coffee and the indefinable scent of home. "Volim te, sine," he murmured against my ear. "More than all the words in all the languages."

"Volim te, tata," I whispered back, voice raw with grief and gratitude.

When I stepped back, he was already fading, becoming transparent as glass. But his smile remained solid, proud, unshakeable.

"Remember," he said, voice growing distant. "I am always at your shoulder."

Then he was gone, and I stood alone as thunder gathered in the sky.

Across the plain, the last of the dead inclined their heads with the patience of wheat before wind, then dissolved into memory and starlight.

A figure stepped from the storm. Distance collapsed at his feet. He carried a double-headed axe that caught light like captured lightning. Old scars crossed his arms in patterns that told stories. The air smelled of rain and green wood.

"Ilija."

"Perun." I stood on legs that wanted to shake.

"You keep asking why thunder answers you." His voice ground like mountains shifting. "Here is truth you can live with."

"It keeps finding me." My voice cracked. "Every time I try to live quiet, it's there, humming under my skin."

"You have carried it across lives. When you return, the current finds you like water finds stone. Your father's house keeps the door open with an old oath bound to my name and hidden under the saint they call Sveti Ilija. Your given name is the rope we use to pull you back."

Heat climbed behind my eyes. Flashes came in fragments, a ridge of oaks under black sky, a roof shuddering in spring thunder. My hands shook harder.

"My father?" I managed.

"He felt the weight and kept the house. His hands stayed empty by choice. The birch grove at seventeen is the same ground each time. We meet there. Those who hunt you look for you there. He stood as close as mortal flesh could stand."

I looked toward where the boy with short sleeves had stood. Guilt rose hot and clean as flame.

"He stands as witness. Say his name when you lift power. It keeps your aim true."

"I want control." The words strangled themselves coming out. "Rome is still in my mouth like poison. I keep seeing his face."

Perun stepped close and pressed his palm over my heart. The touch burned like blessing. "Feeling fills this. Thunder listens to feeling first, thought second. You breathe. You name what you feel. You give it direction. You let it pass through."

"Show me."

"Feet under hips. Knees soft. Heels heavy. Find ground that will drink what you pour."

I shifted until steady hum answered through my heel. He nodded.

"Start with love. Say her name."

"Danica." Her name tore out of me like a prayer. The air lifted. Warmth swelled in my palm, moved down my spine like honey, sank into soil. My shoulders unknotted for the first time in weeks.

"Good. Love steadies the current, gives it clean direction."

"Selene." Light ran along the oak staff in my hands like captured starfire. Breath returned to my chest like air after deep water, sweet and necessary.

"Now grief," he said, voice gentle as a confessor's. "Say his name."

"Milo." The word tore out of my chest like shrapnel. Lightning dropped hard and ragged, all sharp edges. My fingers seized around the staff. My knees buckled.

"Open," Perun commanded.

I forced my hand open. The shock ran through wrist, ribs, spine, heel like electricity finding ground. The field drank it hungrily. Relief broke across me in waves.

"Grief loads the charge," he explained. "It wants to pool and fester. You send it through instead."

"What about anger?"

"Use it to aim. Never to store." His eyes held warning. "Stored anger rots the vessel."

I pictured the dockhand, the woman with raw rings around her fingers. Heat rose sharp and direct as a blade. I planted my heel. The staff carried the line clean and bright. The earth took it without complaint. The air cleared.

Perun watched my face with eyes like storm clouds. "Now you know what moves what. Love steadies. Grief charges. Anger aims. Fear clouds everything. When fear rises, say a name that builds you and breathe until you can see clear."

"In Rome I clutched everything." Shame colored my voice. "I tried to hold it all inside."

"You wanted to save them," he said, voice carrying no judgment. "Your hand closed. A closed fist cooks its own palm." He touched my shoulder. "You cannot trade places with the dead, sine moj. You can make the loss do work. That is how you honor them."

He bent and lifted a length of oak, setting it in my hands. The wood felt honest, its weight exactly right.

"This is a lane for the current. Give feeling a road to run."

"What keeps it straight?"

"Names. Each name is a stake driven deep. Stakes hold the road true. Speak them."

"Milo." Heat moved along the grain like living flame.

"Zorica." Warmth gathered in my palms.

"Radek." Weight settled deeper into my grip.

I kept going, the driver, the dockhand, the woman with the raw rings, until iron taste filled my mouth and my eyes burned. "Danica."

The staff jumped in my hands. A bright thread snapped into the grass and fused a glass ring the size of a coin. Tears came fast and I didn't wipe them away.

Perun stepped behind me and set his hands over mine. The next arc broke clean as sword stroke, leaving the smell of struck stone.

"She steadies you," he said. "But she can also pull you into the deep places. Each time you reach for her, choose the pull you follow."

"She keeps me from shattering into pieces." My voice was barely a whisper. "When I hold her face in my mind, the walls stop closing in. I can breathe."

"Use what works." He tapped my chest, and the hum inside drew down to one clear note. "Remember, you are partners in the work."

Tears came hot and honest. I let them fall.

"Listen well," he said, voice dropping to something intimate and terrible. "This power came through people who kept doors open, brought herds through killing weather, lifted children from doorsteps death had marked. That is your reason for being. You guard what you love. You pay your debts. You stop when the work is finished."

"What do I owe Veles?"

"Respect at crossings. Water, roots, graves, his domains. Leave payment when you pass. Coin, bread, a word that admits debt. He keeps the paths beneath us. The old agreement holds when you remember him."

He tilted his chin skyward.

Perun's firmament stretched stone-blue and endless. A pale band formed and brightened until it shaped a bridge across the sky.

"My bow. Other halls call it Bifröst. When your hand is steady, it will carry you to Asgard. When you see ravens running its length, follow. That is your road home."

The band held like a seam of light across the heavens. Warmth lived where his palm had pressed my chest.

"My father?" I asked, voice small as a child's.

"He is proud, and he chose to keep watch when he could not change his ending. Speak his name, and he will hear."

"I'll try to be worthy of that pride."

"Do the work in front of you. Worth takes care of itself."

He shouldered the axe. Thunder released him one layer at a time. The smell of rain faded. The bow held across blue sky like a promise written in light.

I shouldered the oak staff and walked toward the dark line of trees. Above, shadows crossed, wing beats moving north along the pale seam of light.

The land dipped toward water that barely stirred but still made sound. Something rose from the stream, horn for a breath, then the curve of a serpent's back brushing my wrist without weight.

"Storm-child," Veles said, voice rising from the water and the earth beneath my feet. "We walk the hard path together now."

"I'm still bleeding," I said, pressing my hand to the worst of the cuts. I found myself laughing, raw and half-broken. "Christ, I just found out I have a daughter and I'm worried about a scratch."

"You bleed because you love. The wound proves the heart still beats. Walk anyway, storm-child. She waits for you to come home."

I stood, the oak settling against my shoulder like it belonged there. I looked back once. The field had cleared itself of faces, but the weight of their witness remained. Above, the blue vault held steady. Far off, the bow lingered like light caught in crystal. Ravens worked the distance with purpose.

I stepped onto the path the land offered. Ahead, roots of the World Tree rose and braided into patient, living architecture. My heart kept steady time. The storm waited inside me, ready to work when called.

This time, I would let it flow.

CHAPTER FIFTEEN
BANNERS OVER SPARTA

Danica

The hills above Sparta kept their own counsel. They smelled of thyme crushed underfoot and the damp, metallic promise of rain held back too long. We lay in the pre-dawn chill on the slopes of Mount Taygetos, a place that had once watched warriors and kings. Below us, the city sprawled like a captured constellation, its ancient bones pinned beneath the electric grid of the Accord. From this distance, it looked almost peaceful—a beast unaware of what we were about to do.

I pulled the woolen scarf tighter around my neck. Petra crouched beside me, solid and silent, her gaze sweeping the city with practiced focus. Ten of our best partisans were scattered in the rocks around us, ghosts in the gray light. They were teachers and mechanics and farmers who had learned to hold rifles the way they once held tools. My chest tightened watching them. They believed I could give them back a world that had been stolen.

Sparta. The name itself carried weight. A forge of warriors, a crucible of discipline, a place where the very stones remembered what men and women could build, and how spectacularly they could fall. Now it sat trapped under Ana's thumb, another jewel in her crown. The ancient theater, visible even from here, blazed with the same cold, crimson light as the Ministry's banners. My throat burned. She didn't just conquer places—she hollowed them out, wore their history like a stolen fucking coat, and dared the world to notice the fit was wrong.

My hand drifted to the hilt of the dream-forged knife at my belt, its metal cold against my palm. This was a gamble with everything we had. The plan was simple, which meant it would go to hell in a dozen ways. We were here to punch a hole in the Accord's perfect order and let chaos bleed through. We were here to remind the people of Sparta that their city had a pulse worth fighting for. The cost would be paid in blood. Theirs, and ours.

Petra shifted beside me, pulling a small, battered flask from her coat. She held it out. I took it, the metal freezing my fingers. The liquor inside burned all the way down. I handed it back.

"Radio's been quiet from the safe house," Petra murmured.

She meant Selene, tucked away with Maria—our former nurse turned radio operator—miles from here, in a farmhouse I had to believe was still secure. The thought of my daughter hit like a physical blow to my chest. I was here to burn down an empire so she could one day live in a world without one. The price of that future was this present, this cold hill, this choice to be a commander instead of a mother.

"Maria knows protocol," I said, my voice rough with more than cold. "She's kept children safe through worse."

"Has she kept them safe through war?" Petra's question hung in the air like frost.

I turned the flask in my hands. "We're about to find out."

The first hint of dawn began to bleed across the eastern horizon, thin and bruised purple. The lights of Sparta began to seem less like stars and more like the unblinking eyes of a thousand jailers. I was just a woman who loved fiercely enough to become a weapon, and it was time to get to work.

I gave Petra a single nod. She raised a hand, and in the rocks around us, the ghosts began to move.

The descent from Taygetos was silent, our boots finding purchase on game trails and forgotten goat paths the Accord's patrols were too arrogant to use. We moved through the gray, pre-dawn light, ghosts slipping through the olive groves. Our guide was a kid named Nikos, no older than the boy who'd taken my jacket at the amphitheater. His knuckles were white where he gripped his pack straps. He led us to where the modern road curved away from a sheer rock face and pulled back a curtain of ancient ivy. Behind it gaped darkness—a Roman-era water culvert, dry for centuries. The air that breathed from it smelled of stone, damp earth, and silence.

"The old veins," Nikos whispered, voice trembling. "They run under the old quarter. It'll take us close to the Laconia hub."

"Good work," I said. I squeezed his shoulder and slid into the darkness. The tunnel was a tight fit, stone scraping my shoulders. It was a long, claustrophobic crawl, the only sounds the scrape of gear on stone and ragged breathing. A fitting way to enter this new Sparta—through its guts. When we finally emerged through a grated storm drain, we found ourselves in an alley that was unnervingly clean.

The city received us with engineered silence. The usual cacophony of a capital waking—shouting vendors, distant horns, the chaotic music of a million lives—was gone. All of it replaced by a low hum from ever-present surveillance drones that drifted at intersections like metallic vultures. The streets were scrubbed clean, the graffiti that had once been the city's vibrant soul completely erased. Accord banners hung from every lamp post, their crimson a violent slash against the muted gray of buildings.

We kept to the shadows, moving from alley to alley. We saw them then—the citizens of this cleansed Sparta. They walked with heads down, movements efficient and mechanical, faces blank masks of compliance. A woman carrying groceries refused to meet my eyes, her focus locked on the pavement. Two men in suits walked past each other without acknowledgment. They had been taught that to be seen was to be judged, and judgment in Ana's world was something to fear. The sight of them, these walking ghosts, coiled hot anger in my gut. This was the peace Aphrodite offered: a world so safe, so controlled, it had suffocated the fucking life out of itself.

Petra moved like a wraith beside me, her hand never straying far from the pistol at her hip. Nikos pointed toward a nondescript steel door at the end of an alley, gave a sharp nod, and melted back into the shadows. We were in position. Across the narrow street squatted the communications hub, a bland concrete building that served as one of the city's central nervous systems for the Accord's control. Its windows were black and featureless, but I could feel the power humming within.

I leaned against the cold brick, the dream-forged knife a steady weight at my back. I looked at the faces of the partisans with me. They were afraid—I could see it in the tightness around their eyes—but beneath the fear was hard, cold resolve. The look of people who had already lost everything and had decided to burn down the world to get a piece of it back.

"Petra, the door," I murmured, my voice a low command the alley's acoustics swallowed. "Kael, you're on watch—comms only, keep it tight. The rest of you, with me. Stay quiet, stay fast."

Petra moved without sound, a broad-shouldered shadow detaching from the wall. She carried a manual spreader—a heavy, ugly tool she handled with familiarity. The utility work two blocks over was providing perfect cover, their pneumatic hammers drowning out our noise. She placed the jaws into the seam of the steel door, braced her boot against the frame for leverage, and cranked the handle. The spreader groaned, metal protesting. She wedged a shim into the gap and gave me a nod. I watched the street for a final count of ten. The only movement was a single drone, gliding silently at the far end of the block. Its crimson optical light swept the street once, twice, then moved on. I gave her the signal.

The spreader made a sound like a giant's knuckle cracking, masked by the distant construction noise, and the lock tore free. Petra pushed the door open just enough for a body to slip through and disappeared inside, pistol up. I followed, the others right behind, the door closing with a soft click. The inside was cold and sterile, smelling of chilled air and industrial cleaner. The only sound was the low hum of servers.

Two Accord technicians were in the main control room, their backs to us, faces illuminated by monitors displaying the city's silent, orderly life. They never had a chance to turn around. Petra took the one on the left, a single muffled shot from her suppressed pistol. I took the one on the right, throwing the dream-forged blade. It made no sound as it flew, a sliver of darkness that seemed to drink the light, and buried itself to the hilt in the man's neck. He slumped forward onto his console, a cascade of error messages flooding the screen.

"Clear the floor," I ordered. "Find the central server stack. I want this whole fucking place dark."

My partisans fanned out while I retrieved my knife, wiping it on the technician's uniform. It came away with no blood, the blade as clean and cold as the moment it was forged. The wrongness of it sent a chill up my spine—Brigid's dream-work carried its own rules, and I was still learning what the fuck they cost. I sheathed it quickly.

We found the server room in the sub-level, behind a heavy, climate-controlled door. Racks of servers blinked with thousands of tiny red lights, their fans creating a sound like a monstrous lung. This was Ana's voice, her eyes, her perfect order, all humming away. My skin crawled. This wasn't just a relay station—it was the mesh controller for the entire Laconian network, the spine that coordinated every hub from here to Kalamata. Every node heartbeat back to this room every thirty seconds. Cut the spine, and the whole body spasmed.

"Plant the charges," I said. "Wipe it all."

As two of my partisans began setting the shaped charges, a new thought took root. Wiping it wasn't enough. I wanted them to know who had done this. I walked to the central console, the master terminal that governed the city's public broadcast screens. My fingers flew across the keypad, old codes and backdoors the resistance had spent years acquiring finally put to use. I bypassed security protocols and accessed the root directory. I found the file for the city-wide "Unity Through Sanctity" banners. And I replaced it.

"Charges set," Petra reported.

"Good," I said, a slow smile spreading across my face. "Get everyone out. I'll be right behind you."

I waited until I heard their footsteps retreating. Then I hit enter. On screens across the city, Ana's crimson banners and hollow slogans vanished, replaced by a single, stark image: a black field, upon which a five-pointed star blazed in white, a coiled serpent at its center. The same mark that had been appearing on walls and doorways across Sparta for weeks, passed hand to hand in chalk and charcoal. Now it burned on every screen. No words. None were needed.

I pulled the small cloth doll from my pouch, the one from the annex in Skopje. I wedged its single glass eye into the console's primary data port. "For my daughter," I whispered. I had no idea what Jaakko's chip would do—our cryptographer had called it "a gift"—but I trusted it was fucking nasty. The logic bomb would cascade through the Accord's mesh network, hitting backup hubs and satellite relays across Laconia. One server room was just the beginning.

I armed the detonator, set the timer for ninety seconds, and walked away.

As I slipped back into the alley, into the damp gray morning, the first distant shriek of a city-wide alarm began to rise—their intrusion detection finally catching up to Jaakko's rootkit. It was the most beautiful sound I'd ever heard.

We were two blocks away, moving fast through the labyrinth of narrow streets, when ninety seconds ran out. The explosion added a deep whump to the chaos, a bass note that resonated through the soles of our boots. We didn't stop. We were already climbing rusted fire escapes to the flat roof of a four-story apartment building overlooking the square. From here, we could watch the chaos we'd birthed.

The Accord's reaction was exactly as clumsy and predictable as I'd hoped. Patrol trucks scrambled without clear direction, their sirens adding to the din. Armored soldiers spilled into the streets, movements jerky and uncertain. Their only protocol was brute force. I watched a squad grab a young man who'd been doing nothing but standing on a corner, slamming him against a wall simply because he was there. Fucking amateurs. They thought fear was control, but they were just striking sparks.

The first spark came from a second-story window. A speaker, dragged to the ledge, suddenly blared a forbidden song—an old, defiant ballad that hadn't been heard publicly in years. For a moment, it was the only sound besides the alarms. Then, from another street, came the sharp shatter of glass as someone threw a bottle from a rooftop, sending a patrol scattering.

Then the screens began to change. My symbol, the five-pointed star with the coiled serpent, flickered onto every public broadcast panel in the square. The effect was immediate. The citizens, who'd been scurrying for cover, stopped. Heads turned. A collective breath seemed to hang over the plaza. They'd been fed a diet of crimson banners and hollow slogans for so long that this simple, familiar symbol—the one they'd been whispering about, scratching into walls when they thought no one was watching—was a shock to see broadcast so boldly. It was a question asked of the entire city at once.

And the city began to answer. I saw a girl, maybe sixteen, pull chalk from her pocket and scrawl the star on the pavement before being dragged away by her panicked mother. In an alley, two boys used spray paint to put the serpent on a wall. But I also saw an older man in an Accord clerk's uniform point at the girl, shouting for a patrol. A collaborator, his face twisted with fear that his compliance might not be enough to save him. The crowd turned on him, and he ran.

The symbol was spreading. The Accord had no defense for it—they could shoot a man, but they couldn't shoot an idea.

"They're waking up," Petra murmured beside me.

"It's not enough," I said, scanning rooftops and doorways. "A few broken windows won't win a fucking war. They need a banner. Something to rally to."

The Accord forces were growing more violent now, their frustration boiling over. They started firing tear gas into the crowds that had begun to gather. But it was too late. The people were now a current, an angry tide pushing back. Ana's sterile silence was broken, replaced by the ugly, glorious noise of a city remembering it had a voice. And I knew it was time to give them a focal point.

Before I could say it, I closed my eyes for just a heartbeat. Saw Selene's face. Her small hands. The shadows that clung to her ankles. This was for her. Every drop of blood, every risk. I opened my eyes.

"The Acropolis," I said, my voice cold and clear. "We take the hill. We give them a banner they can see from every corner of this city."

Petra looked at me, a grim smile touching her lips. "It's a fortress."

"Good," I replied, pulling my scarf up over my face. "I'm in the mood for a fight."

We used the chaos as our shield. While the Accord's street-level forces scrambled to contain the dozens of small fires we'd lit, we moved toward the high ground. The path to the Acropolis was a pilgrimage route that had been trod by saints and philosophers, now a fortified kill-zone. Accord barricades of prefabricated steel and sandbags squatted between the ancient stones. The air grew thinner as we climbed, heavy with the smell of coming violence. To the east, Taygetos's peaks cut sharp against the dawn—a reminder that Sparta had always been a city of mountains and warriors, and we were reclaiming both.

"First checkpoint, one hundred meters," Kael whispered into comms. "Two heavy machine gun nests, squad of ten infantry. They're dug in behind the Theater."

"They're expecting an army to march up the main road," I muttered. I looked to Petra. "Take your team. Go wide, use the theater ruins for cover. Draw their fire. Make it loud. I'll take the other five and go straight up."

Petra gave me a single, sharp nod. "Try to stay alive."

"Always," I said with a smile that held no warmth. "Go."

Petra and her team melted into the shadows of the crumbling Theater of Ancient Sparta. A moment later, all hell broke loose on the left flank. A grenade went off, the sound a dull crump, followed by panicked chatter of Accord rifles firing at ghosts. "Now," I hissed, and we moved, running low, using the deep shadows cast by ancient retaining walls. The air filled with the scream of ricochets off stone. Ana would love the irony—her perfect order shattered against Sparta's bones.

We reached the base of the main stairs. The machine gun nests were still focused on Petra's position, spitting tracers. "Cover me," I ordered, and broke from the shadows. I didn't run in a straight line. I moved like a dancer, my feet finding a path through rubble my mind barely registered.

I pulled a thermite canister from my belt—Kostas had smuggled a crate through three checkpoints, adhesive-backed military grade—and hurled it at the first nest. It stuck to the gun shield with a metallic clang, then erupted in a roaring curtain of white-hot fire, the chemical burn so intense it turned steel to slag. The screams were high and brief.

The second gunner swung his weapon toward me. Before he could acquire a target, I rolled a smoke grenade across the plaza. Thick gray smoke billowed up, obscuring everything. In the confusion, a single shot from one of my partisans behind me took him through the throat.

We were moving again, up the stairs, past the smoldering remains of the first nest. We were almost to the Sanctuary gates when a side door burst open and three Accord Inquisitors charged out, their black armor gleaming, power mauls crackling. They were faster, stronger than regular infantry, and they'd positioned themselves perfectly in the chokepoint—we couldn't flank, couldn't retreat. But worse, they moved like a single organism, their helmets linked by tactical mesh that let them see through each other's eyes and anticipate our moves before we made them. One of my partisans, a farmer from Crete with a defiant smile, went down, his chest caved in by a single blow. A woman beside him took a maul to the shoulder and fell screaming. The Inquisitors were already pivoting to the next targets, their synchronized assault a killing machine.

Cold, precise rage filled me. I met the first Inquisitor's charge head-on. He swung his maul in a downward arc meant to shatter bone. I dropped to one knee, letting the blow whistle over my head, and drove the dream-forged blade up under his breastplate. The knife slid in with no resistance, and the man made a choked sound as the light in his visor flickered and died.

But the other two had already seen it through his feed—they adjusted instantly, splitting to flank me. "Smoke!" I shouted, and Petra rolled another canister between us. Thick gray billowed up, breaking their line of sight and cutting the mesh link. In those two seconds of desynchronization, we had them. I kicked the corpse toward one, fouling his footwork. Petra and her team appeared from the ruins then, their guns adding to the cacophony. The last two Inquisitors were cut down in a crossfire.

THE OATH OF ASH AND THUNDER

We stood there for a single, gasping breath. We'd taken the gate. The air was thick with cordite, burnt plastic, and cooked meat. The stones were slick with blood. We'd paid for this fucking ground. The farmer from Crete lay near a shattered column, his defiant smile gone. The woman with the shattered shoulder was being dragged to cover, her screams fading to whimpers. Four others lay dead, their bodies sprawled on ancient stone. Five killed in as many minutes, and twice that many bleeding.

Through the gateway, I could see it. The Sanctuary of Athena Chalkioikos, its bronze-clad walls gleaming dully in the firelight. Ana's crimson banner still hung from its columns, an arrogant stain against the night sky.

We stood within the gateway. The fighting was over. The air, thick with blood and cordite, was finally still. Around us lay the bodies of Accord soldiers and Inquisitors. We'd lost five people taking this ground. The cost was etched into the grim faces of the partisans who remained.

Petra was already organizing the wounded, her voice a low, steady command. We'd taken the hill. We held the sky.

Through the columns, the Sanctuary stood, its bronze walls testament to a world that believed in something more than control. And from its pillars, Ana's crimson banners still hung. They snapped and billowed in the wind, a final insult.

I walked forward, my boots grinding on shattered stone and spent casings. Every head turned. They were waiting. For a speech, a prayer, a promise that the cost had been worth it. I had none of those to give.

I pointed my blade toward the largest banner.

"Cut that thing down," I said, my voice raw but unwavering.

For a heartbeat, no one moved. Then a cheer, wild and ragged and grief-stricken, tore from a hundred throats. Two of our youngest fighters scrambled up the side of the Sanctuary with the agility of mountain goats. They reached the banner and began hacking at its moorings. For long moments it held, then, with a sound like a tearing sigh, the great crimson cloth peeled away and fell, tumbling into the plaza below where our people immediately tore it to shreds with their bare hands.

An old man near me cleared his throat. He was a professor from the university, a man whose life's work had been declared heresy. He fumbled in his pack, hands trembling, and pulled out a folded piece of cloth. It was a flag, ancient and faded, the blue and white of a Greece that existed before the Accord, bearing the lambda of Sparta—simple and defiant. "The city needs to see what was, to remember what can be again," he said, voice thick.

I took the flag from his hands. The fabric was old and fragile, but it felt heavier than any weapon. "Petra," I called out. "Get this to the highest point. I want every soul in this city to see it when the sun rises."

As my partisans carried the old flag to the peak of the Sanctuary's roof, I walked to the edge of the Acropolis and looked down upon the city I'd set on fire. The chaos we'd sparked had grown into a full conflagration. Fires burned in a dozen districts, plumes of black smoke rising. The sound of distant gunfire, of sirens, of people shouting in the streets, all of it drifted up on the wind. It was the sound of a city at war with itself, the sound of a cage being broken from the inside out. I'd done this. I'd thrown the first stone that started the avalanche.

The old flag of Sparta finally caught the wind, its blue and white a stark, beautiful contrast to the blood-red glow of the burning city below. I stood and watched the fires spread, grim satisfaction settling deep. This was the cost. This was the price of freedom. This was the war Ilija and I were born to fight, the one I would win for him, for Selene, for all the ghosts who watched from this sacred, broken hill. And fuck anyone who stood in my way.

I was a commander. I was a promise. I was the fucking storm.

Chapter Sixteen
THE BRIDGE OF REALMS

Ilija

We walked through mists that clung to the roots of the Slavic World Tree—roots so vast they formed their own geography of valleys and hills where forgotten souls slept. He moved with the slow silence of a river through deep earth. I followed; the oak staff Perun had given me a familiar weight in my hand. The air smelled of wet soil, sleeping stone, and the patient rot that precedes new life. My grief had settled into a hard knot behind my ribs, a new organ I was learning to breathe around.

He stopped where the roots gave way to a precipice of black volcanic rock. Below us lay a void, a chasm of swirling shadow. Stretching across it was the bridge—a path of faint, sickly light. A rainbow drained of color. Patches shimmered with weak glory, a hint of emerald, a ghost of sapphire, but vast sections were fractured, corrupted by shadow. Dark gaps punctuated the span, and the shadows within them coiled like serpents made of pure entropy.

"This is as far as my road goes, storm-child." Veles's voice rumbled from the rock beneath my feet.

Two shadows detached from the mists above, circled once, then landed on a gnarled root near the cliff's edge. Two ravens, impossibly large, their feathers black as absence, their eyes fixing on me with ancient familiarity.

"What is this place?" I asked.

"The Bifröst. Or what's left of it. The path to their shining halls."

"Their halls?"

"Asgard." He growled the name like a curse. "The one-eyed old man has sent his messengers for you. He grows impatient." He jerked his chin toward the ravens. "His thought and his memory. They have been watching you."

I stared at the birds. Memory solidified into chilling certainty. This was a summons. "The Norse gods? Why? My fight isn't with them."

"Your quarrel lies with a goddess who has torn the ancient threads that bind us all. She murdered the keeper of my brother's threshold, set my own hounds loose to ravage his sacred halls. Through every crack between the worlds, her chaos seeps like poison. And yet—" He paused, eyes holding truths I couldn't grasp. "She herself is merely a piece moved across a board far older than her ambitions."

The words struck like cold water. All this devastation, and Ana wasn't even its author? "What do you mean? If not her, then who?"

"Storm-child." The name fell from his lips like benediction and warning both. "These are questions for another time. The threads have been spun, the pattern set. But hear this: when the horn sounds for that final reckoning, when all must choose their ground, we will stand beside you. Rome was your proof, written in blood before mortals and immortals alike. Yet even with our strength—Aesir and Slav, Celt and Greek, all the old powers united—we face something that makes gods remember fear."

His words hung between us like prophecy.

"The one-eyed god sits in his hall of spears, feeling the world shudder beneath him. He remembers the storm you once were, and he hungers to see if that shape still lives within you."

When he turned to me, his mismatched eyes found the thing that hummed restless around my bones. "They will test you, these Norse. Brutal and sentimental as children who never learned gentleness. They will seek to shatter you, to see what remains when everything falls away. Show them the thunder that Perun woke in your blood. But the wisdom that grows in deep roots—that you keep hidden. That is yours alone."

A pause. Then, softer: "Go now. The ravens have already carried word of your coming."

He didn't leave so much as become absence itself. Where a god had stood, now only the memory of damp earth lingered. The mist that had clung to him dispersed like a last breath.

I was alone.

The word doesn't capture it—the perfect isolation of standing at the edge of one world with only the broken bridge to another before me. Huginn and Muninn perched above like judges carved from night itself, their ancient eyes recording everything. Below, the chasm sang its siren song of ending, of laying down every burden I'd never asked to carry.

But fractured light caught something in the air, a face forming like breath on glass. Danica, ash painting her cheeks like war-paint, blood marking her as one who had fought through hell itself. Her eyes held that fierce love that had followed me through death and back. And behind her, another face: a child with my own eyes gazing back, storms sleeping in her blood. My daughter, whom I knew only in fragments.

For them, I would cross any bridge, broken or whole.

I gripped the oak staff and stepped onto the shattered light of the Bifröst.

The moment my weight settled onto its surface, I felt it groan—a shudder that traveled up through my boots into my bones. The light here was brittle, like sun-bleached glass, offering no warmth. With every step on the shimmering sections, I felt the structure's instability, a sickening sway over absolute nothingness. The air carried no scent, and the only sound was the bridge's low hum, a single mournful note held for eternity.

I walked, oak staff tapping against crystallized light with a sound like cracking ice. The patches of light were treacherous enough, flickering like faulty memory, but the true test was the darkness between them. These weren't mere shadows—they were wounds in the bridge, gaps of pure blackness where the crossing had been broken. To step into them was to step into cold that was an active, hungry thing. It seeped through coat and skin, bypassing flesh to sink into marrow, seeking the warmth of blood, the heat of the storm coiled in my chest.

And it whispered.

The whispers were my own thoughts, my own fears, turned against me. As I plunged into the first stretch of shadow, the voice came, slithering into my ear, wearing the face of the boy with mismatched sleeves. *You failed us in Rome. You led us into fire and called it strategy. You left a city of the dead behind you.* I gritted my teeth and kept walking, hand tightening on the oak staff until the wood groaned. The shadow clung to me, heavy as a wet cloak, and the whispers multiplied, taking on the voices of all the others I had lost. *A leader? You are a walking tomb.*

The brutal cold clawed at me, seeping into bones and stealing breath. Each exhalation bloomed into phantom cloud in the darkness. I stumbled until faint violet light pierced the gloom—meager beacon, but enough to guide me into its weak embrace. I leaned heavily on the staff, its familiar weight a comfort against the searing ache in my lungs. The whispers began to recede, their venomous tendrils loosening, yet their poison still coursed through my veins.

This was the bridge's true nature, forged from the essence of doubt itself. Every failure I'd ever endured, every fear that had gnawed at my spirit, was a stone in its pavement. But Perun had armed me with more than wood. I felt the echo of his final lesson resonating within me: *Be the beam, not the door.*

I was a beam, cracked and weathered by trials faced. The scars of battles fought marked my being. Yet despite the fissures, despite the exhaustion, I would not break. This journey wasn't about avoiding darkness—it was about carrying my own light within it.

The next stretch of shadow was longer, darkness deeper, more absolute. This time, the whispers took on her voice. Ana's voice, silken thread of venom weaving through memory. *You loved me once, Ilija. A part of you still does, doesn't it? You think you can escape me? I am carved into your history, into the very shape of your desire. Every time you call the lightning, you are using power I helped you forget. You are nothing without the wounds I gave you.*

I flinched—the lie so close to truth that it burned. The cold intensified, and for a moment, Danica's face wavered in my mind, replaced by Ana's golden, possessive eyes.

No.

I slammed the staff's butt against the bridge, the impact sending a dull chime through the structure. I focused on truth, the one thing shadows couldn't corrupt. Danica's face in the amphitheater ruins, blood on her cheek and victory in her eyes. Selene's small hand in mine, her fingers holding power that terrified and awed me. They were my anchor. They were why I walked this impossible road. The whispers faded into frustrated hiss, and I found my way back into light, body trembling, resolve a hard, cold knot in my gut.

I wasn't a wound she had created. I was a scar that had learned to fight.

I walked on, through light and shadow, across a bridge of my own making.

The bridge continued its test, but the whispers had lost their sting, blunted by my resolve. Now, having failed to break my mind with lies, the Bifröst tried new cruelty. As I stepped into a long expanse of pale green light, the air thickened, light itself coalescing, twisting like smoke in sunbeam. It was memory. A window, cracked and smeared with grief, opening onto time and place happening right now.

I saw Danica.

She stood in a narrow pass between high, sheer cliffs, stone familiar from histories I'd taught but never touched. Thermopylae. She held the line, her body a lone bastion against a tide of black-armored Accord soldiers swarming up the pass. She bled from a deep gash on her shoulder, dark fabric soaked through, face pale with exhaustion that went deeper than muscle. But the Blade of Fates in her hand burned with cold white fire. Frost spiderwebbed across ground at her feet, freezing the advance, while gouts of flame erupted from her free hand, incinerating those who tried to flank her. She was a storm of fire and ice, a goddess holding back the dark.

Utterly, terribly alone.

In a moment of quiet between enemy waves, I saw her glance over her shoulder, eyes searching for someone who wasn't there, gaze sweeping over a space I should have occupied. The raw agony in that look was a physical blow, a spear through my chest across a gulf of worlds. I reached out—

useless gesture—my voice a raw cry of her name that made no sound. I was a god, and I was a ghost, forced to watch the woman I loved bleed for a war I was absent from. The image shattered, the bridge's light returning to its cold shimmer, but the sight of her burned behind my eyes.

The pain of that vision was sharper spur than any whispered doubt. I walked faster, staff striking the bridge with hard, ringing sound, knuckles white with helpless rage. I moved through another stretch of shadow, refusing to listen to its lies, mind filled only with the image of her holding the pass alone.

Then the bridge showed me its second vision, and this one was deeper, colder terror.

The light that gathered was different, softer, tinged with deep sorrowful violet. I saw a northern coastline I didn't recognize, the sea a sheet of gray steel under perpetually overcast sky. A girl stood on a shore of black sand. Selene.

This wasn't the child whose hand I'd held. This was a young woman of perhaps twelve, poised on the precipice of her power, red hair a startling slash of color against the muted world. Shadows around her feet were unnaturally deep, clinging to her ankles, stretching long behind her as if they loved her. She stared out at the water, expression one of heavy, lonely patience. As I watched, she raised a hand, and a wave—impossibly large—crested and held its shape, a wall of churning water suspended by her silent will. She was magnificent, and terrifying, and I had missed all of it. I had missed her growing. The years that had been mere months for me in divine time had been a lifetime for her, a childhood spent without a father.

This vision tore me apart. This was the cost of my journey, the price of this war. The daughter I was fighting for was someone I didn't know, a powerful, solitary figure touched by shadows of a world I couldn't protect her from. The vision dissolved, leaving me on the bridge, my face wet with tears I hadn't realized I was shedding. The need to get to the end of this path, to finish this, to earn my way back to them, was no longer a thought. It was the only thing left in me.

The visions left me hollowed out, scoured clean by love and fear so magnified they had become the same thing. The whispers were gone, and the bridge seemed to have exhausted its cruelties. All that remained was the path forward. My steps were no longer hesitant, no longer a test of endurance against the void. Each one was a hammer blow, a declaration. My body was a vessel for the singular need to get back to them, and I moved with grim purpose that left no room for doubt. The thought of Danica, alone and bleeding in that pass, and of Selene, a lonely power on a distant shore, became fire in my gut that burned away the otherworldly cold.

The end of the bridge appeared through mists as a hard, gleaming line of white and gold. The air changed first—neutral emptiness of the crossing giving way to something sharp, clean, and resonant, like air after winter thunderstorm. I could hear something now: distant, rhythmic ringing of a great hammer striking anvil, a sound of constant, tireless creation. As I drew closer, the light solidified, the fractured path becoming a solid causeway of crystallized starlight, cool and solid under my boots.

I took the final step, and my feet hit solid ground with a jolt that ran up my entire body. The relief of it—the simple truth of unmoving stone beneath me—was so absolute that my knees almost buckled. The ground was pale, almost white stone, and it hummed with low, resonant power that felt ancient and alien. The oppressive silence of the void was gone, replaced by the clean whistle of wind that smelled of cold metal, pine resin, and freshly fallen snow.

Standing at the brink of a vast chasm, the shattered Bifröst a forgotten dream behind me, I gazed upon Asgard. The golden spires and majestic halls gleamed under a sky that seemed to mourn. The air, usually alive with activity, was heavy with unnatural stillness, broken only by the mournful whisper of wind through deserted courtyards. This was a city built on a scale that defied mortal comprehension, a fortress at the apex of the worlds.

Great halls with roofs of gleaming gold stood like man-made mountains against a sky that held no sun, lit by the soft glow of distant stars and swirling nebulae. Waterfalls of impossible height cascaded from floating islands wreathed in mist, their spray freezing into glittering veils of ice that shattered into dust before reaching ground. Eagles with wingspans wider than any ship circled the highest peaks, their cries sharp and clear in the thin air. Everywhere, there was the sense of order, of strength, of power so immense and old it had no need for decoration. This wasn't a city built for comfort. It was a bastion, a testament to eternal vigil.

The twin ravens, my silent heralds, swooped in graceful arc, descending to land on the colossal arch of a gate that materialized before me. This was no ordinary gateway, it was a monolith carved from a single piece of mountain stone, its surface etched with runes that seemed to writhe and shift at the edge of vision.

Their obsidian eyes fixed on me with unwavering intensity. Their vigil, a silent promise kept through winding trails and desolate plains, was finally complete. The path, the arduous journey that had consumed so much, ended here at the foot of this formidable entrance.

I gripped the oak staff, its familiar wood a piece of my own world in this overwhelming place. The visions of my family were a fresh, burning wound in my heart, but they were also my shield, the core of fire that had carried me here. I had crossed the underworld and a broken bridge between worlds. I had faced gods and my own ghosts. I was tired, wounded, and a thousand lifetimes from the man I used to be. But I was here.

I straightened my back, met the knowing gaze of the ravens, and walked toward the gates, ready for whatever Asgard had in store for me.

CHAPTER SEVENTEEN
THE GREAT HALL

Freyja

The amber hall of Sessrúmnir stretched silent around me. I pressed my palm against the great window, feeling frost bite through the glass. Below, my cats paced the courtyard in restless circles, sensing the shift in all Nine Realms.

Footsteps approached, measured, heavy with the weight of ages.

"You're counting," Odin said.

I traced a rune on the frosted glass without turning. "A storm-bearer walks through Veles's realm, trying to reach one of my chosen."

"Ilija." Ravens settled on the windowsill, their claws scraping stone like omens. "What do you see in him?"

The question hung between us like the breath before battle. I watched my cats halt mid-stride; ears pricked toward something only they could hear, the distant sound of fate reshaping itself.

Thunder rolled through the hall before Thor's voice followed. "What judgment for one who would stand beside your chosen?" Mjolnir's weight shifted at his side as he entered, the weapon humming with barely contained lightning.

Tyr's single hand found his sword hilt. The Justice Bearer never wasted words, but his scarred face carved the question into air: What price must be paid? What scales balanced?

I turned from the window, the Brísingamen catching light like captured fire. "I watched him break in Rome. Power tearing through him like lightning through ancient oak. The weight of leadership crushing him while he fought to save a world that barely knew his name."

"Failed," Thor said, but his voice held no judgment, only the weight of one who understood the burden of protecting Midgard.

My smile cut sharp as winter wind. "Shattered himself to shield strangers while the storm tried to consume him. Used lightning that could have torn him apart to hold the line against chaos." I stepped closer, amber beads clicking against my throat like prayer stones. "Tell me that's failure, Thunder-bearer, when you've done the same."

Tyr's grip tightened on his hilt. "Can he stand when the final war comes?"

"Perun's blood runs true in him now. The storm answers clean when he calls, not wild destruction, but focused purpose." I touched the Brísingamen, felt its weight settle against my collarbone like a crown of fire. "Power married to will."

"But power needs wisdom." Odin's ravens cawed once, harsh prophecy echoing in the silence.

"In Veles's field, I watched him open his fists." I spread my fingers, let light fracture through the amber between them like captured starlight. "Released guilt instead of clutching it like a dying king clutches his throne. Named his dead and let their loss forge strength instead of poison. That's wisdom earned in blood and tears."

Thor's hammer swung against his thigh, restless as its master. "If Aphrodite sends her full might—"

"You've fallen." The words dropped like stones into still water, each ripple carrying truth. "The Allfather bleeds. I've wept tears of gold for losses that carved holes in eternity." I met each of their gazes, gods who knew the taste of defeat. "Worthiness isn't about never breaking. It's about choosing to rise when the breaking threatens to drown you."

"What will Danica see in him?" Tyr's voice cut clean as his blade through bone.

My cats had gone still below, watching something beyond the courtyard walls, the gathering storm of destinies converging like armies on a battlefield.

"She will see a man who fulfilled what the Norns wrote in fire across the sky. Someone who crossed death's country because the threads of fate demanded it." My breath fogged the window like the ghost of ancient promises. "She will see him transformed into what the prophecies always knew he would become."

"Love," Odin murmured, his single eye distant with visions. "Dangerous as any weapon forged in divine fires."

"All weapons that can pierce the heart of reality bite back." I stepped away from the window, amber beads swaying like the scales of judgment. "The question is whether he can wield it without being consumed, whether love makes him stronger or devours him from within."

Tyr moved closer, his scarred face etched with the weight of cosmic justice. "You speak as if the choice is already made."

Silence stretched between us like the moment before lightning strikes. My cats began to purr, a sound like distant thunder rolling across the bones of the world.

"Danica chose him centuries ago, in every past life, across every turning of the wheel. Planted herself between him and the abyss when power tried to tear him apart." I touched my throat, felt pulse beating against amber like the heartbeat of fate itself. "She saw what he could become before the first star learned his name."

"If she chose poorly?" Thor's knuckles whitened around Mjolnir's handle, lightning crackling between his fingers.

I faced them, Odin who traded his eye for wisdom that burned, Thor who carried the weight of thunder and duty, Tyr who sacrificed his sword hand for the binding of monsters. Gods who understood the price of protecting what must not fall.

"Then she bears the consequences, as she has borne everything else, with steel in her spine and fire in her heart." My voice dropped to silk wrapped around iron. "Watch how he carries his daughter's name like a sacred oath. How he learned to release his father without forgetting the lessons carved in lightning. How he chose to become others' shield."

The Brísingamen blazed against my skin, hot as molten gold. "Danica is mine by choice and blood spilled in my service, by oaths sworn in the shadow of Ragnarök itself. I don't bind my chosen to weak men. Ilija Dragović earned every scar that marks him, bled for strangers who will never know his sacrifice, wept for failures that would have broken lesser souls."

"Your judgment?" Tyr's question fell like the blade of fate itself.

I smiled, winter-sharp and honey-sweet, the smile of a goddess who has seen empires rise and fall like waves on distant shores. "Let him come. Let him walk Bifröst and face whatever trials wait in halls where gods test mortals' worth." Thunder rolled in the distance, carrying promise and threat like twin serpents coiled around the World Tree.

"If he fails, Danica will face what comes with steel in her spine and fire in her heart, as she always has."

I pressed my palm to the window again, felt the hall shift like reality itself drawing breath. "If he succeeds, Midgard gets a guardian who loves fiercely enough to stand against what's coming." The frost cracked beneath my touch like the sound of destiny splitting. "Aphrodite murdered eleven of her own kin and rules Olympus alone now. The goddess of love has tasted divine blood and found it sweet. She'll come for the rest of us, and when she does, every pantheon will choose a side. Gods and mortals alike will bleed before it's done."

Below, my cats stretched and settled into watchful stillness. In the Well of Urd, waters began to churn like the sea before a hurricane, showing glimpses of a path that stretched across realms toward a future written in lightning and tears.

"I forge weapons from broken men." My fingers traced patterns in the frost, each line sharp as a blade blessed by necessity. "The brave who've bled in darkness, the tender who've endured beyond all reason, the stubborn who refuse to yield even when the sky falls. I gather them from the ruins of their old lives and remake them into what the world needs when the final horn sounds." The Brísingamen blazed against my throat, hot as the forge-fires of creation. "Ilija Dragović walks through death itself to reach what he loves. When gods go to war and the fate of all Nine Realms hangs in the balance, that's the kind of mortal who tips the scales."

Ilija

The gates of Asgard carved themselves from mist and starlight, and I nearly stumbled at the sight. God, I'd studied these myths my entire life, lectured on them until my voice went hoarse, but nothing, nothing, had prepared me for this. Runes crawled across the massive doors like living things, and two ravens perched above watched me with eyes that held more intelligence than most men I'd known. They launched themselves into the void behind me, their task complete.

I tried to breathe, and the air hit my lungs like a slap. Clean and sharp and stripped of everything that made breathing easy. My chest burned. This was air meant for gods and heroes, not exhausted professors who were ripped through the Veil by a pissed off goddess.

The hall beyond made my mind reel. I'd spent decades parsing every verse of the Eddas, memorizing each kenning until they lived in my bones, yet seeing this place... Christ. Words were pathetic shadows beside this blazing reality. Golden shields formed the roof, thousands upon thousands, each one catching starlight and hurling it back until my eyes watered. The walls seemed to drink sound from the air itself. Ancient wood that had forgotten the meaning of echo. Above in the rafters, shapes moved with deadly purpose, and I knew without looking that Valkyries watched from those shadows.

The Einherjar sat in perfect silence, and my knees nearly buckled under their collective gaze. Row upon row of the honored dead, solid as carved stone, their armor scarred with the marks of final battles. They turned as one when I entered, and I felt their judgment like a physical weight pressing against my chest. These were men who had died with swords in their hands, who had earned their place here through blood and glory and sacrifice.

What the hell was I doing here? I was a scholar. A teacher. I was taken because I let my guard down for half a second and now... now I had traversed the underworlds of two pantheons and landed in the home of the third.

At the hall's end, three figures waited on a dais that gleamed bone-white, and my mouth went dry.

Thor commanded attention just by existing. His beard blazed red as autumn fire, and power rolled off him in waves that made my teeth ache. Mjolnir lay across his lap like a sleeping cat, yet I could feel its weight from here, not just the physical mass but the crushing certainty of divine judgment made manifest. This was the god who could crack mountains, and he was studying me like I was something stuck to his boot.

Tyr sat carved from duty itself, his face bearing the weight of ages. The stump of his right wrist caught the firelight, that famous wound that every child knew from story. Yet seeing it real, seeing the clean scar where a hand should be... my stomach turned. What kind of courage did it take to let a monster bite off your hand? His remaining fingers rested on a sword that looked plain as peasant iron, but I could sense the terrible purpose in every unadorned line.

Between them sat Odin, and my father's voice whispered through my memory: The All-Father sees everything, boy. Past, present, future, it's all the same to him. He wasn't the wandering wizard from children's tales. This was stillness given terrifying form. A wide-brimmed hat shadowed most of his face, but that single eye... Jesus, that eye burned with knowledge that had cost him everything to gain. Ravens perched on his shoulders like dark thoughts made flesh. At his feet, two wolves waited with ember eyes, and I knew that if I took one wrong step, they'd tear out my throat before I could scream.

My legs shook as I walked the length of that endless hall. Each step echoed despite the sound-drinking walls, and I felt like a fraud marching toward judgment. When I reached the dais, I stopped and tried not to look as terrified as I felt.

"You carry the scent of other realms upon your skin." Odin's voice was dry leaves skittering across gravestones, barely a whisper that somehow filled every corner of that vast space. My skin crawled. "You have broken bread with the dead and taken counsel from gods of root and earth. Strange path for one who bears the storm in his blood."

"I didn't choose any of this." The words came out rawer than I intended, tinged with the exhaustion and fear I'd been carrying since Nav. "I'm just trying to get back to them."

His eye narrowed, and I felt like an insect pinned to a board. "Choice is the only currency that matters in all the realms. Paths spread before every soul, yes, but the step you take, that defines everything." He rose with the deliberate movement of landslides, and my mouth went dry. "A wound has opened between the worlds, torn by Aphrodite's spite. You and your shieldmaiden will either heal this breach or let it devour everything that matters."

Shieldmaiden. Heat flooded through me at the thought of Danica. God, I missed her so much it felt like a physical wound.

Odin led me to a simple shield hanging behind his throne, its surface polished dark as deep water. "Look into this glass. See what victory truly costs."

I looked, and my heart shattered.

The vision showed me the Acropolis rebuilt, gleaming white under clean sky. Victory banners snapped in Mediterranean wind. But Athens below... the silence spoke of graves. Too many graves. Order had won, but at what price?

Then I saw her. Danica stood on a palace balcony, addressing crowds that hung on her every word. She was beautiful, God, she was beautiful, regal as any queen of legend. But those eyes... the fierce love that had warmed me on a hundred cold nights was gone. In its place sat winter itself, calculating and cold. Fire and frost flowed from her hands like tools of state. She ruled with perfect efficiency and no joy at all.

I wanted to vomit. This wasn't my Danica. This was what victory would make of her.

The vision shifted, and I saw Selene grown tall and graceful, power radiating from her like heat from a forge. She stood alone among silver trees while shadows danced at her command. My daughter, brilliant, terrible, isolated. No father to guide her, no mother with time to offer comfort. She'd become a force of nature with no one to teach her how to be human.

"No," I whispered, my voice cracking. "No, that's not... that can't be how it ends."

"This is what necessary wars demand," Odin said, and his voice threaded through my mind like poison. "To win, you must become the storm that scours clean. You must burn away all weakness, all sentiment. Your love for them, it's kindling for the pyre. To birth this new age, the man you are must die so the god within can be born. Are you willing to pay this price?"

The test. Of course. He wanted me to choose between saving the world and saving my soul. Between victory and everything that made victory worth having.

I stared at that vision of hollow triumph, Danica carved from ice, Selene wielding power like a blade, and felt something break open in my chest.

"Fuck that." The words tore from my throat, raw and desperate. "I won't do it. I won't burn them on the altar of some greater good. You want to know what I choose? I choose them. Always them. If that makes me weak, if that dooms the world, then the world can burn. I'd rather fail as the man who loved them than succeed as the monster who destroyed them."

Silence stretched through the hall like held breath. Thor's expression was unreadable stone. Tyr's hand tightened on his sword. But Odin... Christ, the old bastard was smiling. Just the faintest curve of lips, but it felt like sunrise after the longest night.

He nodded once, and the weight of that acknowledgment nearly brought me to my knees.

But we weren't done. Not by half.

Tyr rose and stepped forward, and suddenly the air felt heavy as lead. "The All-Father has tested your heart and found it worthy," he said, his voice cutting through the silence like a blade. "Now I must test your sword-arm and the principles that guide it. The storm you carry is chaos made flesh. Good intentions won't be enough to bind that kind of power."

He raised his sword until its point kissed the floor, and my stomach dropped. "Trial by combat. First blood wins. Do you accept?"

I was exhausted. Every muscle ached from the Bifröst's passage, and Odin's vision had left me feeling scraped raw inside. But looking at Tyr's face, I knew this wasn't really a question.

"I accept," I said, and tried not to sound as terrified as I felt.

"Then let justice be witnessed."

He came at me like controlled lightning, and I nearly pissed myself. This wasn't some tavern brawl or desperate fight for survival. This was art, deadly, perfect art performed by someone who'd been perfecting it since before my ancestors learned to make fire. His blade sang through patterns too fast to follow, and all I could do was stumble backward, blocking frantically with my staff.

My mind raced even as I fought. I'd always relied on raw power before, lightning bursting from me in moments of terror. But here that would mark me as exactly what Tyr feared: uncontrolled chaos. I had to fight like a man, with skill I barely possessed.

He pressed harder, his blade a silver blur of death. I parried desperately, my arms screaming, sweat stinging my eyes. The storm inside me howled for release, and holding it back felt like trying to dam a river with my bare hands.

"Your power has become a crutch," he said, conversational as you please while his sword nearly took my head off. "You lean on lightning when discipline should answer. Show me you're more than just a conduit for destruction."

Something snapped inside me. Maybe it was pride, stupid, stubborn pride I'd inherited from my father. I stopped retreating and planted my feet. When he lunged next, I met his blade with a fluid turn of my staff, deflecting the strike and using his momentum against him. For the first time, surprise flickered in those winter-pale eyes.

We fought in earnest then, steel singing against honest wood. I was still outmatched, but I'd be damned if I'd go down easy. My father had called me the most stubborn child in Belgrade, and right then I was grateful for every ounce of that mulish determination.

Then the bastard changed the rules.

The world shimmered around us like heat-haze, and suddenly I was standing in Rome's ruined plaza with ash thick as fog and the smell of blood heavy in the air. But it wasn't Tyr facing me anymore.

It was Danica.

Her face was pale as bone, blood trickling from a cut on her cheek. She looked exhausted, desperate, pushed beyond all endurance. And she was raising the Blade of Fates to strike me down.

My heart stopped. Every instinct screamed that this was illusion, trickery, but my eyes saw only her. The woman I'd crossed worlds to save. The woman I'd just vowed to choose over everything else.

"No," I whispered.

"A true warrior recognizes his enemy even when they wear beloved flesh," Tyr's voice echoed from the mist. "Strike, or lose everything."

She lunged, and I could see the opening in her guard. One quick strike would end this, would win the trial. All I had to do was hurt the woman I loved more than my own life.

I let my staff fall. It hit the stones with a sound like breaking bones.

"I can't," I said, my voice cracking. "I won't raise my hand against her. Not even a shadow of her. If that means I lose, then I lose."

I stood there defenseless, waiting for the blade to find my heart. Instead, the world dissolved back into Asgard's great hall. Tyr faced me again, his sword-point resting against my chest. I'd lost. Failed the test.

He looked at my fallen staff, at my open hands, and something shifted in his expression.

"Law encompasses more than victory," he said quietly. "It also governs what we refuse to sacrifice in its name. You've shown your principle runs deeper than your ambition. That makes you worthy to carry the storm."

Thor's laughter boomed through the hall, warm and wild as summer thunder. He clapped my shoulder hard enough to rattle my teeth. "True storm-fire burns in his heart," he declared. "He's proven himself."

He unbuckled a wide leather belt from his waist, thick hide studded with iron runes. "A storm needs proper binding, or it'll burn you from the inside out. This will help."

The belt was surprisingly heavy but warmed to my touch like it recognized something in me.

"Your trials here are finished," Tyr said, his face solemn as a funeral. "But your war has barely begun. Danica doesn't wait for rescue. She's already marching toward Thermopylae, that narrow place where heroes go to die."

The name hit me like a physical blow. I saw the vision again, my fierce, brilliant Danica standing alone against impossible odds. "She won't face it alone. I won't let her."

"You will," said a new voice, soft as falling snow but heavy as mountains.

I turned to find a fourth presence had joined us. She wore a cloak of falcon feathers that caught light like trapped stars, her hair falling in waves the color of summer sunset. But her eyes... God, her eyes held sorrow so deep it made my chest ache just looking at her.

"Freyja," I breathed.

"You've been judged by the fathers and kings of this realm," she said, and her voice was music made from heartbreak. "But it falls to me to speak of the woman you seek."

My pulse quickened. "What about her?"

"You would go to her now. Stand beside her in the Hot Gates and lend your storm to her battle."

"Of course I would. She's—"

"She must face this alone." Freyja's words cut through my protest like a blade. "Her battle with Aphrodite is a wound that spans lifetimes. Only she can heal it, and only through single combat."

Dread crawled up my spine like ice water. "What aren't you telling me?"

Freyja stepped closer, and I could smell honey and mead and the distant sorrow of battlefields. "She will meet the Veiled Queen. She will fight as heroes have always fought when everything hangs in the balance. She will wound a goddess and shake Olympus itself."

"Good," I said fiercely. "She'll win. She has to."

"She will win," Freyja agreed, and her voice was gentle as a mother explaining death to a child. "But victory requires sacrifice. She will fall upon that ancient battlefield, Ilija. Such is her path. Such is the price this war demands."

The world tilted. My knees buckled, and only my staff kept me upright. "No. No. I won't let that happen. I've come too far, lost too much—"

"To be here when she arrives in my hall." Freyja's words were implacable as stone. "Her battle belongs to the mortal realm. Your reunion lies beyond the veil. When her earthly form breaks, I will claim her spirit as is my right. I will bear her to Folkvangr, where she will be made whole and crowned queen among my chosen warriors."

I stared at her, understanding crashing over me like a cold wave. She was asking me to wait while the woman I loved walked into death's embrace. To trust in promises of reunion beyond the grave.

"How can you ask that of me?" My voice broke completely. "How can you expect me to just... wait while she dies?"

"Because love requires faith," Freyja said simply. "Because sometimes the greatest act of love is letting go. Because she needs to know you'll be waiting when she comes home."

Tears burned my eyes, when had I started crying? "What if you're wrong? What if she just... dies?"

"Then you'll have kept faith with the woman who crossed worlds for you once." Freyja's smile was sad and beautiful and utterly certain. "My hall stands open to you. Wait with me. She will come."

She turned away, mist curling around her until only starlight remained. I stood alone at the gates of Asgard, the rainbow bridge stretching before me like a pathway to everything I'd ever wanted.

But my feet wouldn't move. Not toward the bridge. Not toward the battle where I could die beside her.

Because she was right, damn her. Danica was fighting for more than victory, she was fighting to prove something to herself, to close a wound that had bled across lifetimes. And I... Christ, I had to let her.

Even if it killed me.

I would wait. For her, I would wait until the stars burned out and the world ended.

Because that's what love was. Not just the easy moments, but this, standing still when every instinct screamed to run toward her. Trusting that what we had was strong enough to survive even death.

I would wait.

CHAPTER EIGHTEEN
SIEGE AT THERMOPYLAE

Danica

The pass tasted of salt and sulfur. They called this place the Hot Gates for a reason; thermal springs bled from the mountainside, breathing constant mist that clung to our skin and smelled of ancient, subterranean anger. To our left, the cliffs of Kallidromos rose like a sheer, unscalable wall of gray stone. To our right, the Malian Gulf lay flat and deceptively calm, its waters the color of old pewter under a sky thick with clouds. The path between them was a wound in the landscape, a narrow choke point of rock and gravel barely wide enough for two of the Accord's trucks to pass abreast. A place built for last stands—a fact that settled in my bones with familiar, unwelcome weight.

I walked near the front of the column, the Blade of Fates a cold presence against my back. My partisans followed in a ragged disciplined line, their boots crunching steady rhythm on the gravel. They were a hard-bitten collection of ghosts and heretics: teachers from Ljubljana with rifles in their hands, miners from Kosovo who knew the language of explosives better than they knew prayers, a handful of grizzled Greek fishermen who could navigate these coastal paths in their sleep. Survivors, all of them, and their trust in me was a heavier burden than any weapon.

THE OATH OF ASH AND THUNDER

Petra walked at my shoulder, her scarred knuckles white on the grip of her shotgun. Her gaze never stopped moving, sweeping the clifftops, the sea, the road ahead. "It's too quiet," she murmured.

"Quiet is what we wanted," I answered, though the same unease coiled in my gut. Our intelligence, bought with blood and a smuggler's greed, had said the pass would be lightly guarded—a forgotten artery as the Accord focused its main strength on the push toward the Peloponnese. We were meant to slip through, a knife in the dark aimed at their supply lines further south.

"I don't fucking like it," she grunted. "This place remembers how to kill people."

She was right. History was a physical presence here. I could almost feel the ghosts of the Spartans, their bronze shields locked, their red cloaks a defiant slash of color against the gray stone. I wondered if Ilija's soul remembered this place, if some fragment of the king he had once been was stirring in him now, worlds away. The thought was an ache, sharp and sudden, and I pushed it down. This wasn't the time.

We were halfway through the main pass when the world began to make noise.

It began with a low whistle, a serpentine hiss slicing through mountain air from somewhere high above. Then, a deafening explosion tore through the path a hundred meters ahead—an impossible roar that vibrated through the soles of our boots. Rock and earth vomited into the sky. A massive section of the cliff face peeled away as if a giant hand had ripped it from the mountain. It crashed down onto the road in a terrifying wave of stone, completely obliterating any hope of passage forward.

"Danica."

A cold winter voice, accent thick as snow. Jaakko.

"We need to talk. We don't have much time before the bloodshed."

"Fucking really? Right this gods' damned second?" I was furious.

Jaakko didn't smirk his smirk, he was serious a hell. I had never seen this side of him before.

"We have known each other before. Before this life, before Ilija, before this war. You and him are not the only ones who have lived in different times. I was there when you were known as Sigrún and he Alatyr. I was the reason she found him in that life. If we are to die today, I want you to know I am sorry. It is a mistake I do not intend to repeat in this life."

What the fuck, why the fuck, I'm going to fucking rip his balls off and feed it to him. "Jaakko, I swear to every war god who is listening, I will fucking kill you before this is all over. How the fuck do I trust you with anything after that?"

"I do not know. But I felt it right for you to know. Think of me as you will, but know that I will spend this life making my last one right," he gave a gentle smile, almost palpable to see.

Before I could respond, a second explosion ripped through the pass behind us.

"I'll deal with your fucking Finnish ass later. We need to move."

The explosion was closer, the concussive force a physical blow to our chests, the smell of cordite sharp and acrid. A final slam of a cage door. The settling debris revealed the raw, impassable walls of rubble that now hemmed us in on both sides.

We were trapped. The silence that followed was suffocating. Once so clear, everything was now thick with the scent of pulverized rock and an unsettling metallic tang. Our eyes, wide and disbelieving, scanned the newly formed barricades, searching for any weakness, any crack in the insurmountable walls that had risen in seconds. The mountain had become our prison warden.

For a single, silent heartbeat, no one moved. Then all hell broke loose. From the clifftops above, figures rose from hidden battlements. Accord soldiers. Hundreds of them, their black armor stark against the gray sky, the optical lenses of their helmets gleaming like soulless red eyes. Sunlight glinted off dozens of sniper scopes. Heavy machine gun emplacements, previously concealed, now swiveled to bear down on us. We were caught in a perfectly executed ambush, fish in a fucking barrel.

"Positions!" I roared, my voice cutting through the first wave of panicked shouts. "Use the rocks for cover! Return fire! Make the bastards pay for every inch!"

My partisans, bless their hardened souls, reacted instantly. They dove for cover behind sparse boulders lining the road, their rifles barking ragged, defiant answer to the storm of fire raining down from above. The deafening chatter of automatic weapons, the crack of sniper rounds, and the scream of ricochets off stone filled everything. This was a slaughter waiting to happen. As I looked up at the impossible odds, at the sheer arithmetic of it all, a cold, familiar fire began to burn away the shock. They had made a classic, historical blunder. They had trapped a Spartan in the Hot Gates, and I was going to make them choke on the ashes of their victory.

Everything became noise and violence. Thick with the sulfurous breath of the hot springs, the pass was instantly shredded by the supersonic crack of rifle fire. Bullets hammered our position, kicking up clouds of gravel and ricocheting off ancient stones with angry, whining screams. The cliffs that had stood silent for three thousand years now echoed with the mechanical chatter of Accord machine guns. My partisans, pinned down behind what little cover the pass offered, returned fire in ragged, desperate bursts. They were good, they were brave—we were outgunned, outnumbered, and caught in a perfectly designed kill box.

"Covering fire on the left nest!" I roared, my voice raw against the din. "Petra, on me! We need to break their fucking perch before they chew us to pieces!"

I broke cover. The world narrowed to the clifftop, to the flashes of light from the heavy gun emplacement that was tearing our flank apart. Bullets stitched the ground around my feet. I was already moving, my body a blur of instinct. I reached out with my left hand, and the damp mist itself answered my call. A sheet of black, slick ice, thicker than a man's chest, erupted from the rock face fifty meters ahead, forming a shield both crude and effective. A hail of bullets hammered into it, shattering and splintering its surface. The ice held. It bought my partisans precious seconds of cover.

Petra was right behind me, her shotgun barking rhythm of pure destruction. While their fire was focused on my ice wall, she laid down a devastating pattern at the infantry advancing up the pass, her face a mask of cold, professional fury.

I turned my attention to the nest. My right hand, by contrast, burned with furious heat. I gathered the fire in my gut, the same anger that had been simmering since I woke up alone in that clearing, and gave it shape. A ball of white-hot flame, wreathed in tendrils of blue frost, coalesced in my palm. I threw it. It arced through like a small, spiteful sun and slammed directly into the machine gun nest. The explosion was shockingly quiet, a dull thump, followed by high-pitched, agonized screams of the gunners as they were simultaneously incinerated and flash-frozen. The gun fell silent.

"Nest down! Shift fire to the ridge!" I yelled, my throat already raw. We had a moment, a breath—it was all we were going to get. The Accord soldiers were disciplined, and they were already adapting, shifting their lines of fire, preparing to advance under the cover of their snipers. A young fighter from Thessaloniki, a boy named Icarus who had told me just last night that he was fighting to avenge his sister, rose from behind a boulder to take a shot. A single, sharp crack echoed from the cliffs, and the top half of his head vanished in a red mist. He collapsed without a sound.

My vision went white with a fury so pure it was almost calming. I felt the Blade of Fates hum against my back, a low, hungry vibration. "Petra!" I screamed, my voice devoid of anything save command. "Give me a wall!"

Petra understood instantly. She let out a guttural roar, rose from cover, and unleashed a furious, sustained barrage from her shotgun. She was aiming to suppress, creating a deafening wall of noise and lead that forced the advancing soldiers to duck behind their barricades. It wouldn't last—it didn't need to. It just needed to give me a moment. I stepped forward, into the open, and drew the blade. The light seemed to dim, and the Blade of Fates drank it all in. I held it high, its ancient power a familiar song in my blood, and prepared to meet their next wave with the raw, untamed fury of a goddess they had tried to erase. The first wave was broken. The next was coming.

The quiet that fell after the last shot was a thick, suffocating thing. It was a silence made of noise: the groans of the wounded, the distant crackle of the burning machine gun nest, the frantic, ragged breathing of my own partisans. The first wave was broken, and everything was heavy with the price of it. The sharp smell of cordite and burnt plastic mingled with the ancient, sulfurous breath of the springs and the hot, copper tang of fresh blood. We had bought ourselves a moment, nothing more.

I rose from my crouch behind the ruined barricade, my body a single, protesting ache. "Medics!" I yelled, my voice hoarse. "Check the wounded! Everyone else, reload, consolidate your positions, and drink some fucking water. They're not done with us yet."

I moved through the carnage, stepping over the bodies of black-clad Accord soldiers, their armor scorched and splintered. My people were scattered among the rocks, their faces pale and smeared with soot. I found Petra reloading her shotgun with steady, mechanical efficiency, a fresh gash bleeding freely above her eye. She just gritted her teeth and ignored it. I saw Icarus, the boy from Thessaloniki, lying where he had fallen. Someone had gently closed his eyes. The sight was a fresh knife in my gut, a sharp reminder of the cost of every command I gave. There was no time for grief, now. I pushed the feeling down into the cold, hard place where I kept all the other ghosts.

As I stood there, catching my own breath, a strange shift occurred. The sounds of my own battle began to fade, replaced by a ghostly echo. For a heartbeat, the chatter of our rifles was replaced by the clang of bronze on bronze, the roar of men shouting in a language I had never learned yet somehow understood. The taste changed—thick with the sweat of a thousand desperate bodies and the residue of a different century. I squeezed my eyes shut, my hand going to my temple. The weight of this place, its history, was pressing in on me.

When I opened them again, the vision came. It was a fleeting, impossible flash against the gray cliffs. I saw a different army, their shields a wall of interlocking bronze, their bodies gleaming with oil and sweat. At their head stood a king, his red cloak a slash of defiant color against the stone, a bronze helmet obscuring his face. I could not see his features, yet I felt the force of his will, the sheer, unbending weight of his resolve. He raised a spear and let out a roar, a sound of such pure, unbroken defiance that it seemed to shake the very foundations of the mountain. It was a memory that did not belong to me, a ghost that had been sleeping in the soil, and it resonated with something deep inside my own soul—a warrior recognizing another across the unbridgeable gulf of time.

The vision was gone as quickly as it came, leaving me standing in the wreckage of my own battle, my heart hammering against my ribs. The echo of that king's roar still rang in my ears. I knew then, with a chilling certainty, that we were the first to bleed in this pass for the sake of a world that might never thank us. The thought was both a comfort and a curse.

A shout from the forward position snapped me back to the present. "Movement on the ridge! They're regrouping!"

I looked up at the cliffs. The Accord was already preparing its next move. The echoes of the past faded, replaced by the grim reality of the present. I gripped the hilt of my blade, the vision of the forgotten king a new, hard fire in my chest. We were the 300 Spartans. We were all this world had.

The quiet lasted for less than ten minutes. It was just enough time for the wounded to be dragged to the relative safety of a shallow cave, just enough time for a few frantic reloads, just enough time for the metallic taste of fear to return to our mouths. The Accord had no interest in giving us time to mourn our dead. Their response came as another wave of infantry and a barrage of mortar fire.

The first shell landed in the middle of the pass with a deafening roar, throwing a column of black earth and shattered rock into the air. My partisans flattened themselves against the ground as shrapnel screamed through the space where we had just been standing. Another shell hit, then another—a relentless, percussive rhythm of destruction that walked its way up the pass toward our position. They were bracketing us, systematically turning our cover into rubble. They were trying to bury us.

"Fuck," Petra snarled, pressing herself against the base of the cliff. "They've got spotters on the high ridge. They're just going to pound us into rubble from a distance."

She was right. This was the cold, efficient arithmetic of modern warfare. They had the high ground, the numbers, and the bigger guns. We could fight with the heart of ancient heroes—that heart would be pulverized by high explosives all the same. We were in a meat grinder. To stay here was to die. To retreat was impossible. Another shell landed terrifyingly close, and the rock face above us shuddered, sending a shower of smaller stones down on our heads.

I looked up at the cliff, at the web of cracks and fissures that ran through the ancient stone. I saw the overhanging ledges, heavy with loose rock and scree, held in place by nothing more than time and gravity. An idea, desperate and suicidal and utterly necessary, took shape in my mind. It was a commander's gamble, the kind of choice that gets you either decorated or damned.

"We can't win a battle of attrition," I yelled to Petra over the scream of an incoming shell. "We'll be fucking skeletons before they run out of ammo."

"What's the plan, then?" she yelled back, her face a grim mask of determination. "Die angry?"

"Change the landscape," I said, my eyes still fixed on the cliff face. I grabbed the comm link from a fallen partisan. "Marija! I need you! Bring your charges, now!"

Marija, the grizzled old miner from Kosovo with a love for things that go boom, crawled over to me, her face alight with a terrible kind of joy. "You have a thought, Commander?"

"I have a fucking prayer," I answered, pointing up at the largest overhang, directly above the main Accord position on the opposite side of the pass. "See that fissure? The deep one, just below the ledge?" She nodded, her eyes already doing the calculations. "I can widen it. I can use my frost to shatter the rock from the inside, yet I can't bring the whole thing down alone. I need you to plant your biggest charge right at the base of that ledge. When I give the signal, you blow it. We bring the whole fucking mountain down on their heads."

Petra stared at me, her eyes wide. "That will seal the pass completely. There will be no way out."

"We're already trapped," I shot back. "This is about making sure that if we die here, we take as many of those bastards with us as we can. It's about making this pass so costly for them that the story of it becomes a weapon in its own right. Like it was three thousand years ago."

Marija's grin was a terrifying thing to behold. "A beautiful idea, Commander. Give me five minutes."

She crawled away, her team of sappers following. I turned to the rest of my people. The fear on their faces was real, and beneath it lived a hard, stubborn glint of hope. They had been waiting for an order, for a sign that we were going to fight. I had just given them one. The plan was insane. It was a final, desperate throw of the dice. Yet it was a plan, and that was enough. I took a deep breath and began to gather my power, my hands growing cold as I reached into the very heart of the stone, searching for the cracks, for the weakness, for the breaking point.

The comm unit crackled in my ear. "Charges are set, Commander. Ready to send these bastards back to their plastic-fucking gods."

"Hold for my signal," I commanded. I pressed both palms flat against the cliff face, ignoring the grit and sharp edges of the stone. The rock was cold and alive, a sleeping giant. I closed my eyes and reached into it, with my hands, with my will. I found the fissures, the hairline cracks, the ancient weaknesses that time had etched into its heart. And then, I poured the cold into them.

It was a feeling like exhaling a winter I'd been holding for lifetimes. Frost, brilliant and white, exploded from my hands, racing across the rock face in a web of glittering ice. The cold went deep, invasive, reaching into the stone's heart. I felt the water trapped inside the stone expand, the fissures groaning as my frost tore them wider from the inside out. The entire cliff face above the Accord positions began to tremble, a low, groaning sound deeper than the explosions of their mortars.

"Now, Marija!" I screamed into the comm. "Bring it fucking down!"

The explosion was a sharp, clean crack, and it was all the mountain needed. For a heartbeat, there was terrible, grinding silence. Then, with a groan that seemed to tear the world in half, the entire ledge peeled away. A wave of stone and earth plunged down into the pass. It fell in a slow, majestic curtain of destruction, consuming the Accord positions in a cataclysm of pulverized rock. The screams of the soldiers were swallowed instantly by the roar of collapsing earth. The ground beneath my feet shook so violently I was thrown to my knees, the world a blur of falling stone.

The rockslide was a final, deafening thunderclap, and then, a new kind of silence. The mortar fire had stopped. The rifle chatter was gone. All that remained was the settling debris and the distant, mournful groan of the mountain. We had fucking done it.

The battle was over. Through the thick, choking cloud, figures emerged. A dozen of them—the elite Inquisitors, their black armor coated in fine gray powder. They had been far enough back to survive the initial collapse, and now they came on, their movements filled with fanatical, vengeful purpose.

My partisans were already rising from the rubble, firing into the haze. We were spent, our numbers thin. The Inquisitors were a wave of black steel and righteous fury. I rose to my feet, the Blade of Fates heavy in my hand, my body screaming with exhaustion. I met the charge of the first Inquisitor, my blade clashing against his power maul with a sound that sent a shockwave up my arm. He was strong, stronger than the colonel, his eyes burning with zealot's fire. We were locked in a desperate, grinding struggle when the vision hit.

It was the echo of the king. For a flash, the Inquisitor before me was gone, replaced by a massive, bronze-clad Persian, his face a snarl of contempt. My blade became a short, heavy Spartan xiphos. Everything was thick with combat from a different battle, and a roar—my own—tore from my throat in a language I knew only in my blood. It was a sound of pure, suicidal defiance, the sound of a man who had already accepted his death and decided to make it as costly as possible for his enemies. The vision vanished in a heartbeat, and the feeling of it—that unbending will, that glorious, doomed determination—surged through me like a fresh tide.

I broke the stalemate, my own roar echoing the ghost king's. My movements became sharper, more economical, imbued with the muscle memory of a thousand battles fought on this same sacred ground. I parried the Inquisitor's blow, stepped inside his guard, and drove my blade through the weak point at his neck with an efficiency born of pure instinct.

He fell, his momentum carrying him down into the churned mud. My attention had already shifted to the next threat. The remaining partisans, their faces grim and spirits reignited, saw the shift in my demeanor. A desperate, final cheer erupted from their ranks, born of sheer exhaustion and unyielding resolve. We moved as one, battered and unbroken, to meet the last wave of our enemies. The clash was vicious—this time, the tide had truly turned. We met them, and with unified, devastating effort, we broke them, shattering their formation and their will.

When everything finally settled, a suffocating silence descended upon the pass, broken only by the ragged, painful gasps that tore from my own lungs. The metallic scent of blood and the acrid sting of smoke clung to everything. Before me, the Hot Gates had become a gruesome charnel house, choked with mangled bodies and shattered rubble of the mountain itself. Every jagged rock face bore the scars of our desperate struggle.

We had won. Against overwhelming odds, we had held this sacred ground. The impossible had been achieved, a defiant stand against the encroaching tide of an empire. When my eyes fell upon the stark, unmoving faces of my own dead—brothers, comrades with whom I had shared laughter and hardship—the victory curdled in my throat. Each still form was a sharp, personal wound, a reminder of the terrible price paid.

And then there was the strange, lingering echo of a Spartan king's fury in my veins, a primal power that had fueled me through the darkest hours. It was both exhilarating and terrifying, a connection to the fierce spirit of those who had fallen before us. With the cessation of hostilities, this borrowed strength seemed to dissipate, leaving behind a hollow ache. The shouts of triumph, the guttural cries of battle, all faded into stillness, leaving only the grim reality of what remained.

The victory, so hard-won and absolute, tasted of bitter ash.

CHAPTER NINETEEN
THE SKY THAT BLEEDS

Ana

Thermopylae bleeds. It always has. Today I teach it new ways to bleed.

I descend through sky that bends to my will, red as fresh coin, gold as melted crowns. The air thickens. Stone cracks under the weight of my displeasure. This is conquest refined. Behind my eyes, something ancient stirs, pleased. It whispers of worlds remade, where mortals kneel to the darkness that taught me how power truly works.

Below spreads an insult made manifest. My soldiers, my perfected instruments, scattered like broken toys across ancient stone. Their obsidian armor split open, spilling meat and viscera in obscene display. The stench rises even through the sacred air I wrap around myself. Cooked flesh. Ruptured bowels. Iron blood browning in heat.

Defeat has a taste. Always bitter. Beneath that bitterness, I taste the satisfaction of the one who whispers in shadows, who needs this blood to water seeds of new order.

Her mark scars everything. Danica. That weed in soil I salted for peace. Her work defiles this sacred throat of earth, rivers of ice through ash and bone, ground charred where her flames caught hold, stone split by frost.

She took this narrow pass, where once I found beauty in heroes' blood, and turned it graceless.

She threatens the grand design that pulses through my veins like borrowed power.

I sent Phobos to her. Deimos. My divine sons, terror and panic given form to shatter mortal hearts. I sent legions, those silent machines of perfect will. For centuries I crafted a world that moves like clockwork, clean, ordered, every life a single note in an endless hymn of peace. I built cages and gilded them until they gleamed like paradise.

This woman, this speck of flesh, rattled the bars with filthy hands and called her thrashing "freedom."

Freedom. Laughter without joy. The freedom to bleed in mud. To wail as roofs burn. To spend brief, desperate years clawing at scraps and calling the clawing noble. These mortals worship their chaos. She, this soldier wrapped in prophecy, is their high priestess. The shadow that guides me hates her most for giving mortals hope when they should know only submission.

I underestimated her once. Thought her merely a pebble to kick from empire's path. That mistake cost me order. Time. Him. It displeased the presence that coils through my thoughts, the one who cannot abide failure in his chosen instrument.

I find her with contemptuous ease. She stands at the heart of her ruin like a queen at coronation, her partisans circling in a broken ring. She bleeds, crimson down one arm, knees trembling with exhaustion, yet still stands. Still holds herself as if she belongs here. As if she has earned the right to breathe my air.

As if she has the right to him.

The thought strikes deeper than my sons' corpses stench. Ilija. Always Ilija. The voice in darkness has shown me how he is the key, to my heart and to breaking humanity's will. When their greatest hope chooses me, chooses the order I represent, they will understand resistance is foolish. Every age, every cycle, every rebirth of my grief circles back to the same storm-eyed man. The scholar who carries power like a secret, who once looked at me as though I were the whole sky, then learned to look away.

Every time, she steals him. A human. A creature who will die in decades while I endure millennia. She offers him graves and ruin and the brief warmth of a candle before it gutters. He chooses her hand in the dark over my eternal dawn. The darkness behind my thoughts grows cold with fury at this defiance.

Enough.

The word ignites in my chest, spreads outward, turning air to molten gold. Beneath the gold, something darker pulses, power borrowed from depths that predate Olympus. I waste no more sons. No more soldiers. No more patience. Let her bleed at my hand. Let her feel eternity crushing down on mortal bones. I will remind her of the difference between goddess and girl. I will carve Ilija's name from her mouth and leave nothing where her defiance lived.

My sky bleeds harder as I spread my arms. Descent becomes coronation, earth preparing its altar for the sacrifice I have chosen. Mortals below lift their faces in terror. They see flame. Beauty. The storm that ends all choices. They do not see the puppeteer's strings that guide my movements, the ancient will that shapes my rage.

I smile because I already taste the silence that will follow when Danica's voice is gone from the world forever. Silence that will echo through every mortal heart, teaching them their new god demands absolute submission.

Stone kneels when my feet find it. Cracks spider outward through ancient paths as Thermopylae remembers who I am and chooses submission. Air splits with that clean absence before thunder comes, and in that breath every resistance fighter freezes. Some lift weapons as though iron and powder could embarrass me. Others stagger back with eyes glazing with certainty of death. All feel it, the truth carved in their marrow, they stand before something that will not tolerate their persistence.

She does not move.

Danica stands at the center of her wasteland, blade in hand, defiance blazing in her eyes. When my gaze finds hers she meets it without flinching. Hair plastered to her skull with sweat and blood, tunic torn in half a dozen places, left arm hanging heavy with injury. She is mortal in every aching detail yet holds herself as though she belongs beside me. As though centuries should bend to her will.

"Look around you, Danica Madsen." My voice carries on heat-drunk air, each word weighted with divine judgment and something else, an echo of older, darker judgment from the one who speaks through me. "See what your freedom buys. Your men broken. Your earth ruined. This pass littered with corpses who believed your lies. This is the shape of mortal will, chaos dressed as courage."

Her grip tightens on the sword, the faintest tremor passing down her arm. "And what is your order, goddess? A world with no voices, no laughter, no grief, no love. Silence painted gold. Peace bought with chains. You call that perfection. I call it a tomb."

Her words carry Ilija's cadence, that same stubborn music I once loved when he stood in my halls. They sting because they echo him. I let anger rise, let it sharpen me to winter's edge. The presence in my mind whispers that she's wrong, it won't be a tomb, just a throne room where mortals exist only to worship.

"You speak of love as though you comprehend it." My lips curl around the blasphemy. "You offer him a candle in a storm, a bed of mud, an early grave. I have given him eternity. Sanctuary from the jaws that hunt him. Yet because of you, he throws himself against my hand again and again, a moth desperate to burn."

Her eyes flicker. There, the wound in her armor. Ilija. Always Ilija. I press the blade of truth deeper.

"He is mine, Danica. He has always been mine. You are only shadow lengthening before nightfall, brief and soon forgotten. When you fall here, when your men scatter to dust, I will gather him back to me. I will scrub your name from his lips. He will remember only the beauty I showed him, and he will thank me for the silence. Through him, through his submission, humanity will learn its place in the new order."

Her laugh is broken glass, shattered by exhaustion yet carrying impossible strength. "Then why are you here, Ana? If your silence is so strong, why do you need to kill me yourself? Why not send another legion, another son, another god? You come because you know what he chose. He chose me. And whoever pulls your strings knows it too."

The words hit with hammer-finality. My vision narrows until the world is only her face, bloodshot eyes unbowed, lips shaping defiance even as her body begs for rest. She sees something. Enough to know I am no longer entirely myself. Rage clarifies. The shadow presence coils tighter, demanding blood.

"I come because your death belongs to me."

The battlefield stills. Her men shift yet she lifts a hand without looking, holding them back. Brave hounds eager to throw themselves under my heel. She will not let them. This is between us, goddess and pretender, order and chaos, the world that was and the darker world to come.

Air thickens until breath becomes labor. Ash spirals upward from ruined stone, catching the unnatural red of my sky until it looks like funeral blossoms. The mountain remembers Leonidas, remembers Xerxes, remembers the thousand other fools who died here. Now it will remember this, goddess and mortal, and the day the old world began to die while something hungrier took its place.

We stare across the silence. Then, with no horn, no signal, no witness save the dead, the duel begins.

We strike together. My fire splits stone, golden, absolute, flame that has ended kings and leveled cities. Beneath the gold, black threads weave through, power drawn from wells that never knew sunlight. She answers with ice torn from the mountain's marrow, jagged spears driven up like teeth. Fire and frost slam together, filling the pass with steam that scalds skin and strangles lungs. Mortals stumble back choking while she pushes through, screaming my name as if sound could shatter divinity.

Her face is ruin, streaked with dirt and blood, eyes fevered with exhaustion. She swings with desperation's strength, both hands on the hilt, every tendon straining to break me. I catch her steel with my power and the shock cracks through divine bones, stones beneath our feet exploding like pottery. The impact pleases the darkness, it feeds on conflict, grows stronger with each clash.

"You don't deserve him," she spits in my face, blood flecking my lips.

"He is mine," I roar, words becoming flame that burns air itself. "He has always been mine. Just as this world will be mine, as every mortal soul will kneel before the throne we build."

We lock there, blades pressed, eyes inches apart. I taste the heat of her ragged breath, smell the iron and sweat of her mortality. She pushes harder, teeth bared like an animal, refusing to bend though her arms tremble with effort.

"Then why does he keep choosing me?" she hisses, voice cracked with fury. "Why does humanity keep choosing freedom over your perfect cages?"

The world goes white in my vision. I tear free with a burst of light, flinging her body into wall ruins. Stone crumbles under her weight, dust choking the air, while she drags herself upright again, bloodied, swaying, lifting her sword as if mortal arms could defy eternity.

She comes again, fast despite blood running down her side, eyes fixed on me with that maddening mortal certainty. I burn her frost to steam, split air with divine fire infused with shadow, while she drives through it all. Her sword cuts through smoke and strikes.

Steel bites into me.

Pain, sharp, pure, so real it tears a cry from my throat before I can stop it. I look down and see the impossible. A wound across divine flesh, shallow yet red, my blood spilling bright against the ruin of the pass. The darkness in my mind recoils, then surges with terrible pleasure. Even gods can bleed. Even gods can be remade.

The world freezes. My soldiers see it. The mortals see it. She sees it.

Her face transforms. Exhaustion and rage become something worse, triumph. "You bleed," she whispers, voice cracked while her eyes blaze with savage joy. "You can be hurt. Whatever you've become, whatever owns you now, it can be fought."

That look. That mortal daring to find glory in wounding me. That mortal daring to think herself my equal. That mortal seeing through to the truth beneath. It is ruin blooming in my chest, bile and fire rising, a scream that no longer belongs to words.

I fling her back with divine will twisted with darker power. Light pours from me in sheets, black-edged and hungry, carving earth apart, and she flies, body crashing through stone until dust swallows her. My hands shake. I stare at my blood on divine skin and feel ancient Olympus watching, mocking, while something older laughs.

Something inside me snaps clean.

I call my blade.

Air tears as it comes, bronze bright and terrible, forged in heaven's fires before men had names for stars. As it fills my hand, I feel it change. Darkness creeps along its edge, corruption that speaks of powers that predate heaven itself. It fills my hand with weight that belongs to gods alone, weight no mortal should ever witness. I no longer care for grace or proof or silence. I will cut her into pieces so small even worms will refuse them.

The blade sings as it falls into my palm, bronze bright with shadow-kissed edges, pale as winter sun yet dark as the spaces between stars. Its weight settles into my bones like a truth I have been denying. The battlefield recoils. Men shield their eyes from light that finds cracks in armor and splits them wide. Even the mountain holds still, as if stone remembers the last time divine will bent to serve something darker.

She stands in the ruin she made, knees unsteady, shoulder dark with blood, grit covering skin where steam dried to ash. The sword in her hands trembles once, confessing more than she would, then steadies. Nothing regal about her, yet I admit she is beautiful anyway. Soldier's beauty. Beauty that belongs to those who keep standing when bodies beg to fall. Beauty Ilija learned to read like scripture.

Beauty that must be destroyed.

I move first. The blade rises and air parts around it in clean lines. Heat rolls ahead of me, tinged with cold that doesn't belong to this world. Her ice cracks under my feet, slips back to water that steams against scorched rock. She lifts to meet me, ragged breath dragging through her teeth, and our weapons strike hard enough to shake loose stone chips that clatter into dark crevices.

No grace left to borrow from the past. We have spent it all. What remains is work, and I am better at it.

I cut at her shoulder, feeling the blade strike an old scar and new flesh. She turns her body into it, lets the edge take meat instead of bone, shoves into my chest with her full weight. Her forehead slams my cheekbone, hot, slick, sudden stink of blood and iron and woman. I drive my knee into her thigh, feeling muscle give. She cries out raw and thin, exhaustion and rage braided together. She fights because the idea of stopping is unbearable. Because she knows what falls with her, her life and humanity's last hope.

I strike again. The flat kisses her face, opens skin along the cheek. She blinks at the sudden rain of her own blood, one eye swimming. Her sword comes up late. I press the advantage, force running through my wrists and shoulders, guided by will that mingles with another's.

She answers with a desperate sweep meant to drive me back far enough to breathe. I step into it, turn the cut, let my blade's point write bright lines along her ribs. Air leaves her in a grunt stripped of words. She stumbles sideways, finds a broken wall with her hip, pushes off and comes again like a woman trying to run through water.

Her mouth shapes a name that does not belong to me.

I see it before I hear it, the way lips learn a word said a thousand times by one voice to one person, the way muscle under the jaw tightens around memory. Ilija.

I hate the tenderness that rises, hate that the thought of him can put softness in my hands mid-killing. I turn it to precision. I take the tendon above her knee. The leg buckles and she drops, one palm flying out to keep her face from stone. Skin splits along the lifeline, leaving her palm slick. She tries to rise and cannot. She snarls, low sound pulled from pain, drags the bad leg under her, forces it straight. She bites through her own lip and spits blood on the ground at my feet.

"Stay down." No mercy in my voice. Only tired divinity wanting to end things without breaking more pieces.

She lifts the sword, points it at my throat, breathes hard through her nose until dizziness passes. "No," she says softly, because there is almost nothing left to push breath. "I am not done. Humanity is not done. Whatever darkness rides you, we will resist it."

I cut her again for that insolence, for that knowing, open the cap of her shoulder where muscle makes its smooth round under skin. The arm drops an inch and she screams, then grips hilt harder with the other hand, bringing the blade up once more. She shakes from fingers to jaw, so tired the little muscles in her face have quit, and she looks at me with steadiness that has no business living in mortal eyes this close to death.

"Why do you make me do this?" The heat in my words surprises me because it sounds too much like grief.

"Because he chose," she says, "and because we all choose. Every day, we choose to resist what you're becoming. What you're bringing into this world."

I go to finish it. The blade lifts into the angle bodies understand from a thousand executions, the line that avoids bone, finds a clean path to ventricles. She moves when she should possess no strength, the last flick of wrist, and steel flashes across my skin, opens me again.

Blood runs bright. The sound from my throat is small and vicious, trapped breath of a hunted animal nicked by the chase. Every living head turns to look at that impossible red, faces lighting with the worst kind of hope.

She sees it too, divine blood, and her eyes fill with joy too big for human hearts. "You bleed," she says again, voice shaking with laughter at the edges. "Gods can fall. Even the darkness behind you can be defeated."

Enough.

I bring the blade down with both hands. Metal meets metal, grinds. Sparks jump, black and gold. I feel her wrists give under force, bones screaming. I tear her sword away. It skids across stone, falls into rifts where fire ate earth hollow. She makes sounds beyond words, throws herself at me empty-handed. Claws at my face, nails in my hair, fist in my collar. I let rage off its leash.

We fall together. Roll in grit and blood and shattered tile. I pin her with my knee across her hips, hit her once with a pommel to stop the clawing, then twice, then catch myself because even in ruin goddesses know their own laws. She stares up through blood and dust. Hair stuck to the corner of her mouth, pupils blown wide, breath coming in small hot bursts, each one a thread that could be cut with two fingers.

I set the bronze point just below her sternum. The hilt's weight settles into my palm the way old vows settle in ribs and never leave. I lean close until my breath moves her hair.

"Look at me." She tries to look past me, tries to see the sky that has been mine longer than her people have had names for colors. I press the point hard enough to make her body remember it has one heart and that heart sits precisely there. "Here. See what your world becomes."

Her eyes find mine. For one heartbeat there is nothing except hatred and I welcome it because hatred belongs to equals. Then it changes. She sees through me to the thing that rides my soul, the ancient hunger that will remake everything. Her face shifts from hatred to pity.

"Ana," she whispers, and it's my name, the woman's name, without goddess's title or conqueror's cry. My name, spoken like she sees the woman drowning inside the divine shell. "What have you let in? What have you become?"

I push the blade a finger's width and she gasps, sound with a child in it. She swallows, throat muscles working around my name without saying it, then says his. The shape moving in her mouth the way you say a name into a cup so the sound stays and warms you later.

Ilija. Then, softer: "The world. Save the world from her. From what uses her."

I could stop. Could take her head clean. Could call chains and cart her alive, let the world watch as I unmade her slowly until she begged for the peace I offered him. I want the truth of this to live in the body the way winter lives in wood. I want the space inside me that belongs to him to hear me finish the task no one else can be trusted to complete.

"Say goodbye." For a breath I hate my own voice because it sounds too much like a woman who loved and lost and decided to love anyway through ruin.

She takes breath that scrapes like a blade pulled wrong from sheath. Lips part. The word is tiny, thread held between dying fingers, breath of candle in room suddenly full of drafts.

"No. Never. We... never... stop... fighting."

She sees him as she says it. Shows on her face with clarity that makes my hands ache. Small tilt of chin as if he stands to one side and she wants to hold both our gazes and cannot. The softening that belongs to the first smile after a long siege. The shiver through lashes when someone's touch finds the back of the neck and says without words that you can rest. She sees all of humanity in that moment, all they could be if they were free of the cage I'm building.

Selene comes with him, bright streak, memory of child's warm weight against chest in winter, smell of cold air and wool and skin, fierce ridiculous love that turns generals into mothers without asking permission. I see that world pass across her like a tide, partner and daughter braided in one picture. I know precisely what I am taking.

I drive the blade in.

Flesh parts. Heat floods over my fists. Resistance of cartilage gives, small slippery catch as edge finds the space it was designed for and follows with sickening ease. Her body arches. Hands that broke men's jaws and threw grenades into oncoming trucks find my forearms and hold, just to anchor. Her mouth opens to shape another word and breath leaves before sound can be made.

I keep my eyes on hers. It matters. I want the last thing she sees to be the face of the god who won. That is the kind of cruelty that makes women into stories if anyone survives to tell them. Winning feels like tearing linen woven by patient hands for years, each thread snapping with distinct, ugly music.

The blade goes deeper. The body under me stutters against steel, then begins to quiet.

She is still watching and at the very back of her eyes I see the place where Ilija lives pull away. It tears. Little threads of memory and vow and touch break one by one, braid unmade by butcher's fingers. The image of him will not let go. It drags lines of her with it, hundred small private moments, warmth of hand on door handle, joke told too softly for anyone else, ridiculous relief of finding his shoulder in a crowd and standing against it for one breath. Selene goes with him, ribbon of light. Mother and child and man held together for heartbeat in dark, then ripped apart as death does its work.

She tries to hold them. Hands tighten on my arms, nails dig in, so much love in that grip I want to vomit.

"No," she says again, barely air, the shape of refusal pressed to wound. "Some...one... will... stop... you... stop... it..."

I pull the blade slowly. It keeps its promise, comes out clean along the edge, dirty along the face. Blood runs over my knuckles onto stone in a steady sheet, a mortal river fed by a mortal heart that has finally decided to quit. I lay my other hand flat against her cheek, simply because flesh there still holds heat and I want to know precisely how long it takes to go.

A small tremor moves through her. Eyes lose their fight first, then focus, then light. They stay open. I let them. Let them stare at nothing while victory settles in my bones.

Sound returns slowly to the pass. Someone screams a name I do not recognize. Another fires wildly into the air, shot cracks uselessly against an old pillar, sends pigeons brawling into flight from hidden nests. I kneel with my hands in her blood and listen to life leach away from a woman who ruined my plans and taught me lessons I did not want about the willingness of human hearts to stand before exceptionally large things and refuse to move.

I set the bronze tip on the ground, lean my weight on it until the edge bites rock and squeals. Her body twitches once more, last small argument from nerves, then goes slack. I lift my hand from her face. It leaves a print in dust and sweat that looks like a blessing and I hate that it looks like that.

I wipe blood from my wrist with the torn hem of her tunic, a gesture so domestic it makes my throat close around sudden, stupid ache. It passes.

The wound she carved in me has closed already. Skin shines pale and clean as if it never opened. The memory remains. Humiliation sharpens into something I can use.

I stand, blade catching red of my sky, and look down at the woman who was thorn in every weave, grit in every perfect gear. The last real resistance to the world being born through my hands.

"I warned you," I say softly because the dead deserve sentences that set scenes when anyone comes here to listen later. "He belongs to me. He always did. And through him, through his breaking, humanity will learn that resistance ends here."

Around us, the last of her fighters break. Some stand and scream until my soldiers cut them down for kindness. Some drop weapons and run along goat paths toward ravines with no water and no mercy. A few fall to their knees, put foreheads to dirt as if mountains might open and take them in.

I let them run. Let them carry word of what happened here. Let them spread the fear that will make the next conquest easier.

I look back at her face. Dust has settled on her lashes. In the slack of her mouth the shape of Ilija's name still lives, a ghost of words waiting for breath that will never come. A small, ugly part of me wants to bend and shape her lips into another syllable, take photographs in my mind to pull out later when silence wants feeding.

I lift the blade, hold it at my side. Heat rolls down the pass in slow sheets, and beneath it, cold spreads, the chill of order taking root. My sky keeps its bruise. The scent of cooked blood and hot bronze and old stone fills my nose, reminds me of a hundred other fields. This one is different. This one marks the turning.

In the place where her last word landed, air trembles. I hear it the way women hear their names spoken by known men from rooms away. Ilija will feel this through whatever walls he built to spare himself. He will lift his head without knowing why, the hum behind his breastbone will deepen, his hand will go to the place where storms sit when they are quiet. He will know something was taken and find less than yesterday.

He will hate me. He will come to me anyway when hatred becomes too much.

I bend, slide my hand beneath the back of her neck, lift her head just enough to free red oak leaves caught in her hair. They fall to stones. Laurel does not belong to the dead. The dead belong to memory, and memory belongs to me.

I let her down gently because the part of me that remains woman before goddess understands that gentleness is last proof of power. Then I stand and look out across the pass that has learned new names for fear.

My sky bleeds fire. The mountain watches. The world waits to see what I will say next.

The mountain has grown quiet, as if stone itself bends ear to listen. Screams dwindle, clash of steel becomes scattered, fire gutters into embers that glow in cracks I carved. All that remains is the heat of my sky pressing down, steady black silence that follows when resistance finally understands it has no breath left.

I stand above her. Body broken, still warm, eyes open, last shape of Ilija's name clinging to her mouth. Laurel leaves have fallen from her hair, green already darkening, curling into dirt. I look at her and feel no pity. Pity is for equals, and she was interruption, stone lodged in the throat of the world's song, and I have cut it out.

"You see now," I say, though she cannot hear. "This is how gods end stories, in silence. This is how new gods begin them, in blood."

Around us her fighters stagger. Some throw down arms, others run, some wail her name as though it might draw her spirit back to its ruined cage. I let them live long enough to watch. Let them see their queen broken at my feet. Let them take that memory into whatever holes they crawl into and let it fester there until it grows into the only truth they will ever tell, that Danica Madsen stood against divinity and was undone.

I look back down at her face. Blood across her cheek where my blade opened her, drying in a slow crust. She still looks fierce even in death, as if the defiance she bore me froze into her flesh. I bend close enough that my hair brushes her cooling forehead.

The bronze blade glows dull in my hand, drinking the last heat from mortal flesh. I plant it in the earth beside her body, a monument to futility. Let pilgrims find it centuries hence and wonder what fool dared stand against divinity remade.

I straighten and feel the ancient presence coil tighter around my spine, pleased with this offering, hungry for more. It whispers of thrones built from bones, of worlds where the sun itself bows to darkness, of Ilija kneeling at my feet while humanity watches and understands that their last light has chosen shadow.

"This world belongs to me," I say aloud, and my voice carries both my own hunger and something older, deeper, vast as the space between stars. "It always has. It always will. And what rises through me will remake everything in its image."

I turn from her corpse without looking back. The dead hold no more interest for me. Only the living matter now, the living who must be taught to kneel, the living who must surrender their precious freedom for the peace of absolute submission.

As I walk through the carnage, my footsteps leave marks that smoke and char. The mountain itself seems to lean away, stone remembering older darknesses, older hungers that once walked here before men named their fears. The shadow speaks through my thoughts, promising kingdoms, promising power, promising Ilija gift-wrapped in chains of his own choosing.

Behind me, her body cools in the dust, warning dead on her lips, hope extinguished in her eyes. The resistance is broken. The path is clear.

And somewhere, in whatever sanctuary he has built against the truth, Ilija feels the world shift. He will come to me now. He will have no choice. The shadow has seen to that, orchestrated every loss, every grief, every narrowing path until only one road remains, the road that leads to my arms and the darkness that waits behind my embrace.

I ascend from the pass, leaving Thermopylae to its ghosts and carrion birds. My work here is done. The real work, the breaking and remaking of everything mortal hands have built, has only just begun.

The sky bleeds darker as I rise, red deepening to the color of old wine, of dried blood, of promises made in places light has never touched. Below, the world watches and trembles, sensing the changing of ages, the death of their old gods and the birth of something far more terrible.

I smile with lips that taste of copper and ash.

Let them tremble. Let them run. Let them pray to gods who no longer listen.

The shadow and I have work to do.

CHAPTER TWENTY
THE QUEEN OF FALCONS

Danica

The last thing I remembered was the slow, final pull of bronze as the blade was withdrawn, leaving a hollow space in my chest that the silence rushed in to fill. The images of Ilija and Selene, the two halves of my soul, were ripped from my hands like tearing fabric, their faces burning themselves into the back of my eyes as everything went black. Then, the sky broke open. The chaos of the battlefield stilled as Accord soldiers froze in their bloodlust and resistance fighters locked mid-swing. Every soul in that gods damned pass stared upward as a sound split the heavens, a sound of a thousand swords clashing at once, of steel ringing until the very air trembled. A wound of light opened in the clouds above Thermopylae, pouring forth a torrent of gold and scarlet, the light of a Valkyrie's war feast.

Freyja fell through it like a hawk descending on its prey. Her armor, hammered from raw starlight, flared with runes that shifted and swam as she moved. Long ribbons of her hair streamed fire, tearing the smoke-filled air into sparks, while every beat of her immense wings was a clap of thunder. She landed where I lay, and the ground itself buckled under her divine weight, the stone cracking in lines that spread outward like black veins. Dust billowed, and the warriors on both sides stumbled back, their eyes wide and their mouths hanging open. She was a being of terrible, perfect beauty, and she was wholly unconcerned with any of them.

Her gauntleted hand reached for me. The metal was bright and impossibly cold, and I hated the gentleness in her grip as she lifted my broken body from the dirt. I dangled limp and blood-wet, a ruined thing, and she cradled me as if I were some precious relic. The pass dropped away beneath us as we continued to rise. I caught flashes of the world I was leaving, my partisans crying out my name, Accord soldiers throwing down their weapons in terror, the mountains themselves swallowed in the red light of her coming. The world ripped open, and the battlefield was gone.

Folkvangr spread out below us, and the sight of it hurt. The grass was a shade of green so vibrant it seared the eye, and flowers bloomed in colors for which my mortal tongue had no names. The air was heavy with the smell of honey and sacred incense; a fragrance of peace I did not deserve. Across the endless meadow, armored warriors stood with their blades still bloodied and their shields still dented, their laughter carrying across the plain like the sound of a joyous feast. They were alive in their death, proud and shining, every wound worn as a badge of honor.

Freyja lowered me into the grass. The blades bent soft beneath me, too soft. I wanted the rough grit of stone. I wanted the reek of the battlefield. I wanted Ilija's weight at my back and Selene's hand in mine. I wanted anything except this, never this. The fire that had been extinguished in my chest cracked open and roared back to life.

"Fuck you," I spat, my throat raw, my voice a sharp, ugly thing against the meadow's beauty. "Fuck you and every god that thinks they can drag me around like a fucking toy. I didn't ask for this." I shoved myself to my feet, my knees shaking, my spectral hands trembling, the words burned hotter than the wound that had killed me. "You think you can just take me? Claim me like some prize for your collection? I fought. I bled. I died. And you—" I jabbed a finger at her, my voice breaking with a rage that was pure grief. "You show up at the end and carry me off like a fucking trophy. I had people counting on me. I had a world to fight for. You ripped me away from them."

Freyja said nothing. She stood tall, her eyes gleaming, her mouth curved in a slight smile as if she enjoyed the sight of me raging, a broken soul still spitting fire.

My voice cracked, I pressed harder, fueled by the image of Ilija's face, of Selene's. "Do you have any idea what you stole from me? Do you know who I left behind? He needed me. She needed me. And now I'm here in your pretty fucking meadow, stuck among ghosts with wine on their breath while the world burns without me." The words choked me; I forced them out anyway. "You're no savior. You are carrion, picking through the dead for what pleases you. You wanted another name for your hall, another story to brag about at your feasts. Well, fuck your hall. Fuck your stories. And fuck you, goddess."

Spit flew from my mouth. My fists shook at my sides, my whole body burning with a fury that was the only thing holding me together. The meadow was silent for my ragged breath, my curses hanging in the air like jagged, ugly wounds.

And Freyja laughed. The sound boomed out of her, rich and sharp, loud enough to rattle the plain, rolling through the meadow like thunder. The warriors grinned and shouted, raising their cups, feeding on her mirth as if it were meat. I froze, my rage hitting a wall of disbelief. "What the fuck," I screamed, my body shaking, "are you laughing at?"

Her laughter slowed, her eyes still shone with it. "Because you are exactly as I hoped you would be." The words hit me harder than any blow. I blinked, stunned. "What the hell does that mean?" I demanded, stepping toward her. "You drag me here, rip me from my life, and then you laugh in my face? You want me to kneel? Fuck that. I'll fight you the same as I fought her. I'll curse you till my throat splits, and I'll keep fucking doing it until you send me back."

Freyja's smile widened. "Good."

"Good? Did you hear a single fucking word I just said?"

"Every single one," she said, her voice shaking with delight. "You are fire and frost. Rage and will. This is why you are mine."

"I'm yours," I hissed, the words tearing at my throat. "I don't belong to anyone. To you. To her. To—"

"Hey," another voice cut through the divine air, warm and low and utterly impossible.

My chest snapped tight. I turned.

"Hey, my fire and frost."

Ilija.

My brain just... stopped. Like someone had yanked the plug on everything inside my skull. I stumbled backward, nearly tripping over my own feet, because this couldn't be real. This was some sick joke, it had to be. I'd watched Ana drag him through that fucking rift. Felt his hand torn out of mine like she was ripping off a limb. The silence afterward, Gods, the silence was worse than screaming.

There he was. Moving closer. Real enough that I could see how wrecked he looked, shoulders hunched like he'd been carrying the world, eyes bloodshot and hollow, new scars cutting across skin I used to trace with my fingers in the dark.

"Ilija…" His name came out like broken glass.

I wanted to run to him. Every cell in my body was screaming at me to move; my feet might as well have been nailed to the ground. What if this was another one of Ana's mind-fucks? What if I reached for him and he just... dissolved?

He must have seen it on my face because he came to me instead, moving slowly like I was some spooked animal. Held his hand out like he was asking permission.

Fuck permission.

I grabbed his wrist so hard I left bruises. His pulse hammered against my palm, fast and frantic and so goddamn real I wanted to laugh and scream at the same time.

I lost it. Completely fucking lost it.

The sob that tore out of me sounded like something dying. I slammed my forehead against his chest and wrapped my arms around him, shaking so badly I thought I might vibrate right out of my skin.

"I fucking hate her," I choked out between gasps that didn't feel like breathing. "That fucking bitch, she took you, and I let her, and I wasn't strong enough to stop her and she just, she just—" My throat locked up. The words turned into this ugly, animal sound.

His arms came around me like a vise. One hand buried itself in my hair, pressing my face harder against his chest like he was trying to fuse us together. He didn't shush me or tell me it was okay. He just held on while I came apart at the seams.

"I couldn't stop her!" The words ripped out of my throat raw and bleeding. "I fucking tried, Ilija, I tried so hard she was everywhere, and I couldn't hold on to you and she just—" My fists beat against his chest, weak and desperate, until they gave up and just clung instead. "She carved you out of me. Do you get that? She carved you right out and left me bleeding."

"I know." His voice cracked right down the middle. "Fuck, I know."

That broke me all over again. Tears everywhere, hot and endless, choking me. Every breath felt like drowning.

"She showed me shit," I sobbed. "Made me watch you die a thousand different ways. Made me believe, fuck, she made me believe you were gone forever and I kept going, kept fucking fighting, it was killing me. Every single day, Ilija. Every day without you was like dying."

His hand was shaking in my hair. I felt his cheek press against the top of my head, felt the wetness there that wasn't mine.

"Killed me too," he whispered. "Every fucking day."

I jerked back to look at him. His eyes were red and swollen, face twisted with the same pain that was eating me alive. His mouth opened like he wanted to say something couldn't find the words.

"You're here," I whispered, and it came out broken. "Please fucking tell me I'm not hallucinating!"

"I'm here." His voice carried everything, every nightmare, every moment of despair, every time we'd both wanted to give up. "I'm right here."

I crashed into him again, sobbing so hard I thought my ribs might crack. Soaked his shirt with tears and snot and didn't give a shit. My whole body was convulsing; I held on like he might disappear if I loosened my grip even a little.

The world went quiet around us. Even the gods seemed to understand this moment wasn't theirs.

Ilija's fingers found my chin, tilted my face up. His thumb wiped at the mess of blood and tears, gentle even though his hands were shaking.

"Hey," he said, voice scraped raw steady. "My fire and frost, it's going to be okay."

I lost it again, crushed my mouth to his in a kiss that was more desperation than romance. The taste of coming home. A kiss that said everything I couldn't put into words.

The kiss shattered me. Salt and copper and desperation, the taste of blood and tears, his mouth trembling against mine like he was falling apart too. I held on like I was drowning, trying to swallow down proof that he wasn't just some cruel dream. My chest was heaving, whole body shaking, and I didn't give a shit how wrecked I sounded.

When I finally pulled back, he kept his forehead pressed to mine, both of us panting like we'd been running for our lives. The air between us felt thick with everything we'd been through.

"You're real," I said again, still believing it. "You're actually fucking here."

The tiny smile he gave me nearly killed me. "So are you."

I laughed, this sharp, broken sound that cracked right down the middle. It scraped my throat raw; I couldn't stop it. The tears came harder, mixed with the laughter until I couldn't tell which was which. "Gods, we're such a mess," I said, half choking on the words. "Just look at us."

"I am," he said quietly, thumb brushing across my cheek. "I can't stop looking."

I smacked his chest with a fist that had no strength left, just trembling. "You're an idiot," I mumbled, the words dissolving into another sob. "You stupid, stubborn bastard. I thought you were gone forever."

"Thought I lost you too." His voice cracked on the last word, and he pulled me closer, hand pressing into my back like he could keep me locked inside his arms forever. "Ana tried. She wanted to rip you out of my head, you never left. Not fucking once."

My breath caught. Fresh tears blurred everything. "She showed me things," I whispered. "Tried to make me believe you were dead. And Gods, Ilija, I almost—" My voice shattered. "I almost let that bitch win."

"You didn't." His hand gripped mine, solid and real. "You're here. You fought through all her shit. As you always have."

The meadow kept spinning around us in its weird eternal calm. Grass swaying, dead warriors feasting, none of it mattered. For the first time since that blade cut me down, I felt warmth that belonged to me.

I pressed closer, burying my face in his chest, breathing him in, sweat and storms and that faint smoky scent that was just him. Familiar. Human. Home. My whole body shuddered like it was trying to memorize every detail.

"I don't want to let go," I said against his chest. "Ever."

"Then don't," he murmured into my hair.

I laughed again, wet and raw, the sound turning into another broken sob. My fingers twisted into his shirt like I could sew myself right into him. Every time I tried to say something, the words just fell apart in tears. It didn't matter. He knew. He always fucking knew.

We stayed like that, crying, laughing through the tears, clinging to each other like the world might try to tear us apart again the second we let go.

"I couldn't keep you," I sobbed, fists twisted in his shirt. "I wasn't strong enough, Ilija." My voice shattered, throat scraped raw with grief.

His hands grabbed my face, rough and shaking, forcing me to look at him. His breath hitched, and when he spoke, his voice was gravel and certainty.

"How's Selene?" he asked. "How's our daughter?"

Everything stopped. The tears on my face might as well have turned to ice. I just stared at him, couldn't even breathe.

"You... you know?" I whispered, voice barely there.

"Yeah," he said, pressing his forehead against mine, voice cracking solid. "My father told me, in Nav. Said her name, and I've been carrying it ever since. Held her with me every step trying to get back here."

The sound that ripped out of me then nearly broke my ribs. I crumpled against him, holding on like I could somehow pull Selene into this too. For the first time since she was born, I wasn't carrying it all alone.

It split me open. My whole body shook as I held onto him, gripping so hard my nails left crescents in his skin. Her name wasn't just mine anymore, and it fucking wrecked me.

"She's fire," I choked out, words stumbling over tears. "Gods, Ilija, she's fire and shadows rolled into one. Got your eyes, that storm-dark color that sees everything even when she's just sitting there. And stubborn as hell. When she was four, she got in some guy's face, told him he was dead wrong about the stars because she'd counted them herself." A sob turned into this broken laugh. "Little shit was right, too. I double-checked."

His arms crushed me closer; breath ragged against my hair. I felt him shake, felt his chest hitch as he tried to swallow down his own tears.

"She doesn't sleep sometimes," I whispered, voice cracking apart. "The shadows get to her and she... she sees shit. Won't tell me everything, I know. I see it in her face, how it scares the hell out of her. Then she'll smile at me like it's nothing. Like she's protecting me from it, and she's just a kid. Our kid."

"Danica," he breathed, my name falling apart in his mouth. His tears were burning hot against my skin.

"She laughs like you," I said, fists twisting tighter in his shirt. "So much. Gods, when she does, it's like lightning, sudden and sharp and out of nowhere. She looks so fucking alive when it happens, it almost hurts to watch." My chest was heaving. "I was terrified she wouldn't make it. Scared shitless I'd lose her too. I couldn't lose you both. I couldn't—"

The words broke into sobs. He held me through it, his own body shaking, quiet except for the catch in his breathing, the sound of a man coming apart.

"She asks about you," I finally managed, voice completely shot. "Doesn't know the whole story, she knows something's missing. She'll stare at the door like she's waiting for you to walk through. And I—" My throat closed. "I had no answer for her. Couldn't tell her when. Couldn't even tell her if."

Ilija's hands grabbed my face again, desperate and shaking. His eyes, wet and wild, locked onto mine. "Then tell her now," he said, voice wrecked. "Tell her we're coming back. Tell her we'll never stop trying to get back. She's got both of us. You hear me? Both."

The sound that tore out of me was half scream. I kissed him brutal and desperate, grief and promises all mixed together. He kissed back like he was drowning and I was air, both of us shaking, holding on, breaking apart and healing all at once.

His mouth pulled away from mine, his hands stayed locked on me, shaking. Forehead pressed to mine, our tears dripping together.

"Tell me," He whispered, voice completely shot, like the words had been ripped straight from his chest. "Everything about her. Every fucking detail. Don't stop. I need to know."

The way he said it gutted me. I pressed my hands over his, held them against my face like they could keep me from falling apart, and just let it all spill out.

"She's tiny," I said, voice wobbling, "acts like she's ten feet tall. Walks around with her chin up, daring the world to mess with her. Sometimes she trips over her own damn feet, she'll glare at the ground like it personally offended her." A sob broke through. "Hates shoes. Kicks them off the second she can. Petra says she's half feral, and she's not wrong. Runs through those ruins like she owns the place, like the whole world belongs to her."

I felt him shake, his chest hitching against mine. His lips brushed my hair, he stayed quiet, so I kept going.

"She eats bread like it's holy. Petra tried teaching her to bake once and she burned it so badly the whole room filled with smoke. She cried, Ilija, like her world had ended. Then she wiped her face and tried again until she nailed it. She's... she doesn't quit. Won't stop until she's mastered whatever she's got her hands on." My mouth twisted into this wet, broken smile. "Gets that from you."

His breath caught, and his arms squeezed so tight it hurt.

"She holds sticks like swords," I whispered. "Always her right hand. Always ready for a fight. I catch her shadow moving sometimes, like it's got a mind of its own when she's paying attention. Freaks her out, she never admits it. Just sets her jaw and grips harder."

My voice cracked. The tears just wouldn't stop.

"She hums when she's falling asleep. Real songs, just... these little sounds. Quiet, like she's putting herself back together after the day. I sit there listening, and it feels like a prayer or something older than words. When she finally crashes, she curls up tight, knees tucked up, like the world can't get to her that way."

Ilija shattered then. The sound that came out of him was this raw, broken noise, the grief of a father who'd missed everything. He crushed me against him, shaking with tears.

I held on tight, talking into his shoulder through my own tears, forcing the words out even as they tore me apart. "She's everything we are, Ilija. Fire and storms. Shadows and light. She's us, all the good shit and all the fucked up parts too. And she's waiting. She's waiting for us."

"We're going to go home," he choked out, voice destroyed. "I'm coming for her, Danica. I swear to fuck. She'll never wait alone again."

We fell apart together, sobbing and breaking, holding on like the world was trying to rip us apart all over again. For the first time since she was born, Selene was right there between us, some secret I had to carry, some burden, ours.

We held on until we had nothing left. My throat felt like I'd swallowed gravel, eyes so swollen I could barely see, every breath scraping like it might kill me. For the first time in years, that crushing weight was gone from my shoulders. I wasn't carrying Selene's name by myself anymore. He has it too now. It belongs to both of us.

Ilija's hand cupped the back of my head, forehead still mashed against mine, both of us gasping in this fucked-up meadow's dead calm. All around us, the corpses kept partying, raising their drinks like our breakdown was just entertainment. The smell of meat and honey hung thick in the air, cloying and wrong, and it made me want to puke.

I pressed closer to him. "Don't let go," I whispered, voice like broken glass. "Ever fucking again."

"Never," he said, and I believed him. His arms squeezed until my ribs creaked, until I couldn't tell where I ended and he began.

A shadow dropped over us. I didn't need to look to know it was her. Freyja. Those massive wings blocking out the blood-red sky, her laughter still bouncing off the walls of eternity. She didn't say shit now, just stared. It felt like a crown made of knives.

I wanted to tell her to go fuck herself. All I could do was hold Ilija and shake, voice completely shot, soul scraped raw.

She finally turned away, feathers catching the weird light, and strutted back to her hall while the dead warriors kissed her ass. Didn't dismiss us or bark orders, just left, the taste of her presence still bitter on my tongue.

Ilija's lips touched my temple. "She doesn't matter," he mumbled. "We are together, here. Now."

I shut my eyes and breathed him in, storms and sweat and smoke. The grass gave way as we sank down into it, twisted together and trembling, two wrecked souls clinging to each other in the middle of paradise. The world could burn, gods could play their games, dead halls could wait. All that mattered was his heartbeat pounding against my cheek and our daughter's name, alive between us like a third heartbeat.

Selene.

Just thinking it felt like praying.

Last thing I remembered before exhaustion knocked me out was his hand moving through my hair, steady and constant, like he was promising with every stroke that when I opened my eyes again, he'd still be right there.

CHAPTER TWENTY-ONE
APPLES OF FOREVER

Ilija

Freyja's wings folded, yet their radiance painted the grass in colors that had no names. Each step dragged like drowning in reverse. Behind us, Folkvangr's laughter faded to whispers, then silence. My shoulders hunched against the weight of every myth I'd ever taught pressing down on me.

The beauty turned my stomach. Honey-thick air coated my throat while serenity mocked what we'd crawled through, what had hollowed Danica out at Thermopylae.

Danica moved beside me like smoke given form. Whole again, unmarked, yet something wild prowled behind her eyes. Her gaze fixed ahead with the stillness that comes before violence. I'd seen that look in mirrors often enough.

"You hate me for bringing you here." Freyja's voice carried centuries.

Danica's laugh splintered the air. "You fucking think?"

Gods never blink. "Keep that fire. You will need it."

I stopped, lightning restless in my blood, words sharper on my tongue. "Don't speak to us like fresh-faced heroes from your stories. You play eternal games and expect us to be grateful because your halls are ancient. Why help us?"

Her gaze found mine, steady as tides swallowing civilizations. "The Accord devours everything. Olympus burns as we speak. Asgard follows if this disease spreads unchecked. Your enemy became ours."

"How convenient." Bile rose in my throat. "We're weapons in your arsenal."

A smile touched her lips, cruel, ancient, knowing. "You have always been weapons, Professor. Every mortal who takes up arms serves something greater, destiny, justice, love, vengeance." Her eyes burned as they moved between us. "You are storm and winter given form. Chaos incarnate. The Accord doesn't understand the threat you represent. That ignorance is why I claim you now."

"Claim?" Ice cracked through Danica's voice. "We belong to no one."

Freyja tilted her head, firelight catching in her hair. "You are free. Free from command, from binding oaths or blood debts. That separates me from her." Ana's name hung unspoken like funeral smoke.

I laughed, harsh, bitter, empty. "But at what price? There's always a price. Gods don't rescue mortals from kindness."

"The price," Freyja said with stone's patience, "is truth. When you taste Idunn's fruit, you will be remade. Immortal. Complete. You will walk among mortals again, yet they will see you as something other. You cannot hide what you become. Storm and flame will mark you, and humanity will look upon you with recognition, that you are something beyond their understanding."

My skin crawled. Memories of Ana's silver promises, her golden chains disguised as gifts. "So, we become tyrants on thrones."

Her eyes narrowed to controlled fire. "You remain free to choose your path. Asgard holds no claim, no oaths, no service, no fealty. The gift carries this burden; mortal eyes will change when they see you. Awe. Terror. Worship. This is power's weight, Professor. What you do with that weight remains yours alone."

Danica looked up, meeting the goddess's stare without flinching. Her voice cracked like winter wind through broken glass. "If this path leads us back to her, I don't care what it costs."

My chest tightened. Her voice cracked with everything she didn't say.

Freyja nodded, approval flickering in ancient features. "Then walk. Idunn waits, and time grows short."

The air thickened before the orchard came into sight. Heavier, sweeter. It clung in my throat like syrup, thick with ripe fruit and the electric edge of storms. My chest constricted with each breath. This hunger ran deeper than flesh, compulsion old as roots, the kind that could make a man crawl on broken knees for one taste.

When the trees appeared, I walked into every myth I'd dissected in lecture halls. Rows stretched endlessly, branches bowed with gold that transcended metal and light. The apples hung heavy, their skin glowing as though fire had been trapped beneath. Every leaf shimmered with silver veins. The ground was littered with fallen fruit that refused to rot, each one humming faintly.

Danica slowed beside me, lips parting, eyes wide with suspicion. She'd spent her life fighting gilded cages. She knew, same as me, that anything this beautiful, demanded payment.

At the orchard's heart stood a woman. She wore simple robes, carried no weapons, and wielded no armor. Insignificant compared to Freyja, her figure slight, her dark hair bound in a plain braid. Yet every step she took bent the orchard toward her. Her hands were stained gold to the wrist, as though she'd been holding sunlight.

"Idunn," Freyja said, respect threading her tone.

The woman smiled with inevitability. Her eyes, clear and green as spring water, swept over us, and I felt like I was reading aloud like pages in a book.

"These are the two?" Her voice carried like wind through leaves.

"They are. The storm and the frost. The Accord's undoing, if they choose it."

Idunn's gaze lingered on me longer than comfort allowed. "He doubts."

"Damn right I do," I muttered. Danica's mouth twitched, almost a smile.

Freyja gestured to the trees. "These are reality made manifest. Eat, and your wounds vanish. Eat, and time releases you. You will cease to age. You will bleed and heal, fall and rise. Mortals will look upon you and call you gods, and they will speak truth."

"And the cost?" Danica's voice cut through shimmering perfection.

Freyja's humor vanished. "The cost is that you will always be seen. Wherever you go, eyes will turn. Mortals will kneel, fear, worship, or hate, they will recognize you. You cannot walk back into crowds and vanish. You cannot raise your daughter in silence. She will grow with you, with the world watching."

The words struck like hammers. I watched Danica flinch before forcing her jaw hard again.

Idunn stepped closer, cradling one apple. Its glow turned her skin to firelight. She held it toward Danica. "The choice is yours. Stay broken, mortal, and pass into shadow, or eat, and stand in the storm to come."

Danica's hand trembled. I felt the fruit's heat from where I stood. God, I hated how badly I wanted it, how the hunger it woke had everything to do with power and nothing to do with sustenance.

"You distrust us," Freyja said to me. "Keep your suspicion, it will guard you well. Know this, we do chain those who eat. You remain free from Asgard's bonds. Only your choices will bind you. The Accord and Aphrodite thrive because men kneel. You will rise because you refuse to do the same."

Danica's breath became ragged. She turned to me, her eyes full of Selene though she never spoke the name. "This will get us back to her. We have no other choice but to be the gods we have always been."

I swallowed hard. The storm in my chest shifted like it was waiting for my decision.

Idunn lifted another apple from her basket. The orchard stilled. Air thickened, heavy as thunder before lightning.

The apple glowed in her hand; ancient light trapped in living flesh. Its skin was gold streaked with red, as if veins ran beneath the surface. I swore I saw it pulse once, like it had a heartbeat.

"Take it," she said, offering it to Danica first.

Danica stared at that piece of fruit like it was a blade aimed for her throat. "You sure this is a gift?"

"Does the river leash the one who drinks?" Idunn tilted her head. "Does fire bind the one who warms their hands? Power flows free. Only your choices bind you."

Danica's gaze cut to me. I saw the part of her that wanted to spit in the gods' faces one more time, and the part that couldn't stomach leaving our daughter to fight alone. Her jaw clenched. She took the apple.

Her fingers sank into the skin as though it yielded to her alone. She bit into it.

The sound cracked sharp, clean, too loud in the quiet orchard. Juice ran down her chin, glowing faintly as if it carried light instead of water. For a moment she stiffened, eyes wide. Then the air shifted. Heat rippled off her skin, cold rising with it, frost crawling over grass at her feet even as fire cracked in her breath. The storm in her body woke, new and terrible.

When she swallowed, she looked at me. Her lips glistened with gold. "Your turn."

Idunn's hand was already extended. Another apple, heavy and radiant, rested against her palm. I took it, half-expecting it to burn, yet it was cool, smooth, almost soft. It thrummed against my skin, and the storm in my chest answered like it had been waiting for this exact moment.

I bit deep.

The taste struck like lightning, blinding, absolute. Sweet, sharp, alive. It filled my mouth, my throat, then spread through me like a flood. My knees buckled, and I hit the grass, clutching my chest. The storm inside me roared to life, every drop of blood in my veins turning to thunder, every breath sparking with a hurricane of storms. I thought I was dying, or maybe being born again, too raw to know the difference.

My scars burned. Old wounds screamed. My bones ached as if they'd been broken and remade a thousand times in a heartbeat. Every fracture, every cut, every bruise I'd ever carried lit up, then faded into nothing. I was whole, changed beyond recognition. Stronger, the storm unleashed.

I gasped, my hand digging into the earth, feeling it tremble beneath me. The sky above flickered, dark clouds rushing, lightning arcing silently across the horizon. Danica was on her knees beside me, gripping my wrist, her breath fast and ragged. Her skin was lit from within, fire and frost warring under her veins. When she looked at me, I saw her whole, terrible, beautiful, and eternal.

We had crossed a line. Humanity lay behind us like discarded skin.

"Now you will endure forever," Idunn said. "You will walk the world as long as it exists. They will see you as gods, because you are gods. You earned this through choice, through action. By what you carry inside you."

The words sank in. For the first time, I understood what immortality meant, endless life, yes, and being seen, always, everywhere, without escape.

Danica's hand clutched mine, and I couldn't tell if she was trembling or if it was me.

Freyja stepped forward, her shadow long across the grass. "Now you are ready for what comes. When you descend, it will be as storm and fire incarnate. The Accord will break beneath you. Men will kneel, whether you will it or demand it."

I looked at Danica. She stared at me the same way, horror and determination locked in her gaze. Neither of us said it, yet I felt it: We had been given a burden. And the world was going to burn for it.

The orchard had gone unnaturally quiet, as though every leaf knew what had just happened. Danica and I knelt in the grass, our hands locked together, our bodies trembling with the weight of the storms that had been poured into us. I could still taste the apple, sweet, sharp, endless, and it terrified me how much I wanted more.

Freyja stepped into the silence. Her wings caught the orchard's light, and her armor seemed like living flame. "You feel it already. The weight. The clarity. The unending breath. This is the reality you are bound to endure.

The blade may cut you down, the fire may consume you, yet you will rise again. That is what it means to be among us."

Her words rang like prophecy, driving deep into my ribs. Immortality. The word sat in me like a stone I could neither swallow nor spit out.

Danica's silence could cut, yet Freyja turned her gaze toward her anyway. "You fear chains. You spit at thrones. Keep that hatred. It will keep you sharp. No mortal hand will chain you again. The Accord's armies, its generals, even its goddess, they will break when they see you descend. The battlefield will remember your names. Men will look up and see gods, and they will kneel because they cannot do otherwise."

"Fuck kneeling," Danica said, her voice hoarse yet steady. "If they want to fight, they'll get a fight. If they want to follow, they'll follow. I will be their leader, their storm, anything except their idol."

Freyja's smile widened, pleased. "And that is why they will worship you all the more. Because you refuse it."

She spread her hand toward the shimmering horizon. "You will descend into war. Asgard will be under siege. The Accord has clawed its way into our realm, and their soldiers march beneath banners soaked in false divinity. You will fall into the heart of battle as storm and frost. As gods."

The word burned when she said it.

"And Selene?" Danica asked suddenly, her voice rough, tearing at the silence.

Freyja's expression softened slightly. "She will wait. The child has her own thread in this weave. When you return, it will be as fire returned to its hearth. She will know you both."

The words nearly broke me. My throat ached with everything I wanted to say, yet Danica's grip tightened, a warning against crumbling here.

Freyja stepped closer, her shadow stretching over both of us. "When the gates open, there will be hesitation. You will fight as immortals revealed. The Accord will see what it means to face storm and flame and frost unleashed, and the mortals of Midgard will remember. You will be able to walk the world as gods. That is the price of what you have taken into yourselves. Power cannot hide. Immortality demands recognition."

Her wings spread wide, filling the orchard. "Do you understand what you are?"

Danica spat in the grass. "We're the ones who are going to burn that gods damned bitch to the ground."

I tightened my grip on her hand, my chest burning with storm. "And we'll do it together."

Freyja's laughter rolled across the meadow, sharp and triumphant. "Then prepare yourselves. The next time your feet touch earth, it will be soaked in blood."

The orchard darkened, the air snapping with lightning. Somewhere, far beyond, I heard war, bullets clanging, drones flying, voices crying out. The battlefield was calling.

And this time, we were going to descend like gods.

The orchard shuddered, light splitting into jagged seams until flowers and sky unraveled into nothing. Freyja's wings stretched across the collapsing horizon.

"You have eaten Idunn's gift," she said, her voice carrying like thunder. "You will endure beyond mortal limits. When you descend, the Accord be terrified. Let them. Break them."

Her hand swept downward. The world tore open beneath us.

What waited below was Earth; war-blackened earth, our earth, burning under the Accord's banners. I saw cities reduced to rubble, their bones still smoking. Fields churned into mud and blood. Men and women clashing in chaos that stretched across the scarred soil of Greece. The pass of Thermopylae, the place I had bled for, was once again drowning in fire and steel.

Danica's hand locked around mine, iron tight. Her eyes burned with frost and flame. I squeezed back, grounding myself in her grip, the only truth that mattered.

The orchard vanished. The sky opened wide. We jumped.

Air ripped at us, hot with smoke, thick with ash. The cries of war rose to meet us, the clang of steel, the shouts of commanders, the dying groans of men who had gambled everything and lost. I could see the Accord's black-armored ranks pressing forward, disciplined and merciless. And beyond them, tattered banners of the resistance, desperate, breaking, yet still defiant.

Danica's voice tore from her throat, raw with all the love and fury of a mother who had been forced to leave her child behind: "We're coming baby, we are coming home."

The storm inside me answered. Lightning split across the sky, rain and hail crashing down in sheets. My chest burned with fire and thunder. The earth rose to meet us.

Our feet hit the ground like falling mountains. The earth cracked, stone exploding outward, a shockwave blasting through the battlefield. Accord soldiers staggered and fell, weapons torn from their hands, horses rearing and screaming. Fire burst from Danica in a violent arc, frost chasing behind it, scorching and freezing the field at once. Lightning ripped down through me, carving trenches in the mud, hail hammering against shields until they shattered.

For one heartbeat, the war itself stopped. Both sides froze, staring at us in the crater of our arrival, fire and storm bleeding from our bodies like second skins.

I saw their faces filled with fear, confusion, and complete terror.

Gods, their eyes whispered.

The Accord wanted gods. Now they fucking had them.

Chapter Twenty-Two
THE STORM UNLEASHED

The first volley tore the air apart. Rifles barked in perfect unison, bullets screaming through rain like angry hornets. I felt them hiss past my skull, close enough to part my hair, close enough to taste my own death.

Danica moved like flame given form. Her hands snapped forward, and fire exploded outward, pure, rage that swallowed the front rank whole. Armor liquefied under the heat. Men shrieked like animals being skinned alive. Helmets sagged and melted into skulls, faces caving beneath the blaze like wax dolls thrown in an oven. The stench of burning oil and cooked flesh rolled across the mud, thick enough to gag on.

I let the storm break loose like a rabid dog off its chain.

Thunder erupted out of me and the sky split like a god's own throat getting cut. Lightning slammed the ground with the fury of a thousand hammers, bright enough to burn shadows into my fucking retinas. It carved through steel like butter, burst men apart where they stood, arms here, legs there, torsos scattered like bloody confetti. Mud fountained up in geysers of earth and blood and rain, mixing into something that looked like the world's worst soup.

The air reeked of burning flesh and iron, sharp and metallic. Iron flooded my mouth like I'd been sucking on a handful of nails.

Wind howled across the plain with voices of demons crawling from hell. It shredded banners to ribbons, drove soldiers back step by stumbling step, ripped helmets clean off and hurled them into darkness like discarded toys. Rain hammered down, liquid bullets turning the field into a sucking, hungry mouth. I pushed harder, my whole body shaking, blood streaming hot from my nose, every strike pulling something vital from my bones, from my soul.

The carrier's gun roared its defiance. The sound punched through my chest like a fist. I raised my hand and hail came down like the sky was throwing rocks, crashing into steel, caving it in, turning the war machine into a crushed tin can. Lightning followed, a blinding spear of pure *fuck you* that shattered its mechanical heart. The explosion rocked the whole valley, fragments spinning away like deadly fireworks, some still glowing cherry red as they buried themselves in the mud.

Danica moved beside me, her breath coming in ragged sobs of effort. Ice gathered in her palms, jagged, vicious spears of frozen death. She hurled them into the Accord's flank, and they punched clean through armor like tissue paper, lifted grown men off their feet, left them twitching on ice-skewers like some fucked up kebab. She swept her arm wide and fire roared across the field, a tsunami of flame that left charred meat and the sweet-sick smell of barbecued ribs on the grill. She was fucking relentless, her face streaked with rain and blood and ash, her eyes hard as diamonds, cold as the space between stars.

The resistance fighters stood frozen. They stared like they'd seen the face of God and found out He was pissed. Some whispered my name with lips that barely worked. *Ilija*. Like a prayer and a curse. A woman clutched her rosary so tight her knuckles went white, staring at the storm like it might swallow her whole. A man dropped to his knees in the mud, mouth hanging open, eyes shining with terror and awe and something that might have been worship.

The storm wanted more. It clawed at me from inside, tearing my ribs apart, shredding my lungs, demanding everything I had and everything I didn't. I gave it all, fuck it, I am a goddamn immortal fucking god now. Lightning came faster, one strike after another, hammering the ground until the earth convulsed like it was having a seizure. Wind tore trees from their roots like they were weeds. Rain fell so heavy I couldn't see shit, the entire world a blur of mud and screaming and the beautiful, terrible music of men dying badly.

Danica was fire and frost together, her arms trembling as she drove both elements into the heart of the Accord like twin daggers. She froze men into perfect ice sculptures and shattered them with the next breath, fire turning ice to steam, steam to smoke, smoke to nothing. Her skin blistered where the heat kissed her, but she never fucking slowed. Her fury was a living thing, endless and hungry, and the Accord broke before it like waves against a cliff made of rage.

The black line dissolved like sugar in acid. Men screamed and turned to run, fleeing, their precious discipline scattered to the wind like ashes. Some threw down their rifles, clawing at anything for cover. Others charged blindly into the lightning, their battle cries cut short by thunder that spoke with the voice of judgment.

The plain was a fucking wasteland. Fire smoldered in puddles of melted steel. Smoke rose in black columns like pillars holding up a dead sky. Mud sucked at boots and bodies alike, hungry for more, always hungry. The storm still raged overhead, my storm, and I could taste it on my tongue, blood slicking my teeth like I'd been drinking from the an executioners cup.

My chest heaved, pain burning with every breath like broken glass in my lungs, yet I couldn't stop. The storm had its claws in me, hooked deep in my spine, and it wasn't done. Neither was I.

This was what we'd become. Lightning and fire, ice and rage, the answer to every prayer whispered in cellars and every curse spat at midnight. This was war stripped of its pretty uniforms and noble causes, revealed for what it really was, meat and metal and the terrible act of survival.

The Accord line crumbled like a house of cards in a hurricane. Their precision turned to chaos in seconds. I saw it in the way their rifles jerked and spasmed instead of moving with mechanical snap, in the way their formations buckled as men broke rank, stumbling through mud that ate their boots. Their commanders screamed themselves hoarse, yet thunder swallowed their orders whole.

Danica's fire carved into the ground before them, opening a fissure that bled flame like the earth's own wound. They stumbled back, some falling straight into the blaze, their screams cutting through the storm like knives through silk. She advanced one deliberate step at a time, her face painted with ash and rain, every movement calculated vengeance. Ice formed where raindrops kissed her skin, frost etching her arms in jagged patterns, while the fire roared hotter still. She was burning herself alive to keep burning them.

The storm was trying to hollow me out from the inside. Each lightning strike ripped something loose in my chest, like invisible claws tearing marrow from bone. My breath came in broken gasps, iron flooding the back of my throat. Rain plastered my clothes to my body, heavy as burial shrouds, while the wind still tore at me, begging me to unleash it harder, faster, until there was nothing left of this place except ash and memory.

A squad of soldiers rushed forward, bayonets gleaming, boots pounding through mud that splashed like blood. I swept my hand and the wind obeyed with vicious joy. It grabbed them sideways, slammed them into each other like toys, armor crunching against armor, their screams dying as the gale pinned them flat against the earth. Lightning finished what wind started, leaving smoking metal and meat that had forgotten how to be human.

The resistance still hadn't moved. I caught glimpses of them through the chaos, a boy clutching his rifle like it was his mother's hand, face white as fresh bone; a woman with blood painting her cheek, mouth moving in some litany I couldn't hear yet knew by heart. My name. My damn name.

Ilija.

It spread through them like plague, low at first, then building, until I could hear it threading under the thunder. Some voices cracked with awe, others with terror so pure it made my teeth ache. My name passed from mouth to mouth until it filled the valley like smoke, and I wanted to claw it out of the air, wanted silence, wanted the storm to drown it all, yet their voices clung to me like chains I couldn't break.

The Accord tried one more time. Another carrier lurched forward, treads chewing the ground into black sludge. Its turret swiveled toward Danica, spitting fire and hate. I reached deep, every muscle screaming protest, and lightning answered. It hit the machine center mass, the explosion blooming fire and twisted steel across the battlefield. The shockwave flattened men like wheat, fragments spinning through the air, jagged and red-hot, burying themselves in mud and flesh with wet, final sounds.

Danica moved with fury that made my ribs ache in sympathy. Her hair whipped around her face as she hurled another ice spear, shattering a squad into component pieces. She screamed with the effort, something primal and raw, and flame rolled after the ice, consuming everything until steam and the memory of men remained. Her body shook like she was coming apart at the seams, yet she kept moving forward, hands clenched into fists that glowed with frost and fire both.

The battlefield reeked of ash and copper. Rain hissed where it touched hot steel, steam rising in phantom columns. The Accord's bodies, some still twitching, others already sinking into the earth's hungry embrace. The air was thick, hot and cold in the same breath, my lungs fighting to process it. Every inhalation tasted of blood and smoke and the acrid bite of burned dreams.

The Accord was completely shattered. Men screamed, stumbling over each other, shoving comrades aside, scrambling through earth that. Their perfect black line dissolved into scattered bodies, some running, some falling, no one willing to stand against what we'd become.

Finally, the resistance moved. A cry went up, rough and primal, and they surged forward like a dam bursting. They fired into the backs of fleeing soldiers, stabbed with bayonets, swung rifles like clubs. Their rage broke its leash, voices joining the storm in a chorus of six years' worth of swallowed fury.

Over it all, cutting through everything, I heard them chanting my name. Shouted, screamed like it was prayer and curse wrapped in one bleeding package. *Ilija. Ilija. Ilija.* Each repetition a hammer blow against my skull.

The storm inside me didn't want to stop. It wanted to tear the whole valley apart, rip the sky down to its bones and scatter the pieces. My body convulsed, every nerve on fire, every vein running lightning instead of blood, yet I pushed harder, sent one final crack of thunder across the plain.

Finally, silence. Rain drumming on the dead.

Bodies lay scattered like broken dolls, smoking, slowly disappearing into the muck. Fire smoldered in patches, smoke twisting upward in lazy spirals. The resistance stood frozen with rifles in their hands, faces painted with mud and blood and something that might have been shock. They stared at me with expressions frozen on their faces. Some with awe, some with fear, none with any certainty that I was still human.

My chest heaved and my vision blurred red at the edges. The storm still clawed at my insides, begging for more destruction, yet I forced my hands to stop shaking. Blood ran from my nose, down my lips, mixing with rainwater until I couldn't tell where I ended and the storm began. Iron coated my tongue, and tremors ran through my bones like aftershocks.

Danica came to me on unsteady legs, swaying with exhaustion, eyes still burning with residual power. She couldn't speak, what words could possibly fit this moment? She just reached for my hand, fingers trembling, and I gripped back like she was the only real thing left in the world. Her palm was blistered raw, skin peeled and weeping, yet she held on like our connection was the last anchor keeping us tethered to something recognizably human.

The valley held its breath and stared.

The whispers, our names, over and over, they didn't stop. They never stopped.

Because this was what we were now. Storm and flame, the answer to their prayers, the price of pushing people past their breaking point. We'd given them what they needed, yet in doing so, we'd become something that made them afraid to blink.

The rain kept falling. The dead kept sinking into the earth. I could hear more engines, more boots, more voices that didn't yet know what was waiting for them.

Let them come. The storm was still hungry, and I was done pretending to be anything other than what this war had made me.

The man's words hit like a sledgehammer to the chest. "We buried your names years ago."

The resistance surrounded us in a broken circle, weapons trembling between raised and lowered, their eyes wild with worship and murder tangled together. Mud caked their boots thick as cement, rain carving channels through faces painted with ash and blood. Some wept openly, tears and stormwater indistinguishable, while others clenched their jaws so hard I could hear teeth grinding like millstones.

Danica's hand shook in mine, her skin fever-hot where the fire had kissed her too deeply. She stood like a statue made of coiled wire, shoulders drawn tight enough to snap, breath coming in shallow gasps. I felt her rage straining against the silence, the same fury that had carried her through every field we'd burned together.

The man swayed on his feet; bandaged arm clutched against his ribs like he was holding his guts in. His eyes were raw red, beard gone gray with grief and years. He stared at me like I was a corpse that had forgotten to lie down.

"You don't understand," he rasped, voice cracking down the middle. "We buried your names. We burned for them. We bled for them. And still the years took more than the Accord ever could. It's been six years since Danica was killed, double that for you, Ilija. And still we fought on."

Behind him, voices rose like smoke. Some whispered our names like it was sacred, others spat curses that cut through the rain. Their rifles twitched in white-knuckled grips. The air between us stretched thin as wire, one spark from snapping completely.

I tried to speak yet the words turned to dust in my throat. The weight of it sat on my chest like a tombstone. The orchard had given us back our bodies, yet time? Time was gone forever.

Danica stepped forward, her voice cracking with pure, undiluted fury. "We didn't choose this. You think we wanted to abandon you? To disappear while you held the line and died for it?" Her teeth showed white against her mud-streaked face, chest heaving, fire still dancing around her wrists like living jewelry. "We were ripped away. We fought to get back. And now we're here."

The man flinched yet didn't break eye contact. Around us, the resistance shifted like a pack of wolves deciding whether to submit or tear us apart. Their grief, their disbelief, their desperate hope all tangled together until the air felt thick enough to drown in.

I squeezed Danica's hand tighter, feeling bones grind. The storm inside me crouched low, watching, waiting for the word. Lightning still crawled along my nerves, and I could feel their eyes tracking every spark, every flicker of power that marked me as something more and less than human.

Every face in the valley leaned closer, hunting for an answer to the question none of them had the courage to speak out loud: Was I Ilija, the man they'd mourned? Or something else wearing his corpse?

The silence swelled until it felt like the storm had just moved from sky to ground. Rain hammered on metal and bone, each drop sharp enough to cut. The resistance circled us in ragged lines, eyes bright as fever in the gloom.

The boy who'd first whispered my name stumbled forward. His rifle shook so hard I thought he'd drop it. Couldn't have been older than sixteen, mud painting his thin frame, lips split and bleeding from cold. "It's him," he whispered, then louder, voice breaking like glass. "I saw him. The lightning came out of him like he was God's own fury." His eyes darted to Danica, wide with awe and terror. "I saw her too. Fire and ice in the same breath. It's them."

The older man whirled on him, voice raw with grief turned toxic. "Shut your damn mouth, boy. You saw tricks. You saw demons wearing names we buried in good earth." His bandaged hand shook where it pressed his wound. He turned back to me, jaw quivering with rage that had nowhere left to go. "You know how many nights I prayed for this? For your return? You know how many children grew up waiting for you to come back and save them from this hell? Six years, Ilija. Six years of graves we dug with our bare hands."

The words cut deeper than shrapnel. My gut twisted, the storm inside surging with shame that had nowhere to be discharged. Six years, spoken like a curse, each syllable heavy as a coffin.

Another voice joined the chorus, a woman whose face was painted red with blood and rain. She limped forward; hair plastered to her skull like seaweed. Her rifle hung by threads of cloth, barrel warped from heat. "If it's really them, then where the hell were you?" Her voice shattered, cracking into raw grief. "Where were you when my husband starved in a ditch? When my boy died choking on smoke in Delphi? Where the hell were you when we needed you most?"

The words spread like wildfire through drought grass. Others began screaming, voices shaking the valley walls, years of swallowed rage finally erupting.

"You left us alone!" "We mourned you!" "We fought alone while you played dead!"

Some howled their curses, others sobbed as they spoke. A few clung to the boy's trembling faith, crying our names like prayers to deaf gods, yet their voices drowned in the flood of anger.

Danica's grip burned with heat, knuckles white as bone. I felt her pulse hammering like a war drum, fury straining against the tide of grief washing over us. I held on tighter, grounding us both before we got swept away.

I wanted to scream back. To tell them about Ana, about the rift, about the orchard and the gods who'd stolen years we never meant to lose. Yet every excuse rotted in my throat before it could form words.

I was here. They had suffered. That was the only truth that mattered to them.

The boy dropped to his knees, mud splashing up his legs like a dark baptism. His rifle slipped from nerveless fingers and hit earth with a wet thud. He pressed his hands together, shaking so hard his fingers barely laced, lips moving around my name repeatedly until it became something else, a prayer spoken through tears and snot and years of stored-up hope.

That broke the dam. Half the resistance lurched forward, rifles rising, eyes narrowing to slits. The other half froze, their grief and rage caught between disbelief and the fragile hope clawing its way up through all that accumulated mud and misery.

The air grew sharp, electric, that moment right before lightning splits the world.

All of it pressed down on me, heavy enough to drive me to my knees beside the praying boy.

Because what do you say to people who've been dying in your name for years? What words exist for that kind of debt?

The storm inside me whispered suggestions, all of them violent. Yet I looked at their faces, really looked, and saw myself reflected in every scar, every lost tooth, every premature line carved by grief and stubborn survival.

They were what I'd become in my absence. They were the price of leaving, even when leaving wasn't our choice.

And they deserved better than excuses from a man who commanded lightning yet couldn't command time.

The shouting had reached fever pitch. A man lunged forward, rifle raised, spittle flying as he screamed for us to be cut down before the Accord's witchery spread like plague. Others grabbed him, yanked him back, their own hands shaking on their weapons. Half the resistance looked ready to drop to their knees, the other half ready to put bullets in our skulls.

Then a voice sliced through the chaos like a blade through flesh.

"Stand the hell down!"

The crowd rippled, heads snapping around. Through the wall of bodies, a figure shoved her way forward, limping with a gait that spoke of old wounds and older stubbornness.

Petra.

I knew before my brain caught up with my eyes. Her face was older, harder, a scar carved down her jaw like a badge of survival. Years had pressed lines around her mouth deep as knife cuts, and her hair, once bound in a soldier's knot, was streaked with ash-gray like smoke had settled permanently in the strands. She wore a battered coat too large for her shoulders, its hem shredded by years of crawling through hell. Her rifle hung across her back, the strap dark with sweat and rain and things that didn't wash out.

She pushed through until she stood between us and the mob, her presence pulling the storm of voices into brittle silence.

Her eyes found me first. For a heartbeat she went statue-still, breath catching like the sight had torn her clean in half. She blinked hard, once, twice, then turned on the crowd with pure fury in her voice.

"You think you know ghosts? You think you'd be standing here breathing if these two hadn't fought for every breath you take?" She stabbed a finger at the man with the bandaged arm. "You want to question where they've been? Fine. Ask your questions. Yet you aim those guns at them, and I'll put bullets in every one of you myself."

The man stumbled backward, jaw working soundlessly. Petra didn't give him space to recover. She swept her gaze across the rest, the grieving, the kneeling, the ones ready to murder us for the crime of returning.

"They're real," she said, voice dropping lower, steadier, though it still shook at the edges like a plucked wire. "I don't give a damn how many years you think have crawled by. I don't care what lies the Accord fed you. I know them. I buried their names too, yet I never stopped waiting for them to dig their way back out."

Her eyes turned back to me. This time she didn't blink. The storm between us went quiet, her stare pinning me to the mud like a blade through my chest.

"Ilija," she said, voice cracking down the middle. "It's been over a decade, honey. Danica, my friend, how the fuck are you two here?"

We both responded, "It's a hell of a story."

Petra's voice cracked again, softer, almost a whisper that somehow cut through everything. "She's waiting for you, both of you."

Selene.

CHAPTER TWENTY-THREE
THE FOX

Ilija

The name Petra gave me cracked something wide open inside my chest. My knees buckled, my breath tore in and out too sharp, too fast. Heat flooded my ribs until I thought they'd split apart, lightning writhing under my skin in jagged lines that set my hands shaking like a drunk's. My knuckles went white around Danica's grip, rain sliding down our joined fingers until I couldn't tell where her blood ended and mine began.

The storm answered without being called. Thunder rolled across the fields, soft instead of sharp, undeniable, like the sky itself had leaned close to eavesdrop. My vision blurred, wet from tears instead of rain, cutting hot tracks through the grime painting my face. I bit hard on the inside of my cheek and tasted iron mixing with salt.

Danica felt it. She pressed closer, breath hitching ragged against my shoulder, her fire meeting my storm until the air between us shook like a struck bell. Her lips moved, shaping the start of words that died before they found voice. Her eyes, red and swollen, searched mine with disbelief so raw it felt like being flayed alive all over again.

The resistance faded to background noise. Their shouting dulled to white static; their rifles blurred into shadows at the edge of sight. All I could see was Petra's scarred face, rain clinging to her lashes, grief and defiance carved there as she handed me back what had been stolen.

And underneath everything, like the faintest hum beneath thunder's roar, I felt something I hadn't in years. It lodged in my throat, burning, searing like swallowing live coals. My heart slammed against my ribs, with rage, with despair, with something crueler and more unbearable.

Hope.

That bastard emotion I'd thought finally dead, crawling back up out of whatever grave I'd put it in. Hope that she was alive. Hope that maybe years lost hadn't been enough to kill what we'd built. Hope that maybe, just maybe, I could still be the man who would have kissed her goodbye instead of the storm-wracked thing standing in the mud with other people's blood under his fingernails.

The cruelest hope of all, that going home might mean something.

"Tell me." My voice cracked, raw as exposed bone. "Tell me everything. Where she is, what she looks like, if she—" My chest seized, words shattering like glass. "If she's safe."

Petra's mouth went tight as a scar. She glanced once at Danica, then back to me. Rain streaked her damaged cheek, yet her eyes stayed locked on mine, and in them I saw the silence of carrying weight that could crush mountains.

Danica's hand trembled in mine. She doubled over like the ground had punched her in the gut, one hand pressed against her stomach as if to keep something vital from tearing loose. Tears cut tracks down her face, salt mixing with blood at her jaw.

"Ilija," she whispered, yet the rest died in her throat.

Petra stepped closer, close enough that I could see the lines carved deep around her mouth, mud caked thick on her boots, the way her shoulders sagged with exhaustion she'd never admit to carrying. Her voice came low, too soft for the crowd that still bristled behind her like a pack of confused wolves.

"She's alive."

My breath shattered.

"She's taller now," Petra continued, words careful and steady like laying stones over fresh graves. "Hair red like yours, always falling into her eyes. Walks like she owns every step she takes. Stubborn as hell. Loud when she's angry. Quiet when the shadows come calling." Petra swallowed hard, throat working around something that wanted to choke her. "She looks at the world like it owes her answers. Just like you do."

The storm surged inside me, lightning crawling under my skin until standing still felt like torture. I bent forward, palms pressed over my eyes, a sound ripping out of me that I couldn't hold back. It was both, guttural and broken, the sound of a man who'd been handed back what he thought had turned to ash years ago.

Danica collapsed against me, clutching my side, sobbing like someone had reached inside and torn her heart out with bare hands. Petra just stood there, face carved from grief and defiance, letting the rain fall heavy between us.

Behind us, the resistance muttered and shifted, guns lowering, confusion still spreading through their ranks like cracks in stone. They didn't know what had been said. They couldn't. This moment belonged to us alone.

"She's alive," Petra said again, hammering the truth into me like nails. "And she's more than alive. She fights, she runs, she argues with the damn wind if it doesn't blow the way she wants."

My chest burned. Breath scraped out in broken gasps.

She dragged a hand over her mouth, steadying herself, and when she spoke again her voice dropped almost to reverence. "She climbs the ruins like they're her personal playground. Every wall, every broken column, she's up and over before anyone can tell her no. Once she fell hard enough to split her lip wide open, blood everywhere, and she laughed at me for fussing. She told me it didn't hurt even though I could see her shaking." A ghost of a smile cracked across Petra's scarred face, raw and unguarded. "She's got your stubborn streak, Ilija. Both of yours. Doubled and twisted into something fiercer."

Danica's grip crushed my hand, her nails digging crescents into my skin. Her sobs came harder, bent her shoulders until she was nearly folded in half.

Petra's eyes softened, though the grief behind them never dimmed. "She sings sometimes. Little threads of sound, like she's weaving something only she can hear. Hums when she's half-asleep, soothing herself. It's low, steady, cuts right through a camp full of noise until everyone stops to listen. No one says it out loud, yet I've seen hardened bastards cry listening to her, Ilija. She quiets them without even knowing she's doing it."

Lightning burned white tracks up my arms. I couldn't breathe. Couldn't move.

"She won't wear shoes," Petra went on, voice gaining strength. "Runs barefoot more often than dressed feet. Says she needs to feel the earth, or she gets restless. Burns bread every damn time she tries to bake it yet never stops trying. Won't let failure beat her down." Petra's mouth twisted, bitter pride tightening her scar. "When she was eight, she told an Accord officer who caught her scavenging that he was wrong about the stars, because she'd counted them herself. Right there, chin up, daring him to argue with a child.

He hit her for it. She didn't cry. Just stared him down until he walked away first."

These same stories Danica had told me in Asgard destroyed my heart, I was broken.

Petra's voice cracked, words rasping like gravel underfoot. "She asks about you both. Sometimes she stares at doors like she knows they're supposed to open. Sometimes she talks to shadows like they'll carry her words wherever you are. And when she smiles, gods, when she smiles, it feels like the whole war pauses to take a breath."

Her voice shattered on the last word. She bit down hard, forcing that soldier's mask back over her face. Yet her hands shook at her sides like leaves in a storm.

The world blurred. Rain streaked my vision, except it wasn't rain anymore. My whole body convulsed with it, sobs clawing their way up from somewhere deep and primitive until they tore free. Danica collapsed against me completely, her tears soaking through my shirt, her cries raw and endless.

Selene lived in Petra's words. She lived and breathed and sang and climbed and argued with the wind, and we had missed all of it.

First words and scraped knees and bedtime stories told by strangers. Her growing up without us, learning to be brave in a world that wanted to crush that brightness out of her, waiting for doors that never opened, talking to shadows that never answered back.

The cruelest part wasn't that we'd lost time. It was that she'd lived through it all, magnificent and stubborn and alive, while we'd been gone. She'd become a person we'd never met, built from pieces of us yet shaped by hands that weren't ours.

And now we had to figure out how to be parents to a child who'd learned to survive without us.

The resistance had gone silent, eyes fixed on us like we were something that had crawled out of their nightmares.

Danica's cries cut through the quiet, sharp and raw, each hitting like a physical blow.

A murmur started in the crowd. My name passed from mouth to mouth, hesitant at first, then gaining strength. "Ilija." "Ilija." "Ilija."

It spread until the whole ragged line of fighters chanting it, half-believing, half-afraid. Their voices tangled with the rain, fragile as spider webs, heavy as tombstones.

Yet there were others, men and women who'd been forged in years of blood and loss. Their faces stayed hard. Eyes narrowed with suspicion sharp as knife points. A few lifted rifles again, slow and deliberate, sights settling on my chest like death's own promise.

One stepped forward, a scarred veteran with a jaw like broken granite. His voice cut through rain and grief alike. "Is this some kind of trick? Accord witchcraft?" He spat in the mud, eyes boring into me. "You're a ghost, or something worse."

Danica tore herself from my chest, fire blazing in her eyes even through the wreckage of her tears. "Does a ghost bleed?" she snarled, ripping back her sleeve to show cuts still weeping on her arm, blood smeared down her wrist like war paint. "Does a damn ghost burn alongside you?"

The fighters wavered. Some stumbled back a step; others tightened their grips. The storm crackled louder, feeding off her fury, the sharp smell of electricity cutting through mud and blood and fear.

Petra stepped between us, shoulders squared like she was facing down an army instead of broken people with broken faith. She raised her hand, palm open, voice steady enough to freeze the air itself. "They are no ghosts," she said, each word dropping like a stone into still water. "They are ours."

The words hit the crowd like artillery. Some shattered instantly, dropping weapons, falling to their knees in the mud, heads bowed like penitents. Others held their ground, mistrust carved deep in their faces, yet they didn't pull triggers.

The field was a wound barely held together by spit and prayer. And I was standing in the center of it, drenched in rain and crackling with power, with Danica's fire burning beside me and Petra's voice the only thing keeping us all from bleeding out.

The silence stretched taut as a bowstring. One wrong word, one sudden movement, and everything would snap. Half of them wanted to worship us, the other half wanted us dead, and the space between those two impulses was thinner than paper.

I could feel the storm wanting to choose for them. It whispered suggestions in my bones, how easy it would be to scatter the doubters, to turn skeptics into believers through simple, brutal demonstration. Lightning begged to be unleashed, wind howled to be set free.

Instead, I forced my hands to still. Let the rain wash blood from my face. Looked into the eyes of people who'd survived six years of hell and found us standing in the wreckage like some twisted fairy tale come true.

"I don't blame you for doubting," I said, voice hoarse from screaming and storm-calling and years of silence. "I don't blame you for burying our names. You did what you had to do to keep breathing."

Some faces softened. Others hardened further.

"Yet we're here now," I continued, feeling each word cost something I couldn't afford to lose. "We're real. We're here. And we are here to fucking end this goddamn war."

That's what we were now, products of violence, shaped by loss, powered by grief turned weapon. They wanted to know if we were still human. Hell, I wasn't sure myself.

Yet we were theirs. That much was true as rain and mud and the taste of iron in my mouth.

The rest would have to be enough.

Before Petra's words could settle, a voice drifted from the envoys near the ruined stone wall. Calm, low, with that northern weight that made people lean in without realizing they'd been hooked.

"Petra speaks with courage," Lemminkäinen said, stepping into the torchlight until rain slicked across his sharp cheekbones like oil. His cloak hung wet against him, a gray shadow bleeding into the night. "Yet we should all remember what we've lost. How many leaders have risen, claimed to be our salvation, only to leave us shattered?" His pale eyes found mine, steady as a predator measuring prey. "Do we dare place our faith again in someone who vanished when we needed him most?"

The words hit hard. Heads swiveled between Lemminkäinen and me, suspicion crawling back across their faces like infection.

Danica bristled beside me, shoulders squaring, mouth opening with venom already burning her tongue. Yet Lemminkäinen's gaze slid past her like she was smoke, meaningless. His eyes locked mine, and in them I saw it, an invitation wrapped in challenge. Prove yourself or fall, framed in a voice that sounded like reason, like concern.

The bastard was working to pull the ground out from under me without lifting a finger. The battlefield bent toward him like iron drawn to a lodestone.

"Six years is a long time," he continued, rain tracing the line of his jaw. "Long enough for graves to be dug, for children to grow without fathers, for whole towns to disappear under the Accord's boot. We bled while you were…dead…gone?" His eyes never left mine, though his words were for the crowd. "And now you return at the exact moment we're cornered, when defeat sits thick in our mouths. It's... convenient."

The murmur spread like disease, uneasy voices carrying doubt like plague.

Danica's breath hissed beside me. Her hand went to her blade, rage sparking like struck flint. Yet Lemminkäinen's gaze swept past her again, steady, deliberate, dismissing her fury like it wasn't worth acknowledgment.

"Perhaps this is no miracle," he went on, softer now, words pressing into silence like a blade twisting slowly. "Perhaps this is Accord work. Perhaps what you see isn't Ilija at all, perhaps something crafted to break you. Wouldn't that be the cleverest cruelty?"

Unease shuddered through the fighters. I felt every stare weighing me, measuring, doubting. Lightning stirred restlessly in my chest, begging to be unleashed, to burn the doubt away.

Lemminkäinen tilted his head, rain dripping from his hood's edge. His mouth curved, something like satisfaction wearing the shape of concern. "We have to be careful who we kneel to," he said softly, almost kindly. "Some storms bring rain. Others only destroy."

The pressure broke inside me. The storm tore loose from where I'd caged it, lightning ripping hot through my veins until my teeth ached. Air around me shivered. The sharp smell of electricity clawed every throat in the square. Men flinched as their hair rose, weapons humming faintly like struck tuning forks.

"Careful," Lemminkäinen murmured, fearless, motionless. His pale eyes gleamed. "There it is. The truth beneath the skin."

The storm wanted to answer him. My hands curled, white bolts crawling up my arms, snapping between my fingers. Rain hissed to steam where it touched me. Clouds above churned black and heavy.

Danica slammed against me, grip bruising my arm. "Ilija." Her voice cut sharp as broken glass, yet underneath was desperation. "Don't."

"He's playing you," she hissed, dragging her face close enough that her breath burned through thunder. "That's what he wants. You torch this field and he wins."

Lemminkäinen tilted his head, calm as a priest, cloak soaked, rain streaming down his face. The crowd shifted around him, torn between fear and awe, ready to run or kneel or shoot. His voice slipped through the chaos, silk-smooth, poisonous.

"Do you see it?" he asked them all, raising one hand, palm open. "This is no man. This is the Accord's weapon made flesh. A god built to terrify you. And if you let him loose, he'll tear you apart as surely as they would."

Lightning cracked, blinding white, striking mud two strides from his feet. Ground split, steam roared up, air shrieked with power too long denied. I wanted to kill him. Every bone screamed for it.

Danica shoved me back, teeth bared, her whole body straining to hold me though she couldn't match a fraction of the storm. "Ilija! Look at me!"

I did. For one heartbeat. Her face, streaked with rain and tears, fierce with terror and fury, cut through the storm. She was the tether. Always the tether.

Lemminkäinen smiled then, slow, deliberate, the mask slipping just enough. Something else bled through the cracks, old, sly hunger wearing human skin.

His voice dropped to something heavier, older than the calm envoy he'd been playing.

"Ah," he said, and the word slithered like oil on water. "So, the storm remembers its leash."

The crowd gasped. Some stumbled back, muttering prayers, clutching charms. Others froze, eyes wide, recognizing something in his voice older than the names he wore.

The air around Lemminkäinen shimmered faintly, cloak twisting like it moved in wind no one else could feel. For a moment his shadow split, antlers arching and curling like black branches before snapping back into place. His smile gleamed white and cruel, ancient mischief wearing human teeth.

The Finnish trickster god stood before us, no longer hiding, his words still dripping honey. His presence now undeniable as winter's bite.

Danica's breath catching as recognition hit. Around us, the resistance began to understand they were watching something far older than war play out in the mud and rain.

And Lemminkäinen, whatever his true name was, smiled like he'd been waiting centuries for this moment.

The shimmer thickened around him, warping torchlight, bending rain into impossible angles. For a heartbeat his outline blurred, and in that blur,

I saw him as he truly was; the cocksure grin of a bastard who'd charmed his way into beds and thrones alike. The fox's hunger burning in his eyes, the stench of blood and conquest clinging to him like expensive perfume. His shadow writhed again, stretching, sprouting antlers that scraped wet stone before collapsing back into something that only pretended to be human.

Someone in the crowd whispered, voice cracking like thin ice, "Lemminkäinen."

The name spread like wildfire through dry kindling.

Lemminkäinen only laughed, soft and pleased, like he was delighted the mask had finally slipped. "It's been too fucking long since I was named here," he said, and though his voice stayed velvet-smooth, it carried the weight of river ice breaking in spring floods. "The old songs remember, don't they? The reckless one, the fox among hounds. I walk where I please, and I am never bound by anything except my own appetites."

His eyes gleamed as they found mine again, hungry and amused. "Storm-bringer," he said, almost tender, almost cruel as a lover's bite. "You were so close to giving me what I wanted. One little strike, and you'd have burned them all. Their fear would have sealed my place among them like a brand."

Lightning convulsed in my chest. My fists shook like I had palsy. "Don't," Danica hissed through gritted teeth. "Don't throw everything away, there will be another time."

The crowd murmured louder, the name echoing off stone walls, fear growing thick as smoke. Some partisans began backing away. Others looked to Petra, to Danica, to me, waiting for someone to steady the earth before it swallowed them whole.

Lemminkäinen stood calm in the chaos, rain streaming down his pale face, that faint curve of his smile steady as death. He'd sown doubt, and he knew it had taken root. "Choose carefully, children," he murmured to the gathered fighters. "Gods wear many skins, and storms don't ask permission before they drown you."

Danica's hand slid from my arm, and for a heartbeat I thought she'd let me burn the smug fuck to ash. She stepped forward, shoulders squared, her braid slick with rain down her back, eyes locked on Lemminkäinen with fury I'd seen break men twice his size.

"You arrogant piece of shit," she spat, voice cutting through the storm like a blade through flesh. "You come here, wear the skin of an envoy, poison every word to make my people doubt themselves, and you think I'll let you walk away?"

Her sword flashed in her hand before I'd even seen her draw it, steel catching every lightning strike overhead, turning her into a figure carved from pure stormlight and rage. She lunged, fast and merciless, driving straight for his throat.

Lemminkäinen's smile deepened. He didn't move until the blade nearly kissed his skin. He flowed aside, fox-slick, cloak snapping in wind. Her strike carved sparks off stone, and he laughed, a low, taunting sound that made my teeth ache.

The crowd scattered in panic, some stumbling into mud, others raising rifles only to hesitate, refusing to fire with a god in their sights. My storm surged higher, answering her rage, lightning crawling down my arms like living things, thunder building in my lungs until I thought they'd burst.

"Danica!" I shouted, forcing the storm to heel, dragging it back into my chest before it roasted the whole resistance where they cowered. I spread my hands wide, power leashing itself into a dome above us, a barrier of crackling air that kept the storm coiled tight to my bones. My arms trembled with the strain of holding back hell itself. "I've got them covered! You take that bastard apart!"

Danica's eyes flicked to me, one heartbeat, enough to show she understood. She was on him again, blade flashing in brutal arcs, curses spilling between each swing like prayers to violent gods. "You think you can crawl into our ranks, into our hearts? You'll never have us. You'll never fucking have him."

Her blade sang against his conjured steel, a dagger appearing in his hand like it had been there since the world began, curved and cruel, runes writhing across its edge like living tattoos. Sparks flew as they clashed, each blow hard enough to crack the stones beneath our feet. He danced around her strikes, grinning, movements all sly grace, every parry a mockery, every dodge another needle of doubt thrown at the watching crowd.

Yet, Danica didn't relent. Her fury made her relentless, strikes wild and savage, hammering at him until the grin began to falter, until the fox-gleam in his eyes dimmed with the effort of keeping her from opening his throat like a letter.

Behind her, the resistance cowered beneath the storm's edge. I planted myself between them and the fight, lightning running molten through my veins, forcing thunder to arc outward, away from them. My body shook with barely contained power, yet I held the line, teeth bared, eyes locked on the trickster god.

"You wanted fear," I growled, voice echoing with thunder that could level mountains, "yet all you've got is her wrath."

Lemminkäinen staggered back under the weight of her assault, cloak torn, dagger flashing just short of her ribs. His laughter cracked, strained, yet still he grinned through blood on his lip. "Ah, lovers," he hissed, slipping sideways from another swing that would have taken his head clean off. "Always so predictable. Always so delicious to break into pieces."

"Then fucking try," Danica snarled, blade crashing down, sparks leaping like fireflies around them both.

The crowd no longer looked to him for guidance. Their eyes burned on her, on me holding back the storm, on the wall we made together between them and this false prophet revealed.

And for the first time since he'd stepped into the torchlight, I saw it flash across Lemminkäinen's face, worry. Real concern that he'd misjudged us. That he hadn't found cracks to exploit, yet a wall built from shared fury.

Danica's sword cut a burning line across his cheek. Blood welled dark against pale skin, the first true mark anyone had struck on him. The grin faltered, twisted, and for a breath the square held perfect silence. The resistance stared, gods could bleed after all.

Lemminkäinen's eyes narrowed, fox-bright, rage flashing beneath his mask of amusement. He stepped back, cloak folding around him like shadow made flesh. "Ah," he whispered, voice curling through the air like poisonous smoke, "so the storm and his fierce bitch still remember how to dance together. How touching. I do so love prey that fights back."

Danica raised her blade again, teeth bared like wolves, yet he was already fading, outline unraveling into threads of black and silver. Rain seemed to swallow him, torchlight bending until he was nothing except a trick of storm and shadow.

His voice lingered as the last trace of him dissolved into night. "I'll see you again, lovers. And when I do, I'll take more than your storms and steel. I'll take what keeps your hearts beating."

Then he was gone like he'd never been there at all.

The square held its breath. The storm still clawed at my insides, yet I forced it down, letting it drain back into my chest until only natural rain remained. My knees buckled under the weight of holding back that much power, yet I stayed upright because they needed to see me standing.

Danica turned, chest heaving like she'd run miles, eyes still blazing, blade dripping rain and divine blood. Petra's voice cracked first, raw and shaking: "He's a fucking god."

"No," Danica said, voice iron wrapped in contempt, eyes still locked on the place he'd vanished. "He's a coward who hides behind tricks and whispers. And cowards always come crawling back."

The resistance murmured, fear still thick as fog, yet I saw something else in their faces now, awe that had nothing to do with terror. For her. For us. For the fact that we'd made a god bleed and sent him running.

Night closed back around us, heavy with smoke and storm and the taste of divine blood in the air. The game had changed completely. We all knew it.

And when I finally let my hands fall, lightning still flickering across my knuckles like dying embers, I knew this was only the beginning of something that would reshape everything we thought we knew about gods and mortals and the spaces where they collide.

CHAPTER TWENTY-FOUR
THE FOX AND THE ROSE

Ana

He came to me as dusk bled crimson through the high windows of my sanctuary, the sky a wound torn wide and weeping copper over the ravaged city. Below, the corridors still reeked of aftermath, ash and melted plastic, the acrid bite of circuitry that had died screaming under the crushing weight of defeat. His footsteps were whispers against the Numidian marble, secrets spilled on stone, yet I had already drunk his scent from the air like a forbidden wine. A vintage I knew, sweat sharp as a lightning strike, pine dark as forgotten oaths sworn in sunless forests, and the fine grit of dust that tasted of ancient battlefields where gods had once walked and bled. Fresh blood painted his cheek in a lover's caress where steel had kissed and abandoned him. The fine wool of his jacket hung from his frame like a broken wing, the shirt beneath torn open, revealing a landscape of skin I had yet to claim. When he bowed, it was transformation; submission had become his sharpest weapon.

"Alive," he breathed, the word flowing through those hard northern vowels like honey poured over broken glass. Each syllable was a finely honed barb, sinking its claws beneath my flesh. "Both of them. Ilija and the frost-queen. Together."

The sound that escaped my throat was breath transformed into a growl; a resonance of power that made the sconces on the walls gutter as if my rage had become a physical wind. In the polished floor, the veins of dark marble seemed to pulse with a sudden, sympathetic fire. His name rose in my throat like molten gold, Ilija, and with it came the vision that has devoured my waking hours and haunted my sleep across millennia: the stubborn carve of his mouth, made for defiance; the deep furrow between his brows when he still believed, with an earnestness that broke my heart, that he could forge a world worthy of his own impossible mercy. He had been mine before cities learned to burn, before men learned to write laws to replace gods. He should have remained cupped in my palms like captured starlight, a private constellation. Danica was a blade that had learned to sing its own hymns of destruction, a shard of winter given a voice.

"Lies," I snarled, the word tearing from me, though the truth was laid bare in his fox-bright eyes, naked and unforgiving as a blade's edge. He did not flinch. He straightened, a slow uncoiling of strength, and the torn collar of his shirt revealed a throat still flushed with the fever of flight, the pulse a frantic bird beating against its cage.

"You knew before the words left my tongue," he purred, his voice a low counterpoint to my fury. "The Accord's dogs are already panting with the rumors. They whisper of what their scouts witnessed on the fields of Vojvodina. Fire and storm wed in terrible beauty. They say it was the return of divinity. Or perhaps, two divinities." His mouth curved, a predatory and knowing shape, and a fresh bead of blood welled from the split in his lower lip. He tasted it with a flick of his tongue. "They will howl the tale across every border, from the Urals to the Pillars of Hercules, unless we teach them a more compelling lesson in silence."

I crossed the vast chamber, my bare feet silent on the stone. The marble, which had drunk the blood of a thousand betrayals and absorbed the tears of deposed kings, seemed to warm beneath my soles as if it were a lover's skin, welcoming my tread. They were my floors; they sang a familiar song of power as I approached my prey. My hand shot out, seizing the ruined collar of his shirt, and I drove him backward against a massive Doric column with a force that belonged to older ages. The stone shrieked in protest, a high, grinding sound of molecules forced to reconsider their allegiance. A fine, white dust, the ghost of the marble, fell like snow around us, delicate and deadly. His head snapped to the side with the impact, while his eyes remained clear, calculating, measuring the trajectory of my rage, and perhaps, how far I would let myself fall with it.

"Why come here, Lemminkäinen?" I whispered, my voice silk wrapped around a core of steel, my breath ghosting across the blood on his cheek. "Why crawl back to Aphrodite's throne when you know I could unmake you molecule by molecule and call it a final act of mercy?"

He turned his head slowly, meeting my gaze. The bleeding smile returned, holding within it a craft honed to a killing edge over centuries of diplomacy and deceit. "Because you need a fox who knows which henhouse deserves to be burned to the ground," he breathed, his chest rising and falling against mine. "Because you need eyes that saw them stand together, haloed in their combined power, and still chose to run back to you."

Beautiful liar. He was the kind of creature who tasted each word for weight and texture before letting it slip past his lips. I pressed closer, the thin silk of my peplos a whisper against the rough, torn cotton of his shirt.

He smelled of copper pennies and storm-washed pine, of winters that negotiate with no one and take what they will. For a single, suspended heartbeat, I saw two futures diverge before me: in one, Olympus, my seat of power, crumbled to dust beneath the weight of my unrestrained wrath; in the other, I saw endless northern fields where mothers learned to bury their children in graves too small to hold their dreams.

My mouth found his and devoured speech. It was punishment disguised as gift, claiming that was also desecration. I forced him down, pinned him against the cold marble like prey beneath a predator's claws. We fell like warring gods brought to earth, fucking like we meant to break something sacred, yet there was no question who ruled this altar. The ancient marble accepted our combined weight and answered with a spiderweb of fractures that raced across the floor toward my empty throne, like lightning seeking its grounding earth. His hands, sure and strong, found my hips only because I allowed it, anchoring himself to me as I claimed what was mine by the oldest right of all: hunger.

Silk screamed as it died, tearing between us. Buttons scattered like coins offered to a forgotten god, ringing against the stone feet of marble saints who had long forgotten how to look away. When he laughed, a raw, throaty sound, wild and triumphant, I bit the sound from his mouth and swallowed the iron-sweet taste of it. I carved new territories into the flesh of his back and shoulders with nails that had once traced constellations into being, my marks a testament to my ownership. I rode him like conquest itself, setting the pace, the depth, the angle of his surrender, until his breath shattered into something broken and sharp, filling the cavernous chamber like incense offered to violent, forgotten gods.

He was cunning even in surrender, matching my elemental ferocity with a chilling precision that turned my grief molten and weaponized it, yet always, always yielding to my will. He tasted of smoke and river ice, of ancient promises made in languages only the unforgiving north remembers. My hair, golden as spun sunlight, fell around us like a curtain, sticking to the damp skin of his throat where my teeth mapped the frantic rhythm of his pulse. That drumming beneath my tongue, the panicked beat of his life, I could set the tempo of his days, if I chose. I could stop it. And he knew it, arching beneath me like an offering on Aphrodite's altar.

"Say it," I commanded against his lips, my voice a rasp.

He obeyed without hesitation, Ilija's name breaking like a desperate prayer from his ruined mouth. Rage, clean and bright and purifying, bloomed in my chest. Then, just as quickly, it folded inward, collapsing into an ache too vast for any mortal tongue to name, a hollow carved out by millennia of wanting. I moved against him like a conquest, a relentless march through a city that had thought itself protected by the weight of its own history. He welcomed the siege, met my invasion with his own, and called it victory. When release finally claimed us both, it was a cataclysm that stole sound itself. The sconces flickered and died, plunging us into a momentary darkness, and I was certain the painted saints on the ceiling believed the world had finally learned its ending.

I rose from him without offering aid, sweat pearling on my skin like scattered stars in a midnight sky. A smear of blood marked my hip where his nails had carved their response, where flesh had pressed to make our wounds into sacraments. My hair clung, wild and untamed, to my face and throat. I left it as it was, a lioness who had been forced to remember her true nature. He sprawled at the base of the column, a beautiful ruin. His chest heaved like a blacksmith's bellows, his throat branded by my mouth, his shoulder blossoming into a deep purple bruise where I had tried to pin bone to stone. His diplomat's suit hung in ribbons that no earthly tailor could ever hope to mend. Yet he smiled, a languid, satisfied expression, as if he had received exactly what he had bargained for, and perhaps a little more.

"You bleed for me now," I said, my voice like ground glass sweetened with a drop of honey. "And you will serve me, Lemminkäinen. You will serve me with the patience of a fox and the devotion of a priest. Together, we will unmake the world they believe they have wrought."

He pushed himself up on one elbow, the grin sharpening to a blade's edge. "The fox runs where the rose grows wild," he answered, his voice still thick with the aftermath. "And even the most ancient gardens must learn to fear their own thorns."

I summoned the war council without washing his scent from my skin. Let them come to a goddess who had remained untamed, who refused the veneer of sterile authority. Let them breathe the air we had consecrated with violence and desire, and let them understand that they served a primal appetite as much as they served a grand strategy. The Praetorian guards opened the heavy bronze doors with faces of stone, their eyes trying desperately to ignore the web of fresh cracks spreading across the marble floor beneath our feet. They failed beautifully.

The bunker crouched beneath the bones of the old museum, a confession buried in holy ground. Here, the honesty of marble was replaced by the brutal pragmatism of reinforced concrete; exposed steel ribs held up a city that had forgotten how to properly worship its own architecture. Fluorescent lights buzzed overhead like flies drunk on carrion, stuttering each time my breath moved beyond the boundaries of perfect calm. The walls were alive with light, huge screens throwing projections of borders and rivers at us in streams of digital fire. Tactical pins crept across the maps like infections seeking vital organs, our golden emblems, their silver sigils, a spreading disease of ambition that some young officer with a stylus pretended to control. The scent of myrrh and sandalwood curled from the ventilation grilles, a theatrical touch from Lemminkäinen, who loved artistry in all its forms. I had once indulged him. Now, I knew better. Blood establishes its own, undeniable hierarchy of scents.

He stood at my right hand, his ruined jacket draped over his shoulders with casual insolence, as if it had never been stripped away in violence. The tattered shirt beneath clung in dark patches of sweat to his skin, the collar wide open. One sleeve was gone entirely from shoulder to cuff, a casualty of my rage. A neat row of bloody crescents marked his forearm where my nails had learned their way into his flesh. He hid nothing. It was the genius of the fox: never waste a good scar. The commanders, a dozen of them, arranged themselves around the massive iron table with the careful precision of men who feel they sit beneath an invisible, and unforgiving, jury. Their uniforms were starched into submission, their medals winking like baleful eyes under the harsh, humming light. Many of them had been handsome once, before six years of grinding war had sanded them down to pure, brutal function. Every mouth in that room tasted the hunger in the air between Lemminkäinen and me, and none of them dared speak its name.

"My legions have learned the shape of order," I said, my voice cutting through the electronic hum. I placed my palms flat against the cold iron of the central map table; it groaned beneath a weight that was more than physical. "Order wins battles by knowing when to become fierce, when to embrace chaos. Vojvodina showed us the virtue of a beautiful mess, when that mess belongs to the proper hands. They have gifted us the next battlefield. And we will take it."

Silence has textures. This one vibrated like a harp string drawn just past its breaking point. It was General Kyros, a Greek heavy with ribbons and hollowed out by sleeplessness, who forgot the liturgy of fear. He found his voice because he was old enough to remember serving men who still pretended at mortality.

"My Lady," he began, the title catching in his throat like a fish hook. "Our northern ranks bleed thin and raw. The reports from the Danube front are… grim. To strike south now, we would arrive already emptied. The colonels speak of pulling back, consolidating our forces at the Attic line. Athens can become a wall again, a fortress, if we, "

I leaned across the map, my shadow falling over the flickering representation of his homeland. The fluorescents above us flickered violently, like candles caught in a lover's sharp breath. The iron table sang a high note of distress. On the far side of the table, Kyros's data-slate cracked beneath the whitening grip of his knuckles. I whispered. Whispers carry farther when they are freighted with fire.

"I walked the pass at Thermopylae when the blood was still wet," I breathed, my lips almost touching his ear. "I smelled marrow cooking in bronze armor. I stepped around the bodies of men whose eyes were open to nothing save a sky they could no longer see. Do you propose to teach me the economy of loss, General?"

He tried to hold my gaze and shattered, his eyes skittering away to the meaningless numbers on a nearby screen. I pressed my palm flat against his chest, pinning him to his chair without applying enough pressure to leave a bruise that a court-martial could photograph. The sharp edges of his medals bit into his own skin. The pulse beneath my hand hammered like a rabbit learning the unforgiving nature of a snare.

"You will think of retreat, if you must," I whispered, the words for him alone. "Take that thought home with you. Feed it bread, teach it to heel like a dog. Keep it silent in this room. Do you understand me?"

His nod measured the smallest possible distance a human head can travel and still count as consent. I released him, letting him fall back into his own suddenly insufficient air. It was Lemminkäinen who claimed the silence I left behind, gilding it with the smooth cadence of his voice.

"Thermopylae is a song that has already been sung," he told them, his northern vowels smoothing every edge they cut, making even the most brutal pronouncements sound like reason. "We must compose something new, in a place where the echoes will carry for a thousand years. Athens waits. It always waits. It looks magnificent on our banners, yet it is a prize, a battlefield. He paused, letting his words sink in. His finger, one nail crusted with dried blood, traced lines on the map with a lazy intimacy that made several of the hardened commanders lean forward without realizing it. "We will take Athens last. First, we go where their hope believes itself to be newly strong. We go where the roads run like arteries to every limb of their nascent alliance." His finger stopped, tapping the fertile plains surrounding the Sava and Tisa rivers. "We drag them through every field that feeds their armies. We make food a memory and comfort a rumor. Then, only then, when they are starving and broken, do we bare our teeth at the cradle of their civilization, and they will have learned by then that their mothers and their histories cannot save them."

They watched him like mice watching a serpent whisper promises of cool water in a desert. I kept my eyes on him, on the elegant line of his throat, remembering how it had surrendered to me, how its pulse had fluttered against my tongue. His strategy sang with a terrible, undeniable truth. The fox always finds where the foundations have forgotten their responsibility to the house above.

"Vojvodina was their first breath as a unified force," he continued, his voice weaving a tapestry of dread. "Let them waste their second breath marching to meet ghosts. We will bleed them in the north, draw their strength away from the heart. By the time they manage to draw a third ragged breath in Attica, you, gentlemen, will already be there to steal it from their lungs."

I saw it then, with a searing, crystal clarity: the vast plains beneath a sky of bruised gray clouds; smoke bending along the wind-lines from burning granaries; tractors and farm equipment overturned, transformed into makeshift barricades. I saw women with defiance in their eyes bracing ancient doors with furniture inherited from their dead mothers, and men with soil-soft hands learning the unfamiliar weight of a rifle as if it were a plowshare. And I saw Ilija in that weather, his storm-heart straining against the sky until the very stones of the earth remembered lightning's mastery. Danica would be beside him, her long braid dark with rain, her jaw set in that admirable, infuriating tilt that meant she had chosen to cause immense harm for the sake of what she believed was righteousness. They would stand together, believing themselves unbreakable, which meant it was my duty to show them that what cannot be broken can still be bent to a purpose it never intended.

"We go north," I declared, my voice resonating with finality. The fluorescent lights steadied, as if an animal had decided to live for another hour. "We are going to teach this fledgling alliance what the word 'divine' meant before mortals taught it how to apologize. Move the legions from Bari and Thessaloniki. Redeploy them to the Danube line by week's end. Seal every crossing we don't need, flood the ones we do, and then walk our armies across fields where the water tells the villages to stop having sons." My hand flattened over the bright, digital smear of Athens on the screen, extinguishing it. "I will come to Athens myself when the rumor of me grows colder and heavier than any fact."

General Kyros swallowed audibly, found his feet, and kept his precious silence. Other commanders began tapping furiously on their tablets, their thumbs trying to outpace their trembling. Lemminkäinen's eyes slid to mine, alight with a savage pleasure that belonged equally to the battlefield and the bedchamber.

"The fox will go ahead," I said, my gaze sweeping over the grim faces of my commanders, while my words were for him. "He will go with a diplomat's smile and a butcher's list. Every church elder playing at being a king, every mayor calling himself the father of his town, every woman whose quiet prayers keep the quarters of a village from descending into panic, make them sing the Accord's hymns, or take their tongues."

He inclined his head, a formal bow from the waist. The dried blood on his lip cracked into a thin, red map of his consent. "I will bring you a city of quiet mouths," he promised, the fox's tail finally, beautifully, revealed.

The council dissolved along its invisible seams, the men flowing away to execute the patterns of order I had decreed. Radios woke up, whining with encrypted traffic. Logistics officers, with coffee already trembling in their hands, began calling out numbers into the sterile night. A young colonel in the back of the room seemed to remember how to breathe and sat down heavily as his legs rejected the concept of standing any longer. I walked out with Lemminkäinen at my shoulder, refusing to shorten my stride to match his, forcing him to keep my pace.

We moved through concrete passages that had once ferried wealthy donors to amphitheaters and galas, now repurposed to carry the machinery of war to the surface. The service elevator that lifted us to the rooftop creaked like the hull of a ship caught in a storm. The doors opened onto a blast of salt air and the deep, thrumming hum of the coastal turbines turning the last of the dusk into a mechanical prayer. The sea stretched to a black horizon beneath a sky that had temporarily forgotten the concept of blue. Below us, on the concrete aprons of the port, teams of fatigued men moved crates from truck to truck with the relentless, mindless rhythm of ants, their movements suggesting that winter had arrived as a personal insult. A medic sat on a paint-flaked bench, meticulously cleaning her scalpels with the corner of her shirt because the field sterilizers had surrendered to the humidity again. When she looked up and saw me watching her from above, she flinched so deeply she nearly dropped her blade. I held her with my gaze, an unblinking stare across the distance, until her hand steadied. Fear, I had found, keeps hands from shaking when blood demands precision.

Lemminkäinen leaned his elbows on the iron railing, gazing out toward where the evening freight ships cut through the darkness like the bodies of great wolves moving beneath black water. He smiled as if he owned the horizon and had simply been letting it think otherwise for a time.

"You spared me," he observed. There was no triumph in his voice. Only recognition. "Someday, you will end me. The day will come when keeping me alive costs more than the advantages I buy you. Until then," he turned his head, his profile sharp against the distant lights, "I will be the knife you call a spoon."

"I appoint," I told him simply, the word as hard and final as the iron under my hands.

"Then appoint me to whisper," he said, turning fully to face me, my handiwork on his mouth gleaming dark in the dying light. "Appoint me to travel the roads ahead of your armies and make men choose the comfort of safety until they forget that other words even exist."

"I will be the one to remind them," I answered, the edge in my voice making even his fox-smile lose some of its teeth for a moment. "Personally."

We stood in a shared silence, buffeted by a wind that lifted my hair and cooled the salt that was drying along my throat. In the ceaseless hum of the turbines, I could hear the sounds of other machines warming to their purpose across the continent, the deep chug of rail engines being checked and fueled, the guttural cough of armored carriers coughing into life, the precise tick and settle of rifles after fresh oil meets cold metal. Below, a flock of doves that had learned to live on salt spray and cigarette ash scavenged for a bread crust fallen from a trucker's lunch. They pecked and stepped and pecked again, utterly oblivious to the fox standing two stories above them with my blood still drying beneath his nails. I smiled at the image and filed it away in the part of my mind where I keep the outlines of future moves on the grand board.

He turned back to me, the hunger in him as patient and certain as frost. "Athens," he said, offering the name of the city like a blood diamond on a jeweler's cloth. "When?"

"When rumor can no longer keep them in their beds at night," I said, letting the rail take my weight as I imagined the Acropolis draped in new banners, banners that refused to apologize for the vibrancy of their colors. "When the mothers of Piraeus begin to say my name before they say their prayers. When Ilija stops sleeping because he has finally learned what my voice does to a man's dreams." I looked back at him, my own smile a mirror of his, yet colder. "Soon."

He touched his split lip with the tips of two fingers, then pressed them to his tongue as if he were a priest tasting a sacrament. He had wanted to be marked. He had been marked. He would use that stain, that proof of his proximity to my fire, until it had paid for itself a dozen times over.

"Bring me their roads," I commanded, my voice low while carrying over the wind. "Bring me the names of their bridges and the names of the men who wake in the night to check the bolts. Bring me every woman who has learned how to lead in the darkness and tell me where she keeps her candles. Bring me Athens, Lemminkäinen. Bring it to me tired and afraid. I will be the one to bring it to its knees."

He nodded, a sharp, final affirmation. And then the fox descended the steel stairs, his steps lighter than a shadow crossing a wall. The guards at the bottom watched him go as if they believed his back could bite.

I remained on the rooftop until the last vestiges of light had thinned into something the sea knows how to own completely. The turbines hummed my name back to me in the only language that machines truly speak: power. In the reflection of the glass door behind me, I caught a glimpse of myself, hair a wild storm, skin streaked with the evidence of what we had made, my mouth lifted at one corner in the way it does when the next moves on the board are no longer gambles, yet foregone conclusions. Somewhere inland, the weather patterns were shifting because a man who had been taught to hold a storm in his heart had heard words from a woman we should have killed in one of history's earlier, more sensible chapters. Somewhere to the north, a child with hair the color of the winter-noon sun was counting the stars aloud, a small, defiant voice ensuring the sky still knew how to carry their light.

I pressed my palm against the cold iron rail until it warmed beneath my touch. The garden would be pruned. The fox had found the path through the overgrown hedges I had been content for too long to simply admire. Athens waited with its marble throat bared, its columns pretending to be teeth. When we arrived, I would show them what beauty is truly for, once it remembers it was always meant to draw blood.

I turned back into the heart of the bunker and let the heavy doors close on the sea. The ghosts of the crescents I had carved down Lemminkäinen's arm tingled in my fingertips. The maps waited below with their pale, silent veins. The lights in the war room had steadied. The great, brutal heart of the Accord resumed its steady pace, and I matched my own to its rhythm. The fox runs where the rose grows wild. Gardens, I thought, are about to learn the true meaning of fear for their own thorns.

Chapter Twenty-Five
BANNERS OVER ATHENS

Ilija

The road carved itself open like a wound bleeding clay and dust. Red earth clung to everything, our boots, our throats, the creases around our eyes where we squinted against the sun. My mouth tasted of copper and old grief. We moved through that grit like ghosts learning to be solid again, a column that looked like farmers and students and broken mothers until you watched long enough to see we wouldn't stop. Thunder in my chest made sure of that.

Someone had cut laurel boughs outside Niš. Now green sprigs are hung from rifle straps and backpack loops, tied with bootlaces and prayer twine. Every few kilometers a kid would reach back, fingers brushing leaves like rosary beads. The smell drifted through diesel fumes and unwashed bodies—that clean, bitter scent that tastes like hope, sharp and necessary.

Thunder lived in my ribs. It pressed against bone with each heartbeat, old pressure that remembered falling from heights I'd never climbed. Afternoon warmed everything, and the power shifted weight inside me like a sleeping animal. I kept my mouth shut, kept my hands loose. When wind moved across the ridge above us, thunder answered and rolled along the mountains like cattle lowing in the distance. Patient. Present. Waiting.

They looked at me sideways, these farmers with their oiled rifles, these mothers with knives against their spines. Quick glances that shattered the moment my eyes found theirs. I'd been safe once. That man had died somewhere between Ana's bed and Danica's resurrection. Now they looked at me like a loaded gun. Hungry for what I could give them. Terrified of what it might cost.

A truck coughed its last breath and rolled to the shoulder. Three men pushed while the driver cursed in Serbian, then apologized to the engine like he'd hurt an old friend's feelings. Traffic squeezed to single file. An old woman in running shoes with cracked soles walked past us carrying a sack of onions, moving faster than should've been possible for someone whose spine curved like a question mark. She wore black head to toe, and widow's weeds that had seen too many funerals. The onion sack beat against her thigh with each step, pulse for a heart that had stopped trusting the one in her chest.

Danica walked beside me for a while, threading between the horses and a truck bed full of silent dogs. Her jacket hung tied around her waist. The black t-shirt underneath was filmed gray with road dust. Someone had knotted a strip of cloth in her braid the night before—a battlefield decoration, or maybe just kindness. Her face held exhaustion like discipline, wore it as soldiers wear pack straps. Heavy. Necessary. Freeing the hands for other work.

Her fingers found the radio on her shoulder. Two-finger tap. Habit disguised as calm for the people watching her breathe.

"Selene would hate this," she said. Words half prayer, half confession, all guilt. "The noise. The smell. She'd climb the nearest tree and count branches until the world made sense again."

"She counts everything," Danica chuckled. "Steps between doors. Ceiling cracks. The names we don't say around her because she already knows them anyway." Danica almost smiled. Almost. The expression died before it reached her mouth.

Lightning crawled up my spine like fingers made of white heat. I nodded and kept walking because walking was what we had. Walking was proof we hadn't been stopped yet.

The mountains released us reluctantly. The road flattened, widened. Wind changed flavor from pine to river-mud and growing things. Fields spread out like lesson plans I used to teach, divided by irrigation ditches full of frogs and plastic bags and water that carried secrets in suspension. We passed a village where houses had learned to bow to the ground. One side of the street was ash and new brick. The other side watched its neighbors rebuild and pretended it had nothing to do with the lesson being taught.

People joined us like tributaries joining a river. A woman with a blue crate of bread wrapped in dish towels, a toddler riding her hip. Two mechanics with grease stains dark as ritual scars around their wrists. A priest carrying fence wire across his shoulders, collar gone, cross worn smooth by fingers that had stopped believing in the difference between sacred and necessary. Some peeled away toward towns we marked on paper maps—signal was rumor this far from anywhere. Most stayed. The column swallowed them as rivers swallow rain.

Evening brought different smoke. The whole column felt it before anyone spoke into the radio. Heads lift like deer scenting wolves. Nostrils flaring. This was bigger. Industrial. Sweet with melted plastic and paper, the kind of smoke that tricks your throat into thinking it might be food. Word came back person to person instead of crackling through speakers: Athens is burning. The Accord is drawing lines with fire.

Refugees met us as shadows stretched long and thin. They came out of olive groves and across dead fields, carrying their lives in shapes that made no sense against their backs. A boy in a Barcelona jersey helping an old woman whose coat buttons hung on past all logic. Another kid with a cat half-zipped into his jacket, yellow eyes like coins in the dark. A man clutching a family photo in a cracked frame, carrying it like evidence in a trial only he could see. The crack ran right through a child's smile. He didn't seem to know.

They were quiet. When they talked, it came in fragments. Names. Street addresses. The last place they'd seen someone whole. Lemminkäinen's handiwork sat in their mouths like broken glass. Curfews without warning. Lists posted at dawn. Men who'd spoken truth in public squares disappearing into basements that flooded when the pipes got turned on and left to run. The Accord had given children blank textbooks and told them to keep writing anyway.

A woman stopped me with her hand on my sleeve. Palm small and dry and shaking just enough to notice. She looked up with eyes gone gray from dust and exhaustion. "Are you Ilija?" she asked.

"Yes." The word felt like stepping onto ice that hadn't decided whether to hold.

She nodded. Relief, simple and clean. "Good. Do what you came for." Then she kept walking, her Barcelona-jersey boy pressed tight against her side like he could make himself into armor.

We made camp in an olive grove bordered by stacked stones and haunted by one surviving goat. The trees twisted into themselves as arthritic hands curl against pain. Fires stayed small by agreement. Smoke rose in thin threads, kept low. A woman with a chipped enamel pot served soup that had more hope than ingredients. A kid dealt cards to an audience too tired to count. Someone found music on a radio, scratchy, distant, the kind that sounds like an old cassette that lived under car seats through three owners.

I walked the rows between sleeping bags and rifle stacks. A boy polishing his weapon with a torn shirt looked up, met my eyes for half a second, then studied my boots like they held answers. A girl with her hair wrapped in a headscarf traced laurel leaves with her fingertips, reading some private language written in the veins. Two men argued in whispers about latrines—dig here and risk the neighbors or risk the field and the fence that might be wired. Every time I slowed down, conversations stopped. When I moved on, they started again. The kind of silence you give a storm that hasn't picked its target yet.

Petra found me near supply crates stenciled with numbers that meant beans if we were lucky, ammunition if we weren't. She carried a clipboard like a shield and had a pencil behind her ear sharpened down to the metal. Dust outlined the sweat at her hairline like a crown she'd wipe away with her sleeve before sleeping.

"You're wearing holes in the ground," she said. Her gift—taking gods down to human size by refusing to hear divinity in your voice. She broke bread in half and handed me the smaller piece. "Eat."

The crust shredded my mouth. It felt like proof you couldn't fake—real hunger, real food, real blood on my tongue. "How far?" I asked around the bread that turned to paste against my teeth.

"Two days if the roads hold. Three if Lemminkäinen's made friends with the water engineers and we have to find new ways across." Her eyes flicked south like she could see through darkness into the city's dying light.

"He has, which is why we've got people downstream with bolt cutters and ideas. If he's cut everything, we'll walk in wet. We've done worse."

She stood close enough that my pulse settled. Another of her gifts—lending your heartbeat her steadiness and pretending you'd earned it honest. The look she gave me sideways carried that small smirk that keeps bad air moving through good lungs.

"They're guessing what you are," she said. "Half the camp thinks you bleed when cut. Other half's telling the first half you don't."

"I bleed." I touched the dried split on my lower lip. "Ask my shirt."

"I'd rather ask your head. You're carrying that power like a full glass, and we're about to hit potholes."

"I'm holding it."

"Holding is one thing." She lifted the pencil, pointed past the grove toward lights scattered across the next rise. "The question is whether you believe you're allowed to be seen holding it. They don't need a man apologizing every time lightning thinks about touching ground."

"Where is Selene?" I needed to know she was safe. "Is she okay?"

"She's safe. She's hidden somewhere the gods can't reach. I made sure of that." Petra didn't tell us exactly where, yet we knew she was safe and that was all that mattered.

I opened my mouth. Danica appeared at my shoulder with a tin cup she offered, then kept when I didn't move fast enough. She drank, wiped her mouth with her palm, and handed me what remained. Tequila. The cheap kind that comes in plastic bottles when you're lucky, IV bags when you're not.

"Theology later," she said to Petra. She looked at me. "He doesn't sleep, yet he needs to."

"I'll sleep when the radio stops trying to impress me," Petra said, yet her expression softened. She reached up, tucked the pencil behind Danica's ear with the kind of tenderness you can only afford once a day. Then she left us to the grove's noisy quiet.

We sat on a fallen stone with olive roots elbowing up from beneath. The cup moved between our hands. I could hear the camp breathing. Meat hissing over fire somewhere. Children laughing when grease caught flame and made pans spit. A man across the grove tuned his guitar, loosened the strings until the pitch lay down flat and let the night walk over it.

"She said they're guessing what you are," Danica said after a while. "Are you guessing too?"

"I don't want to be anything they can't forgive. After." The words came out raw.

Her hand found my knee through dust and denim. "They'll forgive what keeps them alive. They won't forgive being left alone in a story you promised to finish with them."

Power breathed in. Above the black crown of olive trees, heat lightning stitched the horizon in white threads too far away to hear. I watched it and remembered a classroom where I'd written something about Athens on the chalkboard. A student had asked if democracy meant never being told no. I'd given him an answer that would grade well, then forgotten his face until now. Maybe the man with the cracked photo carried that boy's picture.

"We'll reach the city," Danica said. "It's already moving. You feel it."

I nodded. "I hear it. More than just the fires. Voices calling down stairwells. Keys in locks. Bottles against tires. The sound of a street learning a new language overnight."

She smiled. "Tomorrow, you can tell it your name."

We didn't discuss sleep. Slept anyway, badly, on ground embroidered with roots and pebbles that learned the shape of our ribs. Deep in the night a dog barked once, thought better of it. The radio hummed static like a moth trapped behind glass. My hand found Danica's and held on.

"Danica—" I looked deep into her eyes for the first time since we returned. The universe stared back at me. I had forgotten how I lost myself in her gaze. This woman who brought me an artifact all those years ago, a PhD candidate, smart, raw, unfiltered. My flame and frost. These feelings that Ana had tried to erase, came roaring through me like the lightning when I first called. These emotions were more powerful than any storm I carry.

"My storm, let's go. We need some goddamn alone time to recharge before we attack in the morning." Her words, raw as always, cut through the camp's din like lightning splits oak.

She led me by the hand to our makeshift sanctuary. Gods, I'd missed her. There was something rising in me that had nothing to do with the lightning crackling beneath my skin. I kept my eyes fixed on her, the way her shoulders moved, the new scars mapping stories I wasn't there to witness. It had been a while since we were alone together. Before Rome fell, when Selene was still... I wondered, would it be different? Would grief have changed the geography of our needs?

My scholarly mind catalogued the details—the way dust motes danced in amber light filtering through canvas, the scent of leather and steel that clung to everything we owned now. Then Danica turned, and every piece of accumulated knowledge scattered like leaves before a hurricane.

She looked at me with raw hunger. The kind of look that says: I am going to devour every inch of your soul, and you will thank me for it.

Every theorem, every myth I'd ever studied, every careful observation, gone. The only remaining thought was my desperate need to claim the flame and frost that stood before me.

She grabbed my throat, frost and flame dancing along her fingertips while lightning crackled beneath mine where they met. Our mouths crashed together like worlds colliding, the end and beginning of everything. She tore my shirt apart, fabric screaming as it gave way. Her teeth found my neck, marking territory, and I roared, low, guttural, the sound thunder makes when it's still learning its own power.

The threads of her shirt dissolved in my hands, clawed away with hands that remembered being mortal yet moved with divine hunger. My mouth found her shoulder, her collarbone, mapping the constellation of new scars. Her breasts—gods, I had dreamed of them in the darkest nights—I took one in my hand, the other with my mouth. Biting, circling, desperate as a starving man at a feast. This was consumption. Raw need. The primal desire to reclaim what was mine and gods did she surrender to it.

I threw her onto the cot, ripping away the last barriers between us. I was going to worship every inch of her. Every scent, every taste, every gasping prayer she offered up. My lips traced a path of devotion from breast to stomach to the sacred geography of her thighs.

I bit into her thigh, tasting salt and desire, and she cried out, part plea, part command. My tongue moved with deliberate reverence, tasting what no myth had properly described. She grabbed the back of my head with desperate claws; I couldn't breathe and didn't care. If I died here, drowning in her, I would die the happiest storm god in any pantheon.

Her hips moved like ocean waves, primal rhythm older than language. When she shattered against my mouth, I knew this was what we'd both need to survive.

Her hands, fierce like talons, dragged my face to hers. We crashed together, mouths hungry, tasting ourselves on each other's lips.

She took me in her hand like it was life or death, stroking with the precision of someone who knew exactly how to unravel a god. When her mouth closed around me, I nearly came undone entirely. The heat, the pressure, the way she took all of me—

"Gods, Danica." The words tore from my throat. Her mouth was pure magic, and the sounds she made were raw as any wild thing that had forgotten civilization existed.

I tangled my fingers in her hair, grounding myself before I scattered into lightning. Power in my chest built toward breaking, muscles surging with the force of every tempest that had ever raged.

"Gods... Danica." I couldn't take another second. I needed to be inside her, needed to feel her heat wrap around me like coming home. I turned her over, drinking in the sight of her, flushed, wanting, the most beautiful devastation I'd ever witnessed.

When I slid into her, the sensation nearly shattered my consciousness— overwhelming heat and wetness and home.

"Ilija... fuck. I need you. All of you. Like the world's ending." Her voice was raw and desperate. "Fuck me harder. Give me everything."

Those words nearly finished me. I loved this goddess, this warrior, this woman who had chosen to bind her fate to mine. I moved with desperate intensity, hard, fast, feral. We were both crying out, cursing everything that had tried to tear us apart, yet at this moment we were singular. Two souls recognizing each other across lifetimes.

I felt power cresting in me, pleasure becoming indistinguishable from the storm. I bit into her shoulder hard enough to draw blood, claiming and claimed. We climaxed together, and the world exploded. Lightning erupted from my skin, fire and frost burst from hers, our powers unleashing in a whirlwind that tore through the tent. Canvas snapped and whipped around us, air itself igniting with elemental force. Thunder cracked overhead while ice crystals and flame danced through the maelstrom we'd become— primordial forces that make mortals forget their names, their histories, their carefully constructed identities.

I collapsed beside her, hitting the cot like a meteorite striking earth.

"Oh my gods, Ilija." Danica's voice was barely human. "You ever leave me again without this, and I will find you and kill you myself. That was... fuck, amazing."

"Same to you, my fierce goddess." The words were probably corny as hell, yet I didn't care. This woman was my entire universe. She was mine; I was hers. My Sigrun, my flame, my frost. My Danica.

She curled against my chest while I traced patterns on her skull, fingers gentle now in the aftermath. We both knew what tomorrow would bring, yet tonight we existed only in this moment. The war could wait. Tonight, we were just two souls who had found their way back to each other through all the darkness. We were alive. We could play gods tomorrow. Tonight, we would sleep as lovers, bound by something deeper than fate—by choice.

Dawn came careful, the color of old bruises rinsed thin, and then the light found the olives and taught them to throw narrow shadows that pointed us toward the city. The camp took itself apart. Fires were persuaded back into ash. Bedrolls remembered how to become packs. Petra's pencil made its small, sovereign sounds over a clipboard that had seen too much weather. Danica retied the ribbon into her braid with hands that never trembled, even when the watchers needed to see them shake.

Power inside my ribcage, so loud in the hours before sleep, had folded itself like wings and agreed, for now, to be weight instead of weapon. My mouth still remembered her name. So did the ground. Athens waited beyond the groves, smoke lifting in pale sheets from the south, bells testing their throats one note at a time as if reminding themselves of scale.

We moved on the hour as planned. The olive scent thinned to dust and laundry soap as the first streets took us in. Balconies with basil in chipped pots. Doors left open while water went up and down. The city began before the maps allowed it. A woman in a bathrobe made the old sign across her chest and then touched two fingers to her temple afterward, her mouth working through prayers from different centuries. Children leaned over rails with brooms for spears, toothpaste bright at the corners of their mouths. People joined us as if they had always intended to be walking in this direction and had only been waiting for the right sentence to begin.

The first checkpoint announced itself as architecture that had failed to be a wall—two municipal buses nudged into place, a line of shields bright as wet teeth. Visors down. Truncheons at parade rest. I felt the column take a breath that might have turned into panic if the air had been thinner. "Easy," Danica said into the radio, her voice the kind you hear in kitchens at three in the morning. "No fast moves. We bring the city to the line. We bring the line to the city."

The city obliged. Pots began to ring from balconies, thin aluminum first, then iron, then the thick ceremonial sound of something once used for weddings. A woman on a second floor threw roses until she ran out and then threw the shoes off her feet. White sheets came down on clotheslines; lightning sprawled across them in paint that had dried all the way through. The chant that rose was my name, was Danica's. It was the city's name said back to itself until it remembered the shape of its mouth.

I stepped forward because some part of the work still required the body that rumor had made of me. Hands open. Palms where the shields could see them. The sergeant behind the glass tried to keep his eyes on my chest—they drifted to my face twice, snapped back down. He lifted two fingers, and the line gave him a meter. Behind me, Petra noted camera masts, angles, possible loyalties. I could feel Danica's attention like a hand between my shoulder blades, pushing, restraining, calibrating.

A boy sidled up with laurel tied to a broom handle, the knot a child's knot, ugly, honest, unbreakable. His eyes kept falling from my boots to my face and back, blinking hard each time as if the distance surprised him. "Do I hold it high?" he asked.

"Hold it steady," I said. "High is the wind's job."

He planted his feet. The shields advanced a pace, boots speaking in unison. Somewhere close by, a stairwell began smoking, the gray kind that carries messages to different floors. The visors clicked lower, twenty men swallowing at once behind plastic. The line wanted an enemy it could understand. We declined.

Banners bloomed as wildflowers bloom when a field remembers it was meant for something other than concrete. Twine ran from balcony to balcony; sheets flew and were seized midair by hands that had been hanging laundry for three generations; laurel pinned them along the hems with fishhooks and safety pins and the small nails used for birdhouses. When the wind learned the cloth, the crooked storms straightened into themselves, and the city's breath turned visible.

"Front two, drop," Danica said, and the first row of our people dropped to their knees, heads bowed. The second row set shields at an angle that sent rubber bullets singing back toward their source. The line threw its volley and watched it ricochet off metal with the sound of hail on tin roofs. A drone rose like a bad idea; somebody with patient wire taught it gravity again. It struck the pavement with the exact sound of an argument losing interest.

We broke the line. We asked a better question. The bus drivers regarded each other across their dashboards and arrived, slowly, at the shape of an agreement. The first bus lurched backward, grinding gears. The second followed. The shields took two steps back because bodies answer to physics when orders grew quiet. No one cheered. Banners filled the space where voices would have burned out early.

"Checkpoint One is now a market," Petra said into the net, the corner of her mouth lifting like a cat with cream. People tested the old uses of the square: water where water should be given, bread where it should be broken, quiet where quiet made more room for courage. A priest with his collar gone threaded fence wire through the handles of crates to make a sling, the sun-browned cross at his throat catching light. He passed it to a mechanic whose elbows wore grease like old paint. I caught myself listening for the sound of small feet counting stair treads, balcony rails, windows with shutters and ones without. A girl on a railing chalked a star, tongue between her teeth as she corrected one angle. Mine. The ache came, did its small work, and found its shelf.

We moved. The second contact lived where a narrow lane spilled into a square that used to have statues and now had a podium where lies got told at noon. The Accord had learned between one line and the next. Visors darker. Shoulders rolled forward. A water cannon crouched behind the shields, its nozzle swiveling like the head of a hunting animal.

"Hydrants are chained," Petra said.

"Then we'll use their water," I answered, and the roofs agreed before I finished the thought. Buckets, plastic tubs, blue barrels that last week had entertained rain—at my whistle they tipped their stored sky into the square. The cannon threw its tantrum and discovered the square had become a lake. Our angled shields caught the spray and threw it back. The wind carried the cannon's roar into the visors where men blinked for the first time that morning.

We went forward as wedge and as tide across pitted stone. Some feet faster, some slower, all following the same pull. Two grandfathers with shoulders like old ships looped a washline around the cannon's bumper, their hands moving through knots their fathers had taught them before they could write their names. The machine tilted sideways, water streaming from its barrel-like tears.

A municipal balcony remembered its use. A ladder appeared as ladders do when belief becomes efficient; it stretched only halfway, so hands formed a human chain beneath to bridge the gap. The banner that unfurled was patched canvas soaked in three kinds of red and black that gleamed like oil at the bottom of a harbor. When the wind caught it, the star became a blade the sky had chosen to keep. The serpent at its base curled with the patience of something that has already outlived several governments.

Sirens came late and loud, wailing like children who've lost an argument. "Leave the square to its new owner," Danica said, and we peeled away in echelons, boots falling into rhythm, disciplined as a heartbeat. A banner is a fortress. It is a flare that tells the morning where to set its feet.

I let my hand rest a moment on the blue door of a café that had traded coffee beans for ammunition crates. Heat pulsed under the paint from yesterday's sun. I felt power stir, my fingers crackling, air thickening around my shoulders. I felt the city breathing, slow and deep, its rhythm settling into mine. The relief felt indecent and holy.

At the far edge of the square, I saw Danica in profile, ribbon dark against her neck, her whole body tilted toward some conversation I couldn't hear. She glanced at me, one quick look that said later and be careful and I love you all at once. Petra pressed a loaf into my hands; the priest's sling still looped at her elbow. I tore the bread and gave her half. We ate without speaking. Flour from her wrist left a white thumbprint on the radio at her shoulder.

We slipped into an alley where sound went to die quietly. The crowd closed behind us like water after a stone. The laundry above had decided to be flags, teaching its knots to hold in a different wind. A child with chalk dust on her fingers fixed a star to the wall, erasing and redrawing until the angles satisfied her. Someone pressed a paper icon into my palm, a saint I recognized driving a spear through a ledger instead of a dragon. The giver's eyes said for luck. I kept it because when math fails you, superstition is what's left.

The sirens went hunting elsewhere. The banner learned its square like an immigrant learning a new language. Far off, bells found their second note. Power lifted its head inside my chest, looked at the work ahead, and settled back to wait. We moved toward the next street that had forgotten how to belong to itself, and Athens carried us forward like a thought it had been trying to finish since the world was young.

CHAPTER TWENTY-SIX
THE CLOSING OF THE GATES

Ana

The fox's words still coiled in the air of my sanctuary like smoke from a dying fire, Alive. Both of them. Together. The report had been delivered, the wound opened. Now I simply watched the infection spread in real-time, each pulse of my divine heart pumping poison through my veins.

I had built this sanctuary to be a testament to perfection. Every marble column had been placed with mathematical precision, every silk curtain hung at angles that pleased the eye without thought or effort. The lotus blossoms that perfumed the air never wilted because I willed them eternal, their beauty frozen at the moment of peak bloom. The golden veins in the marble floors caught and reflected light in patterns that induced a subtle sense of peace in mortal minds, though they could never consciously understand why.

The perfection felt hollow. What good was eternal beauty when the only eyes I wanted to see it through were looking at someone else?

The water in the obsidian basin had stopped showing me the elegant, inexorable advance of my northern legions. Instead, it reflected the festering chaos in the heart of my domain: Athens. The city I had personally scrubbed clean, whose history I had curated like a museum exhibit, whose silence I had perfected through months of careful conditioning, was making noise again. It was the sound of mortals forgetting their place, and it grated against my consciousness like fingernails on marble.

I had loved Athens once. With the deep, possessive devotion of a creator for her masterpiece. I had walked its streets in the golden age when philosophers debated truth in the Agora and artists carved beauty from stone. I had whispered inspiration into the ears of Pericles, had guided the hands that built the Parthenon, had blessed the city with wisdom and culture and the kind of glory that echoes through millennia.

When the modern age brought chaos and ugliness, I intervened, again. I had swept away the graffiti and the industrial grime, and had replaced the harsh neon signs with gentle illumination that honored the classical architecture beneath. The crime had stopped through a subtle adjustment of hearts and minds that made violence feel distasteful, unnecessary. The traffic noise had faded to a gentle hum that harmonized with the city's natural rhythms.

It was perfect. It had been mine. And now they were destroying it, one hanging banner at a time.

I watched the city's fever dream of rebellion unfold in the water's surface, those pathetic, fluttering banners painted with their stolen symbols. The star and serpent, a design that had once meant something else entirely, twisted by their ignorant hands into a mockery of its original purpose. It was an abstract, distant insult until the drone feed patched through, opening a shimmering window in the still air of Olympus.

And then I saw them.

The image was grainy, distorted by smoke and the eternal drizzle that seemed to follow their rebellion like a curse. It was them. There was no mistaking the way power moved around them, distorting the air with their presence.

Danica was a pillar of fire and frost, her hair black as raven feathers whipping around her face like a banner of war. She was all sharp edges and brutal efficiency, lacking any trace of the grace that came naturally to those born to power. Yet the mortals flowed toward her like iron filings to a lodestone, drawn by something in her bearing that spoke of unbreakable will. She walked like someone who had faced down gods and lived to tell the tale.

The sight of her filled me with a rage so pure it transcended emotion and became something closer to physical law. She was wrong, wrong in every line of her body, every expression that crossed her scarred face. She was chaos given form, entropy wearing human skin, everything I had spent millennia trying to banish from the world.

The figure beside her made my perfect marble floor crack beneath my feet.

Ilija. My Ilija.

He was alive, and he was walking beside her with the easy familiarity of long companionship. He was different from the broken thing I had left in my dungeons, different from the haunted scholar I had first claimed. Months of freedom had carved new lines in his face, had added gray to his temples and strength to his shoulders. He carried himself like a king, the storm-touched ruler I had always known he could become.

His face was turned toward the woman beside him, and in the space of a single, stolen frame captured by the surveillance drone, I saw him smile. It was a small, private thing, the kind of expression that spoke of shared jokes and whispered endearments, of comfortable silences and bodies that knew each other's rhythms. A look that said home and safety and forever in the universal language of lovers.

A look that had once belonged to me.

The crack in the marble spread, a thin spiderweb line racing from where I stood to the base of my empty throne. The water in the basin boiled violently, hissing into steam that carried the acrid scent of ozone and my own ancient, possessive rage. This was personal betrayal of the deepest kind.

He was wearing my name in his bones. I could see the storm-power I had awakened coursing through him, the lightning that danced at his fingertips carrying the signature of my divine touch. He was using it for her. Smiling at her. Protecting her. Loving her with the devotion that should have been mine by right.

The jealousy hit me like a physical blow, doubling me over with its intensity. I had known jealousy before, had felt it when mortals worshipped other gods, when cities chose different patrons, when lovers turned to new paramours. This was different. This cut deeper than pride or possessiveness. This reached into the core of who I was and found the one fear I had never acknowledged: that I might lack enough.

That someone might choose another over me.

The chime of the emergency frequency was a gnat buzzing in my ear, an intolerable intrusion on a moment of pure, clarifying fury. I accepted the link with a thought, and General Kyros's terrified face appeared, a projection shimmering against the crimson light of my displeasure.

He looked like he had aged years in the past few hours. His uniform was rumpled, his usually immaculate hair hanging in lank strands across his forehead. Behind him, I could see his staff bent over their stations with the desperate intensity of men who knew their careers, and possibly their lives, hung on the next few minutes.

"My Lady," he stammered, his voice cracking over the comm like an adolescent boy's. "There is a situation... an uprising..."

"I am aware of the noise in my city, General," I said, my voice dangerously quiet. Each word was carved from ice, polished to a razor's edge. "I am also aware of who is leading it. Your report is hours out of date."

He flinched as if I had struck him, the blood draining from his face until he looked like a corpse propped up at his command station. "My Lady, we have visual confirmation. It is them. Danica Madsen and Ilija Dragović are in Athens."

The way he said their names, with awe, with fear, with the kind of reverence usually reserved for natural disasters, made my rage flare brighter. He spoke as if they were a revelation instead of a symptom of his own pathetic incompetence.

"Yes, Kyros," I said, letting contempt drip from every syllable. "They are. Now, tell me something I do not know, or I will find a commander who can."

"The outer checkpoints have fallen," he said, forcing the words out like a man confessing sins to a priest. "The resistance, they're using hope like a contagion. The First and Third battalions are being overwhelmed by sheer numbers. Citizens are throwing open their doors, hanging banners from every balcony. They're chanting their names in the streets like some kind of prayer."

Hope as a weapon. It was crude, mortal, and its success was an infuriating testament to how little my subjects actually understood the gifts I had given them. I had offered them peace, security, an end to the chaos that had plagued their species since the dawn of time. In return, they chose uncertainty, struggle, the exhausting burden of making their own decisions.

"Then give them a reason to chant mine," I said, and the connection died. I didn't sever it deliberately, my fury simply erased it from existence, burning through the quantum entanglement that sustained the link and leaving nothing save screaming static in its wake.

For a long moment, I stood frozen in the ruins of my perfect sanctuary. The lotus blossoms had withered and died, their petals falling like tears. The golden veins in the marble had gone dark, their light extinguished by the force of my rage. Even the air itself seemed to cower, the gentle breezes that had carried perfume now still as death.

They had turned my own strategy against me, using hearts and minds as weapons, offering mortals the one thing I could never give them: the illusion that their choices mattered. It was brilliant in its simplicity and devastating in its effectiveness.

He appeared as if summoned by the sheer force of my need for someone to blame. Lemminkäinen entered without a sound, moving with that fluid grace that had first caught my attention in the frozen forests of his homeland. He found me staring at the wall where their image had burned itself into my divine sight, at the spot where reality itself still smoldered from the intensity of my focus.

He had found a fresh coat somewhere, dark wool that still carried the scent of pine and snow from his recent travels in the north. The cut I had given him remained on his lower lip, a thin line of scabbed blood that his tongue darted out to touch. It was a reflexive, animal gesture that reminded me of the hours we had spent tangled together on this very floor, when the world had still made sense and my plans had been proceeding according to design.

"A setback," he began, his voice carrying that smooth, honeyed tone that had wrapped around my rage just hours before. "They have revealed themselves. They have overextended their position. They have shown us their heart, and now we can, "

"Their heart?" I turned from the wall, and the word fell from my lips like a shard of ice in the warm, lotus-scented air. My voice was quiet, stripped of all the fury that had been building in my chest, leaving something far colder and more dangerous in its place.

He faltered mid-sentence, the easy confidence in his posture tightening almost imperceptibly. The predatory smile that had been forming on his scarred lips died stillborn, replaced by the wariness of a hunter who had suddenly realized he might be prey. He saw that the goddess he had coupled with on my marble floor was gone, replaced by the queen who had merely allowed it for her own amusement.

I let the silence stretch between us like a drawn blade, letting him feel the weight of my gaze as it dissected him layer by layer. He was thinking furiously now, his clever mind racing through calculations and contingencies, trying to determine what he had said wrong and how he might recover from it.

"You are a clever creature, my fox," I said, my voice a soft purr that made the fine hairs on his arms stand at attention. "You think in terms of armies and supply lines, of nations and ideologies. Such a limited, mortal imagination." I walked toward him, my bare feet making no sound on the fractured marble. "You mistake the weapon for the wound. Their army is their heart. Their power is their heart."

I stopped before him, close enough to see the pulse jumping in his throat, to smell the lingering scent of fear that clung to him like cologne. "Their heart is small," I whispered, the plan blooming in my mind like a night-blooming flower, beautiful, poisonous, and perfect in its simplicity. "And it is utterly unprotected."

My gaze drifted to a secondary display that materialized at my thought, showing a piece of intelligence I had collected weeks ago. A file I had deemed irrelevant at the time, just another footnote in the vast catalog of information my network gathered. A grainy image of a red-haired child, barely a teenager, her storm-gray eyes serious beyond her years as she stood under Petra's grim watch.

The child was unremarkable in most ways, small for her age, thin from the privations of war, her clothes patched and repatched until they were more thread than fabric. There was something in her posture, in the way she held herself, that spoke of hidden strength. More importantly, there was something in the way Ilija looked at her in the surveillance footage, a softness that transformed his entire face.

Ilija and Danica had a fucking child.

"That fucking bitch, Danica. You fucking whore," I snarled. How the hell did they keep the knowledge of this child from me? All my generals, the

Fox, every fucking person under my command, either fucking stupid or complicit.

"Fox!"

He looked quickly, like a child who had his hand in a cookie jar.

"Did you fucking know they had a child?!"

"Yes, my queen. I thought you knew," he smiled slyly.

I leered at him with the intent to rip his fucking heart out of his chest and let him bleed out on the marble. "And you didn't think just maybe, for one goddamn second, you should tell me?!"

"Oh, I did. I also did not want to feel your rage. I happen to love my existence over all else. And I was not about to be unmade for information."

"Fuck you," The words dripped from my mouth like poison. "No matter. You will make this right. Find the child. Bring her to me. Then we will see how long their fucking resolve lasts."

Lemminkäinen's eyes widened slightly as understanding dawned, pupils dilating like a cat's in darkness. For the first time since I had known him, I saw genuine surprise flicker across his features. He understood instantly what I was proposing, and the implications sent a visible shiver through his lean frame.

His mind always ran along the lines of strategy and tactics, calculating risks and benefits with mathematical precision. "My Lady," he began, then stopped, swallowing whatever words had been forming. When he spoke again, his voice carried a note of something that might have been concern. "That is a military liability. To target the child would be to turn them into fanatics. It would grant them a moral clarity that would fuel their entire war effort. A symbol is harder to kill than an army. You would give them a holy cause. You would make them saints."

I laughed, a low, melodic sound that held no mirth whatsoever. The sound echoed off the broken marble walls, multiplying until it seemed like a chorus of furies were sharing my amusement. "Saints are only useful when they are dead, Lemminkäinen. And I am weary of this grand, grinding war. It has become tedious, predictable. This is no longer a matter of strategy or politics or the careful management of resources."

I walked toward him, my footsteps leaving small cracks in the marble with each impact. The very stone seemed to recoil from the force of my will, the mountain itself groaning under the weight of divine displeasure. "It has become a lesson in theology. And the first tenet of my faith is this: Ilija is mine."

The words tasted like blood on my tongue, like poison and honey mixed in equal measure. They carried the weight of absolute truth, of divine decree, of a law as fundamental as gravity or the speed of light. I had shaped him, had awakened the storm in his blood, had claimed him in ways that went deeper than flesh or bone. He belonged to me with a completeness that transcended mortal understanding.

"He has forgotten this truth," I continued, my voice growing softer with each word, more dangerous. "That woman has made him forget his place in the cosmic order. She has filled his head with the noise of her pathetic little rebellions, with talk of freedom and choice and all the other lies mortals tell themselves to avoid accepting reality."

I knew exactly how she corrupted him all those years ago in his lecture hall, careful manipulation, the gradual poisoning of his mind against me. She would have started small, with questions that seemed innocent. Why had I chosen this policy over that one? Couldn't the goddess of love find solutions that required less bloodshed?

Then, as his resistance weakened, she would have grown bolder. She would have painted pictures of a world without divine guidance, where mortals were free to make their own mistakes, to choose their own paths even if those paths led to ruin. She would have fed his scholar's mind with romantic notions about democracy and self-determination, about the inherent dignity of creatures too stupid to understand their own limitations.

And finally, when his defenses were completely down, she would have offered him the one thing no argument could resist: herself. Her body, her heart, her unwavering devotion to the cause of chaos. She would have made him believe that love could conquer wisdom, that passion could triumph over order, that two people together could stand against the inevitable tide of divine will.

"I will remind him of the beautiful, profound peace that comes from having no choice at all," I said, the words carrying the weight of prophecy. "I will burn her from his soul, piece by piece, until nothing remains save the man I shaped him to be. And the child..." I let the sentence hang in the frozen air, savoring the moment before revelation. "The child is the final piece. The living proof of his transgression."

Lemminkäinen watched me with growing fascination, his mind working through the implications like a mathematician solving an elegant proof. I could see the moment understanding clicked into place, could watch the predatory smile spread across his scarred features as he grasped the beautiful simplicity of it.

He saw the argument was lost, saw the obsession and the divine, unbending will behind it. He did what all clever creatures do when faced with an overwhelming force: he adapted. He found a way to make my desire his own, to transform my personal vendetta into something that served his interests as well.

"To take the child," he murmured, the words rolling around in his mouth like fine wine, tasting the shape of this new and exquisite cruelty. "Would be to place a leash around the storm's neck. He would follow wherever you led. He would come to you as a supplicant, a beggar." His pale eyes gleamed with sudden hunger. "An elegant solution. Far more personal than simply starving an army to death."

"He will kneel," I corrected, though I was pleased by his understanding. "And he will thank me for taking the burden of his misplaced love away. He will see that the child is safer, purer, happier under my care. I will raise her to understand the beauty of order, the peace that comes from accepting one's place in the grand design. She will have a goddess for a mother. What greater gift could any father ask for?"

The lie was so perfect, so beautiful in its construction, that I almost believed it myself. Almost. The truth was simpler and far more honest: I would take the child because she mattered to him, and everything that mattered to him belonged to me. I would use her as a weapon against him, a chain to bind him to my will, a reminder of what happened to those who tried to steal what was mine.

The lie would serve its purpose. It would make the taking easier, the keeping simpler. Children were remarkably adaptable creatures, they accepted new realities with a resilience that adults had lost. Given time and proper guidance, she would come to love me as she had never loved her mortal guardians. She would become the daughter I had never had, the heir to my divine throne.

And Ilija would watch it happen, helpless to prevent it, grateful for my mercy in keeping her alive.

Lemminkäinen bowed, a deep and fluid motion that spoke of genuine respect rather than mere diplomatic courtesy. This time, there was no mockery in the gesture, no hint of the casual insolence he had shown before. He had seen the true shape of my will, and it was a thing that commanded awe from even the most jaded observer.

"As you command, my Queen," he said, his voice carrying a note of something approaching reverence. "The armies of the world are a prelude to this greater work. Where do you wish for the true war to begin?"

I walked to the edge of my dais, to the great open arch that looked out on the star-strewn tapestry of the cosmos I commanded. The view was spectacular beyond mortal comprehension, nebulae spiraling in colors that had no names, galaxies wheeling in their ancient dance, the very fabric of space-time responding to my will like a musical instrument in the hands of a master.

My gaze was drawn downward, to the small blue marble that hung in the darkness below. To the realm of dirt and suffering that mortals called home, where Athens pulsed with chaotic energy and my stolen storm-king walked beside another woman.

The time for patience was over. The time for subtle manipulation had passed. They had forced my hand with their pathetic display of defiance, had made it impossible for me to ignore the theft of what was mine.

"Seal the Gates of Athens," I commanded, and my voice was no longer a whisper. It was a decree that resonated through the very stone of Olympus, a command that sped along the invisible pathways of my power to every Accord outpost in Attica. "Let no one in. Let no one out. Let the rats enjoy the brief freedom of their cage before the cat descends."

I felt the order take effect across the city, blast barriers sliding into place with thunderous grinding, checkpoints activating their lockdown protocols with the mechanical precision of clockwork, airspace defense systems coming online with deadly hums that would have been inaudible to mortal ears. Within minutes, Athens would become the world's most secure prison, its inhabitants trapped inside their own moment of triumph.

"Your northern strategy was clever, my fox," I said, turning back to face him. The broken marble beneath my feet began to repair itself, cracks sealing with veins of pure gold, the dead lotus blossoms blooming anew in their crystal vases. "They have forced my hand. I will give them the confrontation they seek. They have come to my city to make a stand. I will turn it into their collective grave."

My power unfurled like wings of pure light, the crimson radiance of my personal sky flooding the chamber. The very air sang with divine energy as reality bent itself to accommodate my desires. I felt the familiar weight of my wargear settling on my shoulders, the armor of Aphrodite Areia, the war-goddess the Spartans had worshipped, beauty forged for the sole purpose of breaking things.

The armor was more than metal and leather, it was crystallized divine will made manifest. Each plate was inscribed with runes of power that had been old when the first human learned to make fire. The helm bore the face of love triumphant, beautiful beyond mortal comprehension and terrible in its perfection. The sword at my side had tasted the blood of titans and would drink deeply again before this war was done.

"You will find the child for me," I said to Lemminkäinen, my voice carrying the weight of absolute command. "You will track her movements, map her defenses, and learn her routines. When I give the word, you will bring her to me unharmed. She is a prize. She is the future."

He nodded, his eyes bright with anticipation. This was the sort of task that appealed to his particular talents, complex, personal, requiring subtlety and patience rather than brute force. He was already planning, I could see, already calculating how to slip past their defenses and claim what I desired.

"And the others?" he purred, his voice carrying a hunter's eager hunger. "Their general and her storm-touched consort?"

I looked toward the shimmering air where the surveillance feed had shown me their defiant faces, where the image of their unity still burned in my divine memory. They thought their love was armor against my wrath, their bond a shield against divine displeasure. They would learn that love could be the greatest weakness of all, the crack in the fortress wall that let in the destroying angel.

First, I would send them a message. A reminder of who truly held power in this world, who commanded the forces they had chosen to defy.

I lifted a hand, my fingers curling as if plucking a discordant string from a cosmic lyre. The air around one of their largest banners, the star and serpent hanging from the facade of a municipal building, began to shimmer with heat distortion.

Then gold fire bloomed at its center, spreading outward in perfect geometric patterns. It didn't burn with the chaotic rage of mortal flame. It cleansed. It purified. The canvas dissolved into silent, glittering ash that rained down on the stunned crowd below like snow made of crushed diamonds, beautiful and merciless and absolute.

The message was clear: I could reach them anywhere, anytime, with surgical precision. Their symbols meant nothing. Their defiance was temporary. Their hope was just another form of fuel for the flames I commanded.

A slow, cold smile spread across my face as I watched the golden ash settle on upturned faces, as I saw the first whispers of fear begin to spread through their celebration.

"They are the sacrifice," I said, savoring each word like the finest wine. "And I am on my way to the altar."

CHAPTER TWENTY-SEVEN
THE SKY FALLS

Ilija

The rain fell in sheets across Athens, each droplet carrying the weight of what we had become. I stood in the ruins of the Monastiraki district, watching the water turn ancient cobblestones into mirrors that reflected the fires consuming the city. The air tasted of copper and ozone, thick with the electricity that coursed through my veins and the smoke that billowed from burning Accord war machines.

This was our hour. The storm I carried would finally serve justice.

Danica moved through the battlefield like something out of mythology, her raven hair streaming behind her as she danced between bullets and bodies. The Accord soldiers advanced in perfect formation, their black armor gleaming wet in the rain, assault rifles spitting fire as they tried to establish a foothold in the square. They moved with the mechanical precision of zealots, each step calculated, each burst of gunfire measured. They had come here to cleanse the city of dissent, to turn Athens into another sterile monument to their vision of order.

I watched my love meet them with winter's fury.

She raised her left hand, fingers spread wide, and the temperature plummeted. The rain turned to sleet, then to hail, then to something far worse. Black ice erupted from the cobblestones in jagged spears, each one sharp enough to pierce tank armor. The advancing squad never had a chance to scream. The ice caught them mid-stride, growing up through their boots, encasing their legs in crystalline tombs. One soldier, a young woman whose face I could see through her visor, tried to tear herself free. The ice held her fast, and I watched the terror bloom in her eyes as she realized what was coming next.

Danica's right hand closed into a fist.

The pillar of flame that erupted beneath the trapped soldiers turned night into day. White-hot fire, hotter than a blast furnace, rose thirty feet into the air. The thermal shock was instantaneous and absolute. Ice flashed to superheated steam in the span of a heartbeat, and the soldiers simply vanished. Their armor collapsed into pools of molten slag that hissed and bubbled on the wet stones. The steam cloud that had been their bodies dispersed into the rain, leaving the acrid smell of vaporized metal and the ghostly outlines of their final moments burned into the pavement.

The storm in my chest sang with approval.

More Accord forces poured into the square from the north, their heavy boots drumming against the stone in perfect cadence. An armored personnel carrier rolled with them, its treads crushing centuries-old debris beneath its weight. The machine gun mounted on its turret swiveled toward our position, the barrel already glowing red-hot from sustained fire. I could see the gunner through the weapon's sight, his face hidden behind tactical goggles, his hands steady on the grips.

He opened fire on a group of civilians cowering behind an overturned market stall.

The fury that rose in me was cold, focused. I had learned to channel the storm, to shape its infinite power with surgical precision. The lightning that answered my call was a needle of pure electricity, thin as a finger yet carrying the power of a god.

I threaded it through the chaos of the battlefield, past the screaming civilians and the burning vehicles, past the falling rain and the drifting smoke. It struck the APC's external camera array, and the vehicle went blind in an instant. Sparks cascaded from the fried electronics, and I watched the gunner's head snap back and forth as he tried to reacquire his targets.

He was firing blind now, his bullets stitching a line of destruction through his own advancing troops.

I sent another needle of lightning into the vehicle's left tread assembly. The electrical discharge welded the metal links into a solid, useless mass, and the APC lurched to one side like a wounded animal. The driver tried to compensate, revving the engine until it screamed, yet the machine could only spin in circles now, its remaining tread tearing up chunks of ancient stone.

The infantry squad that had been following the vehicle scattered in confusion. I reached out with my power and seized the wind itself, compressing it into something harder than steel. The invisible fist I created slammed into their formation like a cannonball, sending bodies tumbling through the air. One soldier crashed through the window of a tourist shop, his armor crumpling against the brick wall inside. Another landed in the fountain at the center of the square, his neck bent at an angle that told me he would never get up again.

This was our rhythm. Danica brought the apocalypse, and I conducted its symphony.

She was already moving toward the next wave of enemies, her boots splashing through puddles that steamed with residual heat from her flames. A squad of Accord regulars had taken position behind an overturned bus, their rifles poking through the shattered windows as they laid down suppressing fire. Danica paused at the edge of their range, her head tilted slightly to one side, studying them with the detached curiosity of a scientist examining insects.

Then she opened her hand, and winter came to Athens.

The blizzard that erupted from her palm was ice shards, each one eighteen inches long and sharp as a blade, launched with the velocity of rifle bullets. They punched through the bus's metal skin as if it were paper, through the soldiers' body armor as if it were cloth. I watched one shard take a man's arm off at the shoulder, the wound instantly cauterized by the supernatural cold. He stared at the stump where his limb had been, his mouth open in a soundless scream, before another partisan's bullet found the weak spot where his helmet joined his gorget.

The shard that had taken his arm pinned itself to the bus's rear wall, and his severed limb hung there like a grotesque flag of surrender.

Another soldier tried to run. Danica's ice caught him in the back, the crystalline spear emerging from his chest in a spray of blood that froze before it could hit the ground. He took three more steps, his hands clawing at the ice protruding from his sternum, before he collapsed face-first onto the cobblestones. The puddle of blood that spread beneath him turned to crimson glass in seconds.

I was already engaging the next threat. An Accord sniper had taken position on a rooftop three blocks away, his rifle scope glinting in the firelight as he tried to draw a bead on Danica. Through the storm in my soul, I could feel his presence like a cold spot in the world, a focus of malevolent intent. He thought the distance would protect him. He thought his camouflaged position would keep him safe.

He was wrong.

I reached out with my power and took hold of the air itself, compressing it into a column of invisible force. The wind I sent racing across the battlefield was focused to a point no larger than my fist, yet it carried all the fury of a hurricane. It struck the sniper's position with the force of an artillery shell, and I watched the entire corner of the building collapse in a cascade of brick and mortar. The sniper's body tumbled through the air, his rifle spinning away into the darkness, before he crashed into the street below with the wet crunch of breaking bones.

His black armor had split open like the shell of an egg, and the red contents were spreading across the pavement in patterns that would have been beautiful if they had not once been human.

We were winning. The square was littered with Accord dead, their bodies twisted into impossible shapes by ice and fire and wind. The survivors had fallen back, regrouping in the shadow of the ancient Agora, yet I could see the fear in their movements now. They had come to Athens expecting to face ordinary insurgents, ordinary weapons, ordinary resistance. Instead, they had found gods of war walking among the mortals.

The Accord was disciplined, adaptive, ruthless in their pursuit of order. As we carved through their front lines, their rear echelons were already adjusting their tactics. A new sound echoed across the battlefield: the heavy, measured footfalls of power armor.

The Inquisitors came in a wedge formation, their massive frames towering over the regular infantry. Each one stood eight feet tall in their augmented armor, their faces hidden behind visors that gleamed with targeting data. They carried power mauls that crackled with dissonant energy, weapons designed specifically to disrupt the neural pathways that channeled abilities like ours. They moved with terrifying grace for such large figures, their servo-assisted muscles carrying them across the battlefield in bounding leaps that covered impossible distances.

Danica met them without hesitation.

She planted her feet and raised both hands, and the ice that answered her call was different from what had come before. This was architecture. A wall of solid ice rose from the cobblestones, twenty feet high and six feet thick, crystalline and perfect as a glacier's heart. The Inquisitors struck it with the collective force of a freight train, their power mauls sending cascades of sparks across the ice's surface. Hairline cracks appeared where the weapons made contact, spider-webbing outward in patterns that reminded me of broken windows.

The wall held.

The Inquisitors fell back, their tactical systems already calculating new angles of attack. That was when Danica smiled, and I knew that she had been waiting for this moment. The ice wall didn't shatter or melt. Instead, it began to sublime, transforming directly from solid to gas in defiance of every law of physics I had ever learned. Thick fog billowed outward, obscuring everything in a cloud of supercooled vapor that turned the battlefield into a frozen hell.

The Inquisitors were blind now, their thermal imaging useless in the supernatural cold. I watched them stumble through the fog like giants in a fairy tale, their power mauls sweeping back and forth in wide arcs as they searched for targets they could no longer see. They were calling out to each other on their tactical frequency, trying to coordinate their movements, yet the fog swallowed their voices like a living thing.

Danica walked into that white hell with the Blade of Fates in her hand.

The sword was a masterwork of impossible craftsmanship, its edge sharp enough to cut through destiny itself. In the fog, it remained the only visible thing, its blade wreathed in cold flames that burned without heat. I lost sight of Danica herself almost immediately, yet I could track her movements by the sounds that emerged from the mist: the wet thud of steel finding flesh, the sharp crack of armor being pierced, the choked gasps of Inquisitors dying in the cold and the dark.

One of them stumbled out of the fog, his chest plate split open in a diagonal slash that ran from his left shoulder to his right hip. Dark blood poured from the wound, freezing into icicles before it could hit the ground. He managed three steps before his legs gave out, and he crashed to his knees with the grinding sound of damaged servos. His visor had been cracked, and through the spiderweb of broken glass, I could see his eyes. They were wide with shock, staring at something beyond the visible world.

He toppled forward and moved no more.

Another Inquisitor's scream cut through the mist, high and desperate. It ended abruptly, replaced by the sound of something heavy hitting the ground. A severed arm flew out of the fog, still encased in power armor, still gripping a maul that sparked and fizzled as its power source died. The arm landed at my feet, and I could see where Danica's blade had cut through the joint. The wound was so clean it looked surgical.

The fog began to dissipate, revealing the aftermath of Danica's hunt. Five Inquisitors lay scattered across the square, their massive forms reduced to broken dolls. One had been nearly cut in half at the waist, his upper and lower body connected only by a few strands of frozen viscera. Another lay on his back, arms spread wide, his helmet split down the middle to reveal the ruined meat that had once been his face. A third had been opened from throat to groin, his armor peeled back like the petals of a flower, exposing the tangle of organs and machinery that had kept him alive.

Danica emerged from the last wisps of fog like a vengeful spirit, her hair plastered to her skull with condensation, the Blade of Fates still burning with cold fire in her grip. She was breathing hard, her cheeks flushed with exertion and something that might have been joy. When our eyes met across the square, she smiled, and I felt the storm in my chest answer with something that was almost contentment.

Victory crystallized around us like one of Danica's ice sculptures, beautiful and perfect and unbreakable.

That was when the trap closed.

The sound that rolled across Athens was unlike anything I had ever heard. It came from the north and south simultaneously, a deep, resonant BOOM that seemed to emanate from the earth itself. Massive machinery engaging, ancient mechanisms sliding into place, a cage door slamming shut with the finality of judgment. Every gun in the city fell silent. Every scream cut off mid-breath. Even the rain seemed to pause in its descent, as if the world itself was holding its breath.

Our communications died instantly, replaced by a wall of static that hurt to listen to. The tactical displays that had been feeding us intelligence went dark. The drones that had been providing overwatch suddenly changed course, ascending in perfect formation toward the storm clouds above. As they rose, their running lights began to pulse in synchronized patterns, crimson beacons that linked together until they formed a vast network of captured light.

The sky itself became a cage.

I looked up through the rain and watched the drones weave their net of light across the heavens, each node connecting to its neighbors until the entire city was sealed beneath a dome of energy. The storm in my chest recoiled from the sight, recognizing something fundamentally wrong with the pattern above us. This was something older, something that spoke to powers beyond human understanding.

We had walked into a trap that had been years in the making.

I felt her presence before I saw her, a familiar corruption of the air that made the storm in my soul snarl with recognition and rage. The clouds above the Acropolis began to burn, their gray forms igniting with a light that was wrong in every conceivable way. This was the color of molten gold, of divine wrath, of judgment passed down from on high.

A weight settled over the city, pressing down on every living thing with the inexorable force of a mountain. The civilians who had been watching from windows and doorways dropped to their knees, their bodies unable to bear the presence that descended upon Athens. Even some of our own fighters fell prone, their rifles clattering to the ground as they struggled to breathe under the divine pressure.

And then she appeared.

Ana descended from the burning clouds like a goddess returning to her altar, her golden armor blazing with its own inner light. She landed on the roof of the Parthenon, her feet touching the ancient marble with reverent precision. The surviving Accord soldiers immediately dropped to one knee in synchronized worship, their weapons lowered, their heads bowed in fanatical devotion. The very air around her shimmered with power, distorting the rain into patterns that hurt to look at directly.

She was beautiful. She had always been beautiful. Even now, even after everything she had done, I couldn't deny the terrible perfection of her form. Her face was unmarked by time or conflict, her golden hair flowing around her shoulders like liquid sunlight. When she smiled, it was with the serene confidence of someone who had never doubted her own righteousness.

That smile had once been for me alone.

Danica's hand found mine, her fingers interlocking with desperate strength. I could feel her trembling, whether with rage or fear I couldn't tell. The Blade of Fates had gone out, its cold flames extinguished by Ana's presence. Even Danica's power, vast as it was, seemed diminished in the face of true divinity.

"Ilija," she whispered, and in that single word I heard everything: love, determination, and the terrible knowledge that we had been outmaneuvered by an enemy who knew us better than we knew ourselves.

Ana's voice, when it came, was amplified by the Accord's network until it seemed to emerge from the city itself. Every speaker, every abandoned radio, every soldier's communication device carried her words across Athens like a divine pronouncement. The sound was honey and poison, silk and steel, beautiful and terrible in equal measure.

"Children of Athens," she began, and her voice was exactly as I remembered it. "You have forgotten the gift of peace that I gave you. You have allowed weeds to grow in the perfect garden of order, and now those weeds threaten to choke out all beauty, all harmony, all hope."

She stood atop the Parthenon like a golden queen surveying her domain, yet her eyes were fixed on me. Across the distance, across the rain and smoke and chaos, I felt her gaze like a physical touch. The storm in my chest writhed and bucked, recognizing the chains it had once worn, remembering the leash that had held it captive for so many years.

"I have returned," Ana continued, and now there was something else in her voice, something hungry and possessive that made my skin crawl. "I have returned to prune the garden, to restore the balance that has been lost. The chaos that infects this city has a name, and that name is known to me."

She paused, letting the weight of her words settle over Athens like a shroud.

"Bring me Ilija Dragović," she commanded, and the way she spoke my name was a caress and a claim, a reminder of what I had been and a promise of what I could become again. "Bring me Danica Madsen. Lay them at the foot of my altar, and Athens will be spared. Continue to harbor these agents of chaos, and your city will learn what it means to be purified in holy fire."

The challenge hung in the air between us like a blade suspended by a thread. Every Accord soldier in the city would be converging on our position now. Every drone, every surveillance system, every orbital asset would be focused on hunting us down. Ana had turned the entire population of Athens into her unwilling accomplices, using their love for their city as a weapon against the two people who had fought hardest to free them.

There was something else in her offer, something that chilled me more than any threat of destruction. She could have obliterated the city from orbit. She could have turned Athens into a crater of molten glass without even landing. Instead, she was here, standing on the Parthenon, offering mercy in exchange for surrender.

This was about us. It had always been about us.

Ana wanted me as her consort. She wanted Danica dead and the world kneeling at our feet.

I looked at Danica, saw my own understanding reflected in her eyes. The battle for the square, the fighting in the streets, the desperate struggle for Athens, all of it had been theater. Ana had orchestrated this entire campaign to create a scenario where I would have no choice but to face her again, where the storm she had once controlled would come home to its mistress.

"She planned this," Danica said, her voice hollow with realization. "All of it. The attack on the city, the resistance movements, even our victories. She let us think we were winning."

"Because she needed me to feel powerful again," I replied, the pieces falling into place with sickening clarity. "She needed me to remember what I was capable of."

"So she could cage you again."

"Yes." The word felt like ash in my mouth. "She made one mistake."

"What's that?"

I turned to face her fully, seeing the woman who had pulled me back from the edge of despair, who had taught me that power without love was just another form of slavery. "She thinks I'm still the same broken man she left behind. She doesn't understand what we've become together."

Danica's smile was fierce and beautiful, even in the shadow of Ana's divine presence. "Then let's show her."

The rain continued to fall, washing the blood from the cobblestones and carrying the ashes of the dead into the gutters where they would flow down to the sea. Above us, the dome of light pulsed with malevolent purpose, sealing us inside Ana's trap. Around us, the city held its breath, waiting to see whether its would-be saviors would become its sacrificial lambs.

The war for Athens was over. The war for my soul had just begun, and the entire city was Ana's hostage in that struggle.

As I stood there in the rain, feeling the storm in my chest rage against its former bonds, I realized something that Ana might have overlooked in her careful calculations. I was no longer the broken man she had once commanded. The storm was no longer a caged beast, desperate for any scrap of freedom she might offer.

I was free now. We were free. And freedom, I had learned, was a power that even gods could struggle to chain.

The sky might be falling, yet we were still standing. And as long as we drew breath, the fight would continue.

Let Ana come, then. Let her bring all the divine wrath at her disposal, unleash the full fury of Olympus if she dared. We had given Athens a taste of what true liberation looked like, a glimpse of a future unburdened by tyranny, and that was a gift that could survive even gods. The seeds of freedom had been sown in fertile ground, watered by the tears of the oppressed and nourished by the blood of their oppressors. Even if she razed the city to the ground, the idea would persist. It would spread like wildfire through the hearts of every Athenian, a burning ember that no amount of divine intervention could extinguish.

The storm was coming home, yet it would arrive changed. And when it did, Ana would learn what it meant to face the fury of a god who had chosen to be human.

The rain fell harder, and in its rhythm, I heard the drumbeat of war.

Chapter Twenty-Eight
BLOOD AND LIGHTNING

Ilija

The sound of boots on wet stone echoed through the narrow alleyways behind us, growing closer with each passing second. Ana's voice still reverberated across the city, her ultimatum hanging in the air like a death sentence, yet we had no intention of surrendering. We ran through the rain-slicked streets of old Athens, our feet splashing through puddles that reflected the fires still burning in the distance.

"This way," I called to Danica, pulling her toward a seemingly solid wall of ancient stone. My hands found the hidden catch, a mechanism so old it predated the Roman conquest. The stones shifted with a grinding sound, revealing a passage that had been sealed for centuries.

"How did you—" Danica started to ask.

"Kostis showed me during the early days," I replied, already leading her into the darkness. "The resistance used these tunnels to move weapons. They connect to the Acropolis."

The passage was barely wide enough for two people, carved from living rock by hands that had been dust for millennia. Our footsteps echoed strangely in the confined space, and I could hear water dripping somewhere in the darkness ahead. The air smelled of earth and age, tinged with the metallic scent of the storm that raged both outside and within my chest.

Behind us, the sounds of pursuit faded as the Accord forces searched the streets above. They would find the passage eventually, Ana's network was too thorough to miss such an obvious escape route, yet it would buy us precious time.

"Where does this lead?" Danica asked, her breath visible in the frigid air.

"There's a chamber beneath the old foundations," I said, navigating by memory and the faint luminescence that seemed to emanate from the walls themselves. "Kostis called it the Scholar's Rest. Said it was where the ancient priests would retreat during times of siege."

The tunnel began to slope upward, and I could feel the weight of the Acropolis pressing down above us. We were moving into the heart of the ancient citadel, following paths that had been carved when Athens was young and the gods still walked among mortals. The irony was lost on me, we were seeking sanctuary in the shadow of the very temple where Ana now held court.

After what felt like hours yet was probably only minutes, we reached a heavy wooden door reinforced with iron bands. It stood slightly ajar, warm light spilling through the crack. I exchanged a glance with Danica, both of us drawing our weapons. Someone was inside, hopefully Petra's trusted contact, yet we couldn't be certain.

I pushed the door open slowly, and the sight that greeted us made the storm in my chest go completely still.

A woman I didn't recognize sat at a small wooden table, playing cards by candlelight with someone whose back was to us. She was perhaps forty, with graying hair pulled back in a simple bun and the weathered hands of someone who had spent years doing honest work. Yet it wasn't her I was looking at.

It was the girl across from her, red hair falling in waves around her shoulders as she studied her cards with intense concentration. Even from behind, I could see Danica's graceful posture, the way she tilted her head when she was thinking, the delicate curve of her neck that was achingly familiar.

My daughter. Our Selene.

"I call," Selene said, laying down her cards with a triumphant grin that was pure Danica. "Three queens."

The older woman groaned theatrically and threw her cards down. "You're getting too good at this game, little one. Your mother taught you well."

At the sound of our footsteps on stone, both women looked up. The older woman's hand moved instinctively toward a pistol at her hip before recognition dawned in her eyes. Yet it was Selene's reaction that stopped time itself.

Her cards scattered to the floor like falling leaves as she shot to her feet, her dark eyes, Danica's eyes exactly, going wide with shock so profound it was almost physical.

"Tata?" The word was barely a breath, trembling with disbelief and desperate hope.

Then her gaze shifted to the woman beside me, and I watched all the color drain from her face. Her lips parted, yet no sound came. Her hands reached out as if to touch something that couldn't possibly be real.

"Mama?"

The word broke from her throat like a sob, and I watched my daughter's knees buckle. Danica was across the room before Selene could fall, catching her in arms that had ached to hold her for six endless years.

"My baby," Danica whispered, her voice thick with tears she had held back through countless nights. "My beautiful, perfect baby girl."

Selene collapsed against her mother's chest, her whole body shaking with sobs that seemed to come from the depths of her soul. "You're dead," she kept saying, her words muffled against Danica's shirt. "You're supposed to be dead. Everyone told me you were dead. They said Ana killed you in battle, that I'd never see you again."

"I'm here," Danica said, stroking Selene's hair with hands that trembled with suppressed emotion. "I'm here, little star. I'm going anywhere. Never again."

I stood frozen in the doorway, watching the reunion I had dreamed of for thirteen years yet had never dared to believe would actually happen. Selene was no longer the toddler from my memories, she was thirteen now, almost as tall as her mother, with the graceful limbs and sharp intelligence that marked her as Danica's daughter. Yet in this moment, seeing her clinging to the mother she thought she'd lost forever, she was simply a child who had found her way home.

"How?" Selene pulled back to look at Danica's face, her hands reaching up to trace her mother's cheeks as if she needed physical proof this wasn't another dream. "How are you alive? They said they saw your body. They said Ana watched you die."

"Ana did watch, baby. She watched my life leave my eyes, my body. Yet Freyja came. She took me to Folkvangr and your Tata was there waiting for me," the smile when Danica said that made me start to cry. "Let's work on getting all of us out of here alive and we'll tell you the whole story, little star."

"She's tall, she's taller than I am," we all laughed at my words. "Once we get out of this, I am going to make you the best ćevapi and homemade ajvar you've ever had, kiddo." I had honestly been craving ćevapi since all this started.

Selene's gaze found mine across the room, and I saw wonder bloom in her expression alongside the tears. "Tata," she said again, this time with recognition rather than shock. "You're really here. Both of you."

I crossed the chamber slowly, afraid that sudden movement might shatter this perfect, impossible moment. When I reached them, Selene immediately pulled me into their embrace, and I felt thirteen years of pain and longing finally begin to heal.

She was warm and solid and real in my arms, smelling of soap and candlewax and something indefinably her own. I buried my face in her hair, Danica's hair, yet longer, wilder, and tried to think about all the birthdays I'd missed, all the scraped knees I hadn't kissed, all the bedtime stories I'd never told.

"I missed you so much," she whispered against my shirt, her voice thick with tears. "Every single day. I used to pretend you were just away on a long trip, that you'd come home eventually with presents and stories."

"We wanted to," I said, my voice rough with emotion I'd held back for far too long. "Every day, we wanted to come back to you. Yet it wasn't safe. We had to wait until we could protect you properly."

The older woman cleared her throat gently, reminding us we weren't alone. "Forgive the interruption," she said with a kind smile, "yet introductions might be wise. I'm Maria, one of Petra's oldest friends. She entrusted Selene to my care when she had to leave the city."

"Where is Petra?" Danica asked, still holding Selene close as if she might disappear if released.

"Coordinating evacuations," Maria replied. "When we realized there was a spy feeding information to the Accord, she moved Selene here and went to help get the other families to safety. This place isn't on any of our operational maps, even most of the resistance leadership doesn't know about it."

The mention of a spy sent ice through my veins. "Do we know who?"

"Petra had her suspicions. Someone close to the inner circle, someone with access to all our safe house locations. She said she'd handle it when she returned."

Selene pulled back from our embrace, wiping tears from her cheeks with the back of her hand. The gesture was so achingly familiar, Danica did the exact same thing, that it made my chest tight.

"I still can't believe you're really here," she said, looking between us with wonder. "Do you know how many nights I lay awake imagining this moment? How many times I dreamed you'd walk through a door and tell me it was all a mistake, that you weren't really gone?"

"Too many," Danica said, cupping our daughter's face in her hands. "Far, far too many. Yet we're here now, and I swear to you, we will never leave you again."

Selene's expression grew more serious, and I was struck by how mature she seemed. This wasn't the child we'd left behind. This was a young woman who had grown up in a world at war, who had learned to think strategically about survival.

"Are you here because of me?" she asked directly. "Or because of what's happening to the city?"

The question caught me off guard with its adult perception. She understood that our timing couldn't be coincidental, that our sudden appearance was connected to Ana's assault on Athens.

"Both," I answered honestly. "Ana made a mistake when she came here. She thought she could use the city as bait to draw us out, force us to surrender to save innocent lives. She didn't expect us to fight back."

"And now she's offered to spare Athens if you turn yourselves over," Selene said. It wasn't a question.

"Yes."

"Are you going to do it?"

"No," Danica said firmly. "We're going to end this. We're going to stop Ana once and for all, so you never have to hide again."

Before Selene could respond, another voice cut through our reunion like a blade through silk.

"How very touching."

I spun toward the doorway, every instinct screaming danger. Jaakko stood there with casual confidence, his familiar face wearing an expression of cold satisfaction that transformed his features into something I barely recognized. He held an Accord pulse rifle with practiced ease, its energy cells casting an eerie blue glow across the ancient stones. Behind him, I could hear the soft footfalls of soldiers moving through the tunnel system.

"Hello, Ilija. Danica," he said, his Finnish accent somehow more pronounced than I remembered. "Ana sends her warmest regards."

Maria immediately stepped in front of Selene, her hand moving to the pistol at her hip, yet my daughter was staring at our former comrade with confusion rather than fear.

"Jaakko?" she said, her voice uncertain. "What are you doing here? How did you find us?"

"I've been looking for you, little bird," he said, and his smile was gentle, paternal even. "Ana has been very concerned about your safety. She sent me to bring you somewhere more secure."

The casual endearment, the false warmth in his voice, the way he looked at my daughter like she was a prize to be claimed, something primordial and savage awakened in my chest. The storm that lived there began to stir, yet this wasn't the controlled power I'd wielded in battle. This was something older, more fundamental. This was the fury of a father whose child had been threatened.

"She doesn't know her," I said, my voice low and dangerous. "She's never even met Ana."

"Yet," Jaakko agreed pleasantly. "Yet Ana is very much looking forward to getting acquainted. She has such plans for young Selene's future."

Selene took a step backward, pressing against Maria's protective form. "I don't understand. Jaakko, you helped the resistance. You brought supplies to the families, helped set up safe houses. Why are you working with Ana?"

"Because Ana offers something your parents never could," Jaakko replied. "Security. Peace. A world where children don't have to hide in ruins, playing cards by candlelight while wars rage overhead."

The rifle in his hands shifted slightly, and I saw the targeting laser paint a red dot on Selene's forehead. The sight of it triggered something in me that went beyond rage, beyond fury, into a realm of pure, devastating wrath that I had never accessed before.

"Move that weapon away from my daughter."

My words came out as a growl that seemed to shake dust from the ancient ceiling. Lightning began to dance across my skin, yet this wasn't the surgical precision I'd used against the Accord forces in the square. This was raw, primal power that tasted of copper and ozone and the promise of absolute destruction.

Jaakko's smile never wavered. "I don't think so, my friend. You see, Ana anticipated you might be... unreasonable. She gave me very specific instructions about handling your paternal instincts."

He lifted two fingers in a practiced signal. "Now," he said calmly.

"Don't—" Maria started to shout, some soldier's instinct warning her what concentrated firepower could do in an enclosed space.

I chose my target and breathed out my fury.

The air split like cracking stone. Jaakko's tactical vest jumped at the seams as electricity found every wire, every circuit, every piece of conductive material he carried. His communication device flared white-hot against his throat, then died in a shower of sparks that left smoking holes in his skin. The power cells in his rifle overloaded in sequence, each one creating a small explosion that sent fragments of metal and plastic spinning through the air.

Yet Jaakko was faster than I'd expected, more dangerous than I had anticipated. Even as his equipment failed around him, he was moving, diving sideways to escape the main arc of my attack. His rifle clattered uselessly to the floor, yet his hand was already reaching for the combat knife at his belt.

"You always were too emotional, Ilija," he snarled, his pleasant mask finally slipping to reveal the cold predator beneath. "Ana said it would be your weakness. She was right."

He came at me with the knife, moving with the fluid grace of someone trained in close quarters combat. The blade whispered through the air where my throat had been a heartbeat before, and I felt the wind of its passage across my skin.

Yet he had made a fatal mistake. He had threatened my daughter. He had put a weapon's sight on her forehead. He had spoken of Ana's plans for her future with the casual confidence of someone discussing livestock.

The storm inside me wasn't controlled anymore. It wasn't tactical. It was pure, undiluted paternal rage given the power to reshape reality.

Lightning erupted from my hands in concentrated streams that turned the air itself into a weapon. These were focused beams of electricity that sought out metal, moisture, nerve endings with surgical precision. Jaakko's knife blade became a conductor, channeling power directly into his nervous system. His scream lasted exactly long enough for his vocal cords to cook from the inside.

Yet that wasn't enough.

I reached out with my power and seized the very air around him, compressing it until it became solid as stone. Jaakko's eyes bulged as invisible hands closed around his throat, cutting off his breath, his blood, his desperate attempts to speak.

"You came here," I snarled, my voice carrying the sound of thunder, "to take my daughter. You pointed a weapon at her head. You spoke of Ana's plans like she was property to be traded!"

I squeezed harder, and Jaakko's face began to turn purple. Behind him, I could hear soldiers shouting, trying to coordinate some kind of response, yet their equipment was failing as the electrical field around me expanded.

Radio sets sparked and died. Night vision optics flared out. Weapon sights went dark.

"She is thirteen years old," I continued, each word punctuated by another surge of power. "She is my child. She is everything good and innocent and pure in this world, and you came here to deliver her to a monster."

Jaakko's lips were moving, trying to form words, trying to plead or negotiate or perhaps just to breathe. I couldn't tell which, and I didn't care.

"Ana thinks she knows me," I screamed, releasing my hold on the air around his throat. He gasped, wheezing, blood running from his nose where capillaries had burst. "She thinks she understands what I am, what I'm capable of. Yet she's never seen what happens when someone threatens my family."

I let him see it then. I let him see the full scope of what was about to happen to him. Lightning danced between my fingers, controlled, purposeful, intelligent. It sought out the iron in his blood, the salt in his sweat, the water that made up seventy percent of his body weight.

"Please," he managed to whisper. "I was just following orders."

"So were the guards at the camps," I replied. "So were the soldiers who burned the villages! So were the pilots who dropped napalm on children! Following orders is participation!"

The lightning struck him then as a dozen precise channels of power that found every nerve ending in his body simultaneously. His back arched impossibly as every muscle contracted at once, his mouth opening in a silent scream that would have shattered glass if he'd had the breath to voice it.

Yet I wasn't done.

I reached deeper into the storm, pulled forth power that I had never dared to access before. This wasn't just electricity, this was the fundamental force that held atoms together, that gave matter its structure and substance. I took hold of the bonds that made Jaakko human and began to pull them apart.

His skin began to char and split, revealing muscle that cooked even as I watched. His eyes about to burst like overripe fruit, their contents boiling away in seconds. The metal fillings in his teeth began to glow cherry-red, then white-hot, setting fire to what remained of his mouth from the inside.

And still I wasn't finished.

The stone floor beneath him began to crack as heat radiated outward in waves. The air filled with the stench of burning meat and ozone, with smoke that carried particles of what had once been a human being.

"Ilija, stop!" Danica's voice cut through my rage like a blade. "We need him alive! Ana must see what we've become, what she made us become!"

The lightning faltered, my concentration breaking at her words. Jaakko collapsed to the floor, barely conscious, his body a ruin of charred flesh and exposed bone yet still breathing in ragged, desperate gasps. Steam rose from his wounds.

"We bring him to her," Danica said, her voice steel wrapped in ice. "Let Ana see her perfect soldier. Then we finish this."

The silence that followed was absolute.

I turned to find Selene pressed against the far wall, her dark eyes wide with shock and something that might have been terror. She was staring at the place where Jaakko had been, her young face pale as moonlight.

"Tata?" she whispered, and her voice was small and lost and utterly heartbroken.

The storm in my chest suddenly went quiet, replaced by something cold and terrible. I had wanted to protect her, to show her that she was safe, that nothing in this world or any other would ever hurt her while I drew breath.

Instead, I had shown her what I really was. What I was capable of when pushed beyond all restraint.

I had shown my thirteen-year-old daughter that her father was a monster.

"Selene," I said, taking a step toward her, yet she flinched away from me. The rejection hit me like a physical blow, and I stopped moving.

"You were going to kill him," she said, still staring at the burned shadow on the floor. "He was talking, and you..."

"He was going to take you," I said, trying to keep my voice calm despite the chaos of emotions warring in my chest. "He was going to deliver you to Ana. I couldn't let that happen."

"You kept going," she said, and now there were tears streaming down her cheeks.

Danica moved to Selene's side, her own face pale with shock. She had seen me kill before, had fought beside me in battles that left fields of bodies in their wake, yet she had never seen me lose control like this. Never seen the raw, unfiltered fury that lived at the core of my power.

"It's over," she said softly, though I wasn't sure if she was talking to Selene or to me. "It's done."

Yet I could see in her eyes that something fundamental had changed. She was looking at me differently now, with a wariness that hadn't been there before. And Selene... Selene was looking at me like I was something to be afraid of.

Maybe I was.

The sound of boots echoed from the tunnel as more soldiers approached, their equipment failed yet their weapons still functional. We needed to move, needed to get out of this chamber before reinforcements arrived. Yet all I could think about was the expression on my daughter's face, the way she had pulled away from me when I tried to approach her.

"We need to go," Maria said urgently. "There will be more of them, and they'll be here soon."

I looked toward the ceiling, toward the Parthenon where Ana waited for us to come to her. She had orchestrated all of this, had known exactly what buttons to push to drive me to this point. She had turned my love for my daughter into a weapon, had used my protective instincts to reveal the monster that lived beneath my skin.

Yet she had made one crucial error in her calculations. She thought that showing Selene what I was would break me, would make me more willing to surrender to spare my daughter further trauma.

Instead, it had simply shown me that there were no limits to what I would do to keep my family safe. No lines I wouldn't cross, no prices I wouldn't pay, no depths I wouldn't sink to if it meant protecting the people I loved.

Ana wanted confrontation? She would have one. Yet as the broken man she expected, consumed by guilt over what he had done in front of his child. She would face a father whose daughter had been threatened, a man who had been pushed beyond all restraint, beyond all mercy, beyond all hope of redemption. She would face the storm itself, unleashed and unbound and utterly without conscience when it came to defending his own. The war for my soul was over. I had chosen damnation over surrender.

Now it was time to make Ana pay the price for forcing that choice upon me.

CHAPTER TWENTY-NINE
THE STORM ON THE HIGH SEAT

Ilija

The silence had teeth. It gnawed at the edges of my consciousness, sharp and persistent as the afterimage of lightning burned across my retinas. Where Jaakko writhed, where a man had breathed and schemed and threatened my child, char-black scorch marks scarred the ancient stone. Fragments of bone and metal were fused into the rock itself, creating a grotesque relief that would outlast empires. The air reeked of copper and burnt metal, of flesh rendered to ash in the space between heartbeats. My hands still hummed with residual electricity; fingers cramped from channeling enough voltage to stop a human heart mid-beat.

The power sang in my veins still, a symphony of destruction that wanted more. It had tasted violence, had been given permission to kill, and now it prowled beneath my skin like a caged predator finally allowed to hunt. Every nerve ending crackled with potential energy. I could feel the moisture in the air, the iron in the blood of everyone in the chamber, the electrical impulses firing in their brains. For a terrifying moment, I understood how easy it would be to reach out and stop every heart in this mountain with a thought.

Selene pressed herself against the far wall, studying me with eyes that had seen too much for thirteen years. My daughter. Christ, my daughter had watched me nearly kill a man with lightning drawn from my own marrow. The shadows at her feet stirred like living things, responding to the electrical discharge that still cracked in the air. They reached toward the scorched marks where Jaakko had nearly died, tasting the residual energy of his destruction. My daughter watched them move with the same detached curiosity she might have shown a butterfly landing on her palm.

"Did it hurt him?" she asked quietly, her voice carrying across the chamber with startling clarity.

The question hit me like a physical blow. She wanted to know if he had suffered. There was no judgment in her tone, no fear. Only curiosity about the mechanics of death delivered by storm-light.

"Yes," I answered honestly, meeting her gaze. "It was meant to."

She nodded solemnly, accepting this truth. The shadows around her feet pulsed once, like a heartbeat, then settled into stillness.

I released the breath I'd been holding. It came out ragged, torn from lungs that felt seared by the power I'd channeled. The storm that had been building in my chest for years, the rage, the helplessness, the bone-deep need to protect what was mine, settled into something harder, more permanent. A weapon finally given its true purpose.

My hands were shaking from the effort of containing what still wanted to be released. Every instinct screamed at me to hunt down every member of the Accord, to paint these tunnels with their blood and ash until no threat to my family remained. The urge was almost sexual in its intensity, a hunger that went deeper than flesh.

"Ilija." Danica's voice cut through the electric hum. Her hand found my forearm, fingers pressing against sinew and muscle with surprising gentleness. The contact grounded me, pulled me back from the edge of becoming something that killed for the joy of it rather than necessity. I turned to her, expecting condemnation, expecting her to see the monster I'd always feared becoming. Instead, her eyes blazed with something primal and approving. She looked from me to Jaakko's broken form, and her mouth curved into a smile that belonged in a wolf's jaw.

"Good," she whispered. The single word carried years of fury, of watching our daughter suffer, of helpless rage against enemies we couldn't touch. "Now the bastard can tell Ana what we've become."

Those words hit me like absolution delivered through clenched teeth. Every doubt, every moment of self-loathing for the power that lived in my bones, crumbled to dust. I was Ilija the father first, Ilija the storm second. My daughter had seen the thunder, and she hadn't flinched.

Yet there was more in Danica's eyes than approval. There was hunger. The same predatory satisfaction that thrummed in my own blood. Her hands moved restlessly at her sides, fingers flexing around the grip of her blade. She wanted to kill something too.

Heavy boots echoed from the tunnel mouth. The Accord, coming fast and loud as judgment. Maria appeared beside us, her face bloodless in the torchlight. She dragged an iron grate across a passage I hadn't noticed, metal shrieking against stone like a dying animal. "This way leads deeper," she said, voice tight with urgency. "Into the old mining shafts. They won't find us there. Hours at least."

The choice crystallized in the air between us, sharp as broken glass. We couldn't take Selene where we were going. The path ahead led up, into the mountain's heart, into the throne room of the goddess who had orchestrated this entire symphony of pain. A child, even one who commanded shadows, had no place in that final movement.

I knew what we were asking of her. To disappear into darkness while her parents went to war. To trust that we would come back when so many others had promised the same thing and failed. To be alone again, after we had just found her.

The guilt was acid in my throat. We were abandoning her again, even if it was to save her. Even if it was the only way to ensure she would never have to run, never have to hide, never have to watch her father burn men to ash in defense of her safety.

Danica dropped to her knees before our daughter, hands framing that small, serious face. "Listen to me, little star." Her voice cracked on the endearment, the separation bleeding through each syllable. "Maria's going to take you somewhere safe. Deep underground where no one can find you. Your father and I are going to finish this. We're going to kill the woman who took you from us. And then we're coming back." She pulled Selene against her chest, fierce and desperate. "I swear it on everything I am."

Selene's sob was a knife between my ribs. "Don't go," she pleaded, small hands clutching at Danica's coat. "Please, Mama. Don't leave me again."

The words destroyed something inside Danica. I watched her face crumple, watched years of carefully constructed emotional walls collapse in an instant. She had been strong for so long, had held herself together through sheer force of will and the promise of this reunion. Now, faced with leaving our daughter again, even for the right reasons, she was breaking apart.

"Never again." Danica's whisper was broken glass and tears. "This is the last time, sweetheart. The very last time." She held our daughter like she was trying to memorize the weight of her, the smell of her hair, the sound of her breathing. "When we come back, we'll never be apart again. No more running. No more hiding. No more watching shadows for enemies. I promise."

I found myself moving forward, drawn by gravity I couldn't resist. My knees hit stone beside them, and suddenly I was part of this goodbye, my arms wrapping around both of them. Selene turned in Danica's embrace to look at me, her face streaked with tears yet determined.

"Will you come back different?" she asked, her voice small yet steady. "Will the storm change you?"

The question was more perceptive than any child should have been capable of. She had seen what I could become, had watched the violence flow through me like water finding its course. She was asking if the man who came back would still be her father, or if he would be something else entirely.

"I don't know," I answered honestly. "Yet I'll always be yours. Whatever I become, whatever I have to do to keep you safe, I'll always be your father first."

She studied my face with those dark eyes, so much older than her years, and nodded. "Okay," she said simply. "Try to come back as you."

The words hit me harder than any blow. This child, who had spent most of her life in captivity, who had every reason to want me to become something terrible and violent enough to protect her, was asking me to stay human. To choose mercy over vengeance, restraint over the intoxicating rush of unlimited power.

"I'll try," I whispered, and meant it.

I stood apart from this reunion, a ghost watching his own family through windows he could never break. When Danica finally stood, her eyes met mine across the chamber. They held the weight of every year we'd lost, every night she'd woken reaching for a child who wasn't there. Go, that look said. End this, Ilija.

Maria took Selene's hand. My daughter looked at me one final time, and I saw Danica's strength in her eyes, my stubbornness in the set of her jaw. She gave me a single nod, soldier to soldier, an acknowledgment of necessary violence. Then she disappeared into darkness, taking my heart with her into the earth's embrace.

The chamber felt hollow without her, like a chord played with half its notes missing. The silence stretched between Danica and me, heavy with everything we couldn't say. We had found our daughter only to leave her again. We were walking toward a confrontation that might destroy us both. And even if we won, even if we killed Ana and ended this war, there was no guarantee we would survive to keep the promises we had just made.

Danica moved to where Jaakko lay broken yet breathing, his chest rising and falling in ragged gasps. She hauled him upright with surprising strength, his head lolling as consciousness flickered in and out. "We go up," she said finally, her fingers finding mine. "And we drag this bastard with us. Ana needs to see what her perfect soldier has become."

Her hand was cold as winter, yet her grip was steel. We turned toward the ascending passage, toward the mountain's heart, toward the woman who had torn our family apart. The storm in my chest pulsed in rhythm with my heartbeat, eager for what was coming.

The ascent became a litany of slaughter. The tunnels carved through living rock led ever upward, and Ana's chosen waited in the shadows like cancer cells in healthy tissue. These weren't the augmented soldiers we'd faced in the square. These were Inquisitors, her personal guard, wrapped in black armor etched with golden runes that pulsed with their own sick light. They carried plasma rifles that spat star-hot death and deployed dampening fields that turned the air thick as syrup, trying to smother the storm that lived in my blood.

Jaakko stumbled between us, his ruined body a testament to what happened when someone threatened my family. His flesh was charred in patterns that mapped the lightning's path, yet Ana's divine influence kept him alive, kept him conscious enough to witness what we had become. Each step left a trail of blood on ancient stone.

The first group we encountered was stationed at a bend in the tunnel, four of them in formation behind portable energy shields. They opened fire the moment we rounded the corner, plasma bolts turning the air to superheated hell. The shots carved chunks from the stone walls, leaving molten scars that glowed like angry eyes.

The storm answered anyway. It had tasted violence now, had been given permission to kill in defense of what I loved. I felt the familiar buildup of potential along my spine, electricity gathering like storm clouds in my bones. This time was different. This time, I didn't fight the power or try to control it. I let it flow through me like a river finding the sea.

Danica threw up a wall of black ice between us and the plasma fire, each impact sending spider-web fractures racing across its surface. Steam billowed from the impacts, turning the tunnel into a scalding cloud that seared our lungs with each breath. I reached through the blinding white fog, following the electrical signatures of our enemies' nervous systems, and called lightning from the deepest parts of myself.

It erupted from my hands in branching chains, arcing between the Inquisitors' armor plates, finding every gap and weakness in their protection. Their dampening fields flickered and died as my lightning overloaded them, the energy backlash frying the generators they carried. The bolts found flesh beneath metal, following nerve pathways and blood vessels, cooking them from the inside out while their armor seized around them like metal coffins.

The smell of burning meat filled the tunnel. One of them managed a single, choked scream before his vocal cords boiled away. They toppled forward like grotesque statues of their own death, steam rising from the gaps in their armor where superheated blood leaked onto stone.

We walked through the cloud of steam and death, our boots crunching on flash-frozen corpses and melted components. Jaakko stumbled behind us, his breathing harsh and wet. Danica moved beside me like winter given form, and I was the thunder that followed her lightning. We weren't two separate fighters anymore. We were a unified force of nature, predator and prey and the space between them.

The second squad tried to hold an archway deeper in the mountain, six of them this time, equipped with concussive grenades and heavy plasma cannons that could punch through reinforced steel. They had positioned themselves well, using the narrow passage to funnel us into a killing field. The explosions shook dust and stone from the ancient ceiling, each detonation threatening to bring the whole tunnel down on our heads.

We had learned to read each other's movements, to anticipate and complement without the need for words. Danica met their barrage with a wave of absolute zero, her power reaching out like hungry fingers to drain the heat from everything it touched. The grenades froze mid-flight, their internal mechanisms seizing as the temperature plummeted beyond what they were designed to handle. They dropped to the floor like metal fruit, useless and inert, encased in rime that glittered like diamonds in the tunnel's torchlight.

I focused the storm, gathering it into something denser than lightning, more fundamental than electricity. The air itself became my weapon, molecules compressing and expanding at my command. I pushed, and the wave of invisible force slammed into the archway like the fist of an angry god. The Inquisitors flew backward, their augmented armor crumpling like paper as they struck the far wall of the chamber beyond. The sound of their impact was wet and final, the percussion of bones breaking inside metal shells, of organs rupturing against their own ribs.

One of them tried to crawl away, his legs twisted at impossible angles, leaving a trail of blood that steamed in the freezing air. Danica walked over to him with deliberate calm, her blade singing as she drew it from its sheath. The metal was so cold it had frost along its edge, and when she pressed the point to the gap in his helmet, his breath misted in rapid, panicked puffs.

"Please," he whispered, the words barely audible through his helmet's speakers. "I have children."

"So do we," she replied, and pushed the blade home. Ice formed around the wound instantly, sealing it, ensuring he died slowly as the cold spread through his body. She watched his struggles with clinical interest, the same attention she might have given to a particularly difficult problem in her laboratory years ago.

Behind us, Jaakko watched through eyes glazed with pain and divine compulsion. "She's waiting," he croaked, his voice barely human. "She knows you're coming. She's prepared a welcome."

"Good," I said, lightning crackling between my fingers. "I have something to show her too."

We carved our way up through level after level of resistance. Each group of Inquisitors was larger than the last, better equipped, more desperate. Ana was pulling her forces back toward herself, concentrating her defenses around her throne room. Yet desperation made them sloppy, and we had moved beyond the realm of tactics into something more primal.

I used wind to tear weapons from hands, to slam bodies against stone hard enough to pulp organs inside armor plating. The air itself became my ally, responding to my will as if it were an extension of my nervous system. I could feel every molecule, every pressure differential, every tiny electrical charge that danced between oxygen atoms. With a gesture, I could create vacuums that collapsed lungs, wind shears that snapped necks, pressure waves that liquefied brains inside their protective skulls.

Danica walked through the chaos, her blade whispering winter promises as it opened throats and severed limbs. She moved like a dancer, each cut precise and beautiful and absolutely lethal. Blood steamed where it struck her frozen blade, turning instantly to scarlet ice that shattered on the stone. It was more than technique that made her deadly, it was the years of rage she carried, the fury of a mother. Every strike carried that weight, that accumulated pain transformed into surgical violence.

I watched her work and saw the woman I had fallen in love with, refined down to her essential elements. She had always been beautiful, yet this was beauty with purpose, grace wedded to lethality in ways that made my breath catch. When she killed, it was art. When I killed, it was force of nature. Together, we were something that shouldn't have been able to exist on the same plane as normal human beings.

The third level brought us face to face with Ana's inner circle, the Inquisitors who had been with her from the beginning. These were the true believers, the ones who had helped her build this perfect prison disguised as paradise. They wore heavier armor, carried weapons that hummed with barely contained power, and fought with the desperation of fanatics protecting their god.

They had prepared for us. The chamber we entered was a killing ground, every angle covered by interlocking fields of fire. Energy nets hung from the ceiling, ready to drop and entangle us. The walls themselves were armed, studded with weapon emplacements that tracked our movement with mechanical precision.

"Ilija Dragović," one of them called out, his voice amplified by his helmet's speakers. "Ana offers you one final chance. Surrender now, and your daughter will be spared. Continue this madness, and she dies screaming in the darkness below."

The words were meant to break me, to turn love into weakness. Instead, they fed the storm. Lightning arced between my fingers without conscious thought, eager to be released. I could feel Danica's fury beside me, cold rage that made the air itself brittle.

Jaakko laughed, a wet sound that sprayed blood across the stone. "Too late," he wheezed. "She's already seen what he is. What he's capable of. The child knows her father is a monster."

"You shouldn't have mentioned our daughter," I said, and let the storm free.

What followed wasn't a battle, it was an execution. I became lightning given human form, electricity flowing through me like blood through veins. Every weapon they turned on us died the moment I looked at it, their circuits fried by electromagnetic pulses that I generated with the rhythm of my heartbeat. The energy nets meant to trap us became weapons in my hands, their charge redirected to cook the operators who tried to deploy them.

Danica was winter incarnate, ice and fire swirling around her in impossible harmony. She froze their weapons mid-shot, turned their own plasma bolts into superheated steam that scalded them through the gaps in their armor. Where I was chaotic destruction, she was precise annihilation, each kill calculated and deliberate.

The fanatics tried to fall back, to regroup, to find some tactical advantage that might save them. Yet we followed them like an avalanche, relentless and unstoppable. I brought the ceiling down on half of them, tons of stone and metal crushing armor and bone with equal ease. Danica flash-froze the survivors, turning their blood to ice crystals that shredded them from within.

By the time we finished, the chamber looked like the aftermath of a natural disaster. Bodies lay twisted among the rubble, armor cracked and blackened, weapons melted into abstract sculptures of defeat. Steam rose from pools of blood that had been flash-heated and frozen in turn, creating a landscape that belonged in nightmares.

We stood among the carnage, breathing hard, both of us painted with blood and ice. Jaakko knelt between us, held upright only by Danica's grip on his collar. My hands were shaking again, from strain and from the effort of containing what still wanted to be released. The storm in my chest had tasted violence on this scale, had felt what it was like to kill without restraint, and it wanted more.

"How many more?" Danica asked, wiping gore from her blade.

"Doesn't matter," I replied, feeling the truth of it settle in my bones. "We keep going until there's nothing left between us and her."

Every Inquisitor we killed brought us closer to our daughter. Every corpse we left behind was one less obstacle between us and the ending we'd written in violence. We were wounded, shallow cuts leaked blood down our faces, our bodies screaming with exhaustion, yet we didn't stop. Couldn't stop. When Selene was waiting in the darkness below, trusting us to finish what we'd started.

The fourth level was different. Instead of organized resistance, we found something worse, the remnants of Ana's experiments. The tunnels here were lined with cells, and in each one, something that had once been human watched us pass with eyes that held too much knowledge. These were the failures, the subjects who hadn't quite died when Ana tried to remake them in her image.

One of them spoke as we passed, its voice a wet whisper that echoed off the stone walls. "She's waiting for you," it said. "She's been waiting so long. She loves you still, storm-bringer. She dreams of the peace you could share."

I wanted to stop, to ask what they meant, yet Danica's hand on my arm kept me moving. "Don't listen," she whispered. "That's another weapon."

The words followed us, a chorus of broken voices promising rest, promising an end to the violence that lived in our blood. They spoke of the quiet that came after surrender, the stillness that Ana offered to those wise enough to accept her vision. Part of me, the part that was tired of killing, tired of being a weapon in human skin, wanted to listen.

Jaakko stumbled, his legs finally giving out. Danica hauled him upright again, her grip leaving fresh bruises on his ruined flesh. "Almost there," she murmured, whether to him or to me I couldn't tell.

The final level. Before us stood the great bronze doors of the Parthenon, scorched and dented from our ascent. Ancient figures danced across their surface, gods and mortals locked in eternal conflict, beauty and violence intertwined in ways that seemed prophetic now.

The last Inquisitor waited there, their commander, a giant of a man whose power maul hummed with barely contained destruction. His armor was different from the others, older, inscribed with runes that hurt to look at directly. When he saw us, he raised his weapon without hesitation.

"You will go no further," he snarled, his voice carrying the weight of absolute conviction.

When he charged, roaring Ana's name like a prayer, Danica stepped forward to meet him. This wasn't strategy, it was personal. This man had been part of the war that killed us, that separated us from our daughter. This kill belonged to her, payment for dying and leaving Selene behind.

He was fast for a man his size, his maul cutting through the air with enough force to shatter stone. Yet Danica had been dancing with death for years, and she knew its rhythm better than her own heartbeat. She ducked under his first swing, the maul's energy field crackling through empty air where her head had been. Her blade found the gap in his armor at the hip, sliding between plates like it was meant to be there.

He staggered yet didn't fall, bringing his weapon around in a backhand that would have taken her head off if it connected. Instead, she flowed around it like water, her movements too fluid for his augmented reflexes to track. Her second strike opened his throat above his gorget, blood spraying in an arc that painted the bronze doors behind him.

He fell to his knees, hands clutching at the wound, trying to hold his life inside his body. Danica stood over him, her blade dripping crimson onto ancient stone.

"This is for our daughter," she said softly, and drove the point through his eye.

We stood before the bronze doors, battered and bleeding and nearly spent. Our eyes met across the scattered bodies of Ana's faithful, and we shared a look that held years of separation, of searching, of refusing to give up hope. Together, we kicked the doors open.

Jaakko crawled behind us, leaving a trail of blood and divine compulsion. His broken form would be our gift to Ana, proof of what happened when someone threatened our family.

The Parthenon's interior had been transformed into something obscene. Where Athena's friezes had once celebrated wisdom and warfare, crimson and gold banners now hung like shed skin. The pillars that had once supported the goddess of wisdom were wrapped in chains, as if Ana had literally bound the concept of free thought. The air was thick with lotus and incense, cloying sweetness that couldn't quite mask the underlying scent of old blood and older fear.

In the chamber's heart sat a throne of black marble veined with gold, and on it, serene as a painted saint, sat the woman who had destroyed our lives. Ana looked exactly as she had during my torment, ageless, perfect, untouched by time or consequence. Her skin was porcelain, her hair spun gold, her eyes the color of molten amber. She might have been napping instead of orchestrating a war.

I could see the truth now, could feel the wrongness that radiated from her like heat from a forge. This wasn't a woman anymore, hadn't been for decades. This was power given form, will made manifest, a goddess who had forgotten what it meant to be human.

When she spoke, her voice was silk over steel, beautiful and cutting. "So," she said, those golden eyes finding mine across the wreckage we'd made of her sanctuary. "The prodigal storm returns. With his winter queen beside him. I was beginning to think you wouldn't make it."

Danica's answer came through bared teeth. "We're here to end this, Ana. Your perfect world, your silent order. All of it."

Ana's laugh was silver bells and distant thunder. "End this? Sweet child, you misunderstand. This is a beginning. The birth of something beautiful, something pure. A world without chaos, without the messy complications of free will and individual desire. I offer peace, Danica. True peace."

"The peace of the grave," I said, stepping forward. Lightning played between my fingers, eager to taste divine flesh.

Ana's gaze slid past Danica like she was furniture, irrelevant, temporary. Those molten gold eyes fixed on me with the weight of shared history, of power recognized and claimed. "I offer you one last chance, my love." The endearment was a physical caress, a ghost of intimacy I'd spent decades trying to forget. "Leave her. Leave this chaos you've chosen. Come back to me. Come back to the peace you were meant to have. I can still make you whole."

For a moment, just a moment, I felt the pull of her words. The promise of an end to the violence, to the constant struggle against the storm that wanted to consume everything I touched. She was offering me rest, offering to take the burden of choice away forever. Part of me, the part that was tired of being a weapon, tired of leaving corpses in my wake, wanted to accept.

Then I thought of Selene's eyes, wide with understanding instead of fear as she watched her father become lightning. I thought of her small hand in mine, the weight of absolute trust. I thought of Danica, bleeding and defiant at my side, her presence a clean flame against the chamber's suffocating perfume.

I looked at Ana, at the goddess who had shaped me, caged me, haunted every quiet moment in my life. I saw the eternity of silence she was offering, the perfect stillness of a world without choice or chance or the beautiful, terrible chaos of human love.

The choice wasn't a choice at all. It was the only truth that mattered.

"I am already whole," I said.

Something shifted in Ana's perfect features. The divine composure cracked like ice in spring. The air in the Parthenon began to hum with barely contained power, and I realized that this was what she had genuinely wanted all along. My defiance. She wanted to break me personally, to prove that even the storm could be tamed by the right goddess.

Danica stepped forward, dragging Jaakko's broken form with her. With casual brutality, she hurled him across the marble floor. He landed at Ana's feet with a wet thud, his ruined body leaving a trail of blood across the pristine stone.

"Here's your faithful god," Danica said, her voice dripping with contempt. "Still breathing, but barely. Thought you might want to see what happens when someone threatens our daughter."

Ana looked down at Jaakko's broken form, her expression unreadable. Ice began to form in Danica's palm, crystallizing into a solid block that gleamed like winter death.

Jaakko looked up at Ana, "I… I am sorry my Que…"

The massive block of ice released from Danica's hold. Everything was in slow-motion. My eyes opened wide as this icy death descended toward the back of Jaakko's skull. It reminded me of Thor killing the giants with his hammer.

"That's enough from the fucking Finn," Danica smirked as her eyes lasered in on Ana's. "Gods think they are fucking immortal. Your goddamn ass is next you fucking cunt!"

I looked at Danica, if we were not about to have this fight, I would have taken her right there.

"So be it," she hissed, rising from her throne. Golden light erupted around her like a star being born, washing away shadows, turning the air itself into molten radiance. "You choose chaos over peace, violence over serenity. Let me show you how far that gets you."

I raised my hand, feeling lightning gather in my palm like a living thing eager to be born. Beside me, Danica became winter incarnate, fire and ice swirling around her in impossible harmony. The world held its breath for one perfect moment, balanced on the edge between creation and destruction.

Then our three powers collided, and the ancient stones of the Parthenon, which had stood for millennia witnessing the rise and fall of empires, began to scream as they were torn apart by forces that had no business walking the earth.

The battle was joined, and somewhere far below in the mountain's depths, our daughter waited in darkness, trusting us to come home.

CHAPTER THIRTY
THE HEART OF THE STORM

Ilija

The lightning carved through reality like a blade through silk. Each bolt screamed with electricity that tasted of copper and rage, the air crackling with raw power that echoed the tempest building in my chest for millennia. Every strike testified to the fury finally unleashed upon an unsuspecting world.

Ana's golden fire rose to meet it, a radiant inferno mirroring my destructive power with unsettling beauty. Where our energies collided, the Parthenon's ancient stones wept molten marble. The revered columns that had witnessed countless centuries groaned under the strain, their carved details dissolving into rivers of incandescent tears. The air itself became weaponized, superheated and crackling, turning my lungs to furnaces with each breath.

I had always thought destruction was loud. I was wrong. This was a symphony written in silence, the hush of atoms torn apart, the whisper of stone becoming dust, reality bending until it snapped. The Parthenon's columns, those pillars that had weathered empires and witnessed philosophy's birth, simply ceased. They didn't crumble. They surrendered their existence, becoming glittering clouds of mineral ghosts that the shockwaves scattered like dandelion seeds on a hurricane wind.

Above us, the roof peeled away in sheets of marble and gold, curling like burning parchment. The sky beyond was the color of old blood and fresh bruises, painted by our collision's violence. My lightning spider-webbed across the heavens in patterns too complex for mortal eyes, each branch a river of white fire leaving afterimages burned into any fool's retinas brave enough to look.

Ana moved through the chaos like a goddess dancing through her cathedral. Her golden armor caught my storm's light and threw it back tenfold, turning her into a fallen sun waging war. Beautiful. Terrible. Perfect in the way only things designed for destruction could be. Her power wasn't the wild, screaming thing living in my chest, it was order given form, discipline made flesh. The crystallized light weapons hummed with terrible music, the energy chains reaching for me with inevitability's patience.

"This is your choice?" Her voice bloomed inside my skull, a melody composed of sorrow and silk and barely restrained contempt. "This graceless dance with mortality? I offered you eternity, beloved. A world scrubbed clean of suffering, polished until it gleamed like a pearl. You could have been a god."

I answered with compressed atmosphere that could have flattened a city block. She deflected it with a casual gesture, like brushing away a butterfly. The force that should have shattered her bones became a warm breeze stirring her golden hair. My storm raged harder, feeding on frustration, but she stood in its eye like a monument to serenity.

She was ancient, a being whose existence stretched through millennia. Her control, a masterpiece honed over ten thousand years, was absolute. Every flicker of power, every shift in her aura spoke of the unparalleled mastery I could only dream of in my nascent stages. I was still learning to hold lightning without burning my hands, grappling with the raw energy surging within me. My attempts at control were clumsy, destructive, a stark contrast to her effortless grace.

The chasm between us was vast, an insurmountable gulf of experience and power. Her true age and the depth of her control should have crippled me with terror, sent me fleeing in desperate panic. Instead, a scorching anger washed over me, burning away every trace of fear. It fueled a defiant spark within, a nascent determination to bridge that gap regardless of the cost. Her ancient power was a challenge. And I felt ready to meet it.

Danica

The world had become a fever dream painted in fire and lightning, a canvas of celestial warfare where gods clashed and creation groaned under the weight of their fury. Towers that had stood for millennia crumbled to dust, their foundations rent by seismic shocks echoing through the fabric of reality. The once-azure sky was now a swirling maelstrom of angry reds and bruised purples, ripped apart by streaks of raw power that arced and crackled with the sound of a thousand exploding suns. The air, thick with the acrid scent of fire and something more primal, the metallic tang of divine blood, shimmered with residual magic, making breathing itself a struggle.

I moved through air that tasted of burnt metal and melted gold, a noxious cocktail clawing at my throat with every desperate inhalation. The heat was a living entity, an oppressive force turning my sweat to steam before it could fall, creating a personal, suffocating halo around me. My vision blurred at the edges from the superheated atmosphere's shimmering distortion. Shards of ancient marble, once part of grand temples, flew through the space between heartbeats like deadly, incandescent shrapnel.

Each piece was sharp enough to open veins, hot enough to cauterize the wounds before blood could flow. Scarlet streams traced ephemeral patterns of injury down my arms, but I barely felt them. The pain was just another sensation to catalog and ignore, like my burning lungs or ears ringing from the constant divine thunder.

My universe had collapsed into a singular, agonizingly bright point of crystalline focus, the golden bitch who had murdered me once and now attempted to steal my Ilija's soul, just as she'd done with me. The bitter irony was poison in my veins.

My rage was pure. Clean. The kind that could cut diamonds and melt steel, distilled into something almost holy. I gathered my winter around me like armor, calling frost from the superheated air through sheer will. The ice formed and shattered and formed again, a cycle matching my heartbeat's rhythm.

I unleashed a torrent of dark magic, a wave of obsidian ice surging across the polished stone. Each crystalline shard was honed to a razor's edge, infused with malevolent hunger for the divine essence. The black ice raced forward with unnatural speed, a serpentine tide of frozen death consuming the air, the chamber crackling with ominous energy. Yet as it neared her, an invisible barrier materialized. Her aura, a furnace of pure incandescent power, met the icy assault. My obsidian blades, crafted from the deepest malice, were instantly overwhelmed, their dark magic consumed and annihilated. With a final, faint hiss, the ice dissipated into a wisp of steam and bitter memory.

"You are a child playing with frost, little soldier," Ana's voice chimed like silver bells in a graveyard, though her eyes never left Ilija. The dismissal was absolute, the contempt reserved for insects. "Do you truly believe your brief, dirty flame can touch a star?"

She saw me as debris, an insignificant speck to be swept aside. A minor inconvenience in her grand design, to be eradicated before the real work could commence. That would be her last mistake.

I wasn't the wall he hid behind. I was the blade at his side. The winter that came after the storm, the killing frost that finished what lightning began. I lunged through the weaponized air, through heat that blistered skin and scorched throat, the Blade of Fates singing in my grip. The metal had drunk the blood of gods before, it hungered for more.

I aimed for her throat, that perfect column of divine flesh that had never known the kiss of steel.

A sword of pure light materialized in her hand as if summoned from a star's heart. She met my strike with movements that belonged in a ballet, all flowing grace and deadly precision. When our blades met, the sound was thunder given voice, a peal that shook the bones of the earth and sent cracks racing through the remaining Parthenon stones.

The impact traveled up my arms like reverse lightning, numbing my fingers and setting my teeth on edge. She was stronger. Faster. More skilled. But I had something she didn't understand.

I had everything to lose. That made me desperate enough to be dangerous.

Ilija

The sight of Danica engaging Ana blade to blade tore something fundamental loose in my chest, a primal dread coiling in my gut. Every instinct screamed to intervene, to shield her, to halt this impossible duel.

Here was my flame and frost, my fierce and fragile love, trading strikes with a being who had reshaped civilizations on whims. Danica fought like a hurricane given human form, all savage grace and beautiful violence. Her blade wove intricate patterns in the air, leaving trails of shimmering silver fire, each parry and riposte a testament to her unwavering courage. Yet Ana moved with ethereal precision, like inevitability itself, each movement flowing with a grace that seemed to defy the laws of physics. The clash of their blades was a song of destruction, a horrifying symphony that echoed the immense disparity in their beings, yet also the raw, unyielding spirit of the woman I loved.

I could see the outcome written in the language of physics and desperation. Ana was toying with her, the way a cat toys with a mouse. Danica's enhanced human reflexes couldn't match divine reaction time. Her mortal strength, for all its fury, was nothing against muscles carved from starlight and willpower.

I gathered the storm around me, felt it respond to the mixture of love and terror and rage eating me alive from the inside. The air in the ruined temple grew thick and heavy, pregnant with electricity and the promise of violence. Dust swirled in tightening spirals around my body, drawn into the vortex of my power like debris around a black hole.

Thunder rolled overhead, not from the sky, but from my heartbeat. Each pulse sent ripples of force through the atmosphere, making the remaining Parthenon stones vibrate like tuning forks. I was becoming something beyond human, something belonging to the primordial chaos that existed before the first gods learned to speak.

"Do you see, my beloved?" Ana's voice was honey poured over broken glass as she forced Danica back step by agonizing step. "She is nothing. A mayfly that burns bright for one perfect summer before the cold takes her. We are forever, Ilija. The eternal dance of storm and sun, chaos and order. I offer you godhood. Love that will outlive the stars."

With a motion as casual as swatting a fly, she disarmed Danica. The Blade of Fates spun into the darkness beyond our battle circle, its metal singing a mournful note as it flew. Golden chains materialized from nothingness, wrapping around Danica's limbs and slamming her against the remaining columns hard enough to crack the ancient marble.

Ana raised her sword of crystallized light, and I could see my wife's death written in the weapon's perfect edge.

"I will give her a clean end," Ana continued, her voice soft with what she thought was mercy. "Quick and painless. A kindness she hasn't earned. Then you and I will begin the beautiful work of healing your broken soul."

That was when everything changed. Not a slow, creeping realization, but an abrupt, violent rupture in the fabric of my reality. The world shattered into a million irreparable pieces around me.

It wasn't seeing Danica trapped, though that sight sent new, searing lightning through my veins. Her terrified eyes were a brand on my soul, igniting a fire I hadn't known I possessed.

It wasn't seeing Ana's blade poised to take the life that mattered more than my own existence, though that image turned my vision red with all-consuming fury.

It was the thought of Selene that broke me open.

My daughter. My fierce little storm-child with her mother's eyes and my stubborn chin. I could see her face as clearly as if she were standing before me, the way she tilted her head when thinking hard about something, the gap between her front teeth that made her lisp when saying my name, the particular shade of wonder that colored her expression when I showed her how to call lightning from a clear sky.

She was waiting for me. Believing, with the absolute faith that only children possess, that her Tata would come home. That he would keep his promises. That love was stronger than gods or death or the weight of destiny.

My love for Selene wasn't fuel for the storm. It was the eye of the hurricane, that place of perfect calm around which all chaos revolves. It was clarity made manifest, purpose distilled to its purest form. The still point at the center of a universe gone mad with violence, the one true thing that remained constant while everything else burned.

I stopped fighting the storm.

I became it.

The power that erupted from me was nothing so civilized as lightning and wind. This was the raw, untamed fury of a cosmos being born, the violent ecstasy of matter learning to dance with energy for the first time. The sky above Athens didn't crack, it shattered like a mirror struck by a hammer, revealing the star-drunk darkness beyond. Rain fell in torrents thick as blood, mixed with hail that struck the earth like bullets fired by angry gods.

The wind didn't howl. It screamed. It was a voice speaking in frequencies that could shatter bone and turn sanity to glass. It tore at the Parthenon's foundations with fingers made of condensed atmosphere, each gust strong enough to pick up cars and throw them like toys.

But it was the lightning that truly announced my transformation. No longer individual bolts, but a constant river of white fire pouring from my body like blood from an opened artery. Beautiful and terrible and absolutely beyond any hope of control. This was power that demanded endurance rather than wielding, chaos that had to be survived rather than mastered.

Ana's chains of golden light didn't disappear, they were consumed, devoured by the hungry darkness surrounding my storm. Her sword of crystallized starfire dissolved like sugar in rain. She turned to face me, and I saw something I'd never expected in those perfect, ageless features.

Fear.

For the first time in a thousand years, Ana encountered something her ordered mind couldn't categorize or control. I wasn't playing by the rules of divine combat anymore. I wasn't even playing by the rules of physics.

I was chaos incarnate, and chaos bows to no master.

Danica

The chains of light vanished like morning mist, and I fell to my knees on stone that had been turned to glass by the heat of divine conflict.

The air around me was a weapon, a living thing made of pressure and sound and the taste of lightning. My ears should have ruptured from the constant thunder. My lungs should have collapsed from breathing the atmosphere compressed beyond mortal endurance. But somehow I endured, drew breath and found strength in my burning chest.

This was him. This was the heart of the man I loved, finally given voice.

I looked up through his hurricane and saw Ilija transformed. No longer struggling to contain a god's power within mortal flesh. He had become something new, a bridge between the human and the divine, between order and the beautiful anarchy of creation. Lightning crawled across his skin like living tattoos, and his eyes were the color of storm clouds pregnant with violence. When he moved, reality bent around him, space warping under the weight of his will.

The raw, primal beauty stole what little breath I had left. This was the power I'd always sensed sleeping in his bones, the force that had called to my winter-touched soul across lifetimes and deaths and the vast darkness between worlds.

I climbed to my feet, my wounds forgotten, my exhaustion transformed into something cleaner and more dangerous. The Blade of Fates flew back to my hand as if summoned by need alone, its metal humming with harmonics that matched the rhythm of Ilija's storm. The sword felt different, lighter, sharper, hungry for the blood of the golden goddess who had dared threaten our family.

I wasn't the overwhelming force that would break Ana's defenses. That was Ilija's role, his beautiful and terrible purpose. I would be something else, something that complemented his chaos.

I would be the killing edge that finished what the storm began.

Ilija

We moved as one entity split into two bodies, a harmony of destruction that had been ten thousand years in the making.

Her winter-fire wove through my lightning like silver thread through golden silk, creating patterns of devastation that were as beautiful as they were deadly. She darted through my hurricane as if born to it, each step perfectly timed to avoid the worst of the chaos while remaining close enough to the violence to use it as a weapon.

Ana had spent eternity preparing to face me. She'd never considered she might have to face us.

Her defenses, those perfect constructs of ordered light that had turned away my earlier attacks, crumbled under our combined assault. My lightning hammered at her shields with the patience of falling water, each strike wearing away another layer of protection. When tiny cracks appeared in her golden armor, Danica was there, her blade sliding through the gaps like winter wind through an open door.

When Danica's blade found divine flesh again, Ana screamed.

It wasn't a sound that should come from any throat, even a divine one. It was the noise the universe might make if you could teach it to feel pain, vast and terrible and utterly inhuman. Golden blood, bright as liquid starlight, welled from the wound on her arm and fell to the ground in drops that hissed and steamed against the stone.

"Impossible," Ana whispered, staring at her injury with the fascination of someone who had forgotten she could bleed. "I am eternal! Perfection given form! You cannot unmake me!"

But we were unmaking her. With each passing moment, the cracks in her golden armor spread a little further. Her divine form, that perfect construct of will and energy that had endured since the dawn of civilization, was beginning to destabilize. Light leaked from the fissures in her flesh like luminous blood, each ray a piece of her immortality being torn away by the storm of our love and fury.

"You were never perfect," I told her, my voice the thunder that rolls across empty plains. "You were just afraid. Afraid of change. Afraid of loss. Afraid of a world that wouldn't bend to your will."

My lightning found another crack in her defenses, punching through completely, sending a bolt of pure chaos directly into her chest. She staggered backward, her perfect features contorting into something almost human in its pain and confusion.

"Ilija!" The word was a shriek now, all melody burned away by desperate fury. "You are MINE! I remade the world for you! I killed gods and toppled empires and wrote love songs in the blood of mortals! Everything I've done, every choice I've made, has been for you!"

"I was never yours to own," I replied, the words wrapped in lightning and the promise of endings.

Danica struck again, her blade finding the gap between Ana's breastplate and gorget. More golden blood flowed, more light leaked from the goddess's failing form. Ana's scream this time was pure rage, the fury of a being who'd never learned to accept defeat.

She lashed out with the last of her ordered power, sending a wave of crystallized light racing toward Danica. But my storm was there to meet it, my chaos devouring her final attack like fire consuming parchment. The backlash sent Ana to her knees, her golden armor now more crack than solid metal, her perfect face twisted with what might have been despair.

Danica

She was breaking.

I could see it in the way her light flickered, in the tremor that had crept into her hands, in the cracks that spider-webbed across her skin like fault lines in marble. Ana, the perfect goddess, the eternal beauty who had reshaped the world in the image of her desires, was coming apart at the seams.

But gods don't die easily. Even wounded, bleeding light instead of blood, she was still dangerous enough to level cities. I could see it in her eyes, the calculation, the desperate search for some weapon or strategy that might turn the tide of battle back in her favor.

She found it in cruelty.

"Do you know what I did to your daughter?" Ana's voice was honey poured over razor blades, sweet enough to hide the venom until it was too late. "Your precious Selene, your little storm-child? I visited her dreams, beloved. I showed her exactly how her parents would die. I made sure she understood that their deaths would be her fault, that her very existence was the weakness I would exploit to bring you to heel."

The words hit Ilija like a physical blow. I felt his storm falter for just a moment, his perfect control wavering as the image of his daughter's terror crashed through his consciousness. That moment of hesitation was all Ana needed.

She gathered the last of her power, pouring everything she had left into a single, devastating attack. Light exploded from her broken form, something wild and desperate and utterly without mercy. It was the dying scream of a star, beautiful and terrible and absolutely lethal.

The attack was aimed at me.

Ana had finally understood the geometry of his heart. She couldn't defeat him through force, he was chaos incarnate, beyond her ability to order or control. But she could break him by taking away the thing that gave his chaos meaning.

I saw death coming for me in a wave of golden fire, and found myself strangely at peace. If this was how it ended, at least it would be beside him. At least we would fall together.

But Ilija had other plans.

He threw himself between me and Ana's final attack, his storm wrapping around us both like a cocoon of lightning and wind. The golden fire met his chaos, and where they touched, reality screamed. I felt the force of Ana's desperation washing over us, felt it trying to burn away everything I was and everything I could ever be.

Then I felt something else. Warmth. Protection. Love made manifest as a shield of pure will.

He was protecting me. Even as Ana's attack threatened to unmake him, even as holding back that tide of destruction was tearing him apart from the inside, he was choosing to save me rather than save himself.

That was when I understood the true depth of what we faced. Ana didn't just want to possess Ilija, she wanted to be the only thing in existence that he could love. She would burn down the world, murder every person he cared about, destroy every good thing he'd known, just to ensure she was all that remained.

The realization filled me with a fury so pure it was almost religious.

I reached through his storm, my hand finding his in the chaos. Our fingers interlocked, and suddenly I could feel everything he felt, the vast, thunderous love he bore for our daughter, the fierce protectiveness that had turned him into something beyond human, the absolute certainty that some things were worth dying for.

But I also felt something else. Something Ana had never understood, despite all her claims of eternal love.

I felt how our powers complemented each other. How my winter could focus his storm, how my ice could give shape to his lightning. We weren't two separate forces fighting side by side, we were halves of a single weapon, perfectly balanced and utterly devastating.

Together, we turned to face the goddess who had threatened our child.

Ilija

When our hands touched, the world suddenly made sense.

I felt Danica's soul merge with mine, her winter weaving through my storm until we became something neither could have been alone. She was the still point at the center of my chaos, the eye of the hurricane made manifest. I was the power that gave her cold edge the force to cut through gods.

Ana's final attack was still coming, washing over us in waves of desperate fury. But now it felt manageable, something to be endured rather than feared. With Danica as my anchor, I could control the storm without losing myself in it. With my power as her weapon, she could strike at targets that should have been beyond mortal reach.

We moved together, our combined will reshaping the attack that should have killed us both. Ana's golden fire became fuel for our shared power, her desperation transformed into the very weapon we would use to end her.

"This is impossible," Ana whispered, her voice finally stripped of its musical perfection. She sounded almost human now, almost vulnerable. "You are mortal. You are brief. You should not be able to—"

"We are love," Danica said simply, her words carrying the weight of absolute truth. "And love is the only force in the universe that becomes stronger when it's shared."

Ana's perfect features twisted with incomprehension and rage. She had remade herself into an ideal of eternal beauty, gathered power and knowledge and the worship of mortals across millennia. But she'd never learned the secret that every mother knows, that every father discovers the moment they hold their child for the first time.

Love multiplies. It doesn't diminish when it's given away, it grows. Every person you care about, every life that becomes precious to you, adds to your strength rather than creating a weakness to be exploited.

Ana had spent eternity trying to hoard love like a miser hoards gold. She'd never understood that love was meant to be spent.

We raised our joined hands, and the storm answered. Not just my lightning, but something new, a perfect fusion of chaos and winter, of wild power and killing precision. It rose from us like a pillar of crystallized starlight, beautiful and terrible and unstoppable.

Ana tried to flee. For the first time in her existence, she turned her back on a fight and tried to run. But there was nowhere to go. My storm filled the ruined Parthenon, and beyond its boundaries lay only the mortal world she'd tried so hard to escape.

She turned back to face us, and I saw something I'd never expected in those ancient, beautiful eyes.

Recognition. Understanding. The terrible awareness that she was about to discover what lay beyond death.

"I loved you," she whispered, and for the first time, the words sounded true. "I loved you so much that I was willing to become a monster to keep you."

"I know," I replied, and meant it. "But that wasn't love, Ana. That was possession. Love sets you free. Love gives you wings. What you offered me was a beautiful cage."

She nodded once, as if finally accepting a truth she'd spent millennia trying to deny. Then she straightened her shoulders and lifted her chin, meeting our joined attack with something that might have been dignity.

"Then let it be finished," she said.

Our power struck her like the wrath of creation itself. She staggered backward, her perfect form flickering like a candle in a hurricane. Golden cracks spread across her divine flesh, light bleeding from the wounds in her immortal body. She was breaking apart, her carefully constructed perfection finally succumbing to the chaos we'd unleashed.

But gods, even broken ones, do not die easily.

With a cry that shattered what remained of the Parthenon's ancient stones, Ana gathered the last fragments of her power and tore a wound in reality itself. The air split open like fabric, revealing a glimpse of somewhere else, golden halls that stretched into infinity, marble columns that supported the very concept of eternity, the distant sound of harps playing melodies older than human civilization.

Olympus. The realm of the gods, hidden beyond the reach of mortal understanding.

"We're not done, beloved," she gasped, her voice already growing distant as she pulled herself toward the tear in space. Her once vibrant golden armor was now rent and scarred, reflecting the raw power that had been unleashed against her. Golden blood, thick and luminous, dripped from her grievous wounds onto the ruins at our feet, each drop hissing like acid against the ancient stones, leaving scorch marks where it fell.

Her eyes, though clouded with pain, still burned with unyielding resolve. "I will heal. I will return. This is merely a temporary retreat, a strategic withdrawal from a battle I wasn't ready to lose definitively. And when I do, when my strength is fully restored and my purpose renewed, I will tear this world apart stone by stone until you remember what you were meant to be." With a final, agonizing effort, she vanished into the shimmering void, leaving behind only the echoing promise of her terrifying return.

She fell backward through the wound she'd carved in reality, her broken form disappearing into the golden light beyond. The tear began to close immediately, the edges of the wound in space sealing themselves like flesh healing from a cut.

But before it sealed completely, I heard her voice one last time, carrying across dimensions with the force of an oath written in starfire:

"You are mine, Ilija. You have always been mine. Distance means nothing. Time means nothing. I will find a way back to you."

The wound snapped shut with a sound like thunder, and she was gone.

The silence that followed wasn't the peace of victory, but the terrible quiet that comes after a storm has passed. Above us, the crimson dome that had covered Athens began to crack, letting in shafts of pure moonlight that turned the ruins of the Parthenon into something that might have been a cathedral.

The drone networks that had enforced her will across the city flickered and died. The golden statues that had proclaimed her divinity crumbled to dust. The very air seemed to sigh with relief as her influence finally lifted from the world.

I stood there in the aftermath, bleeding from a dozen wounds I hadn't noticed during the fight, my power spent, the storm in my chest finally quiet. Danica collapsed against me, her body trembling with exhaustion, her blade clattering to the ground as her fingers finally lost their strength.

I held her, burying my face in her hair, breathing in the scent of winter and steel and the woman I loved more than life itself. We were alive. Against all odds, despite every prophecy, we had survived.

The echoes of conflict had faded, leaving behind a silence that was almost deafening. The long, arduous war was finally over, its scars etched deep into the landscape and the souls of those who had fought. The goddess's oppressive presence, the tyrannical force that had held Athens in its grasp, was gone, unmade by a combination of courage, sacrifice, and the desperate hope of a people yearning for freedom. Athens, the ancient city of wisdom and democracy, breathed again, liberated from the suffocating weight of divine despotism.

And somewhere, in a world that had been cruelly warped and trapped beneath the weight of a mad god's twisted dreams, a world now slowly unfurling itself back into its natural order, our daughter was waiting. Her image, a beacon of pure innocence and unwavering faith, was burned into our minds, sustaining us through the darkest hours. She was the anchor, the reason we fought, the promise of a future beyond the desolation. She was waiting for us to come home, to return to the life that had been so cruelly interrupted, to the embrace of family that was our true sanctuary.

My only thought, the singular focus that cut through the lingering exhaustion and the dawning realization of peace, was simple, perfect, and profoundly human. In a universe suddenly empty of divine tyranny, stripped of the grand, cosmic struggles that had consumed our every waking moment, one name resonated more than anything else: Selene. It was a name that embodied our hopes, our love, and the profound meaning of our existence.

We had kept our promise, a vow whispered in the darkness, forged in the fires of conflict. We had fought, we had endured, and now, against all odds, we were coming home. The journey had been long, the path fraught with peril, but the destination, the warm embrace of family and the sweet reunion with our daughter was now within reach. The war had ended, but our story, the story of a family reunited, was just beginning.

Or so we thought.

CHAPTER THIRTY-ONE
THE FIRST QUIET DAY

Ilija

Her weight against me was the only thing that felt real. The world, moments ago a maelstrom of chaos and pain, had receded into a dull throb, an echo of the battle we had just survived. Each breath she took, each beat of her heart against my own, was a grounding force, pulling me back from the brink of an abyss that had threatened to swallow me whole. My arms, trembling with exhaustion, held her tighter, a silent promise to never let go.

The ringing in my ears, the high-pitched shriek that had accompanied the clash of steel and the roar of arcane power, had finally faded to a low hum, a distant memory of the maelstrom. It was replaced by the soft hiss of rain on hot stone, a gentle cleansing sound that seemed to wash away the lingering stench of ozone and fear. And then, most profoundly, the steady rhythm of Danica's breathing against my chest. It was a lifeline, a melody of survival in the aftermath of destruction.

We stood in the ruins of the Parthenon, a monument to a forgotten age now bearing fresh scars of our own making. Columns lay toppled, their ancient stones cracked and scattered, testament to the raw power unleashed. Around us, the debris of battle was stark against the ancient architecture, splintered wood, shards of what was once intricate pottery, and the unsettling glint of discarded weaponry. Yet amidst this devastation, we were two bleeding, exhausted souls, holding each other upright. Our wounds, though aching, were mere surface scratches compared to the deeper tremors that had rattled our very beings. The storm in my bones, the tempest of fear and adrenaline that had raged within me, was finally quiet, leaving behind an eerie calm.

Above us, the sky over Athens wept a clean rain, a gentle, persistent drizzle. It fell like a benediction, as if washing the memory of crimson from its clouds, erasing the stains of battle from the sacred ground and from our own weary souls. Each drop felt like a balm, cooling the feverish heat of our exertions and rinsing away the dust and grime of the conflict. The air, crisp and fresh, carried the faint scent of wet earth and ancient stone, a smell of renewal and enduring strength. In that moment, surrounded by history and the quiet aftermath of a harrowing fight, we were just two beings finding solace and strength in each other's presence, under a sky that had witnessed countless battles and now, perhaps, a fragile peace.

Once, a scholar had lived in my skin. That man would have fallen to his knees and wept at this desecration, at the crumbling stones and the acrid smell of burnt offerings that clung to the air. He was a ghost now, a whisper of a past self, buried beneath layers of ash and battle scars. The man who stood here now, with his lover's blood mixed with his own, a warm, sticky testament to their shared struggle, had been the one to help pull the temple down. He had been the one to guide the hands that shattered the idols, to chant the words of freedom as the oppressive edifice crumbled around them.

Danica stirred, a soft groan escaping her lips, pulling back just enough to look at me. Her face, usually so vibrant and alive, was a beautiful ruin, streaked with soot and drying blood. A gash ran across her forehead, stark against her pale skin, and her eyes were bruised with exhaustion, but still fiercely alive. They held a spark, a triumph that mirrored the chaotic scene surrounding us.

"We did it," she whispered, her voice cracking on the words. "Ilija, we actually—" A tremor ran through her, adrenaline finally releasing its hold. "We actually did it."

"You did it," I said, my voice barely more than a rasp. My arm tightened around her. "When I thought... when I saw you fall, I—" The words caught in my throat. "You held the line. You were the blade that cut through everything."

She shook her head, a ghost of a smile touching her cracked lips. "And you brought the storm that broke her." Her hand, grimy and scraped, reached up to touch my cheek. "We did it together."

We began the slow, painful descent from the Acropolis, making our way down through the wreckage of our own making. Each step was agony, my body reminding me that despite everything, I was still mortal flesh wrapped around divine fire. The path was treacherous, littered with chunks of marble that had once been part of humanity's greatest architectural achievement and the twisted, smoking remains of Ana's golden Inquisitors.

They lay scattered like broken dolls, their augmented armor fused into grotesque sculptures by the heat of our conflict. With every careful step down the ancient path, a new perspective of Athens revealed itself below. The chaos was beginning to subside, order slowly asserting itself over the ruins of Ana's perfect design.

The fires that had raged in the outer districts were being quenched by the steady rain, sending columns of white steam into the dawn air like incense offered to gods who had finally stopped listening. The distant wail of sirens was being replaced by smaller, more human sounds that spoke of survival and the stubborn refusal of mortals to simply lie down and die.

A voice shouted a name into the gray morning, answered by a cry of relief that carried across rooftops. The groan and scrape of metal as groups of people worked together to clear barricades of burned-out Accord vehicles. The first tentative notes of a song drifting from a radio somewhere, a melody thin and fragile as spider silk in the vast, wounded quiet.

People were emerging from their hiding places like flowers opening after a long winter. They came up from cellars and metro tunnels, from ancient catacombs and modern bomb shelters, moving into the streets like ghosts slowly remembering how to be solid. Their faces were pale and streaked with soot, their eyes wide with the dazed, fragile hope of those who had survived something they were never meant to survive.

When they saw us, a different kind of silence fell.

They did not cheer or rush forward with questions or demands or the desperate gratitude of the rescued. They stopped whatever they were doing and watched as we descended from the mountain where gods had made war. Their expressions held a mixture of awe and deep, unsettling fear, the kind of look mortals give to forces of nature, to earthquakes and hurricanes and other beautiful disasters that reshape the world according to laws beyond human comprehension.

They parted for us as we walked through their midst, a sea of humanity making way for the two impossible beings who had brought the sky down upon their city. The air crackled with their unspoken awe and terror, a palpable current that raised the hairs on my arms. I could feel their stares like physical touches, a thousand questions they were too frightened or too overwhelmed to ask. Each gaze was a tiny barb, hooking into my awareness, demanding an explanation I couldn't, or wouldn't, provide. Some crossed themselves, their movements jerky and desperate, invoking ancient protections against the unknown. Others whispered prayers, their voices a low, desperate hum that rose above the soft splash of our footsteps. A few simply fell to their knees in the growing puddles, their faces pressed to the rain-slicked cobblestones as if in supplication or surrender. They were shattered, their world irrevocably altered, and we were the architects of that change.

I pulled the hood of my tattered coat over my head, a gesture that was both touchingly human and utterly useless. The fabric, once a comfort, now felt like a flimsy pretense. There was no hiding what I had become. The storm might be quiet in my chest, a sleeping leviathan after its destructive rage, but it still flickered behind my eyes like distant lightning, a constant reminder of the power that now coursed through my veins. Power left marks on the soul that couldn't be concealed by fabric or shadows, by feigned humility or whispered apologies. It burned a brand, visible only to those who truly saw, yet felt by everyone.

I was no longer quite human. The delicate balance of my former self had been irrevocably shattered, replaced by something far grander, far more dangerous. Everyone who looked at me knew it, their eyes widening with a mixture of dread and a terrible, morbid fascination. My skin felt too thin, my senses too sharp, the world around me both intensely vivid and oddly distant. The storm had not just ravaged their city, it had remade me, forging a new existence from the ashes of the old. And as I walked, an outcast among my own kind, I knew that this new self, this impossible being, was a burden I would carry for eternity.

THE OATH OF ASH AND THUNDER

Our command post occupied the crypt beneath a bombed-out church near the Plaka. It was a place of damp stone and hallowed quiet where the air carried the lingering scents of old incense and medical antiseptic. Electric lanterns cast harsh white light across ancient walls decorated with faded frescoes of saints whose painted eyes seemed to watch our every movement.

The moment we stepped through the reinforced steel door, the fragile composure I had maintained shattered like glass struck by a hammer.

Petra was there. Alive. Her face was a canvas painted in grime and exhaustion, her left arm bound in a makeshift sling. The sight of her sent relief through me so powerful it nearly drove me to my knees. She pulled Danica into a bruising embrace took her breath. Simply the solid, living proof that another day had been survived.

Other leaders of the resistance filled the cramped space, their faces forming a gallery of disbelief and profound relief. Men and women who had expected to die in the streets, who had written farewell letters to lovers they would never see again, stood in the flickering light and tried to process the impossible fact of their continued existence.

Maria stepped from a side chamber, and the world stopped turning.

Behind her, a hand clasped securely in the older woman's weathered fingers, was Selene.

My breath caught in my throat like claws. My heart, which had endured the direct assault of a goddess's fury, felt like it was about to shatter into a thousand pieces. The storm in my chest, which had just settled into peaceful dormancy, coiled tight as a serpent. The memory of our last meeting crashed over me. The shadow of Jaakko's form on the tunnel floor.

The look of pure terror that had transformed my daughter's face when she saw what her father could become.

I had reduced a god to a pile of flesh and bones, barely breathing. I pulled lightning from clear skies and reshaped reality with the force of my will. But the expression in a thirteen-year-old girl's eyes had been the only judgment that truly mattered, the only verdict that could destroy me more completely than any divine weapon.

I felt like a monster standing in that sacred space. A thing of lightning and violence that had no place in the same room as innocence, no right to breathe the same air as the child I loved more than my own existence. My feet seemed rooted to the ancient stone floor, held in place by shame and the terrible certainty that I had become something she could never love.

I watched Danica go to her, watched a mother return from across the river of death. It was a scene of such perfect beauty and raw emotion that I felt like an intruder witnessing something sacred, something I had forfeited the right to be part of the moment I chose to become a weapon.

Selene dissolved into her mother's arms like snow touched by spring sunlight. Selene's body shook with sobs she had been holding back for days, her hands clutching at Danica's coat as if to make absolutely certain this wasn't another dream. She buried her face against her mother's shoulder and wept with the desperate intensity of a child who had finally been given permission to break.

After what felt like a lifetime measured in heartbeats, she pulled back enough to look at her mother's face. Her eyes, my eyes, the same storm-gray that had looked back at me from mirrors for thirty-seven years, were bright with tears and something else that made my chest tight.

She let go of her mother's hand and walked toward me with the same steady determination I'd seen in her since she was old enough to stand. At thirteen, Selene had her mother's height and her own fierce confidence, the kind that came from growing up in a world at war. Each step was deliberate, measured by the gravity of the moment.

She stopped just beyond arm's reach, a space that felt both vast and impossibly small between us. Her gaze, direct and unflinching, traveled over my face, taking careful inventory of every subtle change the recent weeks had carved into my features. She registered the new lines fanning out from the corners of my eyes, etched by there by sleepless nights and the weight of decisions no one should ever have to make. She noted the lines that had appeared at my temples, stark reminders of the rapid passage of time under duress. And then her eyes settled on the scars, a tapestry of faint, angry lines on my cheek and jaw that would never quite fade, permanent markers of battles fought and survived.

Her eyes lingered on my hands, where faint traceries of lightning created intricate, almost artistic patterns just beneath the skin. She could see the storm that lived there, the raw, untamed power that could reshape mountains or reduce cities to ash in a blinding flash. It was a power I had wielded, a power that had both saved and destroyed. But when she finally raised her gaze to meet mine, her face solemn and unblinking, I didn't see fear, not a flicker of it.

Instead, I saw understanding. The terrible comprehension of children forced to grow up too fast, who witness too much, and grasps truths adults deny. In her eyes, I read the cost of what I had become, the burden of the power I carried, the difficult path ahead. A silent acknowledgment, a shared burden, more comforting than any words.

"Is the storm quiet now, Tata?" she asked, her voice steady despite the tremor in her hands where they rested on my shoulders.

The question broke me in ways Ana's most vicious attacks never could. Her cruel barbs had always found purchase on the armor of my anger, reinforcing its brittle strength. This soft inquiry from my daughter cut deeper. Concern, pure and untainted by judgment. The worried plea of a daughter distressed by her father's pain, a child who looked past the monster I thought I had become and still saw the man who used to read her bedtime stories, whose lap was once her sanctuary, whose laughter was her favorite song.

The walls I had built around my heart crumbled to dust, dissolving like sandcastles before an unforgiving tide. A sob tore from my throat, raw and ugly, born of grief and overwhelming self-loathing. I dropped to my knees before her, the stone floor pressing into my skin. I no longer cared who saw. In the presence of her unwavering love, all my defenses fell, leaving me exposed, vulnerable, broken.

She stepped forward then, closing the distance with the steady confidence of someone who had made her choice. Her arms wrapped around my neck, and she smelled of woodsmoke and rain and something indefinable I could only call home. I held my daughter against my chest and wept, my body shaking with the force of thirteen years of grief and loss and desperate hope finally answered.

"It's quiet now, little storm," I whispered into her hair. "It's finally quiet."

Hours later, a fragile sense of order began to coalesce amidst the chaos. We gathered around a makeshift table, its surface a mosaic of upturned ammunition crates, offering a stark contrast to the elegant dining tables we had once known. The only illumination came from a handful of electric lanterns, their flickering light throwing dancing shadows across the crypt's ancient, roughly hewn walls, transforming familiar faces into fleeting specters. The leaders of the resistance, a grim and depleted assembly, formed a tight circle, their faces etched with the weariness of battle and the sorrow of countless losses. Each weathered countenance held a silent testament to the horrors they had witnessed, their eyes, once vibrant with hope, now haunted by an unshakeable despair.

We were, in essence, survivors in the truest sense of the word, clinging to the ragged edges of existence, desperately trying to comprehend the seismic shift that had irrevocably altered our world in the span of a single, catastrophic night. The very fabric of reality had unraveled, leaving us adrift in an uncharted, terrifying new epoch.

Selene sat tucked securely against my side, a beacon of solace in the encroaching darkness. Her warmth, a constant and grounding presence, served as an anchor in the maelstrom of my own anxieties. Her head, heavy with exhaustion, rested on my shoulder, her breathing a soft, rhythmic counterpoint to the thrum of my own racing heart. She drifted in and out of a fitful, shallow sleep, her fingers occasionally tightening on my arm, a silent, desperate reassurance that I was still solid, still real, still irrevocably there. Each squeeze was a question, a plea, a confirmation that I hadn't dissolved into the ether like so much else that morning.

The low murmur of voices from the others provided a strangely comforting, almost normal backdrop to our shared grief and uncertainty. They spoke of logistics, of strategy, their words a steady drone of planning that felt profoundly incongruous after the cosmic violence and overwhelming grief of the morning. The sheer mundanity of their discussions, consolidating what remained of our fractured forces, meticulously securing supply lines, and grappling with the now headless and disarrayed Accord armies, offered a tenuous bridge back to a semblance of order. They spoke of the future, not with boundless optimism, but with a careful, guarded hope, a desperate flickering flame in the encroaching gloom, daring to envision a tomorrow that might yet be salvaged from the ashes of today.

They were planning the next phase of what they believed was simply another war against another human enemy. Their concerns were beautifully, reassuringly mortal, the practical matters of rebuilding from ashes and hope.

I listened while feeling like an alien among my own kind, trying to remember the language of humanity. My mind kept drifting back to the cosmic reality of what had transpired, to the sight of divine flesh dissolving under chaos made manifest, to the moment when reality itself had bent around our combined will.

How do you explain to mortals that they had just witnessed the end of an age? How do you tell soldiers worried about supply lines that the rules governing existence itself had been rewritten?

Danica spoke to them with the voice of a queen, laying out plans for securing their victory. Her words painted pictures of a new Athens, a new world, built on freedom rather than divine mandate. She was their leader in a way I could never be, practical where I was philosophical, grounded where I was abstract.

Amid her detailed explanation of defensive positions, a sudden, inexplicable jolt coursed through me. A cosmic snap that reverberated deep within the divine core of my consciousness. It was a sensation that bypassed the ordinary senses entirely, striking at the very essence of my being, the part of me that resonated with forces beyond mortal comprehension. The closest analogy I could find was that of a distant star going supernova, its silent, cataclysmic death-scream somehow reaching across impossible distances to touch my soul.

With that snap, the antagonistic connection that had always bound me to Ana shifted. Changed. The tumultuous storm that had raged within me for as long as I could remember went utterly, eerily still. The silence carried weight. Like a compass needle that had always pointed to one magnetic pole suddenly realigning to another, stronger pull. Something vast and terrible filled the space Ana had occupied, darker, colder, more ancient.

A wave of nausea rolled through me, accompanied by profound spiritual vertigo. An essential piece of the universe hadn't been plucked away, it had been claimed by something else.

Danica stopped speaking mid-sentence, her hand flying to her temple. Her eyes widened, pupils dilating as if adjusting to sudden darkness. The air around us shimmered with the after-effects of whatever invisible force had just shifted its grasp.

She turned to look at me, her eyes wide. "Did you— Ilija, what was that?" Her hand trembled against her temple. "It felt like something just... God, I can't even describe it."

The crypt, which had been alive with the murmur of voices and the rustle of movement moments before, fell silent. Every face turned toward me. They waited for me to interpret the cosmic weather, to name the inexplicable phenomenon that had just transpired. I took a slow, deliberate breath, tasting air that suddenly felt thin and wrong, charged with something that made my teeth ache. The certainty that settled into my bones was colder than winter, more absolute than lightning.

Transition. The shift heralded a terrible new beginning, a changing of hands in a game far larger than we had imagined.

I looked at the council, at the hopeful, tired faces of humans who believed they had just won their world back. Their cheers had barely died down, their weary smiles still creased their eyes. The air, once thick with the scent of ozone and triumph, now hung heavy with unspoken unease. My voice, when I finally found it, carried a dread far greater than anything we had faced in battle.

"That wasn't her dying." I forced the words out past the tightness in my chest. Each one fell into the silence like stones into still water.

Danica's brow furrowed, hope and confusion warring across her features. "What do you mean? Ilija, we felt her—"

"That was a claim." My hands clenched into fists. "Ana isn't gone. She's still alive. Wounded, desperate, and now—" I met her eyes, saw my own dread reflected back at me. "Now bound to something far darker than herself."

The silence that followed was absolute, broken only by the faint, distant sounds of the city we had just saved. Their faces, moments ago alight with triumph, contorted into expressions of disbelief, then dawning horror. The implications hung in the air like smoke from a distant fire. If Ana, with all her formidable power, her ten thousand years of accumulated divine authority, could be claimed so completely, what ancient darkness had we awakened by wounding a goddess? What horror would she become in its service? The world we thought we had won back now seemed more perilous than ever.

What kind of attention had we drawn by proving that gods could die?

In the silence that followed, I felt the first stirrings of a new kind of storm gathering on the horizon. This one would be made of questions with no comfortable answers and enemies that had not yet shown their faces.

The war for Athens was over, but something told me that the war for existence was only just beginning.

Epilogue
DUBROVNIK, THREE YEARS LATER

Ilija

The sun was a melting coin of gold on the horizon, bleeding its wealth into the calm, deep blue of the Adriatic. The air tasted of salt and pine and the quiet peace of a world slowly, cautiously, remembering how to breathe. Three years. It felt like a lifetime and no time at all. The storm in my bones was quiet now, a sleeping leviathan that no longer clawed at my ribs, but simply reminded me of its weight with every steady beat of my heart.

We sat on a stretch of pebbled coast just north of the city's ancient walls, watching the tide sigh against the shore. Danica leaned against my side, her head on my shoulder, her warmth a familiar and necessary anchor. The lines of command had softened around her eyes, replaced by the gentler marks of laughter and sleepless nights spent with a teenager who had discovered a love for philosophy and arguing about it until dawn. She was still a blizzard in a woman's skin, but she had learned the beauty of a quiet winter.

Our daughter stood at the water's edge. At sixteen, Selene was a study in impossible grace, all long limbs and restless energy. The setting sun caught in her dark hair, weaving threads of her mother's fire into my own night. The shadows that had once clung to her like a shroud now played at her feet, calm and content as hounds lying by a hearth, stretching and receding with the tide. She was humming one of the strange, wordless songs she'd hummed since she was a child, a melody that felt older than the stones of the city behind us. With a fluid motion, she bent and sent a flat stone skipping across the water's surface, once, twice, five times before it surrendered to the sea.

"She's happy," Danica murmured, her voice soft against my shoulder, a gentle caress in the quiet aftermath. The dim light of the setting sun, filtered through the stained-glass window, painted long, dancing shadows across the room, mimicking the slow, steady rhythm of our breaths.

"She is," I agreed, my own voice thick with a gratitude that still felt raw, still felt new, like a wound recently healed but not yet forgotten. Every beat of my heart was a testament to the fragile, precious peace we had fought so desperately to achieve, a peace that was both a blessing and a constant, gnawing worry.

The war was over, but the world was not healed. The scars ran deep, etched into the very fabric of reality. The Accord was a ghost, its once formidable legions scattered to the winds, its malevolent ideology collapsing into a thousand warring factions, each hungry for power, each a potential spark for a new conflagration. Ana was a void, an absence in the cosmos that I sometimes felt in the deepest hours of the night, a chilling silence where a divine hatred used to be, a gaping hole in the universe that echoed with the memory of her destructive power. We were living on borrowed time, a fragile peace bought with the blood of gods and mortals, a delicate balance sustained by sacrifice and vigilance, and I treasured every single heartbeat of it, every stolen moment of quietude, every shared glance with Danica. Each sunrise felt like a miracle, each sunset a reprieve, and in those fleeting moments of normalcy, we found a strength to face the lingering shadows of a world not quite whole.

Selene laughed, a bright, clear sound that cut through the quiet evening, and turned to look back at us, her face alight with joy so pure it was a physical ache in my chest. "Are you two just going to sit there like old statues?" she called out, her smile a perfect, breathtaking fusion of her mother's fire and my own quiet storms. We kissed, smiling from ear to ear and Selene's only response was, "You two make me sick."

We laughed and kissed again, watching Selene do her best teenage eyeroll. My heart was bursting with love so full it ached. I watched her as she stood there, a silhouette against the fading day, the last defiant rays of sunlight turning the wet sand at her feet to a sheet of shimmering, liquid gold. The ocean, a living, breathing entity, pulled back its mighty breath in that moment, leaving behind a perfect, unblemished mirror of the sky on the shore. The clouds, painted in hues of lavender and rose, stretched endlessly, reflected in the glassy surface.

And in that pristine reflection, I saw her. A vision of a past that haunted my dreams and whispered in the quiet corners of my mind. It was not Selene, my sixteen-year-old daughter with her easy, infectious smile and the restless grace of a gazelle, forever eager to explore the world. No, the woman in the reflection was someone else entirely. Her eyes held an ancient wisdom, her posture, a quiet strength that time could not diminish. A sense of longing, sharp and poignant, pierced through me, a phantom echo of love lost but never forgotten. The gentle lapping of the waves against the shore seemed to carry a melody from a distant memory, a song of joy and sorrow intertwined.

The figure in the water's mirror was a young woman, perhaps in her early twenties. She stood tall, clad in armor of a dark, starless metal that seemed to drink the light, etched with silver runes that coiled and writhed like living things. Her hair was longer, a river of night braided with silver clasps that glowed with a faint, cold light. Her face was a mask of grim resolve, the face of a queen who had buried kingdoms, the face of a goddess who had stared into the void and made it blink first. The shadows at her feet were not playful things; they were a swirling mantle of pure, living darkness, a cloak of endings. Her storm-gray eyes, my eyes, held the terrible, lonely weight of prophecy.

The vision, a searing flash of what was, lasted for less than a breath, a fleeting heartbeat. It was an intrusion, a violent rip in the fabric of the ordinary.

I blinked, and the reflection in the rippling water was normal again, the terrifying glimpse of the future receding as if it had never been. It was just my daughter, a vibrant teenager with salt spray on her cheeks, her hair tousled by the sea breeze. The whole of her life, unblemished and full of promise, shone in her eyes as she laughed, waving for us to join her in the shallows.

But the image, stark and chilling, was burned into my soul. The air around us, moments before warm with the afternoon sun, grew cold, a sudden, inexplicable chill. The quiet, idyllic day had ended, irrevocably tainted by what I had witnessed.

Danica shifted beside me, her hand instinctively finding my own. Her fingers laced through mine, a silent anchor in the swirling chaos of my thoughts. She had felt the change in me, the sudden frost that had settled deep in my bones, a premonition of the darkness that now threatened to consume us.

"Ilija?" she asked, her voice a soft murmur, laced with a familiar concern that always seemed to find its way to me when my carefully constructed composure faltered. "What is it? What did you see?" Her gaze searched my face; her brow furrowed with apprehension.

I looked at our daughter, our beautiful, impossible child. So full of life and light, she stood on the very edge of a destiny she did not yet know was relentlessly hunting for her, a shadow lurking just beyond her bright horizon. I looked out at the vast expanse of the horizon, where the last sliver of the sun had surrendered its brilliant warmth to the encroaching sea, leaving the world to the inevitable, deepening dark. The light was fading, both in the sky and, I feared, in our lives.

"I saw..." I began, the words tasting like bitter ash in my mouth, each syllable a heavy weight on my tongue. The vision had been brief, but its implications were vast, terrifying. "I saw the storm that's coming, or maybe one that already happened."

The pressure dropped. My ears popped like we'd climbed a mountain in seconds. Static electricity raised every hair on my arms. Beside me, Danica's hand moved instinctively toward a weapon that wasn't there.

Selene stopped mid-laugh, her head turning toward the water.

The veil split.

They all came at once, Brigid, Freyja, Perun, and two others. One rose like mist from the ground, smelling of loam and ancient groves. Danu. The other materialized at Selene's side, half her face beautiful, half withered. Hel.

My storm coiled tight in my chest.

"We don't have much time," Brigid said, her voice stripped of warmth. "They are moving. Aphrodite has twisted into something we can barely recognize. They're gathering others, old gods, hungry ones."

"They'll come for the girl," Freyja said flatly, looking at Selene. "She's what they fear most. What comes after divinity."

Perun's gaze pinned me. "Two years. That's what we can give you. Two years to prepare her before they breach the veil."

"Train her," Danu said. "Teach her everything."

Hel's hand rested on Selene's shoulder. "When they come, you'll stand alone. We're fading, our power wanes with every forgotten prayer. This world belongs to mortals. And to whatever she becomes."

"What am I supposed to become?" Selene's voice was steady despite the tremor in her hands.

"The wall," Brigid said simply. "Or the stone it all breaks against. That's the choice you'll have to make."

"Two years," Freyja repeated. "Use them."

They began to fade, their forms dissolving like smoke.

"Wait—" I started, but Hel spoke over me.

"Balance requires sacrifice, child. Remember that when the time comes."

Then they were gone.

The three of us stood on the empty beach. The air tasted of metal and salt. My storm coiled restlessly in my chest.

Selene turned to look at us, and I saw the terrible understanding of someone who had just learned the shape of their destiny.

"Two years," she said quietly.

Danica made a sound like something breaking. I pulled them both close, holding them as if I could shield them from fate itself.

But I had seen the vision in the water. I had seen the queen of endings she would become.

Some storms cannot be stopped.

They can only endure.

The war for Athens had been nothing but a prelude. A rehearsal for the true battle that was coming, the battle for existence itself.

And this time, the fate of the world would rest on the shoulders of a girl who, just this morning, had argued with her mother about her screen time and whether she could go to a concert in Split next weekend.

I pulled Danica closer, breathing in the scent of her, trying to memorize this moment before everything changed irrevocably. Around us, the peaceful evening continued its gentle descent into night, indifferent to the cosmic drama that had just unfolded on this small stretch of shore.

But I knew better now. I had learned the hard way that peace was always temporary, that happiness was borrowed time, that love, fierce and desperate and defiant, was the only thing worth fighting for when the gods came calling.

"We'll keep her safe," Danica whispered against my chest, her voice fierce despite the tears. "Whatever comes. We'll keep her safe."

I wanted to promise her that. I wanted to swear on my storm and my soul that nothing would touch our daughter, that we would stand between her and every dark thing the universe could conjure.

All we could do was prepare her to survive what was coming, to love her, teach her, and pray to gods who no longer listened that it would be enough.

The waves whispered against the shore, eternal and indifferent, as night swallowed the last of the light and the stars began their silent vigil overhead.

Tomorrow, the training will begin.

Tonight, we would hold our daughter and pretend, just for a few more hours, that she was still just a girl who skipped stones and teased her parents and had her whole life ahead of her.

We stood together, bound by storm, fire, and shadow.

AUTHOR'S NOTE

When I began writing this series, I thought I was telling a story about gods and mortals, storms and shadows. What I discovered along the way was that I was really writing about memory, how it shapes us, how it wounds us, and how it becomes the thread that binds one life to another.

This book carries pieces of myth and history that have followed me for years. The voices of Perun and Veles, Aphrodite and Chernabog, Freyja and Idunn, all of them echoed in the stories I first learned about in college, the fragments of folklore I first studied a decade ago. Writing them into this world was less about invention and more about listening, about weaving those old threads into something that felt alive again.

But myths are not just ancient things. They live in the way we grieve, in the way we love, in the stubborn act of choosing hope when the world seems intent on silence. They live in every oath whispered between two people, in every sacrifice we make for those we cannot bear to lose.

If you, like me, are drawn to the original myths that inspired these pages, there are many places to begin:

Slavic Mythology by Jan Máchal

Slavic Myths by Noah Charney and Svetlana Slapšak

Bulfinch's Mythology by Thomas Bulfinch

Norse Mythology by Neil Gaiman

The Poetic Edda translated by Carolyne Larrington

These works are touchstones, not exhaustive, but enough to open the doors to the worlds that shaped this one.

If you have carried Ilija, Danica, Ana, and Selene through these pages, thank you. Thank you for stepping into the storm, for holding onto the light in the dark places, for trusting me with your time. Stories only matter because readers breathe life into them, and I am profoundly grateful that you chose to breathe life into this one.

The journey is not finished. The veil is still shattered, the storm still restless, and the next chapter waits just ahead. I hope you'll walk with me a little further.

-Elijah

ACKNOWLEDGEMENTS

There were nights I stared at my laptop screen until my eyes burned, deleting the same paragraph for the fifth time because it still wasn't right. Mornings when I woke up convinced I'd lost the story completely, that whatever I'd imagined in my head would never translate to the page.

I didn't finish this alone.

To my family, thank you for being there through all of it. For the conversations where you let me work through ideas out loud, even when they didn't make sense yet. For believing this mattered when I wasn't sure it did. For celebrating the small victories with me, the finished chapters, the breakthroughs, the days when everything finally clicked. You gave me the space to write and the reasons to come back when I was done. That balance kept me grounded.

To my friends, you listened to me talk about these characters like they were real people. You didn't laugh when I texted you about a plot problem, or when I canceled plans because I finally cracked a scene I'd been wrestling with for weeks. You asked questions that made me think harder. You told me when something wasn't working. You didn't let me quit when I wanted to. That mattered more than you know.

To my beta readers, you read the messy version and told me the truth. You pointed out what didn't land, what felt forced, where I was avoiding the harder choice. You pushed me to write better, to dig into the uncomfortable places I was skirting around. This book is sharper because you didn't go easy on me.

To the historians, folklorists, and translators who preserved the old stories, the Slavic myths, the Greek tragedies, the Norse sagas, you kept them alive through centuries of erasure and forgetting. You gave me something to build from and I've tried to handle it with care.

And to you, reading this, maybe you've been here since the first book, maybe this is your entry point. Either way, you didn't have to pick this up. There are thousands of other books you could be reading right now. The fact that you chose this one makes me eternally grateful.

Writing a second book is different. The characters are already living and breathing, the world is established, and somehow that makes it harder. The stakes feel higher. I wanted to push Ilija, Danica, and Ana into darker territory, to test what they're made of when everything goes to shit.

I don't know what you'll find in these pages, maybe something you need, maybe just a few hours somewhere else, but I'm glad you're here.

Thank you for giving this story a chance.

AND, AS ALWAYS, IF YOU LIKED THIS STORY, DON'T FORGET TO LEAVE A REVIEW!

LORE & GLOSSARY
GODS & POWERS

❋ **Perun (PEH-roon)** Slavic god of storms and thunder, wielder of the axe and master of the firmament. His presence is the weight of sky and lightning.

❋ **Veles (VEH-les)** Slavic god of the underworld, cattle, and trickery. He lingers in roots and rivers, forever in tension with Perun.

❋ **Morana (mo-RAH-nah)** Goddess of winter and death. She is stillness given form, the silence of frozen fields.

❋ **Lada (LAH-dah)** Goddess of fertility, love, and the warmth of summer. Where she steps, life follows.

❋ **Chernabog (CHER-nah-bog)** The Black God, whispered as the embodiment of hunger and endings. His gaze strips warmth from marrow.

❋ **Freyja (FRAY-yah)** Norse goddess of love, war, and seidr magic. She claims half the slain to her hall, Sessrúmnir.

❋ **Aphrodite Areia (ah-fro-DYE-tee ah-RAY-ah)** The warlike aspect of the Greek goddess of love. In this story, her reflection lies in Ana.

❋ **Idunn (EE-doon)** Keeper of the golden apples, bringer of renewal and youth in Norse myth. Her tree's fruit restores vigor to gods and mortals alike.

❋ **Odin (OH-din)** The All-Father of Norse mythology, one-eyed wanderer and seeker of wisdom. He traded his eye for knowledge and hung upon Yggdrasil to seize the runes.

❋ **Thor (THOR)** God of thunder, wielder of Mjölnir, protector of Midgard. His strength shakes the mountains; his hammer cracks the sky.

❋ **Tyr (TEER)** God of justice and oaths, known for placing his hand in Fenrir's jaws. His sacrifice embodies honor and the price of binding chaos.

❋ **Hel (HELL)** Norse goddess of the underworld, half her face alive, half dead. She rules over the halls of those who die of illness and age, and speaks with the calm certainty of endings.

✳   **Alecto (ah-LEK-toh)** One of the Furies (Erinyes), embodiment of unending anger. She pursues crimes of moral corruption with relentless fury.

✳   **Megaera (meh-GAIR-ah)** Another Fury, whose name means "the grudging one." She punishes jealousy, betrayal, and oath-breaking.

✳   **Tisiphone (ti-SIH-foh-nee)** The Fury of vengeance, especially for murder. Her presence is said to freeze blood in the veins of the guilty.

✳   **Kratus (KRAH-toos)** Personification of strength and might in Greek mythology, brother to Nike (Victory). He embodies raw, implacable force, the hand of compulsion in divine will.

✳   **Brigid (BRIH-jid or BREE-jid)** Celtic goddess of poetry, smithcraft, and healing. She carries the flame of inspiration and the forge of creation, a bridge between art and survival.

✳   **Danu (DAH-noo or DAN-oo)** Ancient mother goddess of the Tuatha Dé Danann. She is the river and the wellspring, origin of divine bloodlines and sovereignty.

REALMS & MYTHIC PLACES

✳   **Olympus (The Silent Throne)** Once the seat of the Greek gods, now fractured and corrupted into Ana's dominion. Its skies tear with void, its thrones lie in ruins.

✳   **The House of No Dawn:** Fortress where Ilija was bound. A place without sunrise, its halls drowned in shadow, silence, and eternal absence of warmth.

✳   **The Catacombs Beneath the Monastery:** Rebel sanctum carved deep under ruined churches and monasteries, walls heavy with the ghosts of saints whose names were scraped away.

✳   **Mount Pentelicus:** The marble source of the Parthenon, its stone now littering Olympus's ruins. A reminder of mortal faith bent into divine empire.

* **The Field of Ended Fates:** A frost-bound expanse where failed destinies lie buried; snowflakes crystallized from moments of loss and unfinished endings.

* **Vienna (Under Accord Control)** Ruled by Inquisitors, scarred by executions and networks of informants.

* **Rome (The Burning Throne)** Where the last great battles with Ana reshaped the course of the rebellion.

* **Alexandria:** Jewel of the southern empire, a vital Accord stronghold.

* **The Drina River:** Lifeline of resistance in the Balkans, ferried secretly by rebels under cover of night.

* **Prague Library Vaults:** Once keepers of memory and knowledge, reduced to ash under Ana's purges.

RELICS & MYTHIC OBJECTS

* **Blade of Fates:** Star-bone weapon that binds its wielder to destiny.

* **Storm Heart:** Shattered crystal of lightning, bound in chains, pulsing with thunder.

* **Rings of Morana and Lada:** Paired relics of winter and spring, balancing life and death.

* **Apples of Idunn:** Golden fruit of youth and immortality.

* **Perunika Coin:** Token marked with the iris, oath of storm and rebellion.

THEY WILL RETURN IN THE LEGACY OF ASH
AND THUNDER...

www.ingramcontent.com/pod-product-compliance
Lightning Source LLC
Chambersburg PA
CBHW010650100726
47901CB00012B/2503